Soldiers of Conquest

Books by F.M. Parker

Coldiron *series*
Coldiron
Shadow of the Wolf
The Shanghaiers
Thunder of Cannon
Spoils of War (a.k.a. The Thieves)

Novels
The Highwayman
The Last Orphan Train (a.k.a. Girl in Falling Snow)
Soldiers of Conquest

Coming Soon!
Dream Hitcher

Soldiers of Conquest

F. M. Parker

SPEAKING VOLUMES, LLC
NAPLES, FLORIDA
2024

Soldiers of Conquest

ISBN 979-8-89022-058-5

To Louise for her proof reading of many manuscripts.

Prologue

The Mexican-American War of 1846-1848, in which Ulysses S. Grant and Robert E. Lee were comrades in arms, could well be called the Forgotten War. Few Americans can recall ever hearing of it, and yet it was a war of invasion and conquest in which the United States took from Mexico the land area now encompassing the states of California, Arizona, New Mexico, and parts of Nevada, Utah and Colorado. By including Texas, this huge land area makes up slightly more than one-quarter of the lower forty-eight states.

Chapter One

"Find a flaw, some weakness in the defenses of the fort and city that will allow us to capture them," General Scott, Chief of the American Army, directed his subordinate officers standing with him on the deck of the small naval steamboat Patrita lying on the Bay of Campeche. He made a sweep of his hand in the direction of Mexico's largest seaport Veracruz and mighty Fort San Juan de Ulua a mile distant and standing out in sharp relief under a brilliant tropical sun. General Scott, a huge man at six feet five and huskily built, had arrived the day before from the States on his flagship, the warship Massachusetts. He had brought with him for the invasion ninety-nine large ships crowded with nine thousand soldiers and the holds full of cannons, muskets, and cavalry mounts.

The Patrita rose and fell showing a portion of her copper sheathed bottom as the swells generated by a storm in the Gulf of Mexico forced their way under her keel. Balancing themselves against the movement of the ship, the blue uniformed army officers held their field glasses focused on Veracruz and the huge stone fortress. With the army men was Admiral Conner, Commodore of the American Home Fleet. His naval warships had been blockading the Mexican eastern coast for the past ten months.

Robert E. Lee, Captain of Engineers and one of Scott's staff officers noted the beauty of the city, the scores of ships lying upon the turquoise water of the bay, and Fort San Juan de Ulua located on the western edge of a coral reef one thousand yards directly seaward from Veracruz. The grand vista added to Lee's pleasant feeling from being part of a band of men planning the invasion of a large nation and fighting great battles with its army. He regretted the killing and destruction that would be done to win the war. He pulled away from those dark thoughts and concentrated his attention on Veracruz.

The city lay in the shape of a crescent moon and hugging the shoreline. Its landward perimeter was two miles long and enclosed many tall buildings of whitewashed masonry. Sixteen splendid white domed buildings promenaded along the waterfront and several magnificent Catholic churches pierced the sky with tall steeples each bearing a cross. The city contained such an abundance of white buildings that it glowed with a luminous sheen. Eight stone piers extended out from the quay and dozens of fishing boats with sails lowered were berthed along them. The city from all appearances was immensely prosperous.

Veracruz was protected from an attack from the sea by a massive granite seawall strengthened at the northern end with Fort Conception and at the southern end by Fort Santiago. He couldn't see the opposite side of the city, but had studied reports describing the city's defensive walls as being some fifteen feet high, three feet thick, and with nine well-constructed cannon bastions reinforcing it. Slots in the wall through which muskets could fire upon attackers were spaced every four feet. Besides its renowned fortifications, the city was famous in Europe and America for its pretty, free-spirited women, and for the dreaded and deadly el vomito, yellow fever.

He pictured how this land of the Aztecs might have looked when in the spring of the year 1519 A.D. the eleven ships of the Spanish General Hernando Cortez appeared off the white sand beach. Perhaps there had been a village of brown skinned men, women, and children who watched in awe as the general and his five hundred and fifty soldiers, their blood hot with thoughts of gold and jewels, came ashore wearing their metal armor and armed with muskets and swords, fourteen bronze cannons, stores of powder and shot, and sixteen horses. Cortez had burned ten of his ships, and in a "do or die campaign", built a road following the aged footpaths, the Aztecs had not invented the wheel, and climbed into the mountains where they had been told a fabulously rich city lay. After killing thousands of the Aztecs in battles, the Spaniards forced their way down into the valley where lay the great capitol city of the land. The city was taken and the Spaniards stole shipload upon shipload of the Aztec people's gold, silver and jewels and sent all back to Spain. Cortez named the land Mexico. Spain ruled it for three hundred years, until 1821 when the Mexicans wrested back control.

Lee turned his field glasses away from Veracruz and to the several ships hanging on their anchors and crowding the harbor. Most prominent were the three American battleships, the heavily armed Albany, Potomac, and John Adams showing the open bores of their big cannons to the fort and city, and as a warning to any Mexican or foreign ship's captain that might be considering running the blockade.

Also present were foreign men-of-war, two British frigates, a French frigate and a Spanish sloop. The foreign warships were here to protect their country's nationals and business interests during the coming war. The British were most concerned for they owned most of the gold and silver mines in Mexico, and scores of other business ventures.

Lee turned back to Fort San Juan de Ulua. The massive structure with its strong battlements was made of coral stone faced with tough granite. It had been built by the Spanish two centuries before to protect Veracruz from pirates, and had served its purpose admirably for no pirate fleet had ever captured the city. Stained a dark brown by the ages, the fort rose menacingly from the reef with vertical, sixty-foot tall walls, above which were two additional fortified levels. Towering still higher was a round tapering column of three levels, the topmost level being constantly manned by lookouts watching the sea. The Mexican national flag, a tricolor of red, white, and green with an eagle holding a serpent in its beak, fluttered from a tall staff on the domed peak of the tower. Fort San Juan de Ulua was the last stronghold of the Spanish.

Over the years many modifications had been made to strengthen Ulua's walls and the old Spanish cannon had been replaced with those of larger bore and longer range. At the base of the walls, water batteries lay wherever it seemed possible to make a landing. Lee had spent four years strengthening the American forts along the Atlantic seaboard and knew from that experience that Ulua with its walls bristling with cannon had to be the strongest fortification in the western hemisphere. Capturing it would be a formidable endeavor.

He saw Mexican artillerymen working swiftly at their cannons in Ulua and called out. "General Scott, there are men working at the guns on the second level of the fort."

Scott intently studying Veracruz, now swung his field glasses to Ulua. "Ah, yes. They're sponging the barrels of their pieces and we shall soon have a shot at us."

"Shall we move out of range?" asked Commodore Conner.

"Not just yet, commodore, if you please" Scott said and looking down from his lofty height at the admiral, frail and sickly from old wounds, and the months he had spent blockading the Mexican coast with its inhospitable climate. "The Mexican gunners will need a few rounds to get our range so we'll have time to do our reconnaissance. And reconnaissance of a foe's weapons and defenses is the key to victory."

"The Mexican gunners most often shoot high the first time," said General Worth who had fought the Mexicans with General Taylor in northern Mexico.

Through his field glasses Lee watched the Mexican gunners prepare their cannons. Scott was gambling his campaign by not withdrawing beyond range. The Mexican gunners might get lucky and hit the Patrita with one of their first shots. A shell exploding on the boat could end the invasion before it began for standing on the deck with him were the senior officers of the American Army; Generals Worth, Twiggs, and Patterson who commanded the three army divisions, Chief Engineer Colonel Totten, Chief Of Artillery Colonel Banks, and Major Turnbull Chief of Topographical Engineers. The death of Commodore Conner would decapitate the navy.

General Scott spoke from behind his field gasses to Commodore Conner. "Commodore, what information have you gathered about the current ordnance in Ulua?"

"I've talked with several of the British naval officers who have been in the fort recently and one of them informed me that besides some fine old Spanish guns, there is a new, heavy battery of sixteen British bronze long 24-pounders. That's the worse for us for the British make excellent weapons. In total I estimate the ordnance in Ulua, counting cannon, mortars, and howitzers at three hundred. From what I've seen, nearly half of them, including heavy ten-inchers, could be aimed at any ships I might send against Ulua. We would suffer heavy losses."

"How about the number of men stationed there?"

"My best estimate from what I've heard is around twenty five hundred."

"I see no weakness in the fort's defenses," Scott said. "It may be impregnable from the sea. If the city was taken first, the fort might hold out for months. We have no time for a siege for the yellow fever season will be upon us within the next few days and the troops must be got off the lowland and into the mountains before it arrives. Yet we must have possession of the harbor and shipping facilities for they're needed in all future operations."

"General, the British have just run up flags signaling that they want to come aboard for a parley." Conner said, his field glasses aimed at the frigate commanded by the senior British officer.

"They don't like the war and are itching to know as much of our plans as we would divulge," Scott replied with a wry smile. "We'll signal them when we get back to the Massachusetts and arrange a time. What's your estimate of the Mexican military in the city?"

"I'd say approximately thirty-five hundred. And about eight thousand civilians remaining from the normal population of fifteen thousand. They won't leave for various reasons, mainly from fear their possessions would be stolen."

Scott nodded acknowledgement of the information and turned back to Veracruz. "It's a beautiful city, but I'll capture it even if I have to destroy it in the taking," he said.

Lee knew that he would use all his strength and skill with weapons to help Scott capture the city. The cruelty in which he was about to participate was disturbing. Yet that changed nothing at all for first he was a soldier. Given that he was a soldier, then he would prove his skill and show his bravery and gain promotion.

He was watching the fort when one of its manned cannons blossomed with smoke and flame. Hardly had his mind registered the flash when a shell screamed past some thirty feet over the mast of the Patrita and burst close above the water one hundred yards beyond. The coarse cries of the circling seagulls became shrill and they fled. Wise birds, thought Lee.

In but a few seconds two other shells came arcing down, one landing to the left side of the boat and one just in front, both exploding and flinging up tall geysers of water. Another seven shells fell about the boat but did no harm. Then one landed very close on the starboard side and exploded just above water level. Metal fragments hammered the boat's hull and went whistling across the deck, but hitting nobody.

"Commodore, I think they may have now calculated the powder charge and fuse length," Scott said. "If you're agreeable, we shall withdraw and inspect the landing site you've recommended."

Commodore Conner called out to the naval lieutenant, captain of the Patrita, who was anxiously waiting for the command to move his vessel out of cannon range. "Lieutenant, you heard the general, make way for Collado Beach on Mocambo Bay.

Chapter Two

"An excellent site for the landing," Scott said to Commodore Conner. "It's well out of range of the guns of the fort and city, and more than ample beach for my first wave of troops to all land at one time."

Lee agreed with the general's observation. The Patrita was stopped two hundred yards off shore, and the officers were examining Collado Beach. The shoreline was a smooth, white sand beach some half-mile long and the shoaling water leading up to it appeared quite suitable for the surfboats to run in to land. Still the landing could be hazardous for inland some three hundred feet the dunes rose steeply and just behind them was a dense stand of chaparral in which the enemy could lie in wait and shoot the Americans all to hell as they waded ashore.

"I thought you might approve," Conner said. "I've scouted the shore for miles both to the north and south of Veracruz searching for the best invasion site and this one is my choice."

"I greatly appreciate that, commodore," Scott said. He gestured at Isle de Sacrificios, a coral and sand island lying a mile distant to seaward. "What can we do about the small area between the island and the beach? I don't believe my troopships can maneuver enough here to pull off the landing in a swift manner."

"Much too restricted," agreed the commodore. "I propose that you allow me to bring your troops from Anton Lizard on my naval vessels for they're more ably handled than your transports with their civilian crews. Then once your troops reach here they can unload into the surfboats. And there would be less confusion and it would go much faster if my steamships towed the surfboats into place."

Scott caught Conner's hand in his giant paw and beamed as he said, "With you and your warships to support me, how can we possibly fail to make a successful landing. No, by the Holy Spirit, we shan't fail."

"I'm glad that you approve," Conner said and delighted by Scott's pleasure.

Scott drew himself up to his full height and spoke to his officers. "Gentlemen, we have seen that which we must capture. All principal officers and aids shall meet with me aboard the Massachusetts at two this afternoon and we will draw up the plans for the landing."

* * *

"Good luck to you, Sam," said Lieutenant Bob Hazilitt. "I'll wait here for you." He halted by the ladder down which he and his comrade officer had descended to the lower deck of Talbott's Trader, the much used and abused ocean-going cargo ship converted to a troop ship and under contract to the army. The ship lay sullen and listless on the end of sixty fathoms of anchor chain in the large harbor at the island of Anton Lizardo twelve miles south of Veracruz.

"I'll need all the luck I can get," Lieutenant Ulysses Grant replied to the blond headed man. He and Hazlitt were of the Fourth Infantry, of Colonel Garland's brigade, of General Worth's division. "The colonel has turned me down three times already and I don't think this time will be any different."

Sam wasn't Ulysses correct name. The name had became attached to him due to West Point duty postings often listing him as U. S. Grant, and the other cadets seeing this began to call him Uncle Sam. That was swiftly shortened to Sam.

The two men were each twenty-four years old, had graduated together from West Point two years before, and were fast friends and messmates. They had been with General Zachary Taylor fighting Mexicans for the past nine months in northern Mexico.

He moved toward Brigade Commander Colonel Garland's quarters at the end of the companionway dimly lighted by the rays of sunlight being refracted down from above through the deck by an oculist, a conical glass prism set in the overhead. Colonel Garland had assigned Grant duties as quartermaster for his brigade early in the campaign with General Taylor. Those duties entailed obtaining all the provisions necessary to keep the brigade, consisting of the Second and Third Artillery and the Fourth Infantry, some 1300 men clothed, fed, and tented, and their hundreds of animals tended to. Grant's men also acted as wagon drivers, ferriers, guards, and transported all the provisions from camp to camp. During the voyage south, the soldiers had been provisioned from central stores. Now the brigade was about to land at Veracruz and Grant hated the thought of again taking up the duties of foraging across the foreign land in search of supplies to buy, or take by force if necessary, as the army fought its way inland. The muscles hardened along his jaw. He had come to fight as a line officer and win promotion, and be damned, somehow he would.

Grant came to Garland's quarters and knocked. At a gruff "Enter", he pushed aside the partially open door and stepped across the raised threshold and into the small and cramped cabin with the ceiling made of the beams and planking of the deck above. Garland sat at a small desk holding several sheets of papers, pen and ink well. An open porthole above the desk gave light and a little air. A bunk, a three-foot square table with two chairs, and a large brass bound trunk took up most of the space. The quarters had been that of the ship's first mate until the colonel had commandeered it. Grant saluted the colonel.

"What is it, lieutenant?" Garland said and returning the salute of his senior quartermaster. Garland liked the young lieutenant, standing some two inches below average height, slender, square jawed. He recalled him in the fight for Monterrey with General Taylor in northern Mexico. Garland had been ordered with his brigade to advance into an unknown maze of buildings with narrow, crooked streets against an enemy that was twice their number and behind heavy stone defensive works and with every rooftop full of Mexican riflemen firing down on them. Grant had galloped up and joined in the fighting just as Garland was ordered to advance deeper into the city, and this without allowing the brigade to replenish their ammunition which was in short supply from the first attack. The Americans were brought to a stop as they drew near the center of the town. Mexican riflemen and artillerymen firing canister from two strong forts knocked half the Americans off their feet within a few minutes. A third of the officers were killed or wounded. Returning the heavy fire, the brigade soon ran low on ammunition. Garland asked for a volunteer to ride for ammunition. Grant quickly volunteered. He sprang upon his horse and with an arm hooked around the horse's neck and hanging along the side of the horse opposite the enemy fire, raced away. At every street intersection, the Mexicans poured heavy fire at Grant. Reaching the supply depot, he loaded a packhorse with powder and shot and sped back. The Mexicans flung a hail of bullets at Grant at every crossing. Unwounded, Grant had fought on through the two-day battle for Monterrey.

"Sir, I request to be relieved of quartermaster duties and returned to my company for line duty."

"And why is that, lieutenant?"

"I wish to be part of the landing."

"I can understand your feelings, but the men deserve a skilled quartermaster. You fit that bill."

"Sir, as you know, I've foraged all over northern Mexico for supplies for the brigade. I sincerely request that I not have the same duties here. It seems quite fair to pass the duties on to someone else and allow me to go on the line. There are many other men who can perform the duties of quartermaster."

"Not as well as you. You know animals and equipment and keep accurate accounts of funds. I've heard other officers say that the men of our brigade are the best fed and best clothed in the army. No, I can't do without you as my senior quartermaster."

"But, sir . . ."

"No buts, lieutenant. Your request is denied. Attend to your assigned duties."

Chapter Three

The little steamship Patrita wound a course through the scores of ships housing Scott's army and crowding the harbor of Anton Lizardo and sidled up to the tall hull of the Massachusetts. The steamer's boatswain flung a line to a seaman on the Massachusetts and the little steamer was made fast to the ship.

Captain Lee, waiting on the deck of the ship with the other officers that had been ordered to assemble, watched as General Scott and Commodore Conner came up the gangway to the deck. Scott looked up at his commander's flag with its blue background and red center waving at the main truck. Lee saw a hint of pride come over Scott's face. The expression was swiftly erased. Both men faced Old Glory and gave her a snappy salute.

Conner swept his hand to encompass the gathering of sailing ships and the forest of masts covering the waters of the bay. "General, the day of the windjammer, of every kind of sailing vessel will soon be over. And it's all because of that," he pointed down at the steam driven Patrita with its stack giving off a thin black ribbon of smoke. "I'm glad that I'm retiring," he said sadly.

"Don't retire too soon, commodore. We still have work to do."

"I won't desert you just yet," Conner said with a faint smile upon his wasted, furrowed face.

The two senior officers received and returned the salutes of the officers on the deck and went into the Massachusetts's war room, also used as the officers' mess. The general and the commodore seated themselves at the head of the table.

Scott's cabinet officers and the division generals filed into the room and took seats around the table. Lee began to evaluate these men with which he would fight a war. General Worth was a square built man with a broad face, deeply set eyes, and an erect and commanding military bearing. He had pronounced that he would win a grade or death in the war. General Twiggs, bull-necked, silver bearded and silver headed, was an aggressive fighter whose main tactic in battle was to charge the enemy. General Patterson was the oldest of Scott's generals, and a wealthy man with a quiet and reserved way about him. He had no ambition to attain higher rank and was here to "Participate in the capture of the Mexican Nation" as he put it.

Patterson, due to his age and knowing much of the fighting of his brigade of volunteers would have to be done by his subordinates, had brought his three brigade commanders with him, Generals James Shields, John Quitman, and Gideon Pillow. Shields and Quitman were experienced battle officers. Pillow had no military experience and his only qualification for appointment as an army general was that he had been President Polk's law partner and had helped him become president by bringing about his nomination for that office at the Baltimore convention in 1844.

Lee watched as Scott silently regarded his subordinates. Scott at sixty had been a general officer for half his life, having made his first star as a brilliant artillery officer and had had a substantial part in the Americans beating the British at Chippewa in 1815. Shortly thereafter he had been wounded at Lundy's Lane and made a prisoner by the British for a month. He had commanded the armed forces during the Seminole Indian War in 1839, and had been the American Army's chief officer since 1841. His insistence on military spit-and-polish had earned him the name of Old Fuss And Feathers.

Lee knew Scott would be measuring his officers against what he knew lay ahead. Scott could make plans and give orders, however the execution of them lay with his field officers and the success of the invasion and the march inland to conquer the Mexican capitol depended upon the judgment and courage of the men at this table.

Scott caught Lee's eyes upon him. The captain had the most penetrating look of all the officers. Knowing the engineers were the elite of West Point graduates, Scott had selected three of them for his aids. Lee, Lieutenant Pierre Beauregard and Lieutenant George McClellan. Lee had the best pedigree, his lineage going back a thousand years to England and before that to France. Beauregard, a young, swarthy faced Creole with black hair and eyes came highly recommended. The brainy McClellan, with his slim build and a little below average height appeared even more boyish than his twenty years. He had entered West Point at the tender age of fifteen. West Point rules had been waived to allow for his enrollment.

Scott spoke in a no nonsense voice. "Gentlemen, let us begin. First I want to summarize our position for what lies ahead. Then we shall decide what to do, how to do it, and how quickly. Our greatest foe may well be yellow fever, el vomito as the Mexicans call it that arrives in this low country in early April. Whatever we are to do, must be accomplished before that scourge hits our men for it would destroy our army more efficiently than Mexican grapeshot. We must, and I repeat MUST be off the coast and into the highlands by the end of March. Another reason to swiftly capture Veracruz and Ulua is that Santa-Anna will receive word within a very short time that we are here in force and will march to defend the city.

"Now to the means to capture the city and fort. Our plans for this operation called for twenty five thousand men. Because of a long list of reasons, delays in recruiting, companies of men sent to the wrong embarkation point, the cancellation of some transport ships when they should not have been, our force consists of but nine thousand men. Seven hundred of them are too ill to assist us in the coming battle. Adding to our problems, none of the heavy siege weapons that I ordered have arrived, and but one-third of the ammunition.

"Only sixty-five of the one hundred and forty surfboats we planned for are here for our use. That means that twenty-five hundred men is the largest number we can land on the beach at one time. Once the loading of the surfboats begins, it must be done swiftly and the men taken ashore before the Mexican Army can assemble in front of us in sufficient force to repel the landing. This could well be the most dangerous action we undertake. By our ability to land but a small number of men, the Mexicans will have every chance to kill us piecemeal, or drive us into the sea.

"But even with all that said, I mean to go forward and make a landing and take Veracruz and Ulua. Verazruz will be our first objective for I believe Ulua can't be taken without an unacceptable loss of men. The landing will be a risky endeavor but we shall succeed. Now let us discuss who will lead the first wave of troops ashore, and the following ones."

Scott looked at Worth. "General, your two brigades of regulars shall lead the landing. Can you have them ready by tomorrow noon?"

"Thank you for the privilege, general. My men are ready now. In fact, the longer we delay, the less fit they'll be. Every day more men come down with some illness, much of it from the dirty, crowded ship's holds they must live in."

"Then you shall be first. Take eight artillery pieces with you for you will in all probability need them."

Scott turned to Patterson. "General your volunteers shall be the second party to land."

"Yes, sir," acknowledge the old general. He looked at Worth and Twiggs, and said proudly, "I know your regulars look down their noses at volunteers, but mine may just surprise you."

Scott's spoke to General Twiggs. "General, your two brigades of regulars shall be the third wave."

"Yes, sir," replied Twiggs.

"I shall write out your orders and have them to you later today."

Scott turned to Totten. "Colonel, we must throw a siege line around the city very quickly to prevent Mexican reinforcements from entering. You will insure ample tools are taken ashore for the men to clear away the brush and trees to do that. Immediately upon completion of the siege line, start your engineers in the construction of the sites for placement of our cannon."

"Yes, sir," said Totten.

Conner spoke. "General, my Colonel of Marines has asked for a company of his men be allowed to participate in the landing. I'd be pleased if you would accept three hundred of them. They would be under the command of Captain Watson."

Scott smiled for the first time since the meeting had begun. "With much gratitude, commodore." Scott turned to Patterson. "General, take the Marines under your wing and use them in the best possible way."

"A pleasure, sir."

"Commodore Conner, how much covering fire can you give us?"

"I have seven shallow draft gunboats that I can run in very close to provide covering fire with grape and canister if you are attacked while your surf-boats are running in to the beach. And all my other ships will be standing by with their heavier guns to help as they can."

"Excellent. Now to establish a timetable . . . ." General Scott ceased talking and looked out the hatchway to the main deck as a boatswain's pipe sounded the identifying call of a high-ranking officer coming aboard.

"That will be the British Commander," said Scott. "I wish all of you to stay to hear what he has to say. We shall finish our business after he leaves."

The young officer of the deck appeared in the doorway and self-consciously saluted the interior of the mess. "Sirs, British Captain Matson and British Consul Giffard are at the gangway and request to see you."

"Captain Matson is expected, lieutenant," Scott said. "And I'm glad to see the British Consul is here. Show them the way."

"Yes, sir." The lieutenant again saluted the interior of the mess and hastily left.

Scott smiled with an ironic twist to his lips. "Gentlemen, keep this in mind during any dealings with the British, they are not our friends. The loss of the last war with us still rankles them. They and the French and Spanish objected strongly to our annexation of Texas, and later at Taylor's march into northern Mexico. The "Morning Herald" of London, which is the British government's mouthpiece, and the "Paris Globe" which does much the same work for the French, condemn our campaign against Mexico most strongly. Both have predicted that the United States could not possibly defeat the Mexican Army on its own soil."

* * *

The deck officer appeared at the doorway with the two Englishmen. Consul Giffard was a tall, lean man with a long nose and a wide mouth that turned down at the ends and gave him a sour expression. Fleet Commander Matson was also leanly built, but of ordinary height, and where Giffard appeared a sourpuss, Matson presented an unreadable military expression to the Americans.

Matson came into the room, glanced past the junior officers, and immediately went to Commodore Conner and offered his hand. "Good to see you again, Commodore."

"And you to, Captain Matson." Conner replied. "I would like to introduce you to General Scott."

Matson took Scott's offered hand. "I've heard much about you, General Scott. My father has told me stories about fighting you Americans back in 1815. He met you while you were our guest after the battle of Lundy's Lane."

"That is a very polite way of putting my stay with you as a prisoner, Commander Matson," Scott said.

Matson nodded at that and spoke. "General Scott, I would like to introduce British Consul Giffard."

Scott turned to the second Englishman. "It's kind of you to come, Consul Giffard." He offered his hand to the Englishman.

"Thank you, General Scott." Giffard shook Scott's hand and quickly released it.

Seeming not to notice the brief handshake, Scott motioned at two empty chairs against the bulkhead. "Please both of you draw up seats and be comfortable as we talk. I've asked my officers to be present, if that meets with your approval."

"Most certainly," Giffard said as he and Matson drew chairs up to the table.

"Commander Matson, you signaled that you wished for this meeting, so would you please begin," said Scott.

"The signal wasn't for me, but rather for Consul Giffard," said Matson.

"Ah, I see," Scott said. He focused on Giffard. "Then, sir, would you inform me of its purpose. I suppose they concern your nation's possessions in Veracruz and elsewhere in the nation."

Giffard's dour expression remained. "Yes, that is precisely so for we have many valuable investments here and my government would take it seriously if they were to be damaged. And it appears that from all of the American ships and soldiers gathered here and at Anton Lizardo that you plan to attack Veracruz and Ulua."

"That's correct, should they not surrender to me," Scott said. "That will be my first step to force the Mexican government to the bargaining table and bring about a resolution to our disputes."

"General Scott, that is exactly why I'm here. I'm in a position to help in this situation for the Mexicans officials trust me and I can speak freely with them. So if you should care to enumerate those disputes to me in written form, then I believe I can be of assistance in resolving them without your invasion of the country."

"The disputes and issues are well known." Scott's tone was hard. "And we have tried in many ways to resolve them. There'll be no negotiations with lower level Mexican officials, only with the president himself and the representatives of their congress."

"But, General, I do believe that I can be of assistance to you."

"You can indeed be of help." Scott's voice had hardened another notch. "Recommend to the Mexican military that they surrender Veracruz and Ulua to me, and do it promptly before I launch an attack. In that way your possessions in the city will be spared any damage that might occur by an inadvertent stray cannon ball."

"I couldn't do that. They would think me mad for they are very strongly fortified." Giffard said, and a scowl creased his brow as if the very thought of doing such a thing was painful.

"Then I shall take them by cannon and musket," Scott said icily. "And I shall assume no responsibility for the damage done to anything in the city."

Giffard's scowl deepened and he pinched his lower lip as he struggled to hold back a sharp retort. He caught his emotions and his face became a mask. He removed a large folded paper from a pocket and spread it on the table in front of Scott. "I took note of your comments about stray cannon balls. In anticipation of the invasion going forward, I had this map of Veracruz prepared to assist you in avoiding British property during the battle." With finger pointing, he said. "This is our Consulate, and these are our warehouses, and this is a store house for some of Captain Matson's naval supplies. All of the areas in red are British owned. These other areas in color and labeled are the Consulates of the other neutral nations."

Lee leaned forward to better see the Britisher's map. It was drawn to scale and quite plainly the work of a skilled engineer. The American's best map of Veracruz was one prepared by the Spanish in 1818. This one would be extremely valuable in sighting targets within the city.

Giffard straightened in his chair and focused on Scott. "The map is for your use so you can avoid our property with your cannon fire." He paused. "Since you have a firm plan to invade, when will it occur? If I may ask?"

"You may ask," replied Scott. His mouth closed like a trap and his eyes shot an accusatory look at Giffard, as if to say, that question was out of order.

Giffard spoke hastily. "General, I only ask because there are British nationals who plan to move their portable valuables to Commodore Matson's ships, and to British merchant vessels. And the other nationals to their ships in the harbor. I merely wondered how much time they had to do that. And to further request that you don't attempt to stop them."

"If I should attempt to stop such activity, then I would succeed," Scott said matter-of-factly.

Lee suppressed a smile. General Scott was here with an army and most of the American navy and spoiling for a fight. So that the British wouldn't cause trouble, he was putting them in their place early in the campaign.

Scott added in a conciliatory tone. "All neutrals may continue to come and go to the ships, or go inland if they desire. Mexican citizens may do likewise. We have no quarrel with either."

He smiled ruefully. "In fact, I would suggest that when you have your discussions with the Mexican officials that you tell them that all people, including the Mexican soldiers should leave both the city and the fort. Anything you can do to encourage them to do so would be to their welfare."

"Regarding Ulua," Giffard said, his attitude and words were much subdued. "I've been in the Fort and I don't believe a sea attack could capture it. I believe Captain Matson would agree with me that its many huge cannon could sink the greatest number of warships." He spook to Commodore Conner. "Sir, I say this with no intention to belittle your fleet."

"No offense taken," Conner replied. "It's a strong fortification."

"Counsel Giffard, how many civilians in Veracruz?" Scott asks.

"Many people have left to seek safety away from the city. I estimate that there are between six and seven thousand people remaining."

"And how many soldiers?"

Lee felt the total silence as every American in the room waited for Giffard's response. How he answered this question was critical for it would indicate how the British would act during the coming hostilities, be neutral, or choose a side.

Giffard retained his noncommittal expression and made the most of a situation he couldn't control. "I estimate the number of Mexican troops in the city at four thousand. Further General Morales, commander of the city and fort, expects to soon receive substantial reinforcements that Santa-Anna has ordered from the twenty thousand man state militia."

"Do you think they will actually come?"

"Who knows whether Santa-Anna has indeed ordered the militia here. He has believed for some time that you intended to invade Veracruz, but he may not know that you have arrived. And even if he has ordered the militia, will they come. Often the generals do what they want and not what they are ordered to do."

"Ah, yes, General Antonio Lopez de Santa-Anna. What is your evaluation of him?"

"He's a scoundrel. He's hated by many in Mexico, disliked by most, and distrusted by nearly everybody, other governmental officials, army officers and the officials of the church. And let's not forget husbands with pretty wives for he's a woman chaser. And he's a liar as you Americans fully know after him tricking your president into allowing him to pass through your blockade."

There were nods around the table. It was common knowledge among the officers that Santa-Anna had convinced the American Consul in Havana that should he be allowed to leave his exile in Cuba and return to Mexico that he could again become president and from that position negotiate a peace settlement with the Americans. The duped consul provided the information to Polk who then instructed Conner to allow Santa-Anna to pass through the blockade. Within weeks Santa-Anna was president of Mexico and general and chief of the army. He immediately marched north to battle General Taylor.

"But I must say this about him, for audacity and cunning he can't be matched by anyone in the Mexican army or government. He can sway any crowd to his way of thinking for he is a master with words."

"How large is the city's food supply?" Scott asked.

"General, I know what you're thinking and I tell you truthfully that you don't have sufficient time to starve the city into submission before the yellow fever would strike your men. Further the people expect an assault and the streets are defended with cannon and barricades. Sandbags protect the doors and windows of the houses, and loopholes by the hundreds have been made in the walls. Now I have answered your questions truthfully and I ask you, how much time do we have before you make your attack upon the city?"

"I believe you have been very forthcoming with me," Scott said in an agreeable tone. "You may continue to take onboard your nationals and their possessions until further notice from me. As may the other neutrals." Again his voice took on an edge. "However, be warned that in no way will I allow anything to change my timetable or interfere with my capture of the city and fort. Once the battle begins any person, neutral or otherwise, entering or leaving the city or fort will be fired upon."

Chapter Four

Lee, engrossed in his letter writing, didn't hear the scratch of the iron nib of his pen on the paper, nor the pen of his long time friend, Joe Johnston, sitting across the table from him. The two men were in the below deck cabin they shared on the Massachusetts. A warm, moist draft of air flowed in the open porthole and out the open doorway. Above their heads the coal oil fueled ships lantern with its mica windows hung on its brass chain and pendulumed slowly to the motion of the ship. Light from the lantern casts distorted shadows of the men to roam about on the floor.

Knowing tomorrow would bring battle and danger, Lee was preparing guidance for his wife Mary on the rearing of their children. His firm hand should be on the older ones, but that was impossible with his long army assignments in faraway places. He felt frustrated by his wife's lack of discipline of the children, too lax, too inconsistent, and too yielding to them. With a frown he signed the letter R. E. Lee, folded and sealed it.

Mary and the children lived with Mrs. Custis, her mother, in the huge manor house Arlington situated on the Virginia hills opposite Washington. Mrs. Custis was a strong woman and perhaps she could be of assistance in the matter of Mary's lack of will. He would prepare a short letter to her and request she use her influence to induce Mary to perform her motherly duties. He hoped for, but held little expectation that Mrs. Custis's effort would have much effect upon Mary.

He turned to preparing his will, beginning with listing his holdings; canal and railroad stock, and state bonds of Virginia, Ohio, and Kentucky, and six slaves. He estimated his wealth at thirty-eight thousand dollars. Considering five percent a reasonable rate of return, he calculated the interest on his holding would be more than his annual salary of $1,350 per year, and a sum large enough for his family to live comfortably off the interest should he be killed in the war. In addition, Mary stood to inherit valuable property; the Arlington house, the White House on the Pamunky River, several hundred acres of fertile land, and two hundred slaves. His family should be able to live very well indeed should he be killed.

Lee glanced at Johnston and saw the tall, wiry man staring out the open doorway into the black night on the deck. "Something bothering you, Joe?" he asked.

"There's going to be a lot of American boys killed in this war. Doesn't it seem foolhardy for us with but a tiny army of a few thousand men to land from vessels on the open sea and invade a nation of seven million people?"

"They do occupy a mountainous land affording the greatest possible natural advantage for defense," Lee said. "And the officers will be creoles. But Cortez did it with five hundred and fifty men." Creoles were the descendants of Europeans and numbered about a million. The remaining citizens were Indians, or mixed white and Indian races called mestizos.

"Yes, but the Spaniards had firearms while the Aztecs had bow and arrows. In our case, the Mexicans have weapons as good as our own. And they'll be fighting from behind strong defensive works. And don't forget that the Aztecs thought Spaniards were gods, and men don't fight as strongly against gods as they do against mortal men."

"If any general can lead us to victory, then Scott is the one."

"Even Scott has to have enough soldiers to do it. Some of the officers believe President Polk and Secretary of War Marcy are deliberately withholding troops from him so that he will fail in his first battle. Then they can replace him with a general of the Democratic Party and then that man goes on to be the next president."

"You know that's not so. The newspapers call this Mr. Polk's war. I think they're right about that and winning it is more important to him than who might be the next president. He wants New Mexico and California so that our country extends from the Atlantic to the Pacific. I agree with him on that."

"It has always been more than just settling the Texas boundary."

Lee went back to his writing. His spirit rose as he composed a titillating letter to Tasy Beaumont, a nineteen-year-old girl with whom he had been corresponding for better than a year. She provided the zest and excitement that Mary lacked. He pictured her young body and smiling face as his pen moved over the paper. He frequently used words and phrases that she could interpret as having sexual meanings. He will write Markie, Martha Custis Williams a young cousin of Mary's, tomorrow after the landing on the Mexican shore. He admitted to himself that he found women, young women, ever more interesting as he aged.

* * *

Grant was seated outside on the main deck of Talbott's Trader. The deck was crowded with soldiers, the eighty men of Grant's enlisted quartermasters and teamsters, and Hazlitt's company of infantrymen. Many of the men were writing letters. Others talked. A number were silent, their thoughts turned inward to their private worlds.

Grant was watching the Mexican mainland barely half a mile distant. The beach was a bone white ribbon of sand lying squeezed in between the sea and dense brush. On a regular schedule, a Mexican lancer galloped along the water's edge. The enemy was keeping a close watch on the Americans.

As he watched the shore, the orange ball sun settled onto the inland mountains, and then fell behind them. In the deepening dusk, he moved along the deck among the men and entered his cabin. The space was small, but clean and orderly. In the light shining from a one-candle lamp in a gimbaled mount, Valere, a large black man and Grant's servant, was polishing one of his boots.

Valere also served Hazlitt, and the two officers shared the payment of his salary of six dollars per month. The northern officers used white men or free blacks and paid them. Many of the officers from the slave states had brought one of their slaves as servants.

Grant opened the chest at the foot of his bunk and took out his saber and brace of cap and ball pistols. The pistols were the standard army issue, .45 caliber, nine inch octagon barrel, weighing 32 ounces with fire blue finish, and a stock of curly maple stained violin red.

"What do you think you're doing?" Hazlitt said from the doorway.

"Checking my weapons."

"Why?"

"Oh, just in case I have a need for them."

"Don't do anything foolish during the landing tomorrow."

"I don't intend to."

Hazlitt grunted a disbelieving sound. He opened his chest and took out pistols and saber.

The young warriors cleaned their firearms, and filled their ammunition pouches with paper wrapped powder and ball cartridges. Then for a long time, there was a duet of rasping sounds as they whet the steel blades of their sabers with fine grained sharpening stones.

* * *

Late in the night Grant dreamed of landing with Hazlitt and his men on the Mexican coast. In the dream world where the dead still live, an old man with an ancient flintlock musket was wading ashore beside him. Somehow Grant knew the old fellow was Noah Grant, the grandfather he had never seen, who had fought throughout the Revolutionary War with General Washington.

"Grandfather, are you afraid," Grant asked.

The old man's stride remained firm and straight ahead as he turned his head and aimed penetrating blue eyes at Grant. "No. Are you?"

"No, sir." Grant said. That was mostly true, but off in the corner of his mind there was a tinge of concern for he was a logical man and knew no man was immune to the strike of a bullet. He had always recognized that fact when going into battle, but had always been able to set it aside and go on with the fighting.

Noah nodded. "We Grants are deficient in fear. That's good if you're a soldier. Unless it leads you to do something reckless that gets you killed." Noah smiled at Grant. "But don't worry too much about death for it's but a halfway point."

The old man dashed ahead and disappeared into a cloud of gunpowder smoke made by hundreds of Mexican muskets being fired at them. Grant plunged into the gunpowder smoke behind Noah.

Grant jerked awake with the sulfurous-carbon stink of burnt gunpowder that he knew so well in his nostrils. He lay for a long time in the darkness of the ship's cabin and wondered why he had dreamed of his grandfather. He had never done so before, so why at this point in his life? Was it an omen of his death in the coming battles?

Chapter Five

Lee, dressed in a blue field uniform and with a pistol and saber buckled around his waist, left his cabin on the Massachusetts and came out onto the main deck. He halted in amazement. A swollen red sun had just broken free of the wet Atlantic horizon and its rays had turned the calm waters of the harbor of Anton Lizardo a deep crimson. Every vessel of the American fleet of warships and transports seemed to be anchored in a pool of blood. He recalled the old sailor's adage that went something like "a red sun in the morning was a sailor's warning" of bad weather soon to come. He hoped this sunrise wasn't forecasting a storm that would hamper the landing.

General Scott, Captain Carmichael, skipper of the Massachusetts, and Colonel Totten, Commander of Engineers were talking near the starboard railing forward. Not wanting to approach the senior officers unless invited, Lee walked to the opposite side of the ship. He looked west at the Mexican mainland and found it covered with a dense gray fog that hid everything except the faraway inland mountains with the fifteen thousand foot, snow crowned Mt. Orizaba, "Mountain Of The Stars" the dominant feature.

Lee had his orders. Once Worth and his regulars had driven the enemy from Collado Beach and the surrounding area, he was to go ashore and ride with Scott while selecting a siege line to encircle Veracruz, and then guide Worth's men in the task of clearing the dense brush from the first third of the line. Beauregard guiding Patterson's volunteers would prepare the second third. McClellan with Twiggs regulars would complete the siege line to the sea north of the city. Then Lee and Beauregard, with labor from the infantry, would immediately begin constructing sites for the artillery batteries.

From the deck of the flagship, Lee watched the day swiftly brightened and the true blue-green of the sea return. The fleet came alive. Signal flags were hoisted to mastheads. Dispatch boats dashed about carrying messages. Other small craft ferried officers from their billets on the larger ships to their stations with their troops. Shouted orders of the naval officers preparing their ships for sea, came rolling clearly across the water to Lee.

At the sight of the American Navy and Army preparing to go into battle, Lee's heart beat a pleasant tattoo against his ribs. Finally it was to happen. In but a matter of a few hours, the opportunity would arrive to prove himself worthy of his famous ancestors.

Lee's attention was caught by the three score surfboats with a naval officer in charge and rowed by eight sailors which were spreading out through the troopships. The surfboats were constructed of wood, flat bottomed for stability, and were capable of carrying sixty men with their arms. They would take on board the soldiers and ferry them to the naval ships for transport to Magambo Bay and the landing on Collado Beach.

By mid-morning, Worth's two brigades of twenty-four hundred men were loaded onto the Raritan and Potomac, both steam driven side paddle-wheelers. The remaining soldiers were put onto smaller vessels of the naval squadron. The decks of the ships were massed with troops, with their polished muskets and bayonets flashing bright silver sun arrows.

After unloading their cargo, the surfboats congregated at the stern of the Princeton, the first American propeller driven naval steamboat. There they were tied into two long lines for towing. Throughout the fleet, ships were made ready to move, with steam being fed to the pistons, or sails unfurled and drawn down and sheeted home.

Lee heard Captain Carmichael shout down to the lower deck where a lieutenant waited with six sailors near the windlass, "Mr. Shultz, hoist anchor, if you please."

"Aye, captain," replied the lieutenant. Turning to his men, he called out, "Round you go boys. Bring it aboard."

The measured metal clank, clank of the pawls of the capstan sounded as the men tramped around and around. Foot by foot the anchor chain came crawling out of the sea up through the hawsehole and down into the chain locker.

Conner's flagship Mississippi with its red swallow tail pennant, followed by Scott's Massachusetts with its blue flag, broke from the pack of ships and started north for the nine mile run to Mogambo Bay. Cheers erupted from thousands of throats. The regimental band struck up "Hail Columbia".

The steamers Raritan and Potomac fell into line behind Scott's ship. Then came the Princeton towing the surfboats. The remaining naval ships carrying troops; a frigate, several sloops, brigs and schooners, came next. The hospital ship with its surgeons and their instruments and medicines fell into line, followed by the two munitions ships. The ships transporting the cavalry mounts, commissary and quartermaster supplies, and those with the wagons would sail to Mogambo Bay as soon as the naval vessels could unload and sail out of the restricted waters. The fleet left Anton Lizardo behind, the great spread of white canvass of the sailing ships catching a slow wind that blew them north.

* * *

Lee, on the quarterdeck of the Massachusetts with Scott, Totten, Beauregard, and McClellan, watched the mighty fortress of San Juan de Ulua grow ever larger as the wind drove them into the open water between Isle de Sacrificios and the mainland. He was glad they weren't attacking the forbidding fort. The landing upon the beach would be difficult enough.

Under a cloudless sky and on the sun-burnished waters of Mogambo Bay, Captain Carmichael halted the Massachusetts and dropped anchor with a rumble of chain. He ordered the ship's cannon ranged on the beach, and then came to stand beside Scott and his staff.

"General, my ship is ready and I await your orders," Carmichael said.

"Thank you. Everything seems to be going according to plan."

"Let's hope it continues so," Carmichael said in a voice one would use for a prayer.

Lee glanced at Carmichael and wished he hadn't spoken in that tone. Then he returned to observing the ships. Conner's gunboats, the Vixen and the Spitfire and five armed schooners, had run swiftly in to form a line some ninety yards from the beach and within easy gun range. Each was armed with a single weapon, either a 32-pounder or an 8-inch Paxihan mortar. The sailors were clearing the guns to be ready to sweep the beach with grapeshot to support the infantry. The naval ships that had ferried the troops from Anton Lizardo were moving into position for unloading. The decks of every ship were jammed with blue clad troops.

Lee turned from the activity on the bay and checked the city and fort, and the actions of the foreign ships in the harbor. The British, French and Spanish warships were lying south and east of Ulua, far enough away to be out of range of either American or Mexican stray cannon balls. Near them were merchantmen carrying army contractors such as wheelwrights, blacksmiths, and wagon drivers. And then there were the ships of the less desirable camp followers; the gamblers, the whoremasters and their whores, and the loan sharks.

The decks and rigging of every ship were black with men waiting for the Americans to charge the beach. A British packet had arrived since Lee was last on the bay. It was tied up to one of the British ships for protection. On its deck men were watching, and ladies with glasses and parasols were equally intent. Farther away at Veracruz, the rooftops of the houses and the great city wall were black with people straining to see the coming battle.

"Any second now," Beauregard says beside Lee.

"Yes," Lee agreed. He would soon have his first view of Scott's strategy and generalship. To be defeated here would mean professional ruin for Scott, and a huge black mark on all the officers connected to the campaign.

Scott spoke, as much to himself as to his aids. "If the roles were reversed, I could sweep the beach with five hundred cavalrymen and a thousand riflemen and prevent our force from reaching land. General Morales has twice that number of men under his command in Veracruz. We'll soon know if he is brave enough to come out from behind his walls and fight us when he has the advantage."

Lee felt the tenseness of the men around him as they waited for the general to give the signal to launch the landing. He was anxious to get ashore but must wait until the enemy was driven from the beach. Be patient, you will miss out on the initial fighting but there will be much more. Your skill as an officer will depend on how well you place the solid shot cannon and the howitzers and the mortars with their exploding shells for they are the weapons that will bring about the capture of the walled city.

Carmichael had been eyeing the signal flags on Conner's ship. He spoke to Scott. "General, Commodore Conner signals that all squadron vessels are in position and the guns ready. All are double-shotted for maximum damage. That and the gunboats should give the Mexicans a hot time should they appear in force."

"Thank you, captain. We have but to wait for the surfboats to deploy."

Chapter Six

Grant leaned with his back against the smokestack of the Raritan and waited for the unloading of Garland's blue clad infantry to begin. The steamer was in its assigned station and halted with the big side paddle-wheels churning slowly to hold the vessel against the one knot current flowing between Isle de Sacrificios and the mainland. The smokestack vibrated, the tremor carried upward from the moving pistons of the fire breathing steam engine deep in the bowels of the ship. A light rain of soot settled out of the plume of coal smoke and fell upon the soldiers and the two cannons aft of the superstructure on the main deck. The soldiers gave no sign they noticed the soot.

Grant hadn't been able to endure being left in the rear. He must be part of the landing and the battle that was sure to come. And so he had joined with Garland's infantry when it transferred from the troopship to the Raritan for the two-hour journey to Mogambo Bay. He believed Garland would know that he was with the men readying for the landing. The fact the colonel hadn't make an effort to spot Grant gave him encouragement to continue on with his plan.

A young private jostled Grant and drew hurriedly back.

"Sorry, sir," said the soldier. "I didn't mean to bump you, sir. The ship's packed damn tight."

"That's all right, soldier. We'll soon have plenty of room." Grant chucked a thumb at the beach.

"Yes, sir," said the private.

Every square foot of deck was jammed with soldiers. Each man carried a musket with bayonet attached, cartridge box on a white belt and holding sixty rounds, haversack containing two days supply of boiled beef and sea biscuits, canteen, and a blanket. Grant was equipped in the same manner, except his weapons were a saber and a brace of pistols.

The muskets of the brigade were second rate, and Grant regretted that. The soldiers had the standard army issue, a Model 1822, .69-caliber flintlock, smooth bore muskets. Loading the weapon was done by biting off the end of the paper cartridge, pouring the gunpowder down the barrel, inserting the paper as a wadding, and ramming the lead ball down firmly. Patterson's volunteers were better armed having the Model 1841, a .54-caliber breech-loading rifle. Grant had fired the newer weapon and knew first hand its effective range was at least three times that of the musket, and many times faster to reload.

Hazlitt was near the starboard railing of the ship. He had called his four sergeants to him and was giving battle orders. Grant watched and felt misused that he wasn't granted the same privilege, a lieutenant leading men in a charge onto the Mexican shore.

Shouts arose. Hands pointed. "Look Mexicans. There's Mexicans on the beach."

A company of two hundred or so Mexican cavalrymen, called Lancers due to the ten-foot lances they carried, had appeared riding swiftly along the edge of the sea from the direction of Veracruz. Immediately the gunboats opened fire and dropped exploding shells among the Lancers. A score of horses fell with their riders. Several horses struck by flying iron fragments shied violently and tumbled their masters upon the ground. The Mexicans still mounted fought to control their horses, and to keep them from tramping on the fallen men. The officer shouted trying to bring order. Three more American shells fell among the Lancers. Their courage broke. The men on the ground that were able to mount sprang upon the rear of a comrade's horse and the company fled into the chaparral.

Is that all the resistance we're going to have? Grant wondered.

The Princeton now had the surfboats into position for loading, the sailors with deft movements of the oars holding them against the side of the hull. With Garland leading, the brigade swarmed down the ladders that hung over the side and into the boats.

Grant waited until Hazlitt's company began to load and then went forward and down into the boat and took a seat beside the man. Haziltt was pale and tense, as was his appearance each time he went into battle. Grant wasn't concerned for he knew that once the fighting started, Hazlitt became a brave warrior and forceful leader.

"Sam, you've not been assigned to my company," Hazlitt said.

"Bob, there's going to be a battle and I got to be part of it."

"You're a glutton for fighting."

"It comes with being a soldier."

"I reckon it does."

"And besides I want to get the blasted war over with so I can go home and get married."

Hazlitt gave a weak smile at that. He was pleased to see Grant had come along for his courage in battle inspired both him and his men. In addition Grant was an expert marksman. During the lull before the attack on Monterrey, several officers had discussed their skill with pistols. There was much bragging and friendly arguments arose. A contest to put the boasting to the test was quickly arranged. Grant, though he had remained silent during all the talk, had easily won the shooting match.

Grant's heart was strumming nicely, just a little higher in his chest than normal that proved he hadn't conquered all his concern about being struck by a bullet or exploding shell. He had no guilt from leaving his post and being here. This was war and he was committed to it. Being with the men satisfied something within him. He thought the something came from the belief that life was action and passion, and war contained both.

He checked the troopers and the sailors on the oars. Several men showed fear, their faces pale and taut and their eyes large and showing much white. Those that didn't show fear, were they simply better at hiding it? Or had they done as Grant had, accepted the danger that lay ahead and resigned themselves to whatever happened.

A young soldier not far from Grant spoke to the young soldier beside him. "Billy Boy, you know something?"

"What's that?"

"We're just seven dollar a month targets. And that's all we are."

"That's too damn cheap," replied Billy Boy. "I feel that I'm worth a hell of a lot more than that."

"Then maybe some day you'll make sergeant and be a ten dollar target," said the first man with a boyish laugh.

Grant was a sixty-four dollar a month target and he too felt he was worth more than what he was being paid. He smiled to himself.

The loading of the brigades was completed, and with the Princeton once again hooked onto the surfboats from both the Raritan and Potomac, they were towed into position four hundred yards behind the screen of gunboats.

To the rear of the surfboats, Patterson and his volunteers and marines waited on the steamer Porpoise. Twiggs and his regulars were farther back on another naval vessel.

Grant scanned the anchored foreign warships and merchantmen. The decks were crowded with crewmembers and passengers, with some having sought the highest possible perches on the ships, even the crow's-nests were full, from which to better see the Mexican cannon devastate the foolhardy Americans charging the shore. Beyond the gently undulating water of the bay was the white sand beach framed with dense green brush, and inland Mt. Orizaba with its snow-capped crown rising sparkling and bold above the forested foothills in between.

The grand scene didn't relieve Grant of his worry about the timing of the landing. The day had been eaten away by the loading of the men onto the naval vessels, followed by the trip to Mogambo Bay, and lastly the transfer to the surfboats. Now the landing was being made just before sunset with night but a couple of hours away. That allowed little time to land, fight a battle, and secure the beach. Darkness would give all the advantage to the defenders in entrenched positions, knew the lay of the land, and could be reinforced as needed.

A thunderous roar jarred the air and Grant whirled to look to the north. Ulua and Veracruz had fired a barrage from their big cannon. Every shot fell short, their impacts into the sea sending huge gouts of water leaping skyward. Another six to seven hundred yards range and one of those shells could have struck a surfboat where men, packed like sardines, would have been killed by the scores. Still the barrage was of a benefit to the Americans for they now knew the maximum range of the Mexican's guns and could anchor with the knowledge they were safe.

The signal gun boomed on the Massachusetts. The bands of the regiments struck up the Star Spangled Banner. Cheers rose from the American sailors and soldiers on the ships.

The surfboats cut loose from the Princeton, and with regimental pennons fluttering from the stern of every one, speedily formed in a line abreast the shore. Bull-voiced General Worth gave a war cry and the sailors bent to their oars and the surfboats raced for the beach. The boats darted through the screen of gunboats and into the open where they were fully exposed to the Mexican artillery that would be hidden behind the sand dunes. Grant expected that any moment camouflage would be flung aside and the Mexican cannon would be blasting the Americans with exploding canisters.

The sailors pulled powerfully and the boats sliced landward through the water. Worth, in a sleek gig rowed by four sailors, sprinted ahead of his men. In less than a minute, they were so close to the shore that the American gunboats couldn't fire over their heads to knock down enemies should they suddenly threatened them.

Worth's gig grounded and the general sprang into the water and splashed ashore. Just like the general, Grant thought. He had to be first to set foot upon the hostile shore. The general had courage and spirit, but was too impetuous, too quick to act, and because of that was dangerous to the men he led. Grant hoped the general wouldn't get them killed.

With wooden bottoms grating on the sand fifty feet from the shore, the wave of surfboats came to a stop and the whole brigade jumped into the shallow surf. Holding their muskets and cartridge boxes high, the men ran for the beach.

The captains and lieutenants of the companies, gripping their sabers and the color bearers with their muskets slung over their backs on leather straps, moved out a few yards from the water's edge. The company of soldiers they led hastily formed behind them in battle order.

Worth shouted at Garland and Clark and swung his saber to point at the ridge of tall sand dunes at the end of storm surge a hundred yards inland. He wheeled around and charged toward the dunes. Screaming a mighty battle cry, the brigades of staunch and battle-hardened veterans ran after him in a long blue line.

Grant pulled both pistols and holding them ready to fire ran beside the big sergeant carrying the colors for Hazlitt's company. Any second now the Mexicans would rise up above the ridge of dunes and a blast of muskets and grapeshot and exploding canisters would strike and riddle the Americans.

He veered away from the color bearer. As an officer he would draw more than his share of fire. It was foolish to also be in the storm of enemy bullets the color bearer would draw. Grant crossed the bare beach and plunged into the sand dunes. Slipping on the loose sand, he stormed ahead and scrambled to the crest of the dunes.

The sergeant with the colors had beaten Grant. Now the big soldier was shouting with jubilation and whipping his flag about over his head. He gave a mighty war whoop, made a last proud wave of the flag, and stabbed its staff into the sand.

With heart pumping from the all-out run, Grant swiftly scanned the land between the crest of the dunes back to the chaparral and was amazed that not one enemy could be seen. The Americans had taken possession of the shore without a musket being fired. The Mexicans had had more than ample time to march to the beach in force after the landing place of the Americans could be determined with certainty. They had not and had missed a perfect opportunity to slaughter the American invaders.

The brigade burst into tremendous victory cries. From out on the bay answering cheers come rolling from the soldiers waiting to land, and from the sailors of the American ships. Something within Grant told him that the celebration was woefully premature.

Worth shouted orders at his brigade commanders. The orders came speedily down the ranks to the lieutenants and the men and they moved out to expand and consolidate the beachhead.

Grant cast one glance at the surfboats heading back for Patterson's volunteers, then looked for Hazlitt.

"Well, are you coming?" Hazlitt called.

"Can't," Grant said and shaking his head sadly. "With no fight, I've got to get back to the supply ships. The colonel will expect me to get everything ashore, and have a camp set up for the men in short order."

"You be sure and do that for I don't like to sleep in the rain. And help the commissary fellows get the kitchen set up too so we can have hot food." Hazlitt grinned, waved and ran toward his men held in formation by his sergeants.

Chapter Seven

The lively sea breeze blowing through the open portholes and the doorway of the officers' mess on the Massachusetts had cooled steadily after the setting of the sun. Its gusting breath often reached the vents of the three ships' lanterns hanging above the dining table and sent their flames dancing and flicking. The ship now and again jerked and rattled the dishes on the table as it was brought up short against the end of its anchor chain.

Lee had remained silent during the late evening meal with General Scott, the generals of the divisions, and several other officers. The conversation had flowed freely but Lee had grown tired of it because everybody avoided discussing the situation of the army that was on his mind. As an aid of the general he had to endured the session, still he wished it would end. Lee could see the general was also restless. The mess orderly made the round and poured the final cups of coffee and left.

Scott tapped his coffee mug with a spoon. "Gentlemen, let me interrupt your conversation and discuss our actions for tomorrow. As you know, General Twiggs landed the last of his troops at 10 tonight, and that includes the one thousand Louisiana volunteers that arrived late today. We now have all three divisions on the shore, nine thousand and six hundred men. Pickets and roving patrols are in place."

Scott continued in a pleased voice and his eyes sparkling. "Not one man was lost. General Morales has made a serious error in not attacking us as we landed. Two or three coordinated cavalry charges at us while we were in the water to our crotches could have turned the landing into a slaughter. Now give us another day to dig in and it will take an army twice, no, three times our size to rout us out.

"Because of the late landing, we weren't able to start building the siege line today. Colonel Totten, tomorrow at first light, I want you and Captain Lee to accompany me ashore to select the location of the line. Your engineers will guide the divisions in its construction."

"Yes, sir," Totten said.

"Now let's discuss how we will take Veracruz. And it's ours for the taking. Any army that locks itself behind walls and fights from there can't win. For him to win, he must come out and drive the enemy away. It's obvious that General Morales isn't coming out.

"We have all studied the drawings and written material that is available describing the defenses of the city, and we have examined what we could see from the sea. And we have what the Britisher Giffard told us. So now let's hear recommendations on how to proceed."

"General, we can take the town by storming the walls," said Worth. "Wait for a dark night and steal up close. Then rush the walls in force before the Mexicans could assemble and prevent us from getting over. I'd lead the attack with my regulars."

Twiggs nodded quick agreement. "Right. We can have them in a few hours once we're set to attack."

Lee was dismayed that the two generals would consider charging such strong walls where the defenders would be expecting just such an action. Surely Scott wouldn't agree to it.

Scott spoke to Patterson. "And you general, what do you say to a frontal attack?"

"I wouldn't advise storming any walls that the cavalry couldn't jump and so be able to help the infantry," said the old gentleman and shaking his gray head. "And that means that I wouldn't recommend attacking Veracruz's high walls."

Lee was pleased with Patterson. He would watch these generals and learn much about them during the coming campaign.

Scott caught first Worth and then Twiggs with a penetrating look. "How many men would it cost to take the city by storm?"

The two officers glanced at each other. Then they looked away with neither meeting Scott's eyes.

Slowly rotating his coffee cup on the table, Scott waited for one of the men to reply.

Worth squared his shoulders and faced Scott. "There would be losses but we could immediately march into the highland and avoid the yellow fever."

Scott spoke and his tone grew harder with each word uttered. "I estimate we would lose more than a thousand men killed and wounded. That would leave us with a very small army to fight our way nearly three hundred miles to Mexico City. Could we capture a nation with so few men? And consider this, it may be weeks before we get reinforcements."

Scott eyes smoldered as he looked into the eyes of each of his generals. In a stern voice he said. "Gentlemen, we are greatly outnumbered and that's a hard fact. Every battle will be fought against superior numbers, and most likely with them behind fortifications as here at Veracruz. We can't afford to lose one man unnecessarily. Above all we dare not lose one battle for that would mean disaster, the very end of our campaign.

"I have decided that we will throw a siege line around Veracruz and bottle it up to prevent reinforcements from arriving. Once that has been accomplished, we will take the city by siege and bombardment. We will pound them with every gun we have. If we lose more than a hundred men, I shall consider myself a murderer. Your orders are to establish the siege line and place our cannons where they will do the most damage, and do it swiftly. Once Veracruz is taken, we shall turn our guns on Fort San Juan de Ulua and take it also. Should the bombardment not succeed in a reasonable time, we will be preparing for storming the walls.

"Tomorrow morning headquarters will be moved to the shore. Now, gentlemen it's getting late so I say, goodnight. Go and make preparations for what must be done."

Lee filed out of the mess with the other officers, and then separated and walked to the ships railing. Joe Johnston came up and stood beside him. They silently stared out across the black sea. On the shore a thousand bivouac fires burn with leaping orange flames. The voice of a man raised in song came to them.

"He had better do his singing now," Johnston said. "We're going to have a lot of American blood on the ground before this war is over."

* * *

With the night draped in blackness over Talbott's Trader, Grant seated himself at the tiny table in his cabin. Placing paper close to the frail light of the candle, he began a letter to Julia Dent. She had been his betrothed for two years and in all that time he had seen her but once. Feeling an immense yearning to hold her in his arms, he told her how much he missed her. He continued on to describe the beauty of the harbor and the beach. He told her that the army had arrived at Veracruz and had made a successful landing upon the coast, that he wished for a short war so that he could return to the States and they could be married.

Grant finished his writing and studied the flickering flame of the candle. Julia seldom wrote, and rarely expressed any fondness for him. He reflected upon this characteristic of Julia's, and upon his mother Hannah whom he had never seen cry nor express any feelings for his father. Maybe all women were like that. Reflecting upon that thought, he prepared the letter for the mail packet.

* * *

In the gray gristle of dawn's first light, Grant came awake to the ship trembling and shaking under powerful blasts of wind. He knew a "norther" a fast moving storm with gale force winds had arrived. It was the curse of all sailors on the Mexican coast, and now of the American soldier.

Grant came out of his cabin and into the stiff wind raking the ship's deck. To maintain his footing on the plunging, rearing vessel, he held to the taut, straining rigging with the ropes strumming like piano wires under his hand. Overhead a low mass of dark gray clouds sped south. A gull shot past like a white arrow, barely missing the ship's whipping mast.

All around him the sea was a ribbed expanse of high waves with every crest crowned with white spume. Halfway along the ship's length, the waves crests ran level with the railing. Grant could have scooped up a handful of foam by merely reaching out for it. The Trader plunged its bow into a huge roller and breaking free brought a ton of water aboard that swept the length of the ship in a dense curtain.

All the ships of the fleet, except for three of the supply vessels, had their snouts pointing into the north wind and pulling mightily on their anchor chain. The three supply vessels had been torn from their anchorages by the wind and driven ashore where the huge breaking surf was pounding their ribs upon the beach. Two of them were close together directly opposite Grant, and one a quarter mile farther away along the shore.

Grant recognized the ships on the beach. The two closest vessels carried officers' horses, the third wagons. His mare was in one of the ships. He had captured her from a herd of wild horses roaming the plains north of the Rio Grande and had broken her to ride. He hated to think of the harm being inflicted upon the gentle animal.

He saw Captain Lyford and his two mates standing together and partially protected from the wind on the lee quarterdeck. He made his way to them.

"Captain, I need to take men to those wrecked ships and salvage what I can of the cargo," Grant called through the strident whine of the wind in the shrouds.

"And the sooner the better, I know. But I can't put a boat in the water with the sea running so damn high. However it's been easing up for the past hour. If it continues falling, I'll take a chance on two of my boats and enough men to handle them in half an hour or so."

"I'll get my men ready." Grant said.

Grant descended into the shadow filled lower decks of the Trader and found Sergeant O'Doyle. "Sergeant, we've got ships washed up on the beach. Muster the men and get them prepared to go ashore to help with salvage. We've a lot of work to do and won't be coming back here any time soon so have them carry enough food for a couple of days and a blanket."

"Yes, sir," O'Doyle replied.

"Probably be at least half an hour so have them eat something. I'll call you when it's time to come on deck."

"Yes, sir." The sergeant turned and shouted at the men in the tiers of bunks. "Up and dressed you blockheads. You've been wanting to go ashore and here's your chance. We're to help the lieutenant salvage cargo."

* * *

Grant's men climbed up from the hold of the ship and stood squinting in the light of the upper world. They spread their legs and braced on the heaving deck. Sergeant O'Doyle came to Grant and saluted.

"Lieutenant, all the men are accounted for and ready to go ashore."

Grant returned the salute. "Just waiting for Captain Lyford to give the signal to load the boats." He turned to watch the seamen at the davits and lowering boats.

A young quartermaster with a face strained with fright was eyeing the turbulent, wave tossed sea lying between the ship and shore. He called out. "Sergeant, I can't swim. If the boat sinks I'll sure as hell drown."

"Now, Crowley, buck up. Trust Lieutenant Grant for he'll call it right."

Crowley gave Grant a questioning look.

Grant winked at him and grinned, and hoped he was making the correct decision in putting his men onto the sea in small boats.

Crowley smiled weakly back.

Grant returned to surveying the angry sea. The north wind had slowed to a quarter gale and the waves had decreased to six feet or so. Even so to try to row a small boat across the heaving water appeared extremely dangerous. The captain must know what seas a boat could withstand for him to be willing to risk his sailors. Grant could do no less with his men.

On the shore the wrecked cargo ships with their curved hulls and black bottoms wallowing and bouncing under the surge and wash of the surf resembled giant sea beasts in their final death throes. A handful of crewmen were on the ground and milling about each of the beached ships.

"Lieutenant Grant, I have the boats alongside," Captain Lyford called. "Load your men."

Grant raised his hand in acknowledgement of the captain's words. Then he called to O'Doyle. "Let's get the men over the side."

He led to the railing above the ship's boats riding the waves along the lee side of the Trader. Four oarsmen and a coxswain were already in place in each boat.

Grant climbed over the railing and led the way down one of the swaying ladders hanging along the hull and into the nearest bouncing boat. His men followed.

The coxswain of Grant's boat called out above the water noise of the sea. "You soldiers stay seated and stay low. Now hear me! Don't stand up for any Goddamn reason. You sailors, cast off forward. Push clear and man your oars. Pull on my calls.

"Pull! Pull!"

The coxswain threw the tiller over, the rudder bit water, and the boat pivoted away from the ship and plunged into the sea of waves. The soldiers hunkered low and gripped the gunwales with white knuckled hands. Grant glanced to the side and saw the other boat had shove clear of the ship. The die was cast.

The fragile boat Grant rode fought one tall wave after another. When it sank to the bottoms of the troughs and water towered above on all sides, the shore and the other boat with them disappeared from view. Even more frightening was when the oarsmen on one side or the other would miss a stroke as the sea fell away from under their oars and the boat would yaw and slide into the trough and take on water before the coxswain could swing the rudder and right it. By the time half the distance to the shore had been made good, water above the men's ankles was sloshing back and forth over the bottom. Still the sailors pulled their oars and the boat struggled on.

The bow of the boat grated on sand and the two forward oarsmen quickly shipped their oars and sprang into the surf. Wading water to their waists, they kept the boat from swinging sideways and broaching as they pulled its bow upon the beach.

"Out. Out. Before we're rolled." The coxswain shouted at Grant.

"Abandon ship," Grant called.

In a flurry of arms and legs, he and his men hastily jumped from the boat and waded to dry ground. Immediately he turned and helped push the boat back into deep water, and the sailors bent to the oars. The remaining boat swept ashore and disgorged its passengers to splash to the shore.

Grant shouted his men together and hustled them along the beach toward the nearest wreck wallowing in the surf. As he drew close the pain-filled screams of injured horses made the hair on the nape of his neck stand erect. One of those cries could be his mare's.

"You fifteen men stay with me to unload this ship," Grant ordered and his hand moved indicating those men he meant. His mare was on this ship and he wanted to be here when she was found.

"Sergeant O'Doyle, take the rest of the men and get the horses off that next ship. Move fast! Make the sailors help you unload. Don't take no for an answer."

Grant led his men and the sailors onto the groaning hulk of the old wooden ship and down into its creaking dark holds. He searched hurriedly among the horses, some on their feet, but most lying in tangled mounds on the rounded ship's side.

He came upon his horse and his breath caught at the awful sight. The mare was penned beneath two other horses. A crushed eye hung from a socket. Her right front leg was broken with the end of the splintered bone sticking out through the skin. She breathed feebly. Yet her good eye saw him, and she seemed to plead for his help.

He pulled his pistol and eared back the hammer. He blinked to clear his vision.

"Sorry, girl, there's nothing I can do for you," he whispered to the faithful mare that had carried him hundreds of miles upon her back and never once let him down. With a stifled sob, he pointed the pistol at a spot between the mare's eyes and fired.

He reloaded and went among the horses and shot the ones with broken bodies. God! How horrible it was to shoot a lead ball into those beautiful animals.

He set the men to work to build a strong tripod using spare ship's spars, and then to hang a block and tackle from it, everything being found in the ship's stores. Fighting to control the frightened horses, they began the long and laborious task of hoisting them one by one from the holds and setting them down upon the beach.

Chapter Eight

Early in the afternoon when the storm subsided, Lee came ashore on Collado Beach with Scott, Totten, Beauregard and McClellan in the Massachusetts's gig. Behind them came three boats carrying Scott's army headquarters' paraphernalia; official papers and maps, a small table, four chairs, an oversize cot for the big man, and Scott's personal possessions in two trunks, and his weapons, and lastly three large tents to house everything. All the men were armed with pistols. The three junior officers also carried full knapsacks and rolled blankets across their shoulders for they wouldn't be going back aboard ship for days, and then only to get their private belongings.

As the officers moved up from the beach, Lee scanned the area occupied by the army that was about three hundred yards deep and stretching some half-mile along the shore. Hundreds of brush windbreaks had been built and on the lee side of them off duty men lounged upon their blankets. Lee identified the brigades by the colors of their standards stuck into the sand about each encampment. The sight of the men waiting for the order to move out into hostile ground caused his heart to pick up its tempo. The time had come when he would be put to the test. He felt the ebb of his life running strong and vital and looked forward to whatever assignments might be handed him.

Generals Worth, Patterson, and Twiggs had been waiting on the shore and now came to meet General Scott. They appeared grim, with their eyes red rimmed and clothing dust covered from spending the night out in the fierce windstorm. The three saluted Scott.

Scott returned the salutes. "What's our situation?" His manner was brusk as he glanced about at the enclave of soldiers.

"Our perimeter is well dug in and roving patrols are out in force," Worth replied for all three generals since he was the senior one. "We'll have no surprises."

"Very good," Scott said to Worth. "I'll establish headquarters here in your section." He motioned at the three boats with their bows up on the beach and the sailors holding them against the surf. "Assign some men to bring the headquarters' items ashore. Rig the tents there on that level ground above high tide?" Scott pointed at the location. "From here I can stay in contact with Commodore Conner and also with what is happening on the shore."

"Certainly, general," Worth said.

He called out to a lieutenant standing nearby self-conscious and listening. "Lieutenant Brodworth, take six men and get headquarters set up."

"Yes, sir," Brodworth replied.

"Now we should have a look at Veracruz and its walls," Scott said. "We need horses, have any been brought ashore?" His words came swiftly.

Lee saw Scott look around as if expecting to see some of the animals. Lee had become aware of this characteristic of Scott, of asking a question with which he already knew the answer and didn't like the one he was about to receive.

"No, sir, not yet," Worth said. "The sea has been too rough. But two of the ships that went aground last night had horses and men are working to unload them now."

Scott's face registered disapproval. "I don't believe the sea is too rough for horses to swim. Send word to your quartermasters and cavalry commanders to drop them over the side to swim to shore. We need a company of cavalry on land and out on patrol."

He pulled out his watch and checked its face. "So that we may have a better chance of reconnoitering without drawing fire, I've asked for a few cannon balls to be thrown into the city to divert their attention. We have about half an hour before that begins."

* * *

Grant and his men saved ninety-seven horses and he considered that number a miracle considering the destruction that had occurred inside the ships. Seventy-five had been found dead or so badly injured that they had to be shot. The officers owning those horses would have to wait until Grant could go foraging and find them replacements, or a company of Lancers were fought and killed and their mounts taken. In a separate ship's hold they had found the saddles and bridles for the horses.

Grant cast an eye over the fleet of transport ships, their masts bare and sails furled, anchored in an area stretching for a mile along the coast. Among them were the thirty empty troopships that Scott had not allowed to return to the States. Should the Americans suffer defeat, the ships would be needed to evacuate the men from Mexico. The seventy remaining vessels carried the provisions, arms, and medical supplies for the fighting that would soon begin. The cavalrymen would bring their horses to shore and the artillerymen their weapons. Grant and the other quartermasters were responsible for unloading and transporting everything else, and establishing a central supply depot. A week or more would be required to accomplishing that Herculean task.

"Mount up," Grant called out and yanked himself astride one of the horses. Once their hooves had stepped upon solid ground, the horses had mostly shaken off their ordeal aboard the wrecked ships.

His men had chosen mounts and now swung astride. The extra saddles and bridles had been divvied out amongst the men and were carried along with them.

Grant led the company of men along the beach toward the landing site some half-mile distant. As he drew near, he saw General Scott talking to a score of officers that surrounded him. The general, towering above even the tallest man by half a head, was an impressive figure. Enlisted men were gathering about the general also but keeping their distance from the officers.

Grant noted the boats being unloaded and tents being erected. Scott was establishing his headquarters on the shore and that meant he was here to stay. Now the preparations for the attack on Veracruz would progress swiftly and this pleased Grant. He must hurry his work so as not to be responsible for delaying the attack.

Grant held up his hand to halt his cavalcade of men and horses. "Dismount," he ordered.

The men swung down and stood holding the reins of the animals as Scott and the other officers came to meet them.

Grant saluted the officers. "Lieutenant Grant, Quartermaster for Colonel Garland's brigade," Grant said. It would be to Grant's benefit for these senior officers to know his name, especially General's Worth and Scott, both of whom would have to approve the recommendation for promotion that he intended to win.

Grant recognized Patterson and Twiggs the other two generals with Scott. He had become acquainted with Colonel Totten and his three engineers, Lee, Beauregard and McClellan while they had waited at Brazos Santiago for the transport ships to arrive and carry them to Veracruz. Lee had begun to earn a name for himself by the scouting he did for General Wool in the Mexican state of Chihuahua. Scott must prefer engineers as his staff officers for they made up the bulk of them.

"You're just in time for we need mounts," Scott said. He looked past Grant to the horses. "Is this all you have?"

"Yes, sir. This is all that we could save from the wrecked ships. Some were dead and we had to shoot several others that were badly injured."

"I don't see my horse here," Scott said as he brushed past Grant to the animals. "I hope he wasn't one of those you shot."

Grant shrugged. For now he won't let the general's attitude rile him. He moved away from the officers sorting through the horses and went up the beach a score of yards.

Scott called out as he climbed astride a large grey horse. "I'll temporarily borrow this one for today's ride. I hope the owner doesn't get mad that I used it without asking permission, but we have no time to waste to locate him.

"The rest of you who are accompanying me, mount your horse if it's here. If not, borrow one as I've done and let's get moving."

A half minute later, Lee rode up to Grant and halted his horse. The quartermaster was well respected by his colonel and the officers of his brigade. His penchant for always finding his way into a battle was talked about among the officers, and so too was his bravery at Monterrey.

"Thanks, lieutenant, for saving my mare for I'm partial to her," Lee said.

"You're welcome, captain, for I know how you feel," Grant said. "And you were luckier than me for my mare was injured and I had to shoot her."

* * *

"The siege line must be as close as possible to the city while still affording our men protection from the Mexican guns," Scott told the officers riding horseback with him. "And strong enough to prevent even a large body of enemy soldiers from breaking through and reinforcing it."

Scott was leading the group of three generals and four engineers along the narrow, sandy beach in the direction of Veracruz. The surf lapped noisily at the horses hooves on the right, and close on the left was chaparral made of thorny mimosa and prickly pear matted together in a tall, impassable barrier for long stretches.

Two miles from the city, Scott halted the group and looked at his watch. "About now," he said expectantly.

As if in response to Scott's words, a cannon boomed. Lee looked quickly in the direction of the sound and saw a gray puff of gunpowder smoke rising from a gunboat sheltered behind Point Hornos and a mile closer to Veracruz.

"Ah, right on time," Scott said with satisfaction. "The sailor boys will fire a round at the city every two minutes. That should keep the attention of the Mexicans away from us. Now let's go and choose the site for the siege line."

He guided away from the beach through a break in the chaparral and into the broad expanse of sand dunes lying inland from the city. The men worked across the dunes, trying to stay within a mile of the city, but forced to take a winding course to avoid the chaparral thickets and low areas full of water. They frequently halted and lifted their field glasses to study the walls of the city. They came within sight of Vergara a small seacoast town on the distant side of Veracruz. Scott led his group to the tallest of the nearby sand hills and sent his horse in a difficult, scrambling climb to the summit.

"Where should we build the siege line?" Scott asked. "You have ridden it," he flung his hand out to indicate the land they had crossed over, "and from here can see all of it at one time. Give me your recommendations."

Lee studied the terrain spread out before him under the warm afternoon sun. Veracruz, where five columns of smoke rose from fires started by the American cannonading, was to the northeast. Inland from the city's walls lay a plain approximately one-half mile wide. Beyond the plain were sand hills rising gradually to an elevation of three hundred feet some three miles inland. Then came dense forests cut here and there by roads and open areas of cultivated land and orchards.

The chaparral was not continuous; being absent on the crest of the dunes where the wind kept the sand too active to allow for growth, and also missing where the land was low and stands of water glistened. The water areas would shorten the time needed to remove the chaparral to construct the siege line, but increase the effort to place the cannon. He would worry about the cannon later.

Now where should the siege line run? As the possibilities ran through his mind, a wonderful sensation came over him and his spirits soared. The weight of family responsibilities, of being a husband, a father, and worrying about his children's training and education, of being the son of Light Horse Harry Lee, was lifted off him and he felt sublimely free. He was freer now than ever before, even when but a small boy. He should have a sense of guilt for this, but hadn't the slightest. Now he could apply all his strength of mind and body to simply doing his duties as an engineer and soldier. Did all soldiers feel freedom from personal cares when far from home and preparing for battle?

He controlled the urge to laugh out loud from the sense of freedom for Scott and the other officers would think they had a crazy captain of engineers. Instead he smiled a little and focused on the land lying before him and evaluated the topography for the best place to construct the siege line. During his years improving the American fortifications along the Atlantic coast, he had participated in the firing of every type of cannon, mortar, and howitzer and could picture the arcing parabola of the balls from each one. The solution as to where the siege line should be was as obvious to him as knowing water would run downhill.

Should he be the first to make a recommendation? Would that be too presumptuous for a captain to do in the presence of generals? To the devil with it, he wanted to be noticed. He spoke to Scott. "General, I believe that ridge of sand dunes some quarter mile closer to Veracruz should be the location of the siege line. It stretches from the beach on the south to Vergara on the north." Lee pointed both directions as he spoke. "Vergara should be the northern terminus. The ridge bends and twists some, but overall it runs in a half circle that parallels the city's walls."

Scott didn't respond for a full minute as his eyes roamed the area Lee had pointed out. Then he spoke. "Any agreement, or disagreement with the captain's recommendation?"

"It appears quite plain that's the correct location," Worth said, his tone showing annoyance.

"Anyone have a different suggestion?" Scott asked.

"Captain Lee has recommended the best place," Totten said. He nodded his approval at Lee.

"Captain, another question for you, where would you put our cannons?" Scott said.

"To do the most damage, they should be placed nearer the city, within a quarter mile or even closer. I'd recommend just behind the crest of those hills", again he pointed, "where the cannon balls from the Mexican artillery can't easily strike our men."

Scott nodded. "The Mexican strong points outside the walls will have to be taken so that the batteries won't be in danger of being overrun."

Scott led the group of horsemen down from the crest of the dune.

Chapter Nine

At the last moment the wave tossed sea relented from its efforts to sink Grant's surfboat heavily laden with army stores. A large watery roller ran in under the boat and lifted and shoved and deposited it half its length upon the beach.

Grant sprang onto the shore, caught hold of the craft and steadied it against the large breaking surf. His men already on the beach hastened up and swarmed over the boat and started manhandling the cargo onto the sand.

"Get out and help them," the boat's coxswain ordered his oarsmen.

The men put down their oars and scrambled out and fell in beside the laboring quartermasters.

Grant and the other quartermaster officers and all their men had ferried supplies from the ships to the shore from daylight to dark whenever the conditions of the sea permitted. Now in mid-afternoon of the third day after the landing of the army, approximately one-quarter of the provisions had been brought ashore. Once on the shore the goods were being carried on the backs of men along the beach to the central stores depot at the near end of the siege line.

His brigade of infantry was under tents along their section of the siege line and their personal effects had been delivered to them. He had helped the brigade commissary officer get the kitchen up and hot meals served. He was pleased by his accomplishment considering the almost endless wind and blowing sand and mean sea conditions.

None of the artillery had made it off the ships for it was far too valuable to risk on the turbulent sea. As for the unloading of the horses, several had been hoisted from the holds of the ships by a windlass and boom, swung outboard to be lowered near the water, and dropped into the sea. One in five horses had drowned trying to swim through the waves and the attempt to bring them to land was halted until the sea would become less deadly.

The surfboat was soon unloaded and Grant called out to the coxswain. "The sea's too rough for another trip. Let's call it off until the wind weakens and the waves die down."

The coxswain cut Grant a hard look. "'Bout time you saw that," he said in a surly tone. Because of the rough sea, the other quartermasters had ceased efforts to bring supplies ashore an hour earlier. The small army officer was dangerous to work with.

"Watch the shore for my signal early tomorrow. If conditions have improved, we'll start again."

"Right," said the coxswain. He motioned at his crew and they hastily climbed into the boat.

"Grab a load and let's get it to stores," Grant said to his men.

He hoisted a sack of beans, settled it on his shoulder, and headed along the sandy beach toward central stores some quarter mile distant.

* * *

"I estimate a sixty man garrison," Lee said in a low voice to Beauregard lying in the hot sand beside him. "How many do you think?"

"That's a good guess, unless some men are inside the church," Beauregard whispered back.

The two engineers lay on top of a sand hill two miles beyond the American lines and half of a mile from the walls of Veracruz. A Mexican outpost was less than a hundred yards in front of them. The Mexicans had chosen the front yard of a small, whitewashed church with a cemetery surrounded by a low stone wall at its rear. The voices of the Mexican soldiers could be plainly heard.

The siege line had been constructed and Scott had directed the two men to locate the Mexican outposts between the American lines and the city's walls, and make an estimate of the size of the garrisons, and of any roving patrols. Once the outposts had been destroyed and the Mexicans captured or driven back, the engineers would begin placing the artillery where it could inflict the heaviest damage on Veracruz.

The two engineers had been slogging up and down the sand hills since dawn and it was now the middle of a sweltering day with the fiery orb of the sun directly overhead. Twice they had almost run into squads of roving Mexican patrols and barely escaped being spotted by plunging into the thorny chaparral. Both had received painful stab wounds.

The Mexican outpost consisted of several tents protected by a sandbag breastwork encircling an area of about a quarter acre. A shade had been made of canvass under which several soldiers lounged. Other soldiers were lying about in the shade cast by the front wall of the church. Two soldiers were on lookout in the bell tower. From that elevated position, the lookouts had a clear view of the surrounding sand hills and the chaparral. Lee and Beauregard were most careful not to be seen.

"We'll call it sixty men," Lee said.

"That makes six outposts and the last one and about time too," Beauregard said. He skimmed beads of perspiration off his forehead with a hooked finger and flicked it away onto the sand.

"This looks like a good site for our artillery," Lee said. "What do you think?"

"The eastern walls are within easy range from here," Beauregard said. "To hit the west walls will require us to place other cannon off in that direction a mile or so."

"I agree," Lee said. On the map he had constructed during the reconnoitering, he quickly sketched the church and the surrounding terrain and recorded estimated distances and compass bearings to points on the city's walls.

He took up his field glasses and focused it on Veracruz standing out brilliantly white in the bright sunlight. Beyond the city, many boats were coming and going to the neutral ships anchored on the bay. It was well known that the ships were taking under their protection large quantities of property belonging to influential Mexicans.

"It's a shame to use cannon on such a beautiful city and its people," Lee said with a gloomy feeling at the prospect.

"Maybe they'll surrender the city before we start bombardment."

"I doubt it. Let's make our report to General Scott."

They stole down from the hilltop and away, winding a course through the dunes and chaparral and speedily crossing the openings visible to the artillerymen in Veracruz.

* * *

Grant could feel the tenseness, the girding for battle of the men of his brigade as he moved along the siege line through them. Scott had issued orders for a detachment from each brigade to advance and drive the Mexican's from their forward outposts. This would be the first serious engagement since the Americans had landed.

Grant continued on along the siege line that climbed up and down the dunes and circled about to avoid the boggy stands of water. He reached the beginning of the section manned by Clarke's Fifth Infantry, and a short distance farther along, saw Lieutenant Fred Dent forming up a company of troopers. Dent was the brother of Julia Dent, Grant's betrothed. Dent and Grant had been roommates at West point. Grant had met Julia when he had visited Dent at his parents' home near St. Louis, Missouri. Dent was twenty-four years old, the same age as Grant, slightly above average height, with brown hair and eyes and a short full beard. Like Grant, Dent had fought with General Taylor in northern Mexico.

"Fred, what's with the men? You planning to go somewhere?"

"You know damn well we're to move out and force the Mexicans to abandon their outposts."

"I heard something about that," Grant said and holding a straight face with an effort. He liked to josh Fred.

"What're you up to?" Dent asked.

Turning serious, Grant said, "I just came to see you off and wish you good luck."

"I kind'a thought you came to go with me."

"I'd like to but can't. The sea's calm and I got to get our supplies ashore as fast as possible."

"Tend to duty and you'll stay out of trouble. And anyway, I'd not like for my future brother-in-law get killed while with me for Julia would never forgive me for letting it happen."

Grant started to reply when a mountain howitzer boomed at headquarters and cut him off.

"That's the signal," Dent said.

"Don't let the Mexican cannonballs find you," Grant said.

"I'll duck fast. And we're advancing in fairly heavy numbers so it shouldn't take long to drive their outposts into the city."

Dent motioned with his sword to his two sergeants standing and waiting for his signal to move out. The sergeants shouted at their platoons and led them off.

The long blue line of Americans, single rank deep, left the siege line and moved at the double-quick step toward Veracruz lying two and one-half miles distant. Sunlight glinted from fixed bayonets. The only sounds were the pounding of the men's booted feet, and the shrill, angry cries of the flocks of green and blue parrots flushing out of the chaparral and hastening away. The noise ended as the men disappeared from view into the sand dunes and chaparral.

/ Chapter Ten

Lee came into the headquarters tent, tied the flap shut to keep out the wind and blowing sand, hurriedly slapped some of the dust off his uniform, and found a seat with the other men present. General Scott had called a meeting of his aids, staff officers, and generals. This was the seventh day since the landing.

Glancing around, Lee found he was the last to arrive. When the orders reached him to appear at headquarters, he had been making his final selection of the site for the placement of the American cannons.

"Glad you could make it, Captain Lee," Scott said.

"The messenger found me out in the dunes, sir," Lee said explaining his tardiness.

Scott nodded. He took up a sheet of paper, and without looking at it began to speak. "Gentlemen, we've been hearing for the past few days that General Taylor and Santa-Anna fought a large battle at Buena Vista on February twenty second and twenty-third. So far the accounts have all been from the Mexican side of things and have given a great victory to Santa-Anna. Now I have General Taylor's report just in from the Rio Grande on the mail packet.

"The size of the armies was very uneven with Santa-Anna having seventeen thousand men against Taylor's six thousand. The battle lasted nearly two days. Now as to who won."

Scott paused and looked around at the men all listening attentively. "I ask you, in what circumstances does the victorious army desert the battlefield secretly and in the dark of the night? Well that's what happened. Santa-Anna left the field to General Taylor. Further Taylor lost but six hundred men to Santa-Anna's four thousand. He has now won four victories and against great odds in a foreign land. We must applaud our brave comrades in the north for their victory."

The officers were all suddenly smiling. The reserved Patterson clapped his hands together with a sharp report. Lee was growing to like the old gentleman ever more.

"By now Santa-Anna must be well on his way here for he will know that we're the greater threat to his country than Taylor. He will gather up all the army detachments along the route to reinforce him and will arrive here with a large number of men. We must hurry our capture of Veracruz and Ulua.

"Now as to how to do that." Scott lapsed into a tutorial voice. "There are four stages to a siege of a city or fort. And here we have both fort and city to capture. The first stage is the investment, which we have accomplished. The second is the artillery attack. The third is construction of the approaches our soldiers will use to make the final assault. And the last is the frontal assault itself. And this last one I don't want to have to do.

"We can wait no longer for the storm to end. The artillery bombardment must be started at the earliest possible hour. Colonel Totten, have your engineers begin immediately to construct the sites for our guns. Colonel Banks, have your artillerymen assist them as much as possible. Let us hope our heavy siege weapons arrive by the time the sites are completed."

* * *

Lee worked his nine hundred men silently in the darkness and the windstorm blowing a gritty river of sand over the land. The men and Lee were suffering terribly from the driving sand with each grain striking like birdshot. Their eyes were sore and swollen, and even with neckerchiefs about their face, their mouths were full of grit and throats raw. When the men sought shelter in the lee of a dune, the sand fell upon them like dry rain.

This was the ninth day since the landing and the fifth day of blowing sand. The artillery had been ferried to land every time the storm tossed waves weakened enough so as not to sink the loaded boats. Approximately half the guns, in pieces for they had been taken apart at New Orleans to conserve space aboard ship, were on the beach where the gunners were at work reassembling them and installing the wheels on the carriages.

Of the nine hundred men, three hundred labored with shovels to level the site for the placement of seven 10-inch mortars grouped in three batteries. The batteries were placed on the backsides of the line of sand hills extending east and west from the church and cemetery that Lee and Beauregard had come upon a few days earlier. The distance to the walls of Veracruz was seven hundred yards.

Six hundred men were digging a road sunken below the level of the sand dunes and leading from the mortars back to the beach. The road would be a mile and a quarter long and wide enough to allow the passage of a six-mule team, and sufficiently deep that a loaded wagon could navigate it without being seen from the city. The road would be used to bring the guns and the tons of powder and balls that would be required for the bombardment, and for the coming and going of the relays of artillerymen. To prevent the enemy from discovering what the Americans were doing and open up on them with scores of big guns, all work was preformed at night and with the least noise.

The laboring soldiers cursed and complained that the wind was blowing the sand back into the trenches as fast as they could shovel it out. Lee knew there was much truth in their complaints. He and the infantry officers that were helping him command the men were constantly moving among them prodding and ordering the shirkers and laggards to bend to their shovels.

The wind fell into a lull and the air became clear and Lee could see the lights of Veracruz. In the quietness he heard the sound of a band playing, as if no enemy waited just beyond the walls. On the previous day, Scott had notified Matson, the British naval commander that the traffic of small boats back and forth between the ships and the shore would soon be cut off, and to notify Consul Giffard of this fact. Further that Giffard should notify the consuls of the other neutral nations. The skirmishing between the Mexicans and the Americans was about to end and true war began.

* * *

In the blind night of the waning moon, the three hundred soldiers, divided into squads of thirty, labored and sweated in the sultry heat. They grumbled, but in a low voice for they knew the danger if they should be heard by the Mexicans. The enemy was awake and alert and now and again fired blindly into the night with their heavy mortars. The cannon balls bursting out of the darkness caused concern among the men for one might fall upon them regardless of where they sought safety.

Each squad pulled on one of the two long ropes fastened to the carriage transporting a 10-inch mortar to its prepared firing site. The loose sand made it impossible for the men to gain solid footing. Further multiplying the effort to move the guns, the iron rimmed wheels of the carriages cut deeply into the sand.

A sergeant walked ahead of each gun and led the way through the darkness lying thick as ink in the bottom of the sunken road. Periodically he called a rest period and the men flopped down on the sand to catch their breaths.

Lee led the procession of men wrestling the seven mortars through the sand. These guns would be the first weapons emplaced. Though he felt sad for the plight of the men, the order by Scott to use them as draft animals had been necessary. Scott had grown short tempered as the days passed with the wind blowing almost endlessly and often forcing the unloading of the ships to stop. When Lee and Beauregard reported the sites were ready for the emplacement of the cannon, Scott sourly recounted his problems. The War Department had failed him. He had but half of the soldiers he had been promised, none of the powerful siege weapons had arrived, and he must try to hammer down the enemy's strong walls with light field artillery, and lastly not one of the big draft horses needed to move the artillery was on hand. The general was caught between two forces that could destroy his effort to defeat the Mexicans, the lack of men and proper weapons, and his greatest bugbear the rapid approach of the time of yellow fever. He had declared to his officers, "We can't wait longer. Our soldiers must be the horses."

Reaching the nearest prepared gun site along the sunken road, Lee directed the lead squad of soldiers how to position their mortar. The men finished the task, and then stumbled away along the backside of the sand hill and fell down to rest in the darkness. Lee moved to the next site and waited for the next mortar to arrive.

* * *

"Three minutes remaining," Lee said and snapped shut the front of his watch. He felt his nerves tighten up a notch. He had counted forty-two Mexican cannons that were within range of the American batteries. Also there were the big guns of Fort San Juan de Ulua that could reach them with their shells.

The Mexicans didn't yet know the location of the American guns, but when they did, all hell would break loose.

Captain Bouchard, artillery commander of the batteries, nodded agreement with Lee's comment without taking his eyes off Veracruz. Lee noted the man's face was strained with thoughts of the coming artillery duel and hoped his didn't show such concern.

The gunnery sergeant nearest Lee petted the thick iron barrel of the mortar beside him and spoke loud enough for Lee to hear. "You know, I'm glad the Mexs didn't run up the white flag right off for I like to hear the bark of my faithful bulldogs. After they hear its song, they'll cry uncle."

At first light, General Scott had sent an ultimatum to General Morales demanding the surrender of Veracruz and Fort San Juan de Ulua or face immediate bombardment. Scott had promised safe passage out of the city for all noncombatants. Morales had rejected the ultimatum. Upon receiving the Mexican's reply, Scott sent orders to the waiting gun crews to begin firing upon the city at 2 o'clock.

Lee hadn't expected the Mexican general to surrender. No commanding officer behind Veracruz's strong walls with scores of big cannons, and with mighty Fort San Juan de Ulua with its powerful cannons supporting him would surrender to a demand from an enemy that had yet to prove its strength.

Lee had been ordered to assist the artillery officers in aiming the guns because he had overseen the selection of the battery sites, the placement of the mortars, and knew the location of the targets by the use of the map Giffard had provided. The accuracy of the fire from the mortars would not be great due to the relatively short-barreled nature of the weapons shooting high arcing shells from a distance of nearly half a mile. Rounds would go wild and some would without doubt strike unintended targets killing innocent citizens, or foreigner businessmen, or some of the foreign consuls. Lee had nothing against any of these people, yet he would have major responsibility for killing them with solid balls or exploding shells.

The first targets of the three batteries of mortars would be the barracks of the infantry and cavalry and the forts within range. Scott had learned Fort San Agustin was being used as the main ammunition depot of the Mexicans. For that reason, Lee would stay with the battery that would fire on the fort.

He raised his field glasses and swung it slowly over Veracruz. The city with its beautiful white buildings lay serene on the shore of the blue sea. Airy palm trees were visible over the walls. To the right of the city, the splendor of the white beach could be seen, and the bright sails of fishing boats. In the middle distance was a forest of masts and spars of merchantmen, and beyond was the dark bulwark of Ulua set against the vast blue gulf beyond. He faintly heard shouts coming from the city as if people there were engaged in some kind of party or friendly sport. What would the city's citizens think had they known that less than half a mile away American cannons were primed to fire upon them?

"Light your slow-matches," Captain Bouchard called.

Shortly Lee could smell the fumes from the burning solution of saltpeter that fueled the cotton cords of the slow-matches.

* * *

"Fire your weapons," commanded Bouchard.

The glowing red ends of slow-matches touched the powder holes of the seven mortars. The guns roared and belched flame, and smoke, and iron balls. Shells went howling toward their targets in Veracruz. Standing off a mile seaward from Fort San Juan de Ulua, Admiral Conner's warships with their big guns began a furious cannonading of the fort to knock out some of its big guns. A chorus of joyous shouts erupted from the gunners and powder boys.

Every Mexican cannon in the forts and embrasures and redoubts of Veracruz and within range of the Americans, blasted away with return fire. A sheet of flame capped the walls. Shot and shell and rocket sped toward the Americans whose location was marked by the smoke of their guns. Several cannons at Ulua, firing past Veracruz, opened up on the Americans.

A storm of iron burst upon Lee and the men at the batteries. Fragments of hot metal whizzed about. Shells exploded close by and dug holes in the sand big enough to bury several men. Others landed in the chaparral and shredded it and sent splinters flying like darts. The larger balls could be seen as they slowed at the end of their trajectory. The new recruits cringed and ducked. The veterans smiled hard smiles and cursed and shouted at the recruits to stay at their stations.

Lee saw the three powder boys of the battery hunkered down by the crates of gunpowder. They were frightened and trembling for this was their first taste of battle. He hurried to them and catching them by their thin shoulders drew their quaking bodies to him. They were about the same age as his son Rooney and he felt sorry for them. "Do your jobs, lads, as you've been taught. Grab the powder and run it to your gun." He hugged the boys close for a second and then released them. "Go!" he ordered.

The boys snatched up cloth wrapped packets of gunpowder, each containing the correct charge and ran for the gun he tended.

The American cannons boomed. The earth shook with the explosions of American shells landing within the city's walls, and Mexican shells exploding around the Americans. Large clouds of gun smoke hid the guns of both the defender and attacker. Columns of smoke rose from burning houses in the town.

Lee moved out of the battery's gun smoke and looked at Veracruz. He saw an amazing, frightening thing. A cannon ball was coming straight at him. It grew rapidly in size. By instinct he ducked. A swoosh of air fanned the side of his head as the cannon ball passed but inches away.

He stayed bent to the side for a few seconds, and then slowly straightened. How strange it was to see a cannon ball coming at him. Still the danger had come and gone and he was no less willing than before to be a soldier, and to assume risks that were the steppingstones to distinction and gaining rank.

Chapter Eleven

Grant listened to the roar of the American and Mexican gunners dueling furiously with their cannons as he sat on the crest of a sand hill and looked through his field glasses at Veracruz. The Americans had hurled shells at the city for a full day, then throughout the night and now into early afternoon. He had come into the dunes to see the amount of damage that had been done to the city's walls and forts.

Grant estimated that at least sixty buildings were burning among the homes and businesses within Veracruz. The smoke from the fires, rising and mingling with the gun smoke from the Mexican cannon, shadowed the city with a dark gray pall. The citizens now knew the horror of war, of the pain and death an exploding shell could bring in a blinding flash.

Grant lowered his glasses with a grunt of disgust. Try as he might, he couldn't determine what damage, if any, the Americans had done to the walls and forts of the city. Under a hot yellow sun hanging in a hard blue sky, the air was heavy with moisture and shimmering heat waves distorted his view of all objects beyond a few hundred yards.

He looked up at the sky where the high arcing shells of the contending sides, passing in mid-flight, were marked against the sky by the smoke trails left by the burning fuses. The hundreds of ribbons of smoke had been woven by the slow wind into an arching gray dome that stretched from the walls of Veracruz to the cannons in the dunes.

Grant stowed the glasses way in its leather case. He would have to go closer. He came down from the hill and went toward the battery where the cannons bucked and roared and spewed their metal balls. Lee and Beauregard, and McClellan saw him approaching. Beauregard moved away from the noisy guns to meet him.

Beauregard called out ahead. "Hello, Sam. What are you doing way out here?"

"I wanted to see the damage you're doing to the walls," Grant replied.

"So do I. But you can't tell from here, too much heat waves in the air."

"So I found out. I think I'll go for a closer look."

"Better get permission from the captain before you go out beyond the lines."

"That's what I'm here for."

The two lieutenants drew near Lee, who seeing them coming, ceased working with the chief gunner to aim one of the cannons and walked out from the gun to meet them.

Grant saluted and spoke. "Captain, I'd like to go forward and take a good look at the walls of the city. See how much damage that's been done to them."

"Go ahead."

"I'll go with you to keep you out of trouble," said the black eyed Beauregard. He turned to Lee. "With your permission, captain."

Lee nodded agreement. He almost smiled as he looked into Grant's cool face with the slightly low left eye giving him a quiet, cynical expression, as compared to the emotional Beauregard whose face showed his every thought.

"That house out there should provide a good view point." Lee pointed at the structure situated two hundred yards closer to the city. "I'll join you there when I'm finished here. Keep out of sight of the Mexican gunners for they'll drop a cannon ball on you."

Lee watched the two younger, smaller men go swiftly off through the dunes, Beauregard with a swagger, and Grant with his usual slouched shouldered movement.

* * *

Grant and Beauregard darted from dune to dune as above their heads the screaming shells of the Americans and Mexican cannons ripped the air. They reached the house Lee had indicated, a building with thick adobe walls painted a pale yellow. Though they believed the house would be abandoned with the occupants scared away by the cannonading, they entered warily with pistols drawn. They went quietly thought the four rooms, each with all its furnishings still in place. The house waited silently for the return of its owners.

"We're all by our lonesome" Grant said to Beauregard, and hoping no hostile eyes had spotted them crossing the dunes.

He holstered his pistol, took his glasses out of its case, went to a front window, and focused on the fifteen-foot tall walls of Veracruz. Beauregard came up with his glass to the window on Grant's right.

As Grant studied the southeastern section of the city's walls, the section at which the American cannon fire had been concentrated, his dismay grew. "Why, the walls are hardly hurt at all," he exclaimed. "Just a stone missing here and there. Nothing serious at all."

"And the embrasures and forts aren't damaged one bit," Beauregard said. "Just as if we have been shooting feather pillows at them," he added with disbelief.

Both men froze at the abrupt sound of breaking roof beams and sheathing as a shell smashed down through the roof of the house and buried itself in the earthen floor.

"It's a bomb!" Grant shouted knowing instantly what had occurred. "Get down!"

Grant hurled himself to the side, trying desperately to gain distance from the shell and get low to escape its blast of iron fragments when it exploded.

The shell burst with a brilliant orange flash and a brain jarring concussion. The earthen floor leapt in an exploding brown geyser. A tremendous blast of wind and dirt caught Grant and flung him savagely across the room. He landed hard as a dropped stone and flat on his stomach with his face buried in the dirt of the floor near an outside wall.

Huge pain ran through him, which told him he was still alive. Hurry! Get out of the house before another shells lands. Even as the thought came, a slab of the thick adobe wall collapsed upon him, and splintered roof beams fell on top of that, and the ton weight penned him to the earth.

Grant twisted his head to the side to free his face and sucked at the air. He drew in a little air, and a lot of adobe dust. He heaved and strained to lift the broken pieces of house off him. His battered body ached and creaked and groaned with the effort, but the mass of debris on top of him didn't budge. He was trapped and slowly suffocating. This was a damn poor way to die.

Where was Beauregard? Had he been hurt? Killed? Why wasn't he helping Grant get free?"

Grant heard a dragging sound in the beams and blocks of adobe as some-one moved part of them. Then through the ringing in his ears he heard Lee shout, "Grant, you alive?"

"Just barely, captain. Get the house off me."

He heard the clatter of wood and adobe being thrown aside and felt the crushing weight easing. He thrust his back powerfully upward against the mass. It lifted and his head was free. He heaved again and rolled out from under the heavy chunk of adobe. He looked up into the concerned faces of Lee and Beauregard.

"How bad you hurt?" Lee asked as he knelt down beside the bruised and dust covered Grant.

"I believe I'll live. Good thing you weren't far behind us." Grant looked at Beauregard and found him equally dusty.

"I'm okay," Beauregard said with a wry smile. "I was farther away from it than you and flat on the floor when it exploded. But I think my hearings ruined for my ears are wringing like a hundred bells." He looked steadily at Grant. "Thanks for your warning it made me act quicker than I would've otherwise."

Grant rose to his feet, and stood feeling shaky. "Thanks to both of you for pulling me out before I ate a lung full of dust."

"We can't afford to lose a good quartermaster," Lee said. "Now let's get out of this place before they hit it with another shell."

Lee and Beauregard went out through a gap in the broken rear wall of the house. Grant followed, his head aching terribly, right shoulder feeling like it was half wrenched from its socket, and blowing dust out of his nostrils. He was a lucky fellow.

Reaching a safe distance from the house, Lee halted them behind a dune. "I want to take a good look at the walls and forts," he told them.

"You'll find that almost no damage has been done," Beauregard said.

Lee stared at the city through his glass for a time. Finally he lowered the glass. "The range was too long for our light field artillery to damage either the walls or the forts," he said sadly. "If our heavy siege weapons were here it would be a different story."

Lee looked to the east where Admiral Conner's fleet of war ships was anchored a half mile offshore. "I know where there are guns that can destroy the walls," he said.

* * *

Hidden and protected from the enemy cannons by the depth of the sunken road, Lee, Grant and Beauregard walked swiftly toward headquarters. Reaching the end of the sunken road at the seacoast they came upon Scott and Worth riding horseback in their direction. The three junior officers saluted the generals.

"What happened to you two?" asked Scott looking down at the two dusty, disheveled lieutenants.

"We were standing in the wrong spot when a Mexican shell landed and exploded," Grant said.

"You both are very fortunate," Scott said and amused at Grant's reply.

He spoke to Lee. "Captain, what is our success in damaging the city's walls?"

"Sir, we are averaging one hundred and twenty-five shells an hour with nine out of ten exploding," Lee was proud of the number and wanted Scott to know. "The houses and businesses of the city are suffering badly, and I'm sure the citizens are terrified. But the fortifications and their garrisons are escaping with nothing but minor damage. I saw but a few stones broken loose from the walls. Further, I believe the 24-pounders that we'll have ready by tomorrow morning won't do the job either. We must have more powerful weapons."

Scott cast a look at the sea. "As you know, Commodore Conner and I have discussed the use of his heavy naval cannons in the event that out siege guns didn't arrive in a timely manner."

At those words by Scott, Worth's face hardened and he spoke in a sour voice. "If we use the navy's weapons, then we must share the credit of capturing Veracruz with the sailors. We don't have to do that. I know we can take the city with our infantry, and do it quickly."

Scott continued to stare at the fleet and didn't respond to Worth's words.

Worth turned to Grant. "Lieutenant, you were in the thick of the fighting at Monterrey. I remember your name from Colonel Garland's report. Could you lead a company of men over those walls?"

Grant was surprised, twice; first that Garland had mentioned him in his report of the battle, and secondly that Worth would seek support from him a mere lieutenant. "Yes, sir, if I was strongly supported by attacks at other points along the wall," he replied. What Worth was proposing was damn dangerous.

Scott faced away from the sea and focused gimlet eyes on Grant. It was obvious that he didn't like the way the conversation was going. "Since General Worth has brought up your participation in the fighting at Monterrey, how many men do you estimate that it would cost to take Veracruz?"

Grant didn't want to be drawn deeper into the discussion, almost an argument from the tone of it, between the two generals. To have time to consider how to answer, he turned and looked at the city. There was no way out of the situation for Scott had asked for numbers and now Grant must give his calculation. He faced back to Scott. "The walls are high and strongly manned. Scaling ladders would be required which would slow us in getting over them. I'd guess seven to eight hundred would be killed and wounded."

"Thank you, Lieutenant," Scott said. "My estimate of dead and wounded runs somewhat higher than yours."

Scott spoke to Worth. "General, we'll conduct an assault by infantry only as a last resort. I'll signal Admiral Conner that I accept his offer of his heavy weapons."

Scott spoke to Lee. "Captain, you will see that they are sited as rapidly as possible after they're landed."

"Yes, sir."

"And have these two dirty lieutenants get into clean uniforms." Scott gave Grant and Beauregard a hint of a smile, reined his horse around, and rode off back toward headquarters.

Chapter Twelve

Lee led through the darkness, finding the way among the sand dunes by the pale light of a quarter moon. Behind him in the dunes, a thousand soldiers and two hundred sailors labored, hooked with shoulder straps to long ropes fastened to six giant cannons. He had formed the men into teams of two hundred each to drag the Navy's three 8-inch howitzers, hurling 64-pound exploding shells, and the three 32-pounders firing solid iron balls to their emplacement sites.

Lee halted in the gloom of the night and stared backward. The noise of more than two thousand booted feet churning the deep sand, made Lee think that some great night beast might make the same sound. Above the noise of the boots came the rumbling chant of the men. "Heavy metal" pause "to the front." repeated over and over in rhythm to their strenuous breathing.

General Scott had signaled Admiral Conner aboard the Mississippi that he wished a parley. Conner came ashore accompanied by Admiral Perry who had arrived two days before with orders to relieve the ailing Conner. Perry out of respect for Conner and upon seeing the fierce cannonading in progress against Veracruz, had placed himself temporarily second in command of the war fleet. The two admirals had readily agreed to Scott's request for the loan of their most powerful cannons. They made one condition, their naval gunners must service the six weapons.

By nightfall the seamen had the guns floated ashore. Lee working with Naval Lieutenant Aulick began the tortuous task of moving the guns to their firing positions two and one-half miles distant. The guns were extremely difficult to drag for they were mounted on ship's carriages that had no wheels and thus dug deep furrows in the sand. The men were willing, and with muscles and tendons straining, snaked the weapons onward over the dunes and through the lagoons of water, some of them two feet deep.

In the small hours of the morning, the guns had been dragged to the brush-covered ridge of sand that Lee had chosen. He set Aulick and his sailors to preparing the battery sites on the backside of sand ridges, fill sandbags to build parapets, and dig trenches to dive into when the enemy's shells came crashing down. The soldiers were sent to the beach to bring forward the powder and shot for the weapons.

In the first faint blush of dawn, the sailors wrestled the six guns into the prepared sites. Lee released all from duty. As they walked wearily away among the dunes on the way to the beach, the naval gun crews came into sight.

Lee's heart gave a sudden surge of pleasure for in the front of the sailors was his younger brother Naval Lieutenant Sidney Lee who had duty on Conner's flagship the Mississippi. Lee hastened forward and clasped his brother's hand.

"Sid, so you're going to be with me?"

Sidney, black headed and clean-shaven, beamed happily at the unexpected encounter. " 'ppears so. Until the city falls."

"Which guns are yours?"

"I'm boss of the howitzers. They should knock the walls down."

"We just can't do without you sailors," Lee said with a smile.

"The navy is always there when you need help."

Lee spoke in a serious tone, "Sid, keep your head down. And have your men to do the same for the Mexicans are getting good at hitting what they aim at."

"Right," said Sidney.

"Come and let me point out the targets." Lee said. He put his arms around Sidney's shoulders and they moved toward the howitzers where the gun crews were sponging the barrels to clear out the sand in preparation for action. Lee worried about his brother being permanently located on the coast for yellow fever was running rampant through the sailors of the fleet. One ship had left its blockading station off Tampico for the States with two hundred seamen suffering from the disease. Now Sidney would also be in the thick of heavy cannon bombardment. It was strange to first see combat with his brother. How terrible it would be to see him killed before his eyes. A heavy feeling of responsibility for Sidney's safety swept over Lee.

They stopped by the howitzers and Lee brought from his pocket a copy he had made of the map Giffard had given Scott. He pointed at the map and then at buildings in the city that could be seen and were targets. Others that were also targets but couldn't be seen from the dunes, he marked on the map.

"Now let's set the guns for the first salvo," Lee said. "Cut the fuses of your first shells to ten seconds, and then adjust the length more finely after you see where they explode," Lee said.

"Yes, big brother," Sidney said, his eyes laughing.

* * *

"My, God, look at that!" Lieutenant Aulick shouted excitedly as he stared through his field glasses at the walls of Veracruz.

Yes indeed, a wonderful sight, thought Lee as he too observed the American cannonballs striking the city's walls. He was with Aulick at the battery of naval 32-pounders that he had helped aim for concentrated fire at a section of walls near the Mexican infantry and cavalry barracks.

The brush that had been piled across the top of the sand ridge to hide the naval cannons had been flung aside and the powerful guns had opened fire on Veracruz. The ground shook with the thunder of the guns and the air was full of shells as the bucking and snarling guns let go as rapidly as the men could reload them. The crash of the shells exploding against the city's walls returned sharp and savage. Lee felt satisfaction as the heavy iron balls blasted large segments of wall loose and sent fragments of iron and stone raking the army barracks and nearby casemates.

The Mexican artillerymen returned a terrific fire with every ball aimed at the new American batteries. The city's forts and walls were covered with a dark cloud of gun smoke through which red lances of fire flashed. Cannonballs rained down upon the American gun crews. Deadly iron fragments whined about in all directions. A ball with a sputtering fuse landed and rolled past the guns and exploded harmlessly far behind the men.

The air around the battery of 32-pounders was bitter with the stink of burnt gunpowder, and Lee's eyes and lungs burned. He groped out of the smoke and hastened the hundred yards to the battery of howitzers to be with his brother in this dangerous battle of solid shot and exploding shells.

Sidney was moving among his gun crews and calling out encouragement to them. His shouted orders were swiftly obeyed. Lee thought his brother had become a fine, brave officer.

Sidney noted Lee standing behind the guns and gave him a wave and a white-toothed smile through his smoke begrimed face. He spoke to one of the gun sergeants, and then came and stood beside Lee. Neither brother said a word, simply glad to be near each other and uninjured.

* * *

In the middle of the night, Grant and the other quartermaster officers released their weary men from duty. All of the army's supplies had been ferried from the ships and transported to the central supply depot and stored under canvas. The men kicked sand over the fires that had been built to mark the landing place of the boats on the beach, ships' lanterns had shown the location of the vessels on the water, and went off into the darkness to find something to eat and their blankets.

Grant passed by his tent without stopping and went into the dunes in the direction of the American cannons growling angrily at the Mexicans. Siege and bombardment were the duties of engineers and artillerymen; still he wanted to see the fight. He came to a battery of large naval howitzers and stopped to watch the gun crews at work. Their actions were as smooth as a machine; firing, swabbing the barrels, powder boys running up with the measured powder charge, the powder tamped down, shot shoved into the mouth of the barrel and rammed home with long wooden staffs, and the gun touched off with the slow match.

He left the battery of howitzers and climbed upon a nearby sand hill for a better view of the cannonading. The ground shook incessantly beneath his feet as the battery steadily boomed out. The ear bursting roars and red fire spurting from muzzles constantly shattered the night. The sky was full of shells that seemed to pause at the peak of their arc, then turning and dropping ever more swiftly to their targets. Giant explosions erupted in Veracruz. Scores of fires burned in the city, the flames leaping high above the buildings.

In a short moment of quietness between gun bursts, the screams and wails of women and children in pain and horribly frightened in the city came across the dunes to Grant. His skin crawled at the pitiful cries. This wasn't the right way to fight a war. General Morales may have been correct in a military sense in not surrendering to Scott's demand, however he should have forced the women and children to leave the city. He was glad when the cannon resumed firing and masked the anguished cries.

Grant's weariness overrode his desire to observe the guns at work. He had labored eighteen hours straight and he could hear his blanket calling to him. He climbed down from the sand hill and into the sunken road and walked toward the sea.

* * *

Lee had a bursting headache. He had spent too many hours on the siege line with the earth jarring blasts of the cannons and the shrill whistling screams of the different calibers shells. On this fourth day of bombardment, as it had been for the previous three, the gun crews fired their cannons as rapidly as humanly possible and a storm of four or five explosive shells and solid shot was always speeding across the hot, blue sky. Gray-white banks of smoke were piled above every battery.

The Veracruz defenders were firing three times as many cannons as were the Americans and the walls and forts were alive with flashes of flame and jets of smoke. The preponderance of the enemy balls struck the front of the sand hills and did little damage, or passed overhead to land beyond. The American cannon balls had pounded large segments of the enemy's walls to rubble, and caused great destruction to the buildings within the city.

The number of Americans killed and wounded was but eleven and forty-seven, with the sailors suffering disproportionately large. The young seamen wouldn't obey warnings to keep down behind the parapets, they just had to rise up to see where their shots landed, and four of them had their heads blown off by Mexican cannon balls.

To Lee's surprise, part of the Mexican gun fell silent, and in but a few seconds all were quiet. He quickly raised his field glasses and looked at the city. Atop every fort a white flag rose on a tall staff.

In response to the flags, the American batteries ceased firing one by one. In half a minute, the only sound on the battlefield was the whisper of the slow wind blowing the mountains of gun smoke away.

Were the Mexicans surrendering? Lee struck out for headquarters at a fast pace.

As Lee approached the headquarter tents, he saw three horsemen leaving at a cantor under a white flag along the beach toward Veracruz. He recognized British Consul Giffard but not the other two Anglos both richly dressed and seemingly men of importance.

Lee hurried on and halted near Colonel Totten standing in front of headquarters and watching after the departing riders.

"Colonel, is it a proposal for surrender?" Lee asked.

"No. The consuls wanted a truce to allow the women and children to leave the city. They said they have taken hundreds into their buildings and there is no room for more. Many are hiding in the vaults of the mercantile establishments, in basements, and some are living on the stone breakwater to stay out of range of you guns. Even the priests are frightened and won't leave their churches to perform the last rites for the dead."

"May I ask what the general said to the request?"

"He told them no. And he reminded them that he had given them the opportunity to take all noncombatants from the city and they refused. Further he told them that any person who tried to leave the city would be fired upon. The consuls didn't like that worth a damn. We can't halt our bombardment for we have information that Santa-Anna has already passed through Mexico City with a large army and plans to break our siege of Veracruz."

Scott came out of the headquarters tent, and seeing Lee called out to him. "Captain Lee, go quickly back along the line and tell the artillerymen to begin firing." Scott smiled grimly. "And, captain, aim a few balls somewhat closer to the foreign consulates. Shake those fine gentlemen up even more so that they'll go crying to the Mexican general to surrender the city to stop the bombardment."

Lee returned the general's smile. "Yes, sir, a little closer."

Chapter Thirteen

When General Scott and the aid to British Consul Giffard, a blond headed young man in civilian clothing, came out of the headquarters tent, the score of assembled generals and staff officers ceased talking among themselves and waited expectantly. The Britisher had come out from behind the walls of Veracruz just before sunrise the day following the visit by the foreign consuls and made his way through the cannon fire to the American lines. He had been brought under guard to Scott. After a brief look at the message carried by the man, Scott had sent orders for all his generals and staff to report immediately to headquarters.

Scott raised the consuls' message above his head. "I have news to share with you," he said.

Lee, standing with the officers, saw the general's pleasure in his flashing eyes and the stance of his tall body as he looked down upon his subordinates. "Mr. Campion here has braved our cannon balls to bring us a message signed by all the foreign consuls in Veracruz. They state they are speaking for the Mexican military and desire a truce to discuss surrender. We are requested to cease firing and appoint delegates to negotiate terms. I am agreeable."

Scott gave a broad smile to his officers. "We won't be dealing with General Morales for it seems he has been taken suddenly ill and has turned over the command of Veracruz and Ulua to General Jose Leandro."

The officers broke into laughter. It was a time worn stratagem for a general to protect his name from dishonor by releasing command to a junior officer to surrender a military fortification and thus have that man's name forever tied to the capitulation.

When the laughter died away, Scott spoke to Beauregard. "Lieutenant, ride and order all our guns to cease firing."

Beauregard saluted. "Yes, sir." He hurried toward his horse.

Scott spoke to Campion. "You may return to the city at any time. Those troopers who brought you here will escort you back through our lines."

He turned to his generals and aids. "Come inside and we shall discuss the terms of the surrender and choose our representatives."

* * *

"A magnificent day to accept the surrender of an enemy," General Scott said to his staff officers gathered about him. With Veracruz and Ulua soon to be in his hands, he was in a buoyant mood and a broad smile of satisfaction wreathed his face.

Lee agreed with Scott. It was an enchantingly summer-like day. The drenching rain that had begun during the night had ended at daylight after washing the sky and land to a sparkling newness. A delightfully cool breeze came off the nearby sea. The domes of Veracruz a mile away were gilded with golden sunlight. Directly overhead a sailing hawk held station in a thermal updraft and eyed the goings on of the earth bound men below.

The time was mid-morning on March 29 and twenty days after the landing upon the Mexican shore. The American army was drawn up on the Plain Of Cocos, a green meadow shaded with scores of coconut palms. The general and his officers mounted on horseback had ridden to a position from where they could view the formal surrender. Directly in front of them Worth's two brigades of regulars with their officers were in formation, with Patterson's volunteers opposite and facing them some seventy yards distant. At the end of the space separating the two brigades, the Dragoons and a battery of cannon loaded with exploding canisters, faced the city. All the troops carried loaded weapons and full cartridge boxes. Worth, on horseback, waited near a large white flag waving from a tall pole in the center of the assembled Americans.

Scott had met with his commanders and chose Generals Worth and Pillow and Colonel Totten as the negotiators to meet with the three Mexican representatives for arranging the conditions for surrender. Lee understood the reason why Scott had included Pillow. He wanted Polk's man involved so that he couldn't complain to the president about the terms. The six negotiators had met at Scott's headquarters and haggled for hours. Worth had become exasperated by the interminable argument and had ended the meeting, sending the Mexicans back to the city. He reported to Scott the Mexicans weren't going to surrender, but were trying to gain time for Santa-Anna to arrive and force the Americans to lift the siege. Scott, who had been grimly pacing and waiting, asked Worth whether or not the Mexicans had left a written proposal behind. Worth produced a document and gave it to Scott.

Once Worth had departed, Scott quickly had the Mexican writing translated to English. He saw immediately that the Mexicans wanted a means to save face in the surrender. He therefore stipulated that the Mexican soldiers would not be made prisoner of war, but would be paroled upon their promise not to fight the Americans again. He gave nothing away for he didn't have the means to imprison thousands of men. General Leandro seized upon the promised leniency and signed the document handing over both Veracruz and San Juan de Ulua.

Lee felt proud of his contribution to the victory. He knew he had done well in placing the cannons, selecting targets, and aiming the guns upon the enemy. Danger had been braved, glory won, and his reputation was being built. Perhaps a major's rank wasn't too far off. One thing he wished, that there was a purpose for the war other than that of taking territory from a sovereign nation.

The Americans came to attention as the Mexican soldiers; some thirty-five hundred from the garrison of Veracruz and fifteen hundred from Ulua, in immaculate blue and red uniforms came marching out of the city's gates. They formed up by company with a band at the head of each regiment. Lee judged the officers with their many decorations and pistols and swords a fine sight. As the last of the columns left the gate, the cannons of Veracruz and Ulua gave a final salute and all the Mexican flags came down. The regiments advanced onto the Plain Of Cocos to the beat of their drums and squeal of fife, and onward in between the ranks of Americans to the white flag. There the bands fell silent. The soldiers stacked their arms. A few men, shamed by the surrender, broke their muskets by slamming them down on the ground.

Worth ignored the anger of the soldiers. When the last Mexican had fallen back into rank, Worth saluted the officers and read General Scott's proclamation excusing the forty highest ranking of them from their parole and allowing them to keep their side arms and horses. At this surprise generosity the forty officers came to ramrod attention and saluted Worth. Scott was gambling that his released of the officers from their parole would cause them to tell how powerful were the Americans and yet generous in victory, and this would weaken other Mexican officers' will to fight.

General Leandro released his troops and they hastened to join with several hundred civilians, men, women and children leaving Veracruz and moving along the highway leading inland. The people were loaded with all manner of objects from guitars to baskets of food to household items to pets. Many women cried as they trudged along with their smallest child strapped upon their backs and older ones toddling along beside them.

The American regimental bands struck up "Yankee Doodle Dandy", and Worth, whom Scott had assigned to be military governor of the city, mounted his horse and proudly led the victorious American soldiers in through the open gates of Veracruz.

Lee watching from the Plain Of Cocos with Scott and the other staff officers could see out on the Gulf where Commodore Perry's fleet had sailed in close to San Juan de Ulua and ships' boats were transporting a garrison of seamen and Marines to occupy the mighty fort. Lee thought it a strikingly unselfish gesture by Scott to allow Worth and Perry to have the honor of being first into the two strongholds.

Upon the signal of a cannon shot, the "Stars And Stripes" rose gleaming over the city, and the forts and hundreds of cannons saluted the flag with a thunderous roar on the beach and from the warships of the fleet.

General Scott with his staff officers and escort of thirty mounted Dragoons rode in quietly after all the fanfare was over.

* * *

Grant accompanied by Valere entered Veracruz. Under the sun's harsh eye the cannon battered city stood revealed, and he was astonished at the extent of the devastation. Scores of houses and businesses had been totally destroyed and lay in a jumble of stone and boards, and hundreds of others had been damaged but still stood. Mounds of ashes marked where buildings had once been. Pandemonium must have reined among the frightened people as exploding shells rained from the sky and men and women and children died. Now and again he caught sight of people watching with hostile eyes from shadowed windows.

Grant and Valere came upon a cemetery where at least a hundred freshly dug graves lay open and caskets were placed for lowering into the earth. With the cessation of the bombardment, the burial of the dead could be carried out. Several ceremonies were in progress with people dressed in black standing with bowed heads and priests intoning the rites.

"Lieutenant Grant, we sure killed a lot of them," Valere said in a mournful voice.

"War is hard on the civilians when towns are defended."

"I hope all the rest of our fights are just with their army."

"That sounds good on the face of it. But I'd bet the complaints of the civilians to General Morales to do something to stop our shelling had a lot to do with the Mexicans surrendering when they did. Which saved some of our men too."

Grant had come into the city to find quarters for Hazlitt and himself so they could vacate their tent in the sand dunes and escape the voracious sand fleas and mosquitoes. Scores of other officers were moving with a brisk step along the shell-cratered streets. They had been given permission by Scott to occupy any residence found abandoned by their owners. Knowing few homes had been struck by cannon fire near the waterfront, and wanting to be on the seashore with its cooling breeze, most of the men were hurrying directly there.

Just off the waterfront Grant found a three-bedroom house with all its plush furnishings in place. He staked claim to the residence by writing Hazlitt's and his names on a sheet of paper and tacking it to the door. He set Valere to the task of transferring all their belongings from the tents to the new quarters, and then went off to examine Ulua and its defenses.

* * *

"We are lacking in nearly everything needed to outfit us for the march inland and fight our way to Mexico City," Scott said. "And yet march we must and within the next few days." The euphoria of having captured Veracruz and Ulua had worn off over the past two days and the general was in a foul mood.

Lee was assembled with the generals, staff officers and chief quartermaster in Scott's headquarters established in the mansion of a wealthy merchant who had fled Veracruz for Mexico City. He was now in charge of the army's half hundred engineers due to Colonel Totten having left with Admiral Conner to carry Scott's report of the capture of Veracruz and Ulua to Secretary Of War Marcy and President Polk.

Scott continued to speak. "Shipwrecks from storms have killed many horses and lost essential supplies. That's in addition to having arrived here not fully equipped in the first place. We have less than half of the troops requested. Wagons must come from the States and we need eight hundred, but only one hundred and eighty are on hand. Six thousand horses and mules are required to pull the wagons and siege train. Eleven hundred are available." Scott gave an angry snort. "The wagons and troops must come from the States and we can do nothing except wait for them. However we can do something about the horses and mules. We shall send forces out and strip the land bare of them."

* * *

"From the information we have, the best chance of finding draft horses and mules would be the big ranchos up the Alvarado River and to the north around La Antigua," Colonel Garland said to Grant. "General Quitman will take a sizeable force, including artillery to the river, while Colonel Harney with the same size force will go to La Antigua. However we can't neglect the areas closer to Veracruz. Your task is to make a five day expedition out to the north and west and taking possession of every horse and mule you can lay your hands on."

"Yes, sir," Grant replied. The time was well into the afternoon when he had been summoned to Garland's office at army headquarters.

"Do your best to find draft animals with enough heft to pull the loaded wagons and heavy guns."

"Do I use force to get what we want?"

"Commandeer all suitable animals, that's the general's orders, but pay a fair price for them. Lieutenant Chilton has been ordered to escort you with fifty Dragoons, and Lieutenant Hodding with a hundred infantry."

"Sir, that's a small force of men considering we don't know how much of the Mexicans army is out there waiting to jump us. And neither one of those officers has been in a fight."

"Scott has learned that Santa-Anna is at Jalapa and calling in all the troops stationed at the various outposts between there and Veracruz. So your expedition is not expected to encounter sizeable enemy forces, certainly not Mexican regulars. Now regarding those two lieutenants who will be with you, they both are junior to you. Use them as you see best."

"Yes, sir." Grant didn't like the arrangement. Still there wasn't any gain in worrying when there was nothing he could do about it.

Chapter Fourteen

From the bell tower of the church at the village of Vergara, Grant watched the gray dawn rise up from the wet horizon of the eastern sea. The color had reached a shade of gray that brought to mind the dream about his gray-headed grandfather and the words spoken by the old man of fear and death. He still wondered what the dream about Noah meant.

Below him in the church courtyard, Sergeant O'Doyle and thirty teamsters talked quietly among themselves. Twenty of the men carried muskets and haversacks and would act as infantry until horses were purchased, and then they would become drovers. The remaining men were drivers of the ten horse drawn wagons being taking along to haul food rations, tents, and extra ammunition in the event the detachment got into a fight. The men had been with Grant in northern Mexico and he knew them to be gutsy fighters.

The tromp of marching soldiers and the clatter of iron shod hooves came to Grant and he saw Mathew Chilton's Dragoons followed by Calvin Hodding and his foot soldiers entering the town. They were right on schedule, a good beginning for the foraging expedition. The two men's lack of battle experience concerned Grant. Hopefully luck would favor them and there would be no fighting with battle-hardened units of the Mexican Army.

Grant came down from the bell tower and met Chilton as he halted his Dragoons. Hodding stopped his men just behind the Dragoons and galloped his horse up and reined in beside Chilton.

"Good morning," Grant greeted the men. He had met Mathew Chilton at Brazos. He was a Vermonter and freshly graduated from West Point. He was six feet tall with a lean build, and quite handsome with blond hair and clean-cut features, and though twenty-two years of age, appeared to be a large, overgrown boy.

"And to you," Chilton said.

"I agree it's a good morning, but a little early for me," Hodding said in a lighthearted tone. "But I'm ready." Hodding was strongly built, broad faced, with a high brow above large brown eyes.

"I want to say something before we start out," Grant said. "I've been on these foraging expeditions several times before. You never know what you might run into. It could be regular army units, or maybe militia. Mostly the civilians don't cause trouble. But you got to keep a sharp eye out for ambushes and snipers. One thing for sure, if we run into a company of Mexican soldiers and they outnumber us, we'll have a fight on our hands."

Grant watched the men's faces. "We should come to an understanding right off that. I'm the senior lieutenant and in charge. Once we're jumped and the fighting starts, then it's too late to hash that out, and I have no intention to risk the safety of the men and the success of the expedition. Do either of you have an argument with that?" He held back from mentioning their inexperience.

Chilton and Hodding looked at each other and Grant saw a look pass between them that he recognized as an acceptance of his authority. They looked back at him.

"We both know you've done this before, and have had some hard fighting too," Chilton said. "So I put my men and me under your orders."

"Same here," Hodding added.

"Fair enough. Let's get moving. Chilton your men will lead. Then comes yours Hodding. Mine will come next with the wagons last. Move out and take position."

The two lieutenants reined their steeds away and returned to their men.

Grant went to his mount, borrowed from Hazlitt who was on foot patrol in the city, tethered to one of the tie posts in front of the church and swung astride.

The three officers led the detachment from Vergara and north on the Tampico road, with the sea three miles off on the right, and the first of the sun's rays peeking above the horizon. The cavalcade stretched a quarter-mile with dust boiling up from the pounding of leather boots and iron-shod hooves and hanging in the air behind like a long brown tail. The land was flat with well-tended farms growing grain and vegetables, orchards of oranges, lime, and lemons. No cattle, horses, or mules were in sight, which meant the animals had been driven away to prevent the Americans from taking them. That wasn't a good sign that Grant would be successful.

Grant had mapped out the route for the foraging. It would consist of two days or so north toward Tampico, but never coming anywhere near that city lying one hundred and twenty-five miles distant, then a day or so march west inland, and lastly a turn southward to forage new territory for animals during the return to Veracruz.

They tramped steadily on through growing heat. The land became rolling with the road twisting and dipping into the shallow valleys where every stream ran down to the sea now about five miles away. The farms and orchards had been left behind and they traveled across grassland with narrow strips of trees along the streams. On every hilltop, Grant glassed the land ahead for horses and mules and for congregations of men that could mean trouble, and checked behind to see if Mexican riders were spying upon them.

In mid-morning, they reached the fair size village of San Julian setting on the near side of a moderately large stream running down from the inland mountains. On the upper edge of the town a gristmill sat astride the stream and the big waterwheel was turning and grinding grain. The town was picturesque with brightly colored homes on streets laid out in neat squares, everything clean, and with a prosperous appearance. This would be their first chance to find out if the people would bring their horses out of hiding and sell them to the invading Americans. After a scrutiny of the village from its border, and a look behind, Grant led his men along the main street with the few people out and about giving way before them and watching with sharp, wary eyes from the sidewalks and doorways of the buildings.

He halted his detachment on the street at the border of the town's plaza that consisted of two town blocks shaded by many large trees, mostly eucalyptus, and a bandstand and bleachers. Businesses of various types from a general store to a saddle shop to a bakery lined the cobblestone streets surrounding the plaza.

Grant spoke to Chilton and Hodding, "Go to your men and stay with them. Keep them quiet and under control. Watch everything, the streets, windows, rooftops."

The two officers, their faces taut, rode back along the cavalcade.

"O'Doyle," Grant called. "We'll do this just like we did up north. Send five men to each corner of the plaza to watch for trouble. Then set up the folding table and chair. Put it under that big tree." Grant pointed at the largest eucalyptus throwing a dense shade.

"Yes, sir," said O'Doyle and hastened to carry out the order.

"Hackett, bring my money box." Grant called. Hackett was tall, chesty, with a heavy jaw covered with a bushy bearded, a formidable appearing fellow and was just as tough as he looked. He helped Grant with the lingo.

Hackett broke rank, went to the lead wagon and extracted the steel box from under the canvas covering. Carrying his rifle over a shoulder, he brought the box to Grant and walked beside him to the eucalyptus.

"Watch for trouble," Grant warned Hackett.

"I'll be ready if it comes, lieutenant," Hackett said. "I haven't shot a Mexican since we left Old Zach Taylor and it's about time."

"We want to avoid a fight," Grant said firmly.

"Yes, sir, I know that. But they just might start one,"

With exaggerated movements, Grant placed the box on the table, fished a key from his pocket, opened the box, and put stacks of shiny, Mexican silver dollars on top of the table. He picked up a handful of the coins and shook them above his head to make a bell-like, musical sound.

With no threatening actions from the heavily armed Americans, and now this officer jingling coins playfully, the people's curiosity overcame their fear and they began to draw closer. Other citizens came from the side streets and out of the businesses places to see what the Americans were up to. In but a few minutes, more than a hundred men, women, and children had gathered to view the American soldiers.

The larger boys had pushed out into the forefront of the other townsfolk and Grant called to them and motioned to come closer. They approached, their eyes wide with suspicion and muscles coiled to dash away.

Grant extracted several pennies, large copper coins nearly an inch in diameter, from the moneybox. He spoke to the boys in Spanish. "I'll give each of you one of these if you'll run through the town and call out to everybody that there is a gringo in the plaza who will pay many silver pesos for horses and mules."

Grant looked quickly at Hackett. "Did I say that right?"

"Yes, sir. You're getting good."

Grant looked back to the boys. "Will you do that?"

The boys nodded all in unison.

"Good. Hold out your hands."

Grant pressed one of the coins into a brown palm of each of the boys, and staring into the black eyes, said, "You have given me your word. If you lie, you'll go to hell. Now off with you."

Clutching their money, and with calloused bare feet flying, the boys darted off along the streets with their happy, youthful voices shouting out Grant's message.

As Grant waited and checking the crowd for troublemakers, a group of young men wearing pistols in their belts gathered off to the side of the main throng. They stared with hooded eyes from under big sombreros. Now and again they spoke among themselves with voices too muted for Grant to make out the words. He was certain that if trouble were to come, it would begin with these men.

"Do you see those fellows, Hackett?" Grant asked.

"I see them, lieutenant. I'll make sure they stay good boys."

One of the lads returned with a man leading a horse. Grant gave him another penny and sent him off on another trip.

Within two hours, Grant had examined half a hundred horses and purchased forty, and twelve mules trained to work in harness, for an average price of seven dollars each. When there were no more sellers, he closed his moneybox and led the detachment, with the bought animals tied to the tailgates of the wagons, from San Julian.

On a rise of ground just outside the town, Grant stopped and raised his glasses to the rear. "I thought that might happen," he said to Chilton and Hodding.

"What's that?" Chilton asked.

"Put your glasses on that horseman off there to the left and you'll see that we didn't buy the best horse in San Julian." In the field of Grant's glasses, a rider was bent forward over the neck of his horse running full out to the west.

"He's going to report our whereabouts to the nearest army post," Grant said. "The question for us is will they be regular army of militia and will they have enough men to tackle us. If they do have enough, how long will it take them to catch us?" He thought Chilton and Hodding would soon discover what combat meant.

* * *

Darkness overran Grant and the men on the banks of a tree-lined stream with ample firewood for the evening fires and grass for the animals. They put out sentries, staked out the horses, and made camp. In the light of the bivouac fires, and with mosquitoes swarming with the coming night, the three officers ate their rations from tin plates balanced on their knees.

"Well, Grant, how do you judge the day went?" Chilton asked.

"It's not good that the Mexican Army will soon know, or already knows where we are and our number," Grant replied and looking out across the dark land. "And I'm disappointed in how few animals we managed to buy. Still it's been my experience that the farther we get from the fighting the more willing the people are to sell us horses and food stuffs."

"Well at least the day didn't bring a fight, not one shot," Hodding said.

"Our luck won't hold," Grant replied. "We're a small force moving slowly through a hostile country with men riding to keep the Mexican army informed of our location. And the more animals we collect, the more tempting target we'll be for an attack."

"I don't see that there's much we can do about the Mexicans short of turning back," Hodding said.

"And we won't do that," Grant said. "But starting tomorrow, we'll put riders out in advance and also flankers to give us warning of what's coming at us."

Chapter Fifteen

Lee felt content as he bathed, the water cool to counter the hot day, in the bathtub of the house Johnston, McClellan, and he had taken into their possession. The invasion had gone admirably, and now that he was commander of the company of army engineers, his stature with Scott and the other senior officers had increased substantially. In addition, there was a grand party to attend tonight. The days since the end of the bombardment had been full of making drawings of the fortifications of the city and of Ulua and a party was a welcome event. Yes truly, it was a fine day. He climbed out, toweled dry, and standing naked in front of the mirror, shaved and trimmed his mustache that had grown long during the hectic days of the siege.

Scott and his generals had been invited to a party at the British Consulate. The invitation had not come as much of a surprise for the tone of the relationship between Consul Giffard and Scott had changed markedly after the surrender of the city. This was especially so after Scott issued his proclamation to the "Good people of Mexico", that the Americans came not as thieves, or ravagers of Mexican women, but wanting to be friends of all peaceful people and also of your religion and priesthood. And further that any American who injures you shall be punished, and in turn any citizen who injures us shall likewise be punished. We ask that you sell us supplies, and all who do so will be paid in cash and protected. Our goal is to resolve the two nations' differences quickly and end the war honorably with as little harm done to your fine nation as possible. The rapid change from antagonist to being friends of the Americans, not only by the British but all the foreign consuls, made Lee laugh. But then foreign consuls were selected for their ability to adapt quickly to conditions they couldn't change by subterfuge, bribery, or threat.

What did surprise Lee about the invitation was the request that the American generals bring a few young officers with them. The consuls and their staff members had daughters, nieces, and female cousins with them in this foreign land, and with music planned for the party there would be dancing and the young women would greatly appreciate handsome partners. Lee wondered what Scott had thought about the request. Anyway, and to Lee's delight, Scott had asked his staff officers to join him for the evening.

"Here's your uniform, captain," Connally, Lee's servant, said from the open doorway. Connally was a slender white man whom Lee paid out of his salary. He was a skilled scrounger and kept Lee and himself in the best food available. "I knew you'd want to catch the eyes of the pretty gals at the party, so I put an extra fine press on it and a sharp shine on the buttons."

"I'll need all the help I can get."

"I doubt that, sir. I'll put your uniform on the bed. Is there anything else you need?"

"No. You can take the rest of day off."

"Thank you, sir." Connally's footsteps faded away.

Lee donned his dress blue uniform with its two rows of brass buttons down the front of the frock coat and left the house. The streets were thick with off duty soldiers taking in the sights and searching for pleasure in the conquered city. A limited number of townsfolk were out and moving about quickly to complete their private missions and hasten back to their homes. Most of the citizens hadn't yet gotten used to the foreign soldiers. To enforce everybody's good behavior, Worth had squads of men patrolling the city.

Worth's division was billeted in the Mexican Army barracks on the south side of the town. Patterson's division of volunteers and Twiggs' division of regulars had been pulled out of the dunes and moved close to the city with their tent encampments now on the Plain Of Cocos and other locations where there were trees to provide shade from the sun growing ever hotter as the spring wore away toward summer. Outposts had been left behind on the old investment line, with pickets and cavalry patrols farther afield to provide an early warning of an advancing enemy. The American artillery had been brought in near the city's walls and made ready, together with the captured cannons, to repel any Mexican force trying to retake the city.

Early in the day, Worth had given permission for the camp followers; the gamblers with their cards and spinning wheels, the whoremasters with their whores, stage actors, and sutlers of half a hundred types with their tools of trade and sales goods, to leave their ships and come ashore. They swarmed upon the wharf and swept into the town and hurriedly set up their businesses in deserted buildings or in tents they pitched in parks and vacant areas within the city. The gamblers and the whores showed remarkable quickness in providing instant and convenient vice to the soldiers.

The whores, the imported ones and the brown skinned locals were on the streets parading their well developed bodies and smiling enticingly. They went through the hundreds of soldiers out on the town like fish seiners, and their nets caught many of the fish. Lee passed a brothel with the women displaying their wares in revealing clothing on the porch of a fashionable home with several bedrooms. Lee was struck by the red light hanging from the front of the porch. The English custom of marking a whorehouse with a red light had been brought to the States and now had been transported an even greater distance to the far shores of Mexico.

Lee came to the British consulate building; a splendid, imposing three-story structure built of white coral stone with many tall windows set on a quarter block of land overlooking the beautiful blue Mexican sea. Lee was met at the entrance by one of Giffard's servants in livery who guided the way to the ballroom, a huge room richly appointed with tapestry on the walls, polished wooden floor, and chairs and tables along the borders, and beyond all of that a grand dance floor where fifty couples could swing and promenade.

A large number of people had already gathered, American army officers in blue uniforms, the consulate men in tailored black suits, and the women in dresses as brightly colored as the tropical butterflies Lee had seen and marveled at in this land. People from the foreign delegations and the American officers laughed and held brisk conversations as if thousands of American cannon balls hadn't fallen upon the city from the sky and six hundred soldiers and civilians hadn't been killed. But then perhaps the gaiety existed because there had been a battle and these people had escaped harm. The hum of voices and the smiles brought a wave of nostalgia to Lee for they reminded him of the parties with music and dancing he and his wife held in Virginia when he was home on furlough from the army.

Lee saw Scott and his generals were present and congregated with the British, French, Spanish and Prussian Consuls in a jovial group. He noted Scott was in an expansive manner and had a right to be for he had captured the enemy's most important seaport at the small cost of nineteen men killed and sixty-three wounded. With the victory he gained possession of 400 pieces of artillery and thousands of small arms and ammunition

Lee moved across the ballroom, avoiding Scott and those gathered around him, and staying clear of other groups of men. He saw musicians with their instruments filing onto the bandstand located at the distant side of the dance floor and knew he had judged the time just right, in that he could dance with the pretty women instead of talking war and politics with the men.

He saw a tall brunette with green eyes set in a perfect oval face watching him from a group of women. He recognized Marie Dupois sister of French Vice Consul Rene Dupois. She had been introduced to Lee when he had been at the French Consulate waiting to arrange for a meeting between Scott and the Consul.

She caught Lee's eye upon her and smiled. He considered a smile from a pretty woman a gift of gold. Since he never knew for certain what lay behind a woman's smile, he was drawn to find out. Holding the woman's eyes, he went toward her. As he approached, Marie extracted herself from the group of women and moved a few feet steps away from them.

Lee halted before Marie and gave her a slight bow. "Miss Dubois, perhaps you remember me. I am Captain Lee."

"Oh, I couldn't forget you, captain. You are one of the wicked soldiers who drove me from my home by shooting big cannons at it."

"Never that," Lee remonstrated taken aback by the charge. "I . . . We were always careful where we aimed our guns, though I understand the people living in the city wouldn't know that." If she were going to criticize him about the bombardment, he would apologize and quickly retreat.

"I know you're not a wicked man," she said with a low laugh and her eyes twinkling. "But I did have to leave my home and go to stay on one of my country's ships in the harbor for the last two days of your bombardment."

"I regret you were forced to do that." Lee had done as Scott ordered, aimed some cannon fire deeper into the city and near the consulates.

"Then make it up to me."

"I will do so in any way that I can."

"The penalty is, you must dance with me."

"That wouldn't be a penalty. That would be a great pleasure." Her directness was uncommon. Was it due to her loneliness in a foreign land where eligible white men of her station were few in number? Was her reasoning the same as his that he would be marching away from the city within the next few days and they would have but a little time to build and enjoy a friendship?

"Then I shall think of a penalty later," Marie said.

The room filled with music as the band struck up a waltz. Marie gave Lee an inviting smile, and a nod as if to say, let's dance.

Lee took her into his arms, her flesh warm and soft beneath his hands. He swung her away to the rhythm of the music. Her long silk skirt with its color matching the green of her eyes, rustled with a sound of bird's wings as she moved. He felt a powerful attraction toward this lovely, friendly woman.

During the evening, Lee danced with other women for he knew Scott expected it, and would be watching the behavior of his officers. Often, but not too obvious, when the band struck up a new piece, he found Marie nearby, her doing he was certain, and they would dance to the excellent music. They were dancing together when the music ended for the last time.

As they walked from the dance floor, Marie spoke, "I have thought of a proper penalty for shooting cannons at my home."

"Never at your home. But I accept your penalty nevertheless."

"Then you must show me the city. Not to find fault with you Americans, but just to see all that has happened to it during the bombardment." Marie looked into Lee's eyes and waited for his reply.

"I find the penalty very harsh," Lee said with a frown.

"Too harsh?" Marie asked and taken aback, or a skilled actress.

"Very much so, but I did promise." Then Lee smiled broadly showing he was playing along with her game.

Marie laughed, a lovely bell-like tone, and caught Lee by the hand and squeezed it.

Chapter Sixteen

"Close up your ranks," Grant called to the weary, dust covered men as he rode forward along the length of the caravan. He ignored the unfriendly looks flung at him by the men. This was the fifth day of foraging and he had pushed the troopers hard every hour of daylight not spent bargaining for animals. Now the men were straggling as the heat built under the burning tropical sun.

Grant had stopped his band of foragers at the towns and ranchos they came upon and now had acquired somewhat more than two hundred horses and mules. The men at the ranchos had often refused to sell their animals, protesting bitterly that they needed them to ride to manage their livestock. Grant had his orders and he had one hundred and eighty men with rifles and so he took the horses by threatening force. He paid what he considered a fair price every time, but still he left behind angry, cursing caballeros that would take revenge if they should ever have the opportunity.

He had no saddles or bridles for the purchased animals; still the foot soldiers jumped at the chance to ride bareback. They had fashioned halters from rope and could control their steeds well enough by that means. The animals not ridden were being driven along near the center of the wagon train.

The caravan traversed a road of brown dirt stretching across flat grasslands of the purest green. Ahead and barely visible some three miles away, a small village sat astride the road. Off on the right about a mile the Rio Actopan meandered serpentine-like in the floodplain it had carved from the land. The river's floodplain held a dense stand of woods, and Grant kept a wary eye in that direction. Far off on the left, a small herd of cattle grazed the lush, knee-high grass. If Grant had been after meat, he would turn aside and taken the cattle.

Enemies could come down on the Americans from any point of the compass, and to provide an early warning he had assigned a squad of Dragoons to ride one half mile off on both flanks of the caravan. Regardless of a warning by the flankers, it would be extremely difficult to mount a strong defense against Mexican cavalry because the caravan of horsemen, wagons, and animals stretched for more than half a mile.

Reaching Chilton and Hodding riding in the lead, Grant slowed his horse to match the pace of the mounts of the two officers.

"How does it go back there?" Chilton asked.

"Everybody's hot and dusty and still grumbling about us not stopping for the noon meal," Grant replied. "But I've got a feeling that this isn't one of the times to listen to the men. If we hustle we can deliver these animals to Scott before dark. Then we can give the men a couple day's rest." He had done his best to insure the success of the foraging expedition, and though he had wanted to locate and buy more animals, he wasn't too displeased. Now he must get men, horses and mules safely to Veracruz.

The officers fell silent. The only sound from the caravan was the creak of leather and the sodden plops of the horses' hooves in the thick dust of the road.

* * *

The sound of two distant rifle shots jerked Grant's eyes in the direction of the Rio Actopan. A pair of quick shots was the signal that the flanking Dragoons had spotted an enemy.

"I thought the woods by the river was a dangerous place," Grant said to Chilton and Hodding riding in the lead of the caravan with him.

"Damn I hope it's not true," Hodding said anxiously.

"My boys wouldn't make a mistake about something like that," Chilton said.

"They're too far away for us to see what they see," Grant said quickly. "Best we take it as gospel. If it's Mexican cavalry, it won't be but two or three minutes before they're here. Get your men into position and do it fast." On the second day of the expedition, Grant had joined with the two officers in devising a strategy to resist an attack. Twice the troops had been run through a drill of the plan and he hoped that was sufficient to now get them into place before the enemy struck.

The three officers whirled their mounts and spurred off. Reaching their men they called out orders. With shouts from the sergeants and hurried movement by the men, the lead wagons reversed course while those in the rear continued ahead and the caravan converged upon the ten wagons and the cavalcade of horses and mules at its center.

* * *

"How many of them are there?" Grant asked the corporal of the scouts. The squad had arrived spurring and flogging their mounts.

"Maybe two hundred and fifty and all cavalry, sir," the corporal said in an excited voice. "They were hidden in the woods by the river and we didn't see them until they broke clear. I didn't stick around to try and get an accurate count."

"That's enough to make a good fight," Grant said and looking past the Dragoons toward the river. Behind him the caravan was rapidly consolidating into an eighth of a mile long block of men, horses and vehicles. The wagons and their teams were being arranged in a double column, between which a space had been left and that was now being used to pen the horses and mules, including the mounts of Grant's and Hodding's men who had dismounted. Along the wagons and on the side from which the enemy was approaching, the sergeants were forming up their men two ranks deep.

"I see them now," Grant said. The Mexican Lancers had remained out of his view for a time by following a swale leading from the floodplain toward the Americans. Now they had come up onto the plain and were in sight streaming toward them two abreast and with battle flags snapping. The corporal hadn't exaggerated the number of Lancers; in fact he might have underestimated it by a few.

Grant spoke to Chilton. "There's way too many for your men to fight on horseback."

"I agree," Chilton said as he eyed the large company of enemy cavalrymen racing over the green plain toward them.

"Dismount your troopers and form them up in a double rank there on the end of Hodding's men," Grant directed Chilton.

Chilton moved away shouting. "Sergeants, dismount your men with their arms and cartridges boxes. One trooper out of five will hold the horses. Form the rest there beside those men." He pointed. "Move it, you've little time."

Grant saw Chilton's orders were swiftly obeyed, and he liked that for there wasn't time to sort things out if there was confusion. He looked back at the Mexicans.

The captain of the Lancers halted his column of men on the plain some three hundred yards away from the Americans. He called a command to his two lieutenants. They broke rank and in less than a minute had brought their men up to form a single line left and right of their captain. Grant noted the practiced speed with which the Lancers responded and knew they were drilled and disciplined cavalrymen and would make a hard fight.

Grant turned to his men now in double ranks. Hodding's men were in the center with bayonets fixed, Grant's small squad with muskets ready on Hodding's right, and Chilton's Dragoons with their carbines and sabers on the left. The Dragoon horse handlers with their charges, had worked around back of their dismounted comrades. The drivers of the wagons had set the brakes and climbed down and were holding the bridles of their lead teams to prevent them from bolting when the guns started banging.

"With the wagon drivers and horse handlers out of the fighting, we're outnumbered two to one," Chilton said. He had come up and was standing beside Grant.

"They might ride right over us," Hodding added.

"We'll knock a hundred out of their saddles with a good volley and that'll help even the odds," Grant said.

"Even if we can do that, it'll still be a tough fight," Hodding said in a tight voice.

"There'll surely be some hand-to-hand," Grant said and continuing to watch the Lancers where the captain in his blue and red uniform and black shako hat with its long black feather set at a jaunty angle was riding along the line of his men and gesturing with his hands and arms as he gave a war talk to build courage for the coming battle.

"I found out up north that Lancers, when led by a brave man, fight hard," Grant said. "But we'll stand fast and give them the best we have and try to knock the spirit out of the. Now it's time we tell our men what to expect and what to do."

With the two lieutenants beside him Grant walked along the double ranks of blue uniformed troopers and Dragoons and calling out again and again in a calm voice to them. "We'll give the Mexicans a volley when they're in range. Pick your target and don't miss. Don't fire until I give the signal." He pivoted to retrace his steps. "The Mexicans don't take prisoners. In Texas they massacred every man who surrendered at Goliad. This fight is to the death." He finished in a loud voice, "Wait for my signal to fire."

Grant looked into the tense faces of Chilton and Hodding. This encounter with the Mexican Lancers meant the formula for battle and death had been brewed and there was absolutely nothing that could be done about it. "We must not be defeated so fight to the last man," he said. "Go stand with your troops and lead them bravely."

"If I get hit, take care of my men," Chilton said and looking into Grant's calm, enigmatic face.

"Same here," Hodding said.

"Right," Grant said. What would happen if he were the one to be struck down?

Chilton and Hodding hastened away to take a position in the center of the ranks of their men.

Grant moved to a position in front and midway of the Americans, and watched the Lancers. They came trotting their mounts and gaining sped with each step.

Grant spoke to the men. "Front rank kneel. Smartly now and get ready to fire. We'll give them a volley they won't like. Wait for my call to fire."

He went quickly and took a position beside O'Doyle in the double ranks of his men. O'Doyle gave him a grim look and a nod.

The company of Lancers had closed half the distance. They moved over the green meadow as if on parade, their line straight and their uniform clad bodies erect in the saddle. Their horses were all of a dark color, ranging from dark brown to black. Each man held his carbine across the saddle in front of him. The long lances were fastened by the staff just behind the Lancer's leg and in such a manner that they pointed upward and slanted slightly to the rear. From that position they could be easily unlimbered for close in fighting. Green and red guidons flapped from the staffs of the lances just behind the foot long iron points.

The officer with his black hat with the waving plume was very conspicuous among the rank and file with their white hats. He like, the American officers, would draw many bullets. Field officers who fought with their men lived a very precarious life. Grant pulled his pair of pistols and checked their readiness.

"Prepare to fire on my command," Grant called out above the rumble of the hooves of the enemy's horses.

He cast one last glance along the ranks of the Americans. All preparations were as ready as they would ever be. It was now win or die. He looked to the front at the solid rank of swiftly approaching Lancers. There was always this moment of a few short seconds before the crash of the first shots when he felt vulnerable. After that the battle consumed all his thoughts and strength, and death was a thing that happened always to some other poor, unlucky soul.

The captain of Lancers shouted out and his men replied with high, piercing yells. The captain spurred his horse and his men instantly did likewise and their mounts leapt ahead in a full out run. The company of Lancers, one animal wanting to fight, charged down on the Americans.

Grant heard Hodding calling in a calm voice to his platoon. "Steady, boys. Steady now. Wait for Lieutenant Grant. He'll know when to let go at them."

The distance between the opposing fighters shortened swiftly. The thudding of the horses' hooves was a rumble that swiftly rose in volume. The faces of the Lancers could now be made out; eyes boring straight ahead and mouths open and shouting keening battle cries.

Carbines crackled and puffs of smoke blossomed along the line of Lancers. Grant heard lead balls tearing past him with a deadly, whirring sound. A quick crunching sound of lead cutting flesh came from close on his left. Immediately came a guttural gasp of pain. One of his men was hit. Grant felt guilty thinking the shot was probably meant for him.

He knew the Lancers had fired their short-barreled carbines from too great a range, and shooting from a running horse didn't allow for great accuracy, so hopefully not many Americans had been hit. The Lancers rammed their single shot carbines into scabbards and grabbed their lances from the straps that held them to the side of their mounts. Gripping the shafts fiercely, they lowered the sharp iron points to chest high and charged down on the Americans.

"Fire!" Grant shouted at the top of his lungs.

A crash of musket fire rippled along the American lines. Burning gunpowder flamed red and smoke boiled out in a cloud. Men were half deafened by the thunderous explosion.

Grant saw scores of Lancers scythed away by the concentrated fire of the Americans, ripped from the backs of their running horses as if they had hit an invisible wire. Another two score dropped their lances and badly wounded clung to their mounts. A third that many horses were struck by American bullets and fell with their riders onto the ground in a jumble of kicking and thrashing legs. Frightened and riderless horses veered steeply away from the solid wall of American riflemen and their wagons.

The Captain of Lancers had miraculous ridden through the blizzard of American musket balls. He charged on with the men of his company reining their mounts to fill in the gaps that had been blasted into their rank. His tall black hat was gone; blown away by a bullet. He had jet black hair and a fierce black beard that was split by a gaping mouth rimmed with white teeth. He was locked on Grant, and riding straight at him with his pistol shoved out ahead and aimed.

Grant fixed on the hate filled eyes of the captain and read them as clearly as shouted words. The captain had but one goal, to kill this officer of the enemy and the cost wasn't considered.

Chapter Seventeen

Grant brought his right hand pistol up and sighted down the black iron barrel at the Lancer captain's chest. He fired. The pistol bucked in his hand and flame and smoke chased an invisible bullet that struck the man exactly at Grant's point of aim.

The captain flung both arms wide. An expression of great surprise swept his face. Still holding a grip on his pistol, he fell backward from the saddle, and rolled and tumbled on the ground.

Mounted Mexicans and horses with empty saddles crashed into the American lines. Men were bowled over by the horses, stomped on by iron shod hooves, kicked. The Mexicans attacked with their long lances. Hodding's men fought back with bayonets. Chilton's men swung their sabers. Grant's men reversed their empty muskets and swung them as clubs.

On both sides of Grant the hand-to-hand fighting was savage, with fierce shouts, and thud of blows striking, and cries of pain. He barely heard the sound for his breath was whistling through his teeth as he dueled with a Mexican trooper trying to impale him on the iron point of his lance. Grant had shot a man with his second pistol and now fought with his saber. Sidestepping a powerful thrust by his foe, Grant swung the saber and struck the iron point with a clang of metal on metal and deflected it away. He immediately jumped forward and stabbed out and up at the man. The saber blade slid past the high pommel of the Mexican's saddle and plunged into his stomach. The man's face contorted with sudden pain and he sagged over the blade.

Grant ripped his saber free and whirled to look for another enemy. He found none. The courage of the Lancers had broken. By the twos and threes and then larger groups, they were pulling back from the Americans. As if on some signal that Grant couldn't hear, the remaining Lancers whirled their mounts and spurred away. Those who had had their horses shot from under them ran off on foot, most hobbling or limping.

"Reload! Reload!" Grant gave a stentorian shout that swept over the Americans and snapped them into action.

On both sides of Grant, the men worked swiftly biting off the ends of the paper cartridges, pouring the powder down barrels and inserting the lead balls and seating them with the ramrod jerked from under the barrel of the muskets.

"Get set to fire," Grant called.

Grant watched the Mexicans as he reloaded his pistols. They had reined their mounts to a halt some two hundred yards distant and were bunched and talking and gesturing as they decided what to do next. He estimated that half their original number still sat their saddles. A few gathered around one man and looked expectantly at the others to see what action they would take. No others joined this group. One man wheeled his horse and rode away. A half score followed, and then every one of the mounted men, carrying behind them those who had been unhorsed in the charge, streamed away across the meadow.

Hodding let out a great triumphant yell that was quickly joined by Chilton and all the men. They had broken the will of the Mexicans to fight and they were running, leaving many of their comrades dead and wounded on the battlefield. The two lieutenants laughed at each other knowing they had fought bravely hand to hand with death up close.

Grant saw both had an expression of pride upon their faces. They had just received a lesson in what it took to be an army officer. He called out to them. "The wounded need tending and then got to the hospital as fast as we can. Assign men to do that, and others to gather up the Mexicans' horses and arms."

The laughter ceased and the men began to look for friends, to see if they too had won safely through the hail of bullets and thrusts of lances.

"You've been hit," Grant said to Chilton.

Chilton touched the side of his face where blood ran from a long wound on the cheek. He looked at the blood on his fingers. "Yeh, I know. Burns like hell. That Mexican almost got me with his lance."

Grant faced his own men. "Hackett get out the medical supplies and pass it around. O'Doyle, take some men and empty five wagons by shifting cargo so the wounded and the dead can ride. We're rolling soon as everybody's bandaged up."

"What about their wounded?" Chilton asked as he stared at the Mexicans lying on the green grass, many dead, others alive but wounded and bleeding and groaning.

"Their comrades will come back for them soon as we're gone."

"A man in death looks damn lonely," Chilton said as he stared around at the crumpled, motionless forms on the ground.

"Yes," Grant said. "It's best not to be one of them."

He insured the thirteen wounded were as comfortable as they could be made in the wagons, and the four dead had been loaded, and then left to examine the Lancer captain he had shot. As he passed through the fallen Lancers, he looked down at their brown faces and black eyes, some blank and staring in death and others filled with pain and fearing the Americans would kill them. Three of these dead were by his hand, and he would spill more blood before Mexico was conquered and the war ended. He was a soldier and must not feel regret at his past deeds nor of the future ones to come, for he fought men who had an equal chance to kill him.

He came to the Lancer captain lying crumpled on the grass, his chest bloody and eyes wide and unseeing.

"You were a brave one," Grant said to the unhearing officer.

The captain's horse, a magnificent black animal, approached timidly. Its ears were thrust forward, and gold-flecked brown eyes warily watched Grant. It wanted to be with its master regardless of the strange man standing over him.

Grant picked up the captain's pair of pistols heavily inlaid with silver. They were .45-caliber cap and ball pistols with octagon barrels. He hefted them and found they were excellently balanced, better than the pair he owned. Examining them closely he saw the name Morales engraved in the silver of the butts. Was this young officer the son of General Morales who had been commander of Veracruz? He unfastened the cartridge box from the man's belt. Carrying the pistols and box, he approached the captain's long legged mount.

The animal began to back away. "Steady, old fellow," Grant said in a soft voice. "I'm not going to hurt you. I'm thinking you and I should get acquainted. I need a mount and you need someone to look after you."

The horse stopped, trained not to desert its master. It trembled as Grant's strange hand touched its neck. "Horses have always liked me. You will too."

The bridle and saddle, like the pistols, were resplendent with silver inlays. Here too he found the name Morales. "You look fine with all that silver, but I've got to take it all off. If I don't everything will be stolen some dark night."

"Lieutenant, he's got gold on him."

Grant saw one of Hodding's men squatting beside the officer and holding up a leather pouch heavy with coins. "Soldier, put that back. A dead enemy's weapons and mount are property of war and fair game for a victor. What's in his pockets isn't. That belongs to his family."

"Sir, how do I get it to them," asked the private. The expression on his face spoke clearly that he didn't agree with the difference Grant was making between taking the pistols and horse and taking the coins.

Grant looked about and saw other men were waiting his answer before they too began to search the dead. He turned back to the captain's horse without answering. Let the men take what they wanted for hadn't they won it by their blood? As for him he had drawn a line between horse and pistols and what he considered personal to the man. But was he right, or was he too just a thief scavenging the dead?

* * *

Lee wound his path through the people on the boulevard fronting the sea. Evening shadows were growing, still the streets were crowded with Mexican citizens and American soldiers and all going about the business of buying and selling and the search for pleasure. The fears of the citizens to be out and about in the occupied city had vanished quickly upon Scott's swift execution of the American Issac Kirk who had raped a woman of the city.

Scott had a gallows built in the public square, borrowed the city's public executioner, and with Justus Bustamente, Alcalde of Veracruz, the townsfolk, and all off duty soldiers present, Kirk was hung for all to witness. The executioner, a tall, gaunt man in dark pants and shirt and tall leather boots and a black mask, alone was sufficient to put fear into a man.

Lee came upon a score of Mexican hucksters bawling out their goods at the tops of their voices. One vendor was selling fresh oysters and Lee wished

Connally had been here so that he could buy some for the mess. He walked on passing the camp followers selling zinc coffins and the embalmer. The two men bragged about their wares and promised they would bring you back from the place where you caught the bullet to your home and loved ones. Of course payment had to be made in advance. A few soldiers were inside and talking with the proprietors. A Mexican lad went by selling copies of the American Star. Within one day after the fall of Veracruz, the publisher of the newspaper, John Warland, Quartermaster Sergeant of the Ninth Infantry, had set up his printing press and put out his first edition. Lee bought a copy. The newspaper always quickly sold out for it was immensely popular with the soldiers wanting to know what was happening, be it only rumors.

Farther along the street in front of the row of buildings commandeered by the medical corps for hospital use, several wagons were drawn up. Three officers sat their mounts close by the wagons and watched hospital orderlies unload wounded men and place them upon stretchers and carry them inside for treatment by the surgeons.

Lee recognized Grant, Chilton and Hodding. He was aware that the men had been on a foraging expedition, and wanting to know their success, he lengthened his stride to draw nearer and speak with them. Before he could call out to the three, they galloped off along the street.

Lee arrived at army headquarters just behind Generals Twiggs and Patterson. He fell in silently behind the two and followed them past the armed guards stationed at the entrance and went into the building and along the wide hallway to Scott's office. The door stood open and Lee could see the big man at his desk, his ponderous brow creased with thought as he studied maps spread before him.

Scott, looking up and seeing the generals and Lee, called to them. "Gentlemen, come in."

The three entered and after saluting took seats as directed by Scott beside the officers already there, Henry Scott, Army Secretary, Colonel Banks, Chief Of Artillery, Captain Huger, Chief Of Ordnance, and Colonel Harney, Chief of Cavalry.

"Since we're all assembled, let's get down to business," Scott said. He nodded to Henry Scott who had taken out a pad of paper and was prepared to record the meeting.

Lee was surprised at the absence of Worth, for never had an important matter, and obviously by the attendees this one was, been discussed without his presence. Lee knew Scott and Worth were long time friends, and that Scott had been instrumental in getting the man promoted to major general.

"As you are all aware we've received reinforcements and provisions today, a brigade of 1300 volunteers, our long awaited siege guns, and 1200 horses and mules. We require another 13,500 men to reach our full complement of 25,000 men. We're still short of wagons and draft and pack animals. Further we have more than a thousand men in the hospital, with forty of them down with yellow fever. The chief surgeon estimates that one in ten of our thousand sick will die."

Scott swept the men with a penetrating look, telling them to pay attention for he was going to say something important. "Time has run out for us. We must make a thoughtful and deliberate choice between waiting here in the lowlands for more reinforcements to arrive, with our men dying all the while, or striking out for Mexico City with the force of men and arms that we have on hand. Should we march inland it would be impossible to keep the road open behind us for all the two hundred and sixty miles to Mexico City. So we'd be cutting ourselves off from our supply depot here in Veracruz and must live totally off the land."

Lee listened intently. Over the past weeks he had grown to understand Scott and knew the man had already made his decision of which alternative would be chosen. The reality of the matter was plain, to stand still meant the ruin of the American army, and Scott was a realist of the first order.

Scott continued to speak. "What we must do is as clear as day to me. We will cut ourselves off from the coast and march our men into the mountains. Our first objective is Jalapa seventy miles distant on the inland plateau. At an elevation of 4,000 feet it's above the vomito zone. I have information that Santa-Anna is there with an army of 20,000 men."

Scott focused on Twiggs. "General, reinforce your division with the volunteers that have just arrived. Have it ready to march, infantry, cavalry, and field artillery at first light day after tomorrow. Add the heavy siege guns we've just received to your artillery."

He spoke to Patterson. "General, be ready in all aspects to march with your division and the Marines the navy has loaned us the following morning.

Stay close behind General Twiggs at all times and when he meets resistance from Santa-Anna, you must quickly move your men forward to support him. This should occur at some strong defensive position below Jalapa for Santa-Anna will want to hold us in the vomito zone.

"Now as to your duties," Scott said to Banks, Harney, and Huger. "Your task is to assist the generals in every possible way to be fully equipped and ready to move by the time stated."

Scott spoke to Lee. "Captain, send Beauregard and four other engineers with General Twiggs. They will do his reconnoitering."

Scott turned back to Twiggs and Patterson. "We are short of wagons and draft animals so you'll have only five hundred. Divide the wagons as you see fit among your commissary, ordnance, and medical supplies. Your men will carry their weapons and sixty rounds of ammunition, and rations of hard bread and cooked beef for three days, and hard bread alone for another three. After those rations are used up, you must live off the land. Drive your quartermasters hard to find what you need to survive."

"Yes, sir," Twiggs said in a hardy voice and smiling hugely through his thick white beard.

"Gladly, sir," Patterson said in his gentlemanly manner. "I'm anxious to see Mexico City."

"There'll be much hard fighting before that happens. Santa-Anna will make every effort to destroy us and he can choose the place of battle that gives him the greatest advantage. I believe he'll fight a defensive war astride the National Highway for he'll know that's the only route we can take with our heavy artillery. The odds are high that we will be greatly outnumbered in every battle. I charge you to conserve the lives of your men. Do nothing rash, reconnoiter thoroughly before advancing and don't allow yourself to be drawn into a trap. Keep me informed of your progress by messenger and I will come at once when you meet resistance."

Chapter Eighteen

A broad expanse of the sand plain outside the west wall of Veracruz was crowded with the several contingents of General Twiggs's division assembling for the advance into the distant mountains. More than 3,000 infantrymen stood in ranks as they waited the order to march. Three companies of Dragoons sat the backs of their mounts. Two companies of artillerymen stood by their limbered cannons drawn by two teams of horses, with the big siege guns drawn by three teams of mules positioned at the end of the lineup. Teamsters with long whips sat upon the high seats of three hundred heavily loaded wagons, with each drawn by a double team of horses.

Grant with his right leg thrown around the pommel of the saddle, rested upon the back of his new horse, and watched the final gathering of Twiggs's army. Beside him Chilton and Hazlitt sat slouched upon the backs of their mounts. Old Fuss And Feathers Scott with a gaggle of half his staff, all mounted, were off on Grant's right and also observing Twiggs' doings. Twiggs himself was riding his big sorrel horse from one company of men to another and speaking to the senior officer. From the way Twiggs's sat his horse and the jaunty way he returned his officers' salutes, Grant thought the general was having a grand time.

General Patterson with a portion of his staff was present viewing the show. Worth was absent which was odd and Grant wondered what the reason might be.

Twiggs finished the inspection of the several components of his army and rode to take a position beside the colonel of the Dragoons. His arm rose and motioned at the faraway mountains and his army began to uncoil from their compressed mass near the city. The companies of Dragoons stretched out along the National Highway. The infantry broke ranks, formed into a double column and followed. The artillery came next with its several different size guns drawn by laboring horses and mules. The powder boys rode upon the caissons. The three hundred supply wagons, new and Cincinnati built with white canvass cinched taut over hickory ribs, rolled next. A squad of Dragoons brought up the rear.

The scene was a familiar one to Grant; the soldiers in clean blue uniforms that would soon be sweaty and dust covered, regimental flags snapping in the breeze, rifle barrels and cannon barrels glinting in the sunlight, the creak of wheels on axles, shouts and curses and crack of whips by the teamsters, the rumble of horses hooves, and the muffled tread of marching infantrymen.

Grant rolled a cigarette and then extracted from a pocket a small silver tinderbox. From it he took flint and steel and a short coil of fuse. Striking the flint upon the steel, he dropped a spark on the end of the fuse, which ignited instantly and began to glow. He pressed the red coal against his cigarette and drew it into life, and crushed the fire of the fuse out on the pommel of his saddle.

He sat smoking and watching the men and weapons drawing away in a serpentine column stretching for more than six miles across the sandy plain. The Dragoons located at the front of the army were already lost to view in the moist haze of the coastal lowlands. In four to five days, Twiggs could be upon the high inland plateau. In something over two weeks he could march his army to Mexico City, if Santa-Anna didn't stop him. The Mexican general would most certainly try to do that.

Grant felt let down from being left behind with Worth who was stranded at Veracruz until more wagons and draft animals arrived from the States. He thought the war wasn't necessary, but even so he wanted to get in on the fighting.

"Well, Twiggs is on his way," Chilton said. "Patterson leaves tomorrow and I'll be with him."

"I wish I was going with you," Grant said. "I like to see new country."

"Not me," said Hazlitt. "I can wait for we've got it pretty good here in Veracruz."

"What would you fellows like to do?" Chilton said.

"What's most important, right next to a pretty woman?" Hazlitt said.

"Whiskey," said Chilton.

"Right," said Hazlitt. He turned to Grant. "Want to join us?"

"Just for a sip," Grant said. "Then I've got some letters to write".

* * *

Scott led his staff officers and squad of escorting Dragoons at a grueling pace along the National Highway toward Jalapa. Like his men, the general carried his bedroll, food, and canteen of water tied on the saddle behind him. He wore a broad brimmed straw hat with his blue field uniform to keep off the rays of the blazing sun. In the shade of the hat, his face was creased with worry for his army.

Lee knew the general had a very good reason for his worry. After four days of silence from General Twiggs, a Dragoon riding at top speed had delivered a message from him. The general had encountered Santa-Anna's army in a strongly fortified position in the mountain canyon south of Jalapa near the town of Cerro Gordo. In the message Twiggs informed Scott that he would attack Santa-Anna the following morning. That would have been the day just past and the battle could have already been fought, and lost. Upon reading the message Scott had spoken in a tone of frustration. "Where is Patterson? There's no mention of Patterson and he should be there with Twiggs." The thoughtful, experienced Patterson was senior to Twiggs and could assume command and bring caution to the two armies.

Scott at once directed his staff to prepare for a swift journey to Cerro Gordo. He issued orders for Worth to scrounge up what wagons and horses he could and follow as soon as possible. Worth's division had been reduced in size to 1600 men because of illness and having to leave a company of 500 infantrymen to prevent Veracruz from being retaken by the enemy, and to protect the supply depot and the 1000 ill and wounded men in the hospital,

Within a few hours after receiving Twiggs's message, Scott, riding a big, strong horse to carry his husky body, struck out with his entourage of staff and Dragoon escort for Cerro Gordo sitting nearly half a mile high in the mountains behind the coast. They left the sand plain behind and Scott picked up the pace with the iron-shod hooves of the men's horses rattling on the road Cortez had built up through the mountains to Mexico City.

With a touch of spurs to his horse, Lee held position on Scott. He pondered the situation in which the general found himself. The success of a campaign depended mostly upon the skill and experience of the senior officer present when the enemy was met. Scott, not Twiggs, should have headed the army advancing inland to meet Santa-Anna. However Scott had matters to finish in Veracruz, a last flurry of correspondence with Washington and completion of the negotiations with the city merchants to continue to cash army drafts and supply provisions for his army. Also there were the agreements with the foreign consuls to finalize in which he would protect their possessions if they would use their influence to keep the city officials friendly to the Americans.

Lee thought it a good thing that he personally had left Veracruz, more specifically that he was now separated from Marie Dupois. For a married man, he was becoming much too fond of the lovely woman, though she had in a most delightful way forestalled the loneliness that always came upon him when gone for weeks and months from his wife and children.

* * *

It was near midnight as Scott and his attendant officers and escort rode along the narrow, moonless road tunneling through the dense jungle. The Dragoons held their carbines ready across the saddles in front of them and the officers had their pistols drawn. According to Lee's calculations, they were within five or six miles of the pass below Cerro Gordo where Twiggs had encountered Santa-Anna. Patterson would surely be with Twiggs by now. If Santa-Anna had defeated the two generals, he would have his army positioned to intercept the arrival of American reinforcements.

The Americans broke free of the forest on the brow of a hill and halted their jaded, sweat lathered horses. Below them in a valley at the base of a range of mountains that blanked out a goodly quarter of the night sky to the west in front of them, hundreds of bivouac fires floated in a lake of darkness. There was no crack of rifles, no boom of cannons. The only sounds were the chittering of the night insects and the distant call of a night bird.

Scott spoke from beside Lee. "Captain, what do you make of that down there?"

"I'd say there's enough fires for the men of both Twiggs's and Patterson's divisions." He was swiftly evaluating the possibilities of what it all might mean. "Sir, I don't believe there was a fight. Everything looks too quiet, too orderly."

"My thoughts exactly, and I don't think Santa-Anna would think to stage something that elaborate for our benefit. But still we won't ride down without seeing what's the truth of it."

Scott called out just loud enough for all to hear. "Make camp. Quietly now. Keep you guns and horses close. We'll take a look at first light and see what's what."

Lee rode into a small clearing just off the road and dismounted. He dug a picket pen and tethering rope from a saddlebag and staked out his weary horse in a grassy place. Slacking his thirst from his canteen, he studied the lights below and thinking it all looked peaceful. However there was a problem, the hot breath of the coast on his face and the mosquitoes singing vampiral arias told him that Santa-Anna had penned the Americans in the vomito zone below the plateau. He spread his bedroll, and with his pistol and saber within easy reach, lay resting and eating a piece of hard bread.

Chapter Nineteen

When first daylight defeated late night, Lee stood looking down from Scott's camp on the height and onto the Plan Del Rio where the American army was encamped with its hundreds of canvas tents and covered wagons just visible in the dusk still lingering on the lower land. Part way up the grade of the National Highway to Lee a squad of Dragoons riding picket had halted and sat their horses and watching him. He raised his hand and waved and the rider in the lead lifted his hat in a return salute. The Dragoons wheeled their mounts and hastened down toward the camp.

* * *

The 7,000 men of Patterson's and Twiggs's combined divisions parted to allow General Scott and his staff officers and Dragoon escort to ride through them. The presence of Scott had spread swiftly through the camp and the men had gathered to welcome him. Several of the closest men reached out and petted Scott's horse as it passed. One of Patterson's young volunteers brushed the general's leg with a reverent touch.

"By God, the real general has come to lead us," a sergeant of Twiggs's division shouted out in a stentorian voice.

"Scott! Scott! Scott!" A thunderous chanting began and swept the entire camp of soldiers. Shrill whistles joined the chant. The cheering ended and a buzz of pleased comments of men to nearby comrades began. Scott doffed his big straw hat and waved it left and right to the men as he rode through them.

Lee knew full well the reason for the tumultuous welcome that had risen from every corner of the camp. Scott had taken Veracruz and Ulua by cannon and siege instead of by bloody musket and bayonet assault that Twiggs and Worth had advocated. In so doing he had spared the lives of hundreds of the men now looking up at him, and they knew it. The men acted as it the coming battle with Santa-Anna had been already won now that Scott was here.

Scott led on and as he drew near the cluster of the large tents of army headquarters, his attention left the upturned faces of the men and focused on Twiggs and Patterson standing and waiting for him to approach.

Lee tried to read Patterson and Twiggs thoughts about the welcome Scott had received, but their expressions showed only unreadable military. He reined his horse off to the right and swung down beside Beauregard standing alone and watching the goings-on.

"I don't see any signs of the fight that Twiggs's message to Scott said was ready to start," Lee said. "What's the story?"

Beauregard shifted his feet uncomfortably. "Captain, I would prefer not to talk about the reason, if it's all the same to you."

"It's not all the same to me, lieutenant," Lee said firmly. There was something here that he needed to know. "Speak up."

Beauregard's swarthy face became darker, nearly as dark as his eyes. "Yes, sir, captain. It has to do with Old Davey Twiggs. He almost marched the men into a trap to be slaughtered." He pointed to the northwest where two miles distant the National Highway entered a narrow canyon. "Without reconnaissance he went straight in with Santa-Anna's artillery and troops strongly entrenched on the high ground both sides of the Highway."

"And Patterson hadn't come up yet?" Lee said and turned to look at the abrupt wall of the plateau and just now being lighted by the first rays of the sun.

"That's right. If one of the Mexican forward batteries hadn't fired on us before we were deep in the canyon, it would have been pure and simple murder. As it was we managed to get our vehicles turned around and get the hell out with but a few men who were up front getting wounded. One of them hit was our friend Joe Johnston. He got a bullet through his right thigh and right wrist."

"By the time we pulled back to here, to get out of gun range, it was near dark so we made camp. The next day, Old Davey sends me and the other engineers to do reconnoitering. About dark Patterson comes up with his division. He's sick so he puts his men under Twiggs.

"I reported to Twiggs what I'd seen. Santa-Anna was entrenched with a strong force of men with many cannons and sitting astride the Highway and controlling all the high ground. I advise against attacking him. But the general wouldn't listen. He had command of two divisions and wasn't about to let the opportunity to fight a great battle get away from him. He ordered preparations for a direct assault for the following morning."

Beauregard locked eyes with Lee. "I stewed and stewed about the attack. Then I did something that a lieutenant should never do. It was near midnight, but even so I went and woke Patterson and told him my evaluation of Santa-Anna's strength and the hazard of us trying to dislodge him by a frontal assault. The old gentlemen listened and asked some questions, then he got up out of his sick bed and put on his uniform. He took command away from Twiggs and suspended the preparations for an assault. The following morning, he sent me with some of the other engineers out for a more complete reconnaissance. We found Santa-Anna to be better positioned than we had thought from our first look-see.

"Goddamnit, captain, I'm in big trouble for I've got General Twigs mad at me for causing him to lose command of the biggest force of men he ever had."

"You most likely saved Scott's army and I think he'll greatly appreciate that. So I wouldn't worry about Twiggs too much."

"Then you tell General Scott what happened for you know that I can't."

"I'll do that the first chance I get."

Lee glanced past Beauregard and saw McClellan coming from headquarters. "I'm betting Scott wants a report from you," he said to Beauregard.

Upon drawing closer, McClellan called out. "Captain, General Scott wants to see you and Beauregard."

When the three entered the big tent, Scott spoke without preamble. "Lieutenant Beauregard, General Patterson has told me you did reconnaissance of Santa-Anna's position and strength."

"Yes, sir, with some other engineers."

"Tell me what you saw."

"His line roughly runs north and south and is about a mile and a half long. His right is solidly anchored on the nearly vertical five hundred foot wall of the Rio Del Plan, and his left on steep, rough hills and gorges to the north. He has a large force and cannon well placed."

"Can his position be turned?"

"I don't believe his right flank can because of the deep canyon of the river. Perhaps his left could be. We need more reconnaissance on that end to determine that."

"Then let's get to it. Major Lee, take Beauregard and examine Santa-Anna's front and flanks in detail, and if possible take a look behind him."

* * *

Lee filled his canteen from the rock-rimmed pool of water created by the spring flowing out from a crevice in the ledge above. He straightened and drank deeply of the pure, cold liquid as he looked through the trees to the south across the front of the Mexican army. He had left shortly after receiving orders from Scott to reconnoiter the enemy's positions. He had started on Santa Anna's right that overlooked the river and worked to his left, preparing a sketch map showing the topography and recording what he could see of the entrenched soldiers and cannons and estimating the numbers of each.

Beside Lee, Lieutenant John Fitzwalter, finished filling his canteen and stood up. He drank noisily. "Damn good," Fitzwalter said.

Lee would have preferred to have Beauregard with him, and had started out with him, however near the end of the first day, the Creole had fallen ill and returned to camp. As substitute, Lee had chosen from among his company of engineers the lean, athletic Fitzwalter.

"Fitz, look," Lee said and pointed at the well-trod path coming to the spring from the south, and then at the much trampled grass and soil around the spring and its pool of water.

"This water hole is used by a lot of men," Lee said. "And all come from the same direction. I think we've gotten around Santa-Anna's left and are now behind him."

"Could be, captain, for I don't see any sign of men or guns north or west of us."

Lee scanned the ravines and ridges lying to the east and all running down to the Rio Del Plan. The American encampment lay in the same direction, perhaps a little more southeast than due east. "That land is rough, rocky, and with trees and brush, but I think a trail could be built good enough that men could drag guns over it."

"A few hundred could . . ."

"Quiet," Lee cut in and cocked his head to listen to men's voices that were suddenly audible speaking Spanish on the path just down the hill. The men must have broken above a lip of the hill and their voices now came through the trees to him. The sounds of their steps and conversations swiftly grew stronger.

"Mexican soldiers and it's too late to run," Lee said hurriedly. "Find a hole to hide in."

Fitzwalter sprang across the small clearing that surrounded the spring, dove into a clump of brush, and fell flat. Lee went off to the left of Fitzwalter, jumped over a log lying on the ground and bordered with a thin screen of brush, pulled both pistols, and dropped to the ground. He wedged himself in tight as possible against the bottom of the log, being about half hidden under its out-swelling shoulder.

Lee hazarded a look and rose up to peer over the log. A squad of six Mexican soldiers had come up to the spring and were kneeling and filling canteens. He ducked as three of them turned and came toward the log. They sat down with their backs toward him and their rumps only inches away. He listened to their conversation and heard the words Yankees and Norte Americanos and wished he knew the language.

A voice called out sternly. All conversation died and the men hastily rose and Lee heard them leave the spring.

Silence held only for a moment and then another group of men arrived, drank, and filled canteens. A shadow fell across Lee as one of the men came to the log and stepped across it with his heel landing an inch from Lee's shoulder. He moved on a few steps and relieved himself with his stream splashing on the ground.

Lee prepared to make a fight of it for when the man faced about to return to the spring, he couldn't miss seeing him lying by the log. He would spring to his feet and kill the soldier with a pistol shot, and then run and try to dodge the bullets of the remaining soldiers.

The man turned but not toward Lee. He took a course to pass around the end of the log. Lee let his breath out and his muscles uncoiled a little.

The men left as others come to the spring, and the rotation continued on and on. Often men prowled around as they drank and talked, and some come to the log and sat with their butts just above Lee. He remained perfectly still with the red ants that had found him biting and biting and raising welts that stung like fire.

The long hours passed. The shadows grew long and swung around to point to the east as the sun fell toward the horizon. At last the shadows blurred as twilight came. The procession of soldiers ended and the last loiters shuffled off.

Lee continued to lay and listen for danger as the day burned away to black ash. When the night insects come to life and begin their nighttime chatter and a frog began to croak at the spring, he rose stiffly to his feet.

"Fitz, you still there?" Lee called softly.

"Still here, captain."

"Time to go." He went to the spring and lay down. As he lowered his head to drink from the quiet black pool of water, he saw the stars of the heavens lensed in perfect stillness. Reluctant to destroy the grand beauty of the reflection, he remained poised over the water for several seconds. How strange life was, a short time ago he was close to being killed and now he was alive and looking at the perfect heavens. His engineer's mind said, "no that's not correct" and he smiled a little, he was seeing the heavens in reverse. Then again maybe this was reality and his normal viewing was in reverse. The stars shattered and vanished as he drank sending ripples radiating out across the water.

"Let's get to our lines," Lee said to Fitzwalter who had come up.

"I hope you got cat's eyes, captain. I can't see a thing and we've got some Godawful country to cross."

"I've got it calculated at four miles. First we go east over three ranges of hills and then turn south until we can see our fires."

Slipping on the steep slopes, tripping on rocks and down trees, the two men felt their way over the rough ground. After a difficult trek, they topped a hill and the hundreds of watch-fires of the American encampment came into view below them. It was a fine starry night and a cool breeze stirred and the men were grouped around the fires. Loud voices and laughter drifted up to Lee. If it wasn't for the posted sentinels, the scene might have been taken for some gay festival instead of the camp of American warriors.

Lee called out to the pickets and he and Fitzwalter were let pass. Battered and bruised, they came into the camp. He released Fitzwalter from duty and immediately directed his steps toward Scott's headquarters' tent where a light burned.

Chapter Twenty

In the light of the two oil lanterns hanging from the ridgepole of Scott's headquarters' tent, Lee spread upon a table the map he had prepared of the position of Santa Anna's army. Present to hear his report were Scott and his staff officers, General Twiggs, and General Patterson and his field generals, Pillow and Shields.

Lee began. "General, I started on the enemy's right and found it overlooks the river with its perpendicular bluffs, just as Lieutenant Beauregard said. And I agree with him that a turning action here would have little chance to succeed without a large loss of men. Back from the river, the ground rises fast to three tall ridges that extend out toward our positions. All the ridges are crowned with well-sighted batteries of artillery protected by entrenched men. Just north of the ridges the National Highway climbs up through a vertical walled pass to the high plateau. On a high point is a Mexican battery of guns that could strike any force that we should try to send along the Highway. Two high observations points La Atalaya and El Telegrafo are here about two miles behind Santa Anna's line." He touched the map. "The Mexican general has chosen his ground well for defensive action."

"Did you get behind his line?" Scott asked.

"Yes, sir. We passed around his left flank, but then got penned down until dark by a Mexican patrol and that prevented us from going farther."

"Thanks for you report, captain," Scott said. He leaned over the map and rested his elbows on the table and silently studied the map.

Lee felt the man's deep concentration as his agile mind evaluated what had been told to him and the possible courses of action that could be derived from the facts.

Without looking up, Scott said, "From what you've reported to us, our most logical point of attack is on Santa Anna's left. Is that also you conclusion?"

"Yes, sir, it is," Lee replied. He thought Scott would ask the other generals their opinion. However Scott spoke again to Lee.

"How do we get enough men and guns there for a strong assault?"

"Sir, the land is extremely steep and rough as I described, but give me a company of men and I'll take my engineers and build a trail sufficient to move our men and guns."

"Do you have any other observations to make to us?"

Lee would speak the obvious. "Though Santa Anna is well positioned with a large number of men and artillery pieces, the deep ravines and tall ridges that makes him strong on the defensive would prevent him from reinforcing any sector of his line that we decide to strike."

Scott straightened and swept the gathering of generals with eyes that showed he had come to a decision. "Gentlemen, I am satisfied with what Captain Lee has reported. We can defeat Santa-Anna even though he has much advantage over us. As the captain said, he lacks one important ingredient to successfully repel us, mobility to move his men. Our main attack will be on Santa Anna's left in the hills, however we must hit him in other places at the same time.

"We are very fortunate in that our men are half veterans and have had victories in the north with General Taylor, while Santa Anna's men haven't yet won their first battle. An army that has repeated victories becomes invincible. Hear me plain, when you strike him and he breaks, pursue him as long as your men have strength to follow for an army routed, if hotly pursued, becomes panicked-stricken and can be destroyed by half its numbers.

Now let us plan where we will strike him and how to cut off his escape, to bottle him up and end the war here and now."

* * *

The stomp of booted feet, clank of arms, and muted voices of an army assembling to march to battle woke Lee from his sleep at 4.30 in darkness. All the preceding day and until night stole away vision, he and eight of his engineers had worked with a company of infantrymen to hew out a crude trail through the steep ridges and ravines covered with trees and chaparral.

He pulled on his boots, he had slept in his clothing, and stood erect. Scott's orders to his generals for the assault on Santa Anna's line had been given. During the meeting, there had been one unpleasant incident when

Pillow received his orders to march to Santa-Anna's far right near the river and attack his lines. If Pillow could break through, he was to drive upon the Mexican forward batteries and pursue the fleeing foe until darkness, or halted by fortifications. Pillow had complained that his task was too dangerous, proclaiming it a desperate undertaking. Scott tried to reassure the civilian general. Pillow wouldn't be reassured, and in the end Scott threatened him with discipline. At that, Pillow said he would obey the order even if he left his bones in Mexico.

* * *

In darkness Lee and Twiggs rode their horses in the lead of the division moving with its three gun battery of artillery along the National Highway and climbing ever higher into the hills where lay Santa-Anna's army. To prevent stumbling into the enemy, a rifle regiment of skirmishers was feeling the way out in advance of the mile long cavalcade of men and guns. When daylight broke, they had reached the intersection of the Highway with the new trail and Lee led them off to the right along it.

The sun came up yellow and hot and grew hotter as the men marched steadily on. Distant objects stood out distinctly. The clarity of the day worried Lee for should they be seen by the Mexicans lookouts on La Atalaya, all surprise would be lost.

When they drew near the crest of a high ridge, Lee reined his mount to a stop. Twiggs halted beside him.

"What's the problem, captain?"

"General, we can be seen by the Mexicans when we cross over that," he gestured ahead at the ridge top. "I recommend we build a screen of brush to hide the men and guns."

"We have no time for that," Twiggs said in a rebuking voice and shook his big white head. "Everything depends on us getting into position and taking La Atalaya before dark." He raised an arm and gave the signal to march.

Lee said nothing further and rode on with Twiggs. The lead element of the division was soon on the summit with the cannons and the muskets of the men bright in the sunlight. If the Mexicans were alert, they could not fail to see the Americans moving in strength.

Twiggs called a rest halt and Lee took the opportunity to put his glass on La Atalaya two miles away and El Telegrafo another half mile farther. The men on the two hills, though much miniaturized by the distance, were visible, and hustling about. As Lee had feared, the Americans had been seen.

"General, the Mexicans are hurrying reinforcements to La Atalaya."

Twiggs aimed his glass and studied the hill. After a minute, he said, "Won't do them any good. We'll still take it."

Yes, our stout men will take the hill, but because you wouldn't build the screen, more American blood will stain the ground than should happen.

By mid-morning the three brigades were less than half a mile from La Atalaya. With his army protected for the time being in the bottom between two ridges, Twiggs halted and called Colonel Harney forward.

"Colonel, take two regiments and capture La Atalaya."

"Yes, sir," replied Harney. "How far should I drive them?"

"Drive them to hell!" Twiggs bellowed loud mouthed, and showing excitement now that the battle was commencing.

Harney signaled to his captains who were watching from the front of their men, and led them off the trail and into the chaparral and trees toward La Atalaya.

Colonel Riley rode up. "Captain Lee, help Lieutenant Steptoe take our guns to the top of the hill soon as Harney clears it of the enemy."

"Yes, sir," Lee said. He rode back to Steptoe near the guns that had been dragged along by a platoon of men on each. Now the huge effort of taking them up the long, nearly vertical front of three hundred foot tall La Atalaya lay before them. He and Steptoe organized a three hundred man team for each gun from Patterson's brigade of volunteers.

Lee remained near the artillery and watched Harney and his blue clad men charging the flank of La Atalaya. They slowed with several men falling when the Mexicans opened fire down upon them. The regiments regained momentum and swept on and after a short, stiff exchange of musket fire, chased the Mexicans from the top and down into the valley beyond.

Lee called out to Steptoe and the other two lieutenants commanding the groups of men on the guns, "Let's move them."

At shouted orders from their officers, the men leaned into the drag ropes fastened to the guns and thrashed off through the brush and rocks with them.

At the base of the hill, the guns were removed from the wheeled carriages, and the men began to haul the pieces up the face of the hill where there was no path, no landmarks. When darkness fell, a fire was built at the bottom of the hill and another near the top to mark the route. In the small hours of the night, and after heart bursting labor with scores of men lying exhausted on the hillside, and many sleeping where they had fallen, the guns were in place atop La Atalaya, ammunition brought up, and a parapet built. Everything was ready for the morning when the guns would help Harney capture El Telegrafo by firing upon the men defending it.

Lee staggering with weariness went down the hill and joined Twiggs in the valley where the division had settled to wait for the morning call to action. So far all had gone flawlessly with the troops in an advantageous position for the attack on El Telegrafo.

* * *

In the early dawn, after three hours of iron solid sleep wrapped in his blanket on the ground, Lee joined Riley and his brigade to lead them in the movement to turn Santa-Anna's left flank. With an enemy trumpet blaring reveille on El Telegrafo, and the Mexican red, white and green flag fluttering on a tall pole, they moved out around the north side of the tall hill. Lee recalled it was Sunday, April 18, and a lovely day with the sky a bright blue and a gentle breeze making it all the way from the far off sea.

They had gone less than a mile when the cannons Lee had helped place on La Atalaya opened fire and he knew Harney and his men were advancing on El Telegrafo. He turned away from that fighting and riding beside Riley at the head of the brigade hurried west to cut off retreating Mexicans. Shortly the Americans came upon the National Highway leading to the nearby village of Cerro Gordo and veered onto it and hastened on. They had gone a half-mile when they saw not far ahead a five-gun Mexican artillery battery banging away at Shields brigade marching in from the north.

"We've got to stop those guns," Riley said. "But first I must form up my men." He rode off shouting at his officers to gather their men who had become much scattered by the swift advance.

Lee continued on along the Highway toward a Mexican field hospital of five large tents with many wounded Mexicans lying about on the ground. The sides of the tents were rolled up and tied in pace to allow in light and air and Lee could see the surgeons all frightfully splattered with blood as they cut, sawed, and sewed upon their wounded countrymen.

A platoon of Americans soldiers with muskets and bayonets was bearing down on the hospital. Lee saw their hostile intent and fearing for the safety of the Mexican surgeons, spurred his horse and ran it into the path of the American warriors and sprang down.

"Lieutenant, halt your men," Lee called to the officer at the head of the platoon.

The lieutenant came to a stop with his men bunching up behind him.

"What is it, captain?" asked the lieutenant in a hurried voice.

"That hospital and the surgeons must be protected for our wounded will need their services. Place half your men to guard them. Get the other half started gathering up the wounded and bring them here. I'll talk with the chief surgeon and make sure he'll tend to our wounded as well as his own."

"Captain, we've orders to chase the Mexicans as far as we can. So that's what we're going to do."

Lee put a hand on his pistol. "Lieutenant, I just gave you a battlefield order. That's my right based on the condition as I see them. Are you refusing to obey them?"

The lieutenant saw Lee's hand on the pistol and knew by the steel in his eyes that he would use the weapon. He squared his shoulders. "No, sir. Your order is proper."

"Then get your men to their tasks. I'll explain what I've done if you're ever questioned about your actions."

The lieutenant wheeled around to face his sergeant. "You heard the captain. Divide the men with half guarding the hospital and half bringing in our wounded."

Lee held his position for a minute as the grumbling men split into two squads and were sent off on their duties. Then walking and leading his horse, he went to the hospital.

"Anybody here speak English?" he called to the surgeons laboring over bodies lying on several long wooden tables.

"I do," one of the bloody surgeons answered. "I'm Major Aguilar.

"Those men will keep you safe. In turn I expect you to care for wounded Americans as they are brought to you."

"I saw what you did. There is no need for you to tell me what to do for we are doctors. Your men will receive the same care as my poor wounded comrades."

"I meant no insult," Lee said.

Aguilar gave Lee a short look from angry eyes and lowered them back to the bleeding man on the table in front of him.

Lee mounted and rode in the direction of the Mexican battery still hammering away with rapid shots at Shields's brigade. Near a little house close to the side of the Highway, he came upon a Mexican drummer boy lying penned beneath a wounded and unconscious Mexican soldier. The boy had a shattered leg, the bone protruding stark and white against the red of mangled flesh. A little bare foot girl of five or so, wearing a tattered scrap of a dress, and with black hair in a long plait hanging down her back to the waist, was kneeling beside the boy and crying with tears streaming from her black eyes.

Lee shouted at two Americans and they came and lifted the soldier off the drummer boy and carried them both to the hospital. Lee lifted the ragamuffin girl up in his arms and looked into her face.

"The boy will be all right now," he whispered to her in English and again wished he knew the language of the land.

The girl cried louder and her lips trembled for she was frightened by the big American who held her so tightly. She pushed against Lee's chest with her small hands and wriggled and kicked to be released. Lee sat her on her feet and she darted off and into the house and out of sight.

Lee, seeing Riley now had his men formed up and was ready to move upon the Mexican battery, swung astride his mount and spurred it to take position with the colonel in the front of the men.

Riley led his men closer to the Mexican battery. Then he gave a mighty shout and led the men in a charge upon the guns. Lee riding beside Riley, joined his pistol fire with the musket fire of the lead element of the brigade and the squad of Mexicans defending the battery were knocked off their feet by a fusillade of bullets. He holstered his empty guns, and slashing with his saber, ran his horse in among the defending infantrymen and the artillerymen.

The contest was over after a short, savage fight with bayonets and sabers, and the Mexicans still on their feet threw down their weapons.

The brigade pushed past the captured gun and hurried west, and surmounting a rise saw before them at least three thousand Mexican soldiers and hundreds of tents and wagons on the outskirts of Cerro Gordo. They had come upon the main camp of Santa-Anna's army.

At that moment, Shields and his men broke from the thorny chaparral to the north and charged down upon the camp. Not wanting to be left out of the fighting, Riley shouted a fierce battle cry and led his men forward at a run.

The infantrymen and the artillery battery protecting the camp, loosed a blast at the converging columns of Americans. The Mexican cannons tore viciously at the American front. Shields in the lead of his brigade took a musket ball full in the chest and tumbled to the ground. His men with bayonets fixed, swept past their fallen leader and upon the enemy.

Caught between two full brigades of Americans, the Mexicans ceased firing and stood milling about. The Mexicans on the west broke, streaming off toward Jalapa. The Americans swept around to the west and cut off the bulk of the Mexicans from escape and encircled them. Within minutes the surrounded Mexicans were disarmed and herded together and under guard.

Riley came up to Lee. "Captain, you know where all the fighting was done. Take Lieutenant Colson and his company of men," he pointed out the officer, "and half a hundred of those Mexican wagons and find my wounded, every one of them, and get them to the hospital at base camp for they'll get the best care there. The dead can wait until tomorrow."

"Yes, sir." Lee said and hastened off to give the lieutenant his new orders.

Chapter Twenty-One

The distant crackle of musket fire and boom of cannon and the sight of the tiny figures of distant men in bloody combat held Grant locked to his field glasses. The American attack on El Telegrafo was in progress and he had seen the first charge beaten back by the Mexicans. Now the Americans had regrouped and with a fusillade of bullets and a rush with bayonets swept the enemy from the summit of the hill.

This was the day of the three-pronged assault on the Mexican front of entrenched positions. Grant had considered asking permission from Garland to go forward and join in the fighting, but had dropped the idea knowing he would be denied. He had saddled his horse and ridden to a high point from where he could observe the fighting through his glasses.

Worth had arrived the day before with his infantry, Dragoons, and field artillery, and missing nearly one hundred men who had fallen ill along the Highway from Veracruz. The division had set up camp east of Twigs and Patterson on the Plan Del Rio. The camp followers selected a place to erect their tents as close to Worth's men as they dared. Scott had already made his plans for the battle and Worth discovered he would be held in reserve, to follow behind Patterson and assist him when he struck the Mexican center.

The musket and cannon fire grew in volume as the fighting heated up, and Grant's need to join in the battle increased. He could never be one of the easy-living soldiers of the rear echelon, could not allow the fighting to end without being part of it. He hurried down from the hill and raced his willing horse toward the fighting where bravery was being displayed in heroic deeds and reputations made.

With the mare running hard, Grant soon came up to the battle line, and there found a three gun American battery of 24-pounders setting astride the road. The boyish McClellan was directing the fire of the guns at Mexicans behind stout log breastworks. The American guns were shooting over the heads of a company of Americans advancing for an attack upon the entrenched Mexican position.

Grant dragged the mare to a sliding stop beside an American lieutenant lying dead on the ground near the battery. That would be the artillery officer, he judged.

"You want some help?" he shouted at McClellan.

"Damn right," McClellan shouted back. "Help them aim that gun on the end. They're so afraid of hitting our own men that they keep shooting high."

Grant swiftly dismounted, tied the reins of his horse to a bush, and hastened to the gun. "Shoot and let me see where it lands," he ordered the gunnery sergeant. He raised his glasses to watch the cannon ball land.

The sergeant sighted along the thick iron barrel of his gun, made an adjustment and fired. Grant saw the ball strike several yards behind the enemy position.

"Not too bad," Grant said. "Lower your angle five degrees and swing right three."

Grant continued to call corrections and saw exploding shells fall upon the enemy breastworks, tumbling logs, knocking men down, sending bodies flying into the air. After several rounds from the three guns, the Mexican soldiers scrambled from their battered breastworks and scampered away. The company of Americans broke into a run and whooping loudly surged over the positions and onward in pursuit.

"Look at them skedaddle," shouted the artillery sergeant and laughed and danced a short, happy jig.

"Let's catch them," Grant called out to McClellan. The cannons were no longer of use. Now it would be a chase to round up the enemy before they scattered and escaped. Grant went to his mount and sent it off at a swift gallop.

McClellan swung astride his mount and spurred it up beside Grant. With pistols drawn, they sped along the road. The Mexicans, throwing frightened looks over their shoulders as they ran, saw the two horsemen closing upon them. By singles, then by twos, and then in ever-larger groups, they veered off the road and plunged into the chaparral thickets cloaking the land and vanished. Grant and McClellan, knowing their horses could not navigate the thorny thickets, sped on along the road.

The road soon joined with the National Highway and they saw before them thousands of Mexican prisoners under guard by Americans on the edge of a village of a few houses. They had reached Cerro Gordo. They circled around the men and struck the Highway beyond the town.

"Look at those bastards," McClellan calls out to Grant and pointed at American stragglers, at least a squad, some sitting in the shade of trees and others searching through the knapsacks and pockets of Mexican soldiers lying dead by the Highway.

"Let's get them to the fighting," Grant called back.

"Damn right," McClellan said.

Shouting at the lazing soldiers, the two officers drew their sabers and spurred their horses in among them. The soldiers sprang erect, dodging the iron-shod hooves of the officers' horses. Grant and McClelland swatted the slowest men to rise with the flat sides of their sabers.

"You Goddamn cowards, grab you muskets and form up!" McClellan roared at the men.

The men, some with angry expressions and others with sheepish ones, hastily fell into rank.

"Double time," Grant barked. "You're going to help in the fighting whether you like it or not."

The men marched to the west where hundreds of muskets were popping. The Highway was littered with weapons, cartridge boxes, knapsacks, and articles of clothing dropped by the retreating Mexicans. Among the litter lay some of the enemy, wounded and bleeding. Some lay dead.

Grant and McClellan overtook and passed groups of infantry from Patterson's and Twiggs's commands moving along the highway toward Jalapa. Most of the men, weary after the long chase on foot, were resting in the shade of trees. The Mexicans, having dropped everything that encumbered their flight, had out-run the Americans laden with their arms and knapsacks.

Grant and McClellan noting the exhaustion of the squad of men with them relented and allowed them to fall out to rest. Pushing their horses on, they came within sight of Jalapa lying some two miles ahead. They halted near a company of Dragoons and another of infantry and heard the Dragoon officer telling that he had been to the outskirts of the town and had found it undefended. He suggested the Dragoons and infantry return to the main camp. The captain of infantry nodded agreement and called out for his men to form up. Dragoons and infantry began the fourteen mile trek to base camp.

Grant rode dejected. He had fought no battles, taken no prisoners, won no glory.

* * *

Lee shouted out through the darkness for the medics and stretcher-bearers working with the frail lights of lanterns, to end their search for wounded soldiers. The men called back acknowledgements, and with their lights weaving about to find a path through the trees and brush thickets, came homing in on Lee. The army medics had come up to the site of the fighting as Lee and the infantrymen had started the search for the wounded. The medics had joined in and provided the best treatment they could in the field for men with horrible bullet and shrapnel wounds, and broken limbs and backs from falls in the rugged ground.

Lee had worked the men through the day, and refusing to quit when night came down on them, sent a wagon to the main camp to fetch lanterns. They searched on, shouting out into the blackness and listening for a wounded man to call back. They had looked in all the likely places and it was now time to end the effort. Those men still lying hurting and bleeding must wait until morning for help, or die during the long night. A soldier's life held much peril.

"Mount up and let's go to camp," Lee directed.

The men made their way out to the trail Lee had built for the attack upon the Mexicans, and scrambled up into the wagons to find space among the wounded. The vehicles rolled off with a rumble of iron wheels on the stony ground.

Chapter Twenty-Two

With a huge smile upon his face, General Scott examined the prize his men had brought him, Santa-Anna's personal carriage. He had walked around the four-wheeled vehicle twice and admired its elaborate red and gold paint, iron leaf springs for ease of ride, overstuffed leather seats for softness for the one-legged Mexican general's rump, and a rainproof top with leather side curtains. A troop of Dragoons had found the coach, together with two beautiful horses perfectly matched as to size and charcoal black color, abandoned at Santa-Anna's Encero hacienda north of Cerro Gordo.

Lee, with a group of other officers, was observing Scott in his moment of pleasure. He knew the general would also be feeling a deep disappointment. At the time the troop of Dragoons had found the carriage, and also Santa-Anna's baggage wagon, they had seen a group of Mexican officers riding mules at a swift pace toward the Rio Del Plan. They had given pursuit but the Mexicans had descended into the steep walled canyon of the river where the Dragoon horses could not go. They had learned later that the riders were Santa-Anna and his staff officers. Had they captured the general, the war in all likelihood would have been over.

Still Scott had a rich trophy in the baggage wagon for it contained Santa-Anna's correspondence, many maps, and his money chest holding 20,000 dollars in silver and gold coin, and personal clothing all of which showed the rapidity with which the Mexican commander had fled.

This was late afternoon of the day following the routing of Santa-Anna's army. The battlefields had been scoured for the living and the dead and the three division generals had made their reports to Scott. The Americans had 368 men wounded and 63 killed. Seventy-four were missing, either captured or had deserted.

Nearly 3,800 Mexican troopers had been captured. A thousand had escaped from their guards, which didn't bother Scott for he released the remaining 2,800 on their parole not to fight again. One hundred and ninety nine Mexican officers had been captured, and like at Veracruz, Scott had released the senior ones with their side arms and horses with the thought that they would report his generosity to other officers and weaken their resolve to fight. Forty-three pieces of artillery and 5,000 muskets with considerable ammunition had been taken. Scott had everything destroyed, except for half a dozen of the better cannons.

The general said something that Lee couldn't hear, but set the officers closest to him into a burst of laughter, as if they had already forgotten that the bloody corpses of the 63 dead Americans were sewn into their blankets and stacked like cordwood in two tents but a short distance away. Five of the dead were their fellow officers. The corpses would travel with the army until lumber could be found for the carpenters to make coffins, and then they would be buried in shallow graves here in this foreign land. Once the war ended, the bodies would be retrieved and shipped to the man's home for proper burial.

Lee saw two of his lieutenants, Tower and Beauregard, whom he had assigned to guide Pillow, conversing in low voices and went to talk to them. They saluted when he drew near.

"I've heard some interesting comments about General Pillow's actions on Santa-Anna's right," Lee said. "What do you two know about what happened?"

"Captain, General Pillow really botched it," Beauregard said with disgust. "He wouldn't listen to advice from Tower or me, nor from his second in command Colonel Campbell, so we took the wrong route that led us close to the enemy positions. Then he yelled commands at Colonel Wyncoop so loudly that Mexicans heard him and opened fire. The Tennessee volunteers were caught in cannon and musket fire at almost point-blank range. I saw a cannon ball hit a rifleman and kill him and wound six other poor fellows close by."

"Captain, excuse me for saying this about a superior officer, but the man is no general," Tower said in a contemptuous voice. "He has no judgment. Worse yet he failed to carry out what General Scott wanted because he ordered the assault without getting the columns in proper order. Then to top everything off, he got a slight wound on the arm and left the field with the regiments disorganized. Once he was gone we did the best we could under Colonel Campbell."

"Has General Scott talked with either of you?" Lee asked.

"No, sir," Tower said. "But I know that he called Colonel Campbell and Wyncoop into his tent and I'm betting they told him what happened."

"I certainly hope so," Beauregard said. "Captain, would you be sure to see that General Scott finds out the truth of General Pillow's actions?"

"I'll do what I can."

Just then Scott called out. "Captain Lee, please come into my tent. Bring your two lieutenants with you?"

"Now we'll get our chance," Beauregard said with a pleased tone.

* * *

In the night, Lee wrote his wife and sons of the events since last he corresponded with them nearly a week before. He told about the battle for Cerro Gordo and a little of his role. He made a special statement to his sons, "You have no idea what a horrible sight a field of battle is, and I will not describe it for you because of your tender age. Just be certain that it isn't something you should ever have to be part of."

He turned to a second letter, and began with, "My beautiful Tasy, we have just captured Cerro Gordo, a town in the mountains far inland from the coast." He paused with his pen held over the paper. Tasy's eyes though truly innocent, were the most feminine he had ever seen. As he recalled their liquid depths, the gloom that had fallen on him lifted and a pleasant mood replaced it. All men should have young, pretty women as friends. He smiled and resumed writing.

* * *

The divisions of Patterson and Twiggs broke camp in the newness of the beautiful April day, and with Scott and his generals and Lee and the other staff officers in the lead, lined out on the road for Jalapa. The infantry, proud of the victory they had won, swung along with a light step.

At the entrance to Jalapa, the town officials wearing bright sashes of authority, over equally brilliant trousers and jackets, waited for the Americans to arrive. Scott had earlier sent an armed group to arrange for the surrender ceremony. Patterson having been given the honor of governing Jalapa, now rode forward with an interpreter. He graciously listened to the short speech by the mayor, and then in turn promised the safety of the townsfolk and their possessions as long as no hostile act was made against the Americans.

The Americans entered Jalapa. Scott led followed by his kite-tail of staff officers and an escort of Dragoons. Then came the troops in dress ranks with bayonets fixed, colors flying and regimental bands playing. The streets were thronged with the citizens of the town. A score of church bells rang out a welcome, the welcome totally unexpected.

Lee was surprised by the number of young women with fair complexion, some with hazel eyes and others with blue. Most lovely he thought. Several of the girls laughed and waved at the Americans with their bewhiskered faces and battle worn uniforms. How strange considering this army of men had slain hundreds of their countrymen but two days before. Young women were difficult to understand.

Scott rode to the central plaza of the town and halted in front of Governor's Palace, a grand structure with an impressive array of steps leading up to the entrance. He dismounted from his big gray horse and went up the wide stairway with a chink of spur chains and tinkle of spurs at each step. At the top, he removed his gold braded cockaded hat and waved it in a broad sweep to include the assemblage of townsfolk and soldiers alike, placed it back on his head and strode inside the building.

Scott was an excellent representative for the stalwart American Army, Lee thought. The general had led it to victory and now his men were safe from the sweltering coastal plain and the deadly yellow fever.

Lee left the gathering. As he passed near Patterson who was talking with the mayor and pointing at several large homes near the Palace, he heard the general say he was commandeering the buildings for use as a hospital for the American wounded. The occupation of Jalapa was complete.

* * *

Lee rode alone, pushing his mount for he wanted to overtake Worth's division before nightfall. This should not be difficult for an army on the march was a slow moving creature. He also rode fast because there was safety in speed when traveling without an escort through enemy country. Scott had ordered him to join with Worth in an advance to Perote. Lee, if he judged it safe to proceed further, was to continue on to Puebla another sixty miles and evaluate its suitability as to a station for assembling and storing supplies in the 260 miles between Veracruz and Mexico City. After the reconnaissance he was to return to Jalapa and prepare a plan to occupy and garrison Puebla.

He came upon many women moving slowly with children and bent under heavy burdens of food, cooking utensils, and blankets. A woman with an infant wrapped in her rebozo, and another heavy with child and walking awkwardly didn't bother to look up from the ground as he passed with a pound of hooves. They had followed their men to war and now were retreating, though not as speedily as the men.

* * *

With the Dragoons out front as skirmishers and scouting for Mexican forces, Worth marched his brigade up the National Highway climbing ever higher into the Sierra Madre Mountains. The road curved and twisted in tight bends as it made its route across the steep flank of Cofre De Perote, "Perote's Chest", the broad, round topped mountain rearing 13,000 feet on the left hand.

Grant and several other junior officers rode horseback behind Worth and his brigade commanders, Garland and Clarke. All the officers warily watched the mountainsides above them and now and again caught sight of bands of Mexican soldiers stealing through the woods off at a distance from the road. They were the defeated ones for most had no weapons and were moving in the same direction as the Americans, toward Mexico City.

Lee rode up on a lathered horse and reported his arrival to Worth. The two men talked briefly and then Lee fell back to ride with Grant and the others.

* * *

In the edge of night and half way to Perote's Castle, the army made camp on a restricted section of level ground in a mountain pass at 8000 feet. Dense clouds blanketed the high mountain and the men quickly built fires. With the smell of burning pine wood, they ate rations of hard bread and cooked beef from their knapsacks, and struck up conversations.

The swirling mist made the fires burn poorly and the wintry chill of the mountain soon brought an end to the talking. The men rolled into their blankets and went to sleep with the mist collecting as cool dew on their beards and eyebrows and the wool of their blankets.

Chapter Twenty-Three

"Now that's strange, a Mexican coming to meet us," Grant said. The lone horseman came into sight galloping toward the caravan from off on the right. He rode a fine long legged sorrel and towed behind him three equally fine animals tied nose to tail by short lengths of rope. The rider reached the National Highway and halted in the center and sat horseback facing the Americans.

"That fellow doesn't seem afraid of us," Lee observed.

"He's got horses to sell us," Grant said and designing the man's purpose.

"Our cavalry could sure use them."

"Hackett, back me up with the lingo," Grant called over his shoulder to the man.

"Yes, sir." Hackett said and rode up to stand beside his lieutenant.

Worth's division had come down from the mountains and occupied Perote Castle. With the Americans on short rations, the general had ordered Garland's brigade with Duncan's artillery battery to advance another fifteen miles to the village of Tepeyahuatl and there to gather subsistence for men and horses. Reaching the town, Garland immediately instructed Grant to go foraging. Grant assembled a caravan of wagons and with 300 infantrymen under Hazlitt and 200 Dragoons under Chilton as escort had marched off on the National Highway in the direction of the famous city of Puebla lying sixty miles distant. Lee carrying out Scott's order to scout Puebla as a staging area for supplies was accompanying Grant as far as he went toward Puebla.

"I'd bet he'd be a tough hombre in a fight," Grant said to Lee as he evaluated the Mexican. The man had a burly body, a big head, black curly hair protruding from under a broad brimmed hat, and a full beard. Two pistols were stuck under his belt and a carbine was in a scabbard under his right leg. Expensive clothing showed through a thin covering of dust. Grant noted the man's intelligent black eyes set deeply under a high, weathered brow. He guessed his age at somewhere between forty-five and fifty.

Grant raised his hand and stopped the convoy a few yards from the man. He remained silent, let the Mexican start the conversation.

"I am Manuel Dominguez and I'm very glad to have found you," the man said in Spanish.

Grant nodded and spoke in Spanish, "Why did you want to find us?"

"To sell you these excellent horses." He centered on Grant's mount. "Though you have an excellent mount already."

"How much for each?"

"Twenty pesos in silver."

"Twelve," Grant said. Mexicans horses were beautiful, but in general, as with this man's, they were more lightly built than American steeds.

"I accept twelve," Dominguez said without bargaining.

Grant was surprised at the quick agreement for usually the dickering went on for at least three rounds before a price was agreed upon. "Captain, I think this fellow has come for something other than to sell horses."

"Like what?" Lee asked.

Grant spoke to Dominguez, "What else do you have to sell?"

Dominguez's face turned fierce and his eyes blazed. "I wish to sell you my hate for General Santa-Anna. It would be my honor to help you defeat and hopefully kill him for he is a thief and murderer."

Grant turned in surprise to Hackett. "Did I understand that correctly? Does he want to be our man against Santa-Anna?"

"That's the size of it, lieutenant. He wants to work for us"

"Captain Lee, you should be the one talking with him," Grant said.

"Seems so," Lee said. He spoke to Hackett. "Ask him why he'd help us."

Dominguez grasped the meaning of the English words, and spoke heatedly. "I hate the military for soldiers are protected from the law. Because they have no fear of punishment, they rob the people, kill them. Santa-Anna is the worst of them. He robbed me and burned my hacienda. Now some call me a bandit because I fight the soldiers. But still I have many friends among the people. To have my revenge upon Santa-Anna, I will help you defeat him in battle. I hope to have the chance to kill him."

Dominguez stopped talking and with a struggle composed himself.

"How could you help us?" Lee asked. He had heard of the Mexican law "Fuero" which gave the army and the Catholic Church immunity from the authority of the civil law and its courts. He didn't think a country could be fair and just to all its people if part were exempt from the law. That condition must be one of the reasons responsible for the weakness of the nation.

"I would spy upon his army and bring you information. Or I would be your guide, or carry messages where your riders can't go. And I wouldn't be alone for I have forty men who have also been wronged by the military and have sworn allegiance to me. I could recruit another hundred and fifty to join me if you wanted them."

Lee knew the army needed Mexicans to spy for it, but was the man telling the truth? He spoke to Dominguez. "We need men like you say your are. So come with us now and be our guide and help fill our wagons with food. Then when I return to report to my general, I'll take you to see him."

"Many thanks, captain," Dominguez said and touched his forehead in salute. "To show you I speak the truth, there is a company of guerrillas waiting in those hills to attack you." He jabbed a finger at a range of wooded hills an hour ride ahead. "And I know men with stores of food who will gladly sell to you."

"I think you may now have the beginnings of a spy ring," Grant said to Lee. "Still this could all be a trick."

"We need such men and should take a chance on Dominguez for a time," Lee said.

He turned to Hackett. "Listen closely to what he says when we meet other Mexicans. If he says something wrong, or gives a signal that means trouble for us, shoot him."

"Glad to, sir."

"I'll form up the men to be ready for the attack," Grant said.

He shortened the convoy by rolling the wagons two abreast along the road, the infantrymen marching four abreast, and the Dragoons also by fours. They brushed aside the guerrilla attack with but a few men wounded. During the next day and a half with Dominguez guiding, they filled the two hundred and fifty wagons.

With the vehicles sagging under heavy loads of foodstuffs, flour for bread, meat of several kinds, fresh vegetables and fruits, and grain for the brigade horses, Grant lead his convoy back toward Tepeyahuatl and from there on back to Perote Castle. As he listened to the din of cracking whips, squeal of axles, and the curses of the teamsters, he felt pleased that his job had been well done and his comrades' stomachs would soon be full.

Lee and Dominguez had left the convoy when it turned south. They were miles away and galloping their mounts up the National Highway toward Puebla.

* * *

Lee and Dominguez riding jaded horses arrived back in Jalapa in the early night of the fifth day after receiving Scott's orders to scout Puebla. The darkness filling the streets was broken here and there by the light that escaped from the open windows and doors of the houses and cantinas. American soldiers from the army encampment just outside town roamed about talking and laughing. Music of pianos and guitars and the rumble of men voices and the friendly laughter of women floated out to Lee from the cantinas and he thought it a fine sound. He guided Dominguez on with the darkness a welcome mask for it would prevent Santa-Anna's spies among the townsfolk from seeing the armed Mexican with Lee and possibly ruin his use as a spy.

They had reached Puebla, a city of 80,000 citizens and the second largest in Mexico within one day after leaving Grant and the convoy. Dominguez had obtained Mexican clothing for Lee, and with him wearing these as a disguise, they had ridden through the city and observed its garrison and defenses and evaluated it for use as an army depot. They rode hard all day and into the night to return to Jalapa.

Lee and Dominguez dismounted in front of Scott's headquarters. The sergeant of the guard came up quickly and saluted Lee. "Good evening, Captain Lee."

"Evening, sergeant. Is the general in?"

"Yes, sir, and I've got standing orders to send you straight to him when you got here. Do you plan to take the Mexican in with you?"

"Yes."

"Then I got to have his guns."

Lee motioned for Dominguez to hand over his pistols. Dominguez hesitated, fingering the butts of the pistols. With obvious reluctance he slid them from his belt and handed them to the sergeant.

139

When Lee and Dominguez entered Scott's office, the general was talking with Patterson and Hitchcock at a table littered with maps and papers. Scott rose at once and came forward and pumped Lee's hand heartily. "Glad to see you're back safe, captain."

"Thank you, general."

"Who's this fellow with you?"

Dominguez understood the meaning of the question even thought it was spoken in English. He put out his hand. "I am Manuel Dominguez."

Scott hesitated but a second before taking the offered hand. "I am General Scott," he said. He stepped back from Dominguez and cast a questioning eye at Lee.

"He says he's an enemy of Santa-Anna and wants to help us defeat him."

Scott gave Dominguez an intense stare. The Mexican, looking up at the much taller Scott, returned it without a blink. They stood for seconds with their eyes probing and measuring each other.

Lee was struck by the strangeness of this unexpected convergence between radically different men sharing a critical point in time, the brown skinned Dominguez wanting to betray his country and the white skinned Scott determined to conquer it.

"I've heard Santa-Anna has many enemies," Scott said and broke eye contact with Dominguez.

He turned to Lee. "Captain, what do you know about Senor Dominguez?"

"He's been with me for the past three days," Lee said and proceeded to relate all that had occurred since Dominguez had approached the wagon train.

"What's your recommendation? Should we give him a try as a spy?"

"Judging from his action so far, I say yes."

"Colonel Hitchcock, this would fall in your bailiwick," Scott said. "Take the man and question him. Use my interpreter. Devise a method to test his loyalty to us. If he is what he says he is, then set up a currier service between headquarters and Veracruz. I want every mail packet met and the mail gotten to me as rapidly as man and horse can possible do it. Have spies join Santa-Anna's army. Send others to Puebla and Mexico City to gather information on their garrisons and defenses. And have him recruit all the men you feel we need."

Hitchcock motioned for Dominguez to leave with him. Instead Dominguez went to Lee and saluted him. "Thank you, captain. I shall not betray you."

"Good luck to you," Lee said, understanding only a portion of the man's words, yet knowing what he meant.

Dominguez faced Hitchcock, and with a proud carriage of his body left the room.

"Now, captain, tell me what you've learned about Puebla. Is it suitable for use as a supply depot for us?"

"I'd judge it ideal, general." Lee said.

They discussed what Lee had seen at Puebla. At last Scott shoved back from the table.

"Thank you for the report, and I agree with your recommendation," Scott said. "Now for another subject. Do you think you can find a major's straps?"

"Sir?"

"Major's bars, those small straps that are fastened to you shoulders showing your rank. Do you think you can find some?"

Without waiting for Lee to answer, Scott smiled hugely and continued on, "I'm promoting you to major for your actions at Veracruz and Cerro Gordo. I consider them most brave and contributed greatly to the victory over our foe. Of course the promotion is only temporary until approved by Washington. Which I'm certain it will be."

"Thank you, general. I'm sure I can find a major's bars someplace." Lee tried not to smile and failed completely.

"Then the next time I see you, I shall address you as Major Lee."

Chapter Twenty-Four

Lee looked at the sky to avoid the spectacle on the meadow. But try as he might, he couldn't cut out the sound of the sodden whacks of the leather whips striking the bare backs of the eighteen men tied to posts set in the ground. Well laid on, the blows of the whip tore moans from between clenched teeth. Men from the ranks of Patterson's volunteers had grown restless from idleness and angry from not having been paid for months, and had stolen away from camp and pillaged several homes of Mexican citizens. The officials of Jalapa had filed formal complaints with General Scott. He immediately had the provost martial arrest the men, those that could be identified, and sentenced them to receive a punishment of thirty lashes each. As a lesson to others, Scott had the entire army drawn up on the plain just outside Jalapa to watch the flogging.

The punishment ended and there was an audible release of breath from the assembled soldiers. The floggers cut the whipped men loose. Hospital orderlies came forward and led the bleeding men away to the hospital for treatment of their wounds. Scott released the assembled soldiers and they fell out of ranks silent and thoughtful.

Lee struck out for headquarters. As he crossed the National Highway to enter Jalapa, he saw a troop of Dragoons leading several horses approaching from the north. He recognized Grant and Chilton and went to meet them. Grant was the most experienced of all the quartermasters and Lee had questions for him.

The two lieutenants halted and saluted Lee. "Well, Grant, I see you've had some luck getting mounts for the cavalry."

"Yes, sir, seventy and I believe they're solid animals."

Lee didn't doubt Grant's judgment. It was talked about among the officers that Grant was the best man with horses in the army, and from the way he sat his saddle so easily, so solidly, seeming to be part of his horse, might well be the one of its best riders. He was known at West Point as the cadet who had ridden a big horse that no one else could, and riding the animal had set an all time record for the high jump.

"When are you returning north?" Lee asked.

"Soon as I deliver these horses to Colonel Harney for his troopers."

"Can we talk?" Lee asked.

"Certainly, sir." Grant stepped down from his horse.

"How I can help you, major?" Grant asked. He had observed the new straps on Lee's shoulders.

"Our new spy Dominguez reports Santa-Anna has ordered General Salas, who's reported to be one of his best officers, to organized guerrilla bands to attack our wagon trains. As an incentive, the leaders will receive rank and pay according to how many men they recruit and all plunder will belong to the guerrillas. A good recruiter can earn a colonelcy for five hundred men."

"With that kind of reward, they'll get plenty men. If the Mexicans begin all out guerrilla warfare we would suffer as heavily as Napoleon did in his invasion of Russia."

"You've had a lot of experience moving supplies and fighting guerrillas with General Taylor's army. What's the best way to protect a supply train, some of which as you know will be more than two miles long?"

"I've tried having the escorting Dragoons and infantry divided with part bunched at the front and part at the rear, or spread out along the length of the train. If the escort is spread out, the guerrillas can easily break through and run off with several wagons and their teams, while if the guards are bunched at the ends, they can't reach the spot under attack in time to prevent serious losses. You have to play it to best suit the type of country you're traveling through. One thing for sure, you've got to have riders out a mile or so both sides to spot guerrillas and warn the train so the escort can get ready to defend it. The problem is that we are often traveling on roads squeezed in between mountains or steep, wooded hills and it's impossible to have flankers out."

"We don't have enough men to put heavy guards on every foraging train, and yet we must go out foraging. And there's thousands of tons of supplies at Veracruz that must be brought up."

"There's a way to cut down on the number of attacks, major."

"What's that?"

"Make them stop hitting us."

"How would we do that?" Lee said, surprised.

"General Scott should have the Texas governor send a few companies of Texas Rangers here to escort the trains. We found out up north that those Texas boys are the best at it. After the bloody massacres the Mexicans pulled on them at Alamo and Goliad, the Texans hate them like you can't believe. Our few hundred Dragoons are being wore to a frazzle acting as escort when they should be used for other jobs. Further they never chase the guerrillas far for they're afraid of being ambushed. And that's Colonel Harney's standing orders. But the Texans don't stop chasing the guerrillas until they run them down, whether that's back to their town, or rancho, or wherever. They take no prisoners; just simply shoot the hell out of all they can catch. You'll find that after several hundred Mexicans are killed the fear of the Lord will be put in them and we'll have fewer and fewer attacks."

"Sounds cruel, but I can see that it could work. I'll suggest it to the general. It'll take better than a month for a request to get to the Texas governor and for him to send the Rangers here." Lee knew the Rangers were companies of men organized to travel swiftly with light arms to protect the Texas frontier from Indians, Mexicans, and bandits. The Texas governor had volunteered five hundred Rangers for General Taylor's use when the war with Mexico began.

"I'll feel a lot better when they're riding with me," Grant said. "Is there anything else major?"

"No, that's all."

* * *

General Patterson entered General Scott's office with a hesitant step and a distressed expression upon his face. He halted just inside the doorway.

"Come in, general," Scott said. "It can't be that bad." Scott had been waiting in his office in the governor's palace. With him were Lee and Hitchcock.

"I wish that was true," Patterson replied.

Lee leaned forward as did the other men to hear. The one-year enlistment of Patterson's 3,700 volunteers was due to expire in the first part of June, a month hence. Before Scott ordered the division deeper into Mexico, he wanted to know how many would re-enlist and had instructed Patterson to canvass his men to determine that.

"Tell us straight out," Scott said.

"General, only one man in ten will ship over," Patterson's said in a sad voice. "That leaves enough men to form only one under strength regiment."

Lee felt dismayed. The army had been reduced in one fell swoop from something over 10,000 men to about 6,400. He had heard rumblings of the low morale of the volunteers from their officers but had not expected anything of this magnitude.

Scott broke the silence that had fallen like iron upon the room. "It's their right to go home and I don't reproach them for that natural desire. They have been misled by the War Department and the president as I have been. Reinforcements haven't arrived as promised so we could press the war and that has meant they have been idle far too long. Our strength should be four times what it is.

"The men have served with honor, and now we must protect them on their way home. Though their enlistments don't end for several weeks, prepare them to leave as soon as possible. I want to get them to Veracruz and away on the ships before the peak of the yellow fever season arrives and many of them are struck down."

"General, with the boys gone I'll have no division," Patterson said. "I brought them here and I should see that they get safely home. I request permission to return to the States with them."

Patterson's boys had joined the army for a great adventure, and with the old gentleman leading them, had journeyed to a distant foreign land. There they had "Seen The Elephant", fought battles, made hellish marches, had lived on short rations, saw blood shed and comrades die. Some of the men had survived disease and serious wounds. None had been paid since leaving the States.

"Granted, general, for that is most appropriate," Scott said. "I'll prepare your orders. Don't linger in Veracruz for any reason. Get your men aboard the ships as quickly as possible. Regarding the men who will be re-enlisting, assign them to General Quitman. You will have company on you journey to Washington for General Pillow has informed me that should the volunteers leave that he will also go back to the States to recruit a fresh brigade. I shall give him orders to that effect." Lee saw that Scott wasn't displeased with this opportunity to be shut of Pillow.

Scott came and caught Patterson by the arm. "General, you have given your country and me brave and honorable service. I shall inform the Secretary of War and the President of this in my official report."

"Thank you for those generous words," Patterson said.

Lee was sure he caught sight of tears in Patterson's eyes as the man pivoted about and hurried from the room.

Scott went to the door and watched after Patterson. He wheeled back toward Lee and Hitchcock and swept them with his keen eyes.

"Get those expressions of loss off your faces and those thoughts of despair and defeat out of your hearts," he commanded. "We are a small army, yes indeed, but a valiant one. I promise you that we shall yet succeed in conquering Mexico."

Scott began to pace the room, which Lee had never seen him do, and the tread of his large body shook the floor. His hands were clenched into fists and held behind his back. He stopped and stared at the floor for a moment, and then resumed his pacing. Lee wished he had been released to leave for it was uncomfortable to see the general in such a state.

Scott halted and his voice rang out with conviction. "We shall throw away the scabbard and march inland with the naked blade held ready to strike any one that stands in our path." He paused, smiled grimly, and declared, "I resolve to no longer depend on Veracruz, or the States. I'll render my little army a self-sustaining machine. We are dangerously few in number and have hard campaigning ahead. Reinforcements will be slow in coming. We'll take the necessary weapons from the Mexican Army and our food from the people. I'll write Secretary Marcy and President Polk of my decision. They'll think me mad, but so be it. This is all I have left for I won't retreat."

Scott stepped to the doorway and shouted. "Orderly, go find General Quitman and bring him here on the double."

He faced back to the room. "I shall send him to join General Worth with orders for both to move upon Puebla and occupy the city."

Lee considered the general's plan an extremely risky one. Still one advantage would be gained from the action. By Scott driving his army deeper into hostile Mexico, Marcy and Polk would be under extreme pressure to insure he received the men and supplies needed to prevent his annihilation by the Mexican Army. One thing for certain, should Scott fail in his daring gamble, he and all of his men were doomed.

Chapter Twenty-Five

The four Catholic priests seated at the table were angry men, their faces hard and bodies tense. Three of them were from Jalapa and the fourth, Jesus Campomanes, was a priest emissary from the bishop of Puebla a city of eighty thousand and the second largest in Mexico. The Jalapa men were dressed in clergy garments; the priest from Puebla wore trouser, shirt, jacket and boots. He had arrived at Jalapa on horseback just hours before.

General Scott and Hitchcock and Lee sat across the table from the priests in a large room in the rectory of the Catholic Church on the plaza in Jalapa. Scott had received a request to meet with the priests in the church, with the reason given that the priests should not be seen coming to the American's headquarters. Scott had summoned Lee and Hitchcock, and taking an armed escort because he was always in danger of assassination, had gone to meet with the priests. He had held discussions with the Jalapa church officials before. Campomanes was unknown. He had done all the talking without reference to the others, which showed Scott the man's stature within the Catholic Church.

"The military caste and Santa-Anna in particular must be taught they can't abuse the people and rob the church," Campomanes said passionately, his English excellent. He was thin, almost emaciated, with a long face and black chin beard. His hands lay locked together on the table.

Lee noted the priest had made the statement twice before during the quarter hour meeting. He had never gone any farther to explain the reason he had asked for this meeting with Scott. From the priest's expressions and words Santa-Anna had a powerful enemy in this man and the Church.

"That would meet with our objectives too," Scott replied. "What do you propose?"

Campomanes wasn't to be hurried. "The people of Puebla, and also those of Jalapa, are gentle folk. They don't want to fight a battle with you Americans over their city. And we of the church certainly don't want a battle."

"We wouldn't want to harm your citizens or destroy your city with our big cannon as we were forced to do at Veracruz," Scott said, and knowing the Veracruz battle was the reason for the priest being here. "However I tell you plainly that I intend to defeat your army and occupy Puebla and capture Mexico City."

"It isn't our army!" Campomanes declared, his voice rising. "We disown it because of its brutal ways!"

Lee knew why the priests were so vehement about the army. The spy Dominguez had reported that Santa-Anna had within the past two weeks demanded a loan of two hundred thousand dollars from the church officials in Puebla, under threat that if it wasn't willing given he would take it. The officials fully knew the loan would never be repaid, and further that the general would pocket most of it. The two hundred thousand was in addition to the more than three million taken from the church during the preceding ten months of the war.

Scott spoke. "I promise you this, we Americans desire to have peace and friendship with the citizens of Puebla and the Catholic Church. Further we shall respect private and church property rights and prevent Santa-Anna from taxing you. This is on the condition you convince the people not to resist my army in the occupation of the city."

Lee spotted a look of satisfaction in Campomane's eyes at Scott's words. They had contained precisely what the priest wanted to hear. He wouldn't broach it first. His hands came unlocked. The subject could now be freely discussed. "We of the Church will do our utmost to persuade the people to force the army from Puebla. That won't be easy because the city has strong walls and a large garrison of troops and they'll believe it can be defend against you. Still the bishop has instructed me to tell you that we will make our best effort to influence the people to make the soldiers leave."

"Then we have an agreement."

"I trust your word and will work with the city officials to persuade the soldiers that it is to their best interest to march away. However we must have something to show the people. A proclamation from you as Commander and Chief of the American Army stating your intentions should be sufficient. If you do that, I believe we may be able to have a surrender of the city to you without a man, woman, or child being hurt. The bishop has directed me to assist you with the wording of the proclamation if you are agreeable."

"I would be glad for your assistance."

Lee knew Scott wasn't giving anything away. He would simply be putting in written form what his policy had been all along toward the Mexican people and the Church. He had issued orders in the strongest terms for his troops to treat the people with kindness if they didn't want to starve. Lee did note that Scott hadn't promised not to annex all or part of Mexico to the United States.

* * *

Grant knew action was imminent when General Quitman showed up at Perote Castle with a half company of Dragoons out front as scouts, and four regiments of infantry, and a wagon train behind him. Quitman went at once into consultation with General Worth and his two brigade commanders, Garland and Clarke. This was the sixty-fifth day after the Americans had landed upon the coast of Mexico.

Officers from Quitman's command and Worth's quickly gathered, and the word spread through the group that Scott had ordered an immediate march and occupation of Puebla. The most surprising news was that, just possibly, Puebla would be handed to them without a fight for the reason that Scott and the officials of the Catholic Church had made a pact, though nobody had yet seen a written copy of it.

Garland and Clarke came out of the conference, called their officers before them and gave instructions to prepare to march. Grant hastened to round up his quartermaster and teamsters. It was a stimulating feeling to be moving upon the enemy again. The distance to Puebla was about eighty miles and four days could see the army at the gates of the city.

Worth's army, leaving a garrison of five hundred men to hold the Castle, loaded the wagons and set out on the march in the early afternoon. The soldiers carried their weapons, full cartridge boxes, and knapsacks. Grant, with his pistols and saber buckled to his side and his men armed, rolled his wagons in behind those of Clarke's brigade. Quitman would march a half day behind.

The cannoneers rode the gun carriages or the horses pulling them. The safer riding places on the tops of the ammunition boxes of the limbers were reserved for the powder boys, where they held onto the jostling vehicles, and with their young blood racing through their veins, shouted out excitedly to each. The cannons were loaded and the long slow matches burning, all ready to blast exploding canisters or grapeshot into any Mexican force daring to attack the moving column.

Worth drove his men, as was his habit, and the army passed over the plain around Tepeyahuatl, with its vineyards and orchards and cultivated fields of vegetables and grains. A few big haciendas, walled like small fortresses, made colorful splashes on the land. The highway struck a flat, sandy region that slowed everything down. This gave way to forested hills where the danger was real for guerrillas on horseback could be seen stealing among the trees on the hillsides both sides of the highway. Rain fell for two hours in the late afternoon but no stop was made to find shelter.

The army camped the first night at the small village of Oriental. The thirsty soldiers flocked into the village to fill their canteens. In short order they had drained one of the two wells. Women with empty water pails gathered and finding the well dry shouted abuse at the Americans. A pair of exceptionally angry young women hurled the vilest of curses at the Americans. Grant understood the cuss words, and the other soldiers knew their meaning from the tones. Had the abusers been men, the soldiers would have given them a bloody thrashing, but they stalwartly ignored the women and hastily left.

In the morning of the third day of the American's march, the white tip of Popocatepatl rose above the hills. A few miles farther and the "Sleeping Woman," Ixacihuatal rose up beside Popocatepatl. With these two mountains in front and giant Orizaba behind, Grant rode on in awed silence.

Worth halted his army three miles from Puebla in the evening of the fourth day to let his men rest while Quitman and his regiments caught up. As they were about to settle down for the night, a mounted picket dashed in to report Mexican cavalry approaching from the hills not far off. Worth swiftly formed his men up to meet the attack.

Grant hastily joined Garlands brigade. As they waited for the Mexicans, a heavy, cold rain began to fall on them. The wait was short for the Mexicans were soon seen in the distance, two thousand of them in formation on running horses and sweeping down on the Americans. Duncan and his cannoneers ran their wheeled field artillery out front, took aim, and let go with exploding canisters. The rounds fell true and blasted several score Lancers from their saddles, and knocked down an even greater number of horses. With Duncan's third barrage, the charge of the Lancers broke. In confusion they veered off, and ran their horses back toward the hills.

Grant expected Worth to claim a victory and get his men under shelter. Instead the nervous general kept Garland's men in line in the night of drenching rain and ankle deep mud. Worth sat his horse in the rain with the men, still that didn't lessen the foolishness of being out in it. Grant was disgusted with the general.

Believing the Mexicans wouldn't make an assault in the darkness and rain, Grant went to his men and told them to get out of the rain by crawling under the canvas of the wagons. He did the same and lay on top of sacks of horse feed and listened to the pounding drumbeat of the heavy rain but inches from his face. This was one of the rare instances when he saw a benefit from being a quartermaster rather than an officer of the line standing in formation in blackness and soaked to the skin.

* * *

Lee had pushed his horse hard and now felt it weakening beneath him. He rode slumped with weariness and head pulled down into the collar of his rain slicker to shield himself as best he could against the drenching rain.

Lee and an escort of a sergeant and five troopers had departed Jalapa two days before on orders from Scott to carry an advance copy of the Puebla Proclamation to General Worth to assist him in the negotiation for the surrender of the city and its occupation. The priest Campomanes had left the day before with a copy for the bishop at Puebla. Lee must catch up with Worth and Quitman and their force of men and weapons before they reached the city and began an assault.

His group had change horses at the American garrison at Perote Castle and hurried on. Since then they had stopped twice for a two-hour rest for their horses and themselves. Two hours past as night fell, thick clouds came in and a torrential rain began to fall. In the blackness of the rainstorm, he could see nothing, not even the ears of his mount. He made no effort to guide his steed. It had been set on its course along the National Highway and now kept to it with its night seeing animal eyes.

The rain ceased as the land began to take form in a dreary, damp dawn. In the distance he could make out a gathering of hundreds of wagons, and cannon and horses and men. He felt an easing in his chest for he had succeeded in overtaking Worth and Quitman before they attacked the city.

He led his escort in among the wet and muddy soldiers as they began to mill about preparing to fall into ranks for the march. From the depth of the mud and the amount of it on the soldiers it was obvious that rain had fallen hard and yet he saw no tents and wondered what had prevented them from being erected. He saw the flag that marked Worth's headquarters and worked his way through the horses and men to it.

Worth was seated in the open at a small fold-up table and writing. Standing nearby were General Quitman, the three brigade commanders, and two of Worth's aids. A third aid sat a horse close by the general. He held a white flag on a staff, obviously ready to ride and deliver whatever the general was preparing.

Worth looked up, and seeing Lee riding in, motioned for him to approach.

Lee dismounted and came up and saluted. "Good morning, General Worth."

"What's your purpose in being here, Major Lee?" Worth said brusquely.

"I have a package for you from General Scott."

"Then let's have it."

Lee took an oilskin wrapped parcel from his saddlebag and handed it to Worth. "It's a copy of General Scott's proclamation to the Church and the citizens of Puebla. Representatives of the Church met with him and said they wanted to prevent a fight for the city, and that if he'd state his intentions, they'd try and get the soldiers to leave. General Scott wanted you to have it before you began negotiations."

"I've heard about it. I was just writing a demand to the army garrison, or if there was no garrison, to the city fathers to surrender the city to me. The proclamation will be useful. I'm glad the general saw fit to send me a copy." Worth's tone was sour. He ripped open the oilskin covering off the parcel and began to read.

Lee knew the cause of Worth's bad disposition. "He was mad as hell", those were his aids words, about Scott's official report to Secretary Of War Marcy and President Polk of the battle at Cerro Gordo. Worth had denounced it as a lie from beginning to end because it glossed over Pillow's poor performance during the battle. Further Worth claimed he had been wronged by being held in reserve while Twiggs fought the battle. He had sent what he called a correct report of the battle to the Secretary of War Marcy and President Polk.

Lee believed as Worth did, that Pillow should have been severely reprimanded for his poor leadership and cowardly actions when faced with actual bloody battle at Cerro Gordo. Scott in his jubilant mood after his triumph over Santa-Anna, and not wanting to antagonize Pillow and have him complain to Polk, had used the bland statement that Pillow had performed a service on the enemy's right during the battle. Scott's lack of candor about Pillow's actions had come back to haunt him with Worth's action. That could weaken the morale of the other officers and Lee deeply regretted that. Regrettable also was that Scott and Worth who had been staunch friends were now bitter with each other.

"What are your orders, major?" Worth asked and folding the proclamation.

"To return promptly to Jalapa, general."

"Why not stay a day and observe the occupation of the city? That way you can report first hand how it went."

Before Lee could answer Worth, there was a sudden movement among the soldiers as a Dragoon came riding fast and making the men jump out of the way. The rider pulled rein on his mount near Worth and saluted.

"General sir, Lieutenant Wykoff has directed me to report that there's a delegation of nearly half a dozen Mexicans and a priest outside the gates of the city and that they want to talk to you about terms for surrendering the city. They say they've forced the Mexican garrison out."

Worth spoke to Lee. "It seems that the priest have succeeded in getting the army to vacate the city."

"Yes, sir."

"Are you staying until we occupy the city?"

"Yes, sir." Lee replied.

Worth turned to his brigade commanders. "Form up your men and let's march. We have a city ready to surrender to us."

Chapter Twenty-Six

With one of the regimental bands leading and playing "The Star Spangled Banner", General Worth, with his staff officers behind him, led his mud splattered, raggedy army into Puebla and down the wide, tree-lined main street where townsfolk by the thousands thronged the sidewalks, filled the windows, and looked down from the rooftops. Small boys caught up by excitement dashed about. Here and there, young women laughed and pointed at a soldier who possessed blond or red hair. Older men and women showed dismay at the invasion of their city.

Led was surprised at the size of the Pueblan turnout, and even more so when they arrived at the town's great central plaza where thousands of additional people came pouring out of the side streets and jostling each other for standing room. Regardless of their emotion about the occupation of their town, they seemed anxious to see the ferocious warriors from the North who had captured Veracruz and defeated Santa-Anna at Cerro Gordo and now had marched into their city without having to fight for it.

Lee watched as the muddy, dog-tired soldiers stacked their arms and cartridge boxes. Many went immediately to the fountain in the center of the plaza and drank. A few men wandered off to find something to drink or look for girls. Most men lay down wearily on the cobblestone pavement and went to sleep, totally ignoring the thousands of curious, black eyes looking down on them. Lee saw officers going off into the streets radiating off the plaza to find quarters for themselves and their men. He led his own weary, worn and hungry squad of men away along a street to find them food and a place to sleep for the night. In the morning he would strike out on the return journey to Jalapa to report to Scott.

* * *

Grant awoke to the bugler sounding "Call To Arms". He leapt up from his blanket. He collided with Hazlitt in the center of the tiny room they shared. They moved apart and rushed to buckle pistols and sabers around their waists.

"I hope to God that this isn't another false alarm of our Nervous Nellie General," Hazlitt said.

Grant merely grunted. He sprinted out the door of the cubicle, along the hallway to the outside door, and into the courtyard where the soldiers were snatching up their muskets and cartridge boxes from the stacks. In a flood they poured into the plaza. Hurriedly spotting their company commanders, they formed up in ranks. Hazlitt went immediately to his company. Grant's men gathered before him. Early rising civilians, frightened by the Americans soldiers forming up for battle with their weapons, scattered like quail into doorways and off along the streets.

Troops of Dragoons began to arrive and Worth dispatched squads of them off in several directions to find and obtain information from the roving pickets, and to scout for enemies themselves. The army stood waiting for the reports to come in, as Worth galloped from regiment to regiment checking the men's readiness for battle.

"Lieutenant Grant, what's going on?" O'Doyle asked.

"General Worth must know something."

"I hope so, sir. I was having a fine dream about one of these pretty girls."

A snicker ran through the formation.

Minutes later the squads of Dragoons began to return and report. Worth questioned them. Grant saw the squad leaders shake their heads. The last group arrived also with a negative finding. Worth shouted out to his brigade commander to have the men fall out.

Grant called out. "Sergeant O'Doyle, take the men to the commissary and feed them. Then check all wagons and harnesses and repair anything needing it."

Hazlitt came up and intercepted Grant as he moved away. "This drill," he said with a disgusted expression on his face and waving his hand to indicate the grumbling, dispersing soldiers, "was all based on a rumor that Santa-Anna was approaching with a large army. I think our general is too easily spooked."

Grant smiled ruefully. He didn't respond to Hazlitt for there was nothing to be gained by complaining. During the past two days Worth had made himself appear ridiculous by assembling his regiments on just such a flimsy excuse. This was the kind of dumb action that a young and inexperienced lieutenant might pull. Worth's only saving characteristic was his bravery on the battlefield.

* * *

The courier's horse was dripping sweat lather as it sped past Lee and Hitchcock walking along the evening street in the direction of their quarters. They looked after the horseman and saw him rein his mount to a stop in front of army headquarters. The courier dismounted, untied a mail pouch from behind his saddle, and hastened to the headquarters' entrance where he handed it to the sergeant of the guard.

Both Lee and Hitchcock recognized the man as one of Dominguez's men. The Mexican Spy Company, Scott had officially christened it, had grown to nearly a hundred men and Dominguez was still recruiting. Using a relay of riders, Scott now had mail delivered from Veracruz to Jalapa every two days.

"I'd better go and see if there's something in the mail that needs taken care of," Hitchcock said.

Lee continued on his way and glad he wasn't Scott's chief of staff who was tied to headquarters and at the general's beck and call every minute of the day. As chief of the engineers Lee had much freedom. Especially so just now for most of his engineers were off performing tasks for the divisions.

* * *

"The general is fit to be tied," Hitchcock said to Lee. "In this situation I don't blame him." Hitchcock had just arrived with a bottle of wine to Lee's quarters. He sat down and reached out to fill Lee's offered glass. Then slowly filled his own.

Lee took a drink and waited for Hitchcock to continue. Hitchcock sipped his wine and savored its taste for a moment before he swallowed.

"Well, Ethan, out with it," Lee said. "Or did you come here to just make one statement about the general and then drink wine with me?"

"Okay. A man named Nicholas Trist is at Veracruz. He has written the general that he's a special envoy from President Polk and is here to work toward ending the war."

Lee raised an eyebrow. "Who is this Trist fellow?"

"He's assistant to the Secretary of State. Speaks fluent Spanish, I've heard. The general wasn't notified of his coming, and to make matters worse, Trist has sent instructions for him to deliver a sealed proposal for peace to the Mexican Government."

"I bet the general really like being ordered to do that. But why a sealed proposal? The general is the commander and chief here and it's his right to know what's being offered because it could jeopardize the army."

"Right. He's convinced President Polk has deliberately sent a civilian to supersede his authority as military commander."

"Polk is too shrew to do that in the middle of a war, especially in such a crude way. Do you think there's a misunderstanding on Trist's part of what his role should be?"

"God! I hope it's that simple."

"What's the general going to do about all this?" Lee's sympathies were with Scott.

"I'm worried about that very thing. Usually he's very thoughtful of other peoples feeling, but now his blood is hot. When I left he was writing a harsh letter to Polk and Marcy complaining of Trist acting like he had senior authority of both military and diplomatic actions. He said he would write Trist returning the proposal and telling him that he wouldn't deliver it, and that he was the commanding officer in the field."

"This is bad," Lee said and deeply concerned for the general. "He should be certain of the facts before he does anything."

"There's more. He's had enough of General Worth's shenanigans and is moving headquarters to Puebla. He said to tell you to get ready to go with us in the morning."

"I'll be ready." Scott's senior general was making an ass out of himself. His order of occupation for Puebla had allowed men who had stabbed and robbed Americans to be dismissed by the Mexican courts. He had continued his nervous, unsettling habit of calling his men to arms. Once on unsubstantiated rumors, he had kept the men in ranks all day with their weapons, and haversacks holding three days rations of food. The men were calling the false alarms "Worth's Scarecrows". He had issued a circular accusing the Mexicans of plotting to poison his troops, claiming they had inherited from the Spanish the habit of cowards to poison men whom they wouldn't fight. The Puebla officials and the priests complained strenuously to Scott, pointing out that they were doing everything that had agreed to. Scott sent Worth a letter of reprimand. Worth screamed he was being unfairly condemned and demanded a court of enquiry. Scott selected Twiggs, Quitman, and Perisfor Smith for the court. They found Worth's terms of occupation harmful to public service, and the poison plot circular to be highly improper and the reprimand justified. To which Worth complained even louder and wrote Washington demanding they clear his name. That's where the matter stood.

"What's the plan for the rest of the army?" Lee said. "Tactically it's in a bad situation, being divided into parts as it is at Veracruz, Jalapa, Perote, and Puebla. Such long distances separate them that one part can't come to help another in the event of an attack."

"He's going to pull them together at Puebla. Those at Veracruz will remain there to protect the main stores depot and keep the port open for us."

Chapter Twenty-Seven

"The army keeps getting smaller day by day," said Chilton. "We've had a hundred and thirty men desert since we've been in Puebla, and that's in less than a month."

"That's on top of the three hundred that deserted at Jalapa," Hazlitt said. "That's what happens if you don't pay your men. But besides the money, if we knew the religion of the deserters, we'd probably find that most are Irish Catholics. Isn't that what we found up north, Sam?"

"From what we knew about their religion, that's the way it seemed," Grant replied. "Some Catholic men think were going to tear down all the Catholic Temples, kill the priests, and make the country Protestant. That's what the Mexican newspapers keep drumming into their heads."

Grant and the other two lieutenants had returned a short time before from a successful foraging expedition and were at the Aztec Club located in a large building near the Plaza. The Americans had started the club since they had arrived in the city. He felt genuine pleasure at being here with his comrades, drinking a beer, and drawing on a smooth cigar.

Grant was growing to like the boyish Chilton. He was a brave fighter and was learning quickly how to lead men. Perhaps he was overly concerned about their safety, not fully considering a soldier's life was just naturally dangerous.

"General Scott's here!" a cry sounded from the door.

"About damn time," said Hazlitt and rising to his feet. "Let's go meet the general."

"Right," said Chilton.

Grant followed the others outside.

* * *

Scott and his retinue of staff officers and escort of a troop of Dragoons had covered the ninety miles from Jalapa to Puebla in two and one half days.

They made the journey without incident. Just inside the gate of the city, he sent McClellan ahead to inform Generals Worth and Quitman of his arrival. As McClellan dashed off, Scott continued on at a leisurely pace and commenting upon the fine buildings and the colorful clothing of the people. Lee thought Puebla a grand city, making Veracruz and Jalapa seem but small villages in comparison.

Reaching the plaza they found soldiers gathering by the hundreds. Pueblans were there in an even larger number and wanting to see the commander of all the American soldiers. The troopers quickly formed a ring to hold the civilians away from Scott. The people gawked up at the big, blue uniformed general sitting upon the big gray horse, while he with an expression of amusement, looked out over the townsfolk and his soldiers. This was a change from the past days when he had been silent and withdrawn, anxious about the safety of his men and dreading the encounter with Worth.

General Quitman came pushing through the Dragoons. He saluted the general.

"Welcome, general, it's good to see you here."

"Thank you. Where's General Worth?"

"At headquarters," Quitman said and not liking the message.

Lee was saddened by Worth's absence for it showed disrespect for his commander and chief. The rift between the two men could not but hurt the fighting ability of the army.

Scott's jaws clenched as if to say, so that's the way he's going to play it. His face relaxed and he spoke to Quitman. "General, have one of your people show Colonel Hitchcock the way to the Governors Palace."

He turned to Hitchcock. "Colonel, ride to the governor and ask him to call on me at headquarters later today for we have important matters to discuss. Impress upon him that I want to see him and not a subordinate." Scott was getting straight to the matter of who ruled Puebla.

"Now, General Quitman, lead the way to headquarters."

Quitman called out to the major of Dragoons. "Make a way for us through them." He pointed at the compact mass of soldiers and civilians who had gathered to view Scott.

The major rolled his spurs along his horse's flank and set it prancing and its iron-shod hooves pounding a tattoo on the cobblestones. The mass of people gave way reluctantly from in front of the beast. Scott and his entourage fell into the trooper's wake.

"This is it," Quitman said to Scott as he halted the group in front of a large brick building with a sign over the main entrance identifying it as "American Army Headquarters".

"The governor provided the building for our use. General Worth's office is at the end of the hall."

Scott stared at the sign for a long minute, detesting the task that lay before him. Finally he pivoted around to the men with him.

"General Quitman, you may go on about your duties."

"Yes, sir," Quitman said and his face showing relief. He saluted and walked away.

Scott spoke to his staff officers. "Gentlemen, I will see General Worth alone. You are released to find quarters for yourself."

Without waiting for an acknowledgement or salute, Scott faced away. He dismounted. With a heavy step, he went into the building.

Lee was as glad as Quitman had been not to be a witness to the meeting between Scott and Worth. He felt deeply saddened by the conflict between the two generals. He laid the blame on Worth who seemed to act from shallow thinking and baseless resentment of Scott's intentions.

* * *

In the wagon park the Americans had set up just outside the walls of Puebla, Grant had his teamsters working diligently to harness the hundreds of horses and mules and hook them to the wagons. He watched the men, listened to them curse the stubborn animals, and waited for the Texas Rangers to appear. The yellow ball of the sun was already above the horizon and he wanted to be off on his foraging to Toluca a town some thirty miles away to the northwest.

He had never been as busy as during the past two weeks, not even enough time to go to the Aztec Club and catch up on the latest news and gossip. General Scott had ordered a supply depot be established in preparation for the advance on Mexico City, and every army quartermaster was working full time to fill it with foodstuffs for the men and grain for the thousands of horses and mules. In further preparation for the march upon Mexico capital, Scott now had his entire army, except for the garrison at Veracruz, concentrated at Puebla. General Twiggs had marched in with his division, and the five hundred man garrison from Perote that he had been ordered to pick up along the way. All the camp followers had trailed close behind Twiggs.

For escort Grant would have his Fourth Infantry Regiment, a hundred Dragoons, and a company of some fifty Texas Rangers. Colonel Hays had arrived the day before with five companies of Rangers, 285 men. Grant believed their presence here was due to his suggestion to Lee to have Scott request them from Governor Henderson. The Rangers had been assigned to escort the foragers of the various brigades. The large escort would be needed for as the army had advanced closer to the Mexican capital, the guerrilla bands had become larger in size, numbering in the hundreds, and more aggressive in their attacks on the American wagon trains.

As Grant watched the city gate, a group of Rangers came out and wheeled to come in his direction. The leader, a rawboned six-footer with a freckled face and red hair, brought his band to a stop in front of Grant and dismounted.

"Well, Sam, we meet again," he said and smiled with pleasure.

"Tom Cavallin, it's good to see you." Grant said.

The Rangers were wild looking riders with long, raggedy beards. They were clad in a hodgepodge of leather boots, flannel shirts, cottons trousers and hats or caps. No two were dressed alike except for their shirts that were either blue or red. The Rangers were made up of men with a variety of backgrounds and a wide range of education. Some of them had little or no formal education while others were doctors or lawyers or businessmen who had put their professions on hold to join the renowned group of men to fight in Mexico. Each was armed with a short-barreled carbine in a scabbard under his right leg, a bowie knife, one or two cap and ball pistols, and a pair of Paterson Colts, .36-caliber and each holding five shots. The Paterson guns were worn in holsters strapped to the men's waists, while the holsters for the cap and balls were fastened to the saddles. Grant had fought with Cavallin and his band of rangers at Monterrey and on foraging expedition, some as long as a hundred and fifty miles. He knew first hand that this band of men was the toughest of fighters. Every one of them hated the Mexicans. Many of them had lost a relative at the Mexican massacre of the Americans at the Alamo or

Goliad. Cavallin had lost an uncle and an older brother at Goliad. Grant never knew of a Ranger taking a prisoner, unless ordered to do so for questioning.

"Good to see you too," Cavallin said. "In fact I asked to be assigned to escort you."

"I'm glad that you did. But why're you here? I'd think Taylor would've kept you experienced Rangers for his work and the governor would've sent a new company."

"Taylor knows you fellows down here are the ones that'll win this war. So he's settled down at Monterrey and just waiting for you to get the job done. And besides, he's going to run for president and is saving his strength for that. Wouldn't it be something for our old general to become president?"

"He just might get it," Grant said. "Let me introduce these two men who'll be with us. This is Bob Hazlitt, he's boss of the infantry. This other one is Mat Chilton boss of the Dragoons. Meet Tom Cavallin Lieutenant of Rangers."

"Glad to meet both of you," Cavallin said.

Hazlitt and Chilton stepped up and shook Cavallin's hand, and spoke their greeting.

"Let's decide how we're going to do this," Grant said.

The officers settled upon a plan and, with the road sufficiently wide, the wagons rolled two abreast. Grant thought their arrangement was as good as could be made. Half the infantry marched at the front of the wagon trains and half at the rear. Ten Dragoons were riding as wide flankers with the rest riding close in at intervals along the length of the train. Tom would keep his Rangers together and take them wherever he thought the danger spot might be depending upon the terrain the train was passing through. Even rolling double file, the wagon train would stretch for nearly two miles and would be a tempting target for a guerrilla band.

Grant stopped the train to buy provisions at the big ranchos. By nightfall, they had filled about forty of his two hundred and eighty wagons. They made camp in a flat, grassy meadow beside the road. The wagons were positioned in a square with an open center. The horses were watered and fed grain and corralled in the open space surrounded by the wagons. Mounted patrols began to circle the train, and stationary sentries were posted.

On the second day, the wagon train drew close to Toluca nicely situated on a piece of tableland surrounded by mountains. As Grant with Cavallin, Chilton, and Hazlitt rode down to the Rio Xopanae that lay on the near side of the town, they saw a group of young women bathing in the clear mountain water. The girls smiled shyly at the Americans, and went on swimming with much ease and grace.

"One or two of them are pretty," Cavallin said to Grant.

"Most of them are," Grant replied.

"You've been away from home too long."

"True enough, but even so, I see some lovely girls there."

The Americans crossed on a ford below the girls and continued on to the town. Grant thought the town quite nice with several handsome buildings, and a church made of white free-stone with a slender white steeple contrasting with the fine cornices and turrets that were tipped with red.

Town officials had observed the approach of the wagon train and had come with a score of businessmen to the plaza. Grant introduced himself to the Alcalde, Pedro Calderon, and explained he was there to buy provisions. The mood of the Mexicans improved dramatically at that news. Grant told them what items he wanted, then brought out his moneybox. By evening his wagons were full. As he prepared to leave, Calderon came to him.

"Senor Grant, we appreciate your fairness with us in buying our goods. I know that with your men and weapons you could have taken what you wanted and paid nothing. As a token of our thanks, please come with your officers to my hacienda for food and drink and dancing."

"With pleasure," Grant replied.

* * *

The food was delicious, the wine fine, and Grant was enjoying one of Calderon's cigars. The rhythm of the music meant little to his tone-deaf ear. He sat near the dance floor in the big patio of Calderon's hacienda, a striking structure located beside the Rio Xopanae flowing down from a range of the Sierra Madre Mountains that he could see outlined against the star-studded sky to the west.

On the dance floor illuminated by several glass lamps placed in delicate iron holders on the patio perimeter wall, Cavallin, Chilton, Hazlitt, and twenty or so young Mexican men swung and promenaded with pretty senoritas. The music was that of a violin, delightfully played by a little hump-backed dwarf seated in a chair. The violin was nearly as large as the dwarf, however that harmed his playing not at all, and with his sharp black eyes twinkling in the lamp light, he sawed out quadrilles and waltzes and break-downs with wonderful ease.

The young women were dressed in gaily colored full-length dresses trimmed with lace, pendants about their slender necks, and bracelets and earrings made of silver or gold. Their heeled slippers beat out a lively tattoo on the wooden floor as they spun about with their partners.

The Mexican gallants wore white or black jackets with black pants with buttons down the sides. Around their waists were tied sashes of blue or black. Their hats were high crowned with silver bands. Grant saw the men shone brightly compared with the travel stained Americans.

At tables surrounding the dance floor on all sides were seated older men and women and the chaperones of some of the girls. The people seemed much interested in the Americans merrily swinging their young women.

Grant knew the steps of various dances, but because of his tone-deafness the rhythm of music escaped him and he was awkward on the floor. Still the beauty of one particular girl that had been giving him bright-eyed looks over the top of her tiny fan drew him. She was small and slender with brown hair and gray eyes and a heart-shaped face. Her skin was light in color indicating her Spanish ancestry had been preserved down through the generations residing in Mexico. Her mouth was of a generous size and seemed almost always to be curved up in a smile. As their eyes touched again he felt his courage building to ask her for a dance. The quadrilles and the break-downs were fairly fast and he had doubt about handling one of them. The waltzes, however, were slower with more of a gliding step and some spinning. When the music began for one, he came to his feet and marched across the floor and held out his hand to the girl. She placed her soft hand into his and came close with a heart-stopping smile. Bravery had been rewarded. Now to carry it off without making a fool of himself.

He followed the beat of the music as best he could. The girl was a willing partner and covered nicely when he missed a step. Now and again he felt the gentle guiding pressure of her hand on his shoulder to speed his step or slow it down to bring him back to the rhythm of the music. She smiled and he smiled, both recognizing what she was doing. A second waltz followed the first and Grant had another two minutes of holding the pretty, smiling girl in his arms.

The waltz ended and the musician struck up a fast stepping piece and Grant had to surrender the girl. He felt sad about his lack of skill and dejected by the loss of the girl as he walked back to his seat on the sidelines.

Finally the dwarf ceased to play and tenderly put his violin away in a much-worn case. Everyone came to their feet and gave the little man a loud round of applause for his music. Grant thanked the girl who had danced with him. She offered her hand, which he was pleased to take and gently hold it for a few seconds before propriety forced him to release it. The other Americans gave the girls broad smiles and their thanks, which were returned in equal measure. Grant thought the girls found as much sadness in the parting as did the Americans. He joined with his comrades and they went to Calderon and thanked him for the grand evening.

Chapter Twenty-Eight

A pistol fired near mid-length of the long wagon train. A moment later, the bang of hundreds of carbines and pistols erupted. To Grant riding in the lead of the train with Chilton and Hazlitt, the volume of gunfire meant a strong force was attacking the train. The wagons were moving across an open sweep of grassland with no obvious hiding place for guerrillas for at least two miles on all directions so how had they struck without the flanking troopers sounding an earlier alarm?

Grant shouted out. "Bob, stop the wagons and prepare to defend them. Mat, come with me."

Grant reined his horse toward the fighting. Chilton brought his horse up beside Grant. Raking their mounts with spurs, the men drove them in a flat out run toward the guerrillas.

"Follow me!" Chilton shouted out to each of his troopers as he passed them riding at intervals along the train. They formed up swiftly behind him.

Within half a minute Grant drew close enough to see the attacking guerrillas numbered at least four hundred. They were riding along the wagons and shooting at the drivers, and at the few troopers that had raced up. Some drivers had been killed and their teams were stampeding off over the land. Wagons were overturning and spilling their loads. Other teams tried to run but were anchored by the weight of a dead teammate. Eight or ten guerrilla horses without riders fled the tumult, showing the teamsters' and troopers' shots were taking a toll. Still the overwhelming number of guerrillas would soon swamp the Americans.

A few of the guerrillas left the fight and chased after wagons pulled by runaway teams. The riders caught up with the vehicles and nimbly transferred from their horses and took up the reins. They drove the wagons off across the plain as fast as the horses could draw them.

Grant saw Cavallin and his Rangers riding hard to join the fighting from near the rear of the train. Both he and Grant would be too late to prevent heavy losses of men, horses and supplies.

The gunfire began to slacken. Then it ended as if on a signal, and the guerrillas broke off the assault and streamed away at a fast run across the plain.

Grant shouted out to Chilton above the rumble of the horses' hooves, "Stay here. Tend to the wounded."

He saw Cavallin and his band of Rangers alter their course to give chase to the guerrillas. He reined his horse to follow the Rangers. His blood pounded through his veins. He would catch the guerrillas and take deadly revenge for his men that had been killed.

Ahead of him the guerrillas dropped out of sight as if the land had swallowed them. Then the Rangers vanished. In four or five seconds, the guerrillas popped back into view whipping and spurring their mounts. The Rangers reappeared riding fast. The guerrillas knew the land, and this low place had been where they had hidden until the wagon train had drawn close.

One mile passed under the flying hooves of the horses, two miles, then three. The heart-bursting race was telling on the horses and their labored breaths came as hoarse sucks and blows.

The better horses were showing their quality with the two groups of riders stretching out, the faster horses of each drawing to the front. Grant was pleased with his mare that was clawing her way up through the pack of Rangers' horses.

Cavallin and Grant and some of the speedier riders were gradually closing in on the slower guerrillas. Those men were casting frightened glances over their shoulders at the Rangers. Cavallin pulled his carbine and fired. The tail-end Mexican fell from his running horse. The Rangers let out a shrill cry of pleasure at the kill. Another Ranger took a shot, and missed. A third tried and scored a hit. Other Rangers entered the contest and more guerrillas fell.

Grant doubted the guerrillas would stop to fight even though they greatly outnumbered the Rangers. They were civilians who had become guerrillas and not trained for a standup and shoot it out fight. They wanted to live to raid the Americans another day.

The land turned down and ahead beyond a steep bank a river came into view. The Mexicans rode straight to the bank and over it to a narrow strip of land adjacent to the water. The Americans came up and halted their blowing mounts on top of the bank and looked down on their foes.

Grant stopped beside Cavallin. He thought the river, some eighty yards wide and fast flowing, was a lower reach of the Rio Xopanae. A double column of Mexicans was forcing their mounts into the river on top of a narrow ledge of rock that made a ford. The crossing would be slow and dangerous on the constricted width of the ford with the swift water coming to the chests of the tired horses. Even as he watched, one of the horses was swept off the ribbon of rock and into deep water. Both man and horse came up downstream with the man having lost his saddle and the current carrying them speedily away. The man splashed and desperately fought the water, then slid beneath it and was seen no more.

"This'll be like shooting fish in a barrel!" exclaimed a Ranger happily.

"It's a damn lot of fish and they sure as hell will shoot back," said a second Ranger staring down at the more than three hundred Mexican horsemen.

Grant called out to Cavallin. "We've got them bottled up against the river and now they'll fight."

Cavallin lifted his head and sniffed the wind flowing from the guerillas to him, as if he could smell their intentions on it. "Yeah, they sure will."

At that moment one of the riders below them shouted an order and the bulk of the Mexicans nearest the Rangers on the bank pulled their carbines. Grant saw fear on some faces, anger and the will to fight on most. He recognized the leader of the guerrillas by his strangely marked face. The man was General Alvarez, known as the Pinto General from his pale bleached skin with black spots caused by a type of leprosy. He had skillfully devised a successful attack on the wagon train, however he hadn't known the Rangers would pursue them so relentlessly. Now he was hastily forming up part of his men to hold off the Rangers while the remainder escaped across the river. At the general's command, the Mexicans fired a ragged volley up at the Americans.

Bullets went by Grant with a deadly, whirring noise. He smiled grimly at the sound and drew his two pistols from their holsters.

"They're rattled and can't shoot straight from that range," said Cavallin as he looked down at the Mexicans beginning to hastily reloading. He glanced at Grant. "Now it's time to hit them."

"It's your men and your show," Grant said.

Cavallin nodded and shouted out. "Fan out single rank. We'll take them before they can get ready. Man for man they outnumber us. But with these we outnumber them." He held up his pair of Colt five-shooters.

Grant knew Cavallin's arithmetic was correct. The Rangers and their revolvers had the advantage. He had told Lee that the way to stop guerrilla attacks was to put hellish fear into the Mexican riders. With some three hundred of them corralled against the fast running river and ripe for the killing, it was time to do just that.

"Kill them all," Cavallin shouted at the top of his lungs. "Charge!" He spurred his horse and it plunged down the bank.

Grant and the rest of the Rangers sent their steeds lunging down the bank and onto the level ground with their foes. The rapid bang of the Colts started and rose to an earsplitting din. The line of Mexicans staggered under the fusillade of pistol balls. Men and horses screamed, and fell, and bled as they thrashed in death throes.

Grant fired his pistols at two of the enemy and knew the balls had gone true to their mark. He holstered one gun and reached into his cartridge box for powder and ball. On both side of him, the Rangers' Colt revolvers continued to bang away. He caught sight of the Pinto General and saw the disbelief on his diseased ravaged face as the Rangers pistols fired on and on and his men fell like wheat before the scythe. Grant must somehow obtain a pair of those marvelous pistols.

More than a score of frightened guerrillas ran their horses onto the crowded, narrow ford knocking each other and several riders already there into the swift current of the river. Other men forced their mounts directly into the fast water. Some lost their seat in the saddle and went under not to reappear. Other riders able to swim slid off the backs of their mounts and dropped back to catch the tail of the animal and were towed along toward the opposite bank. Most men and horses that went into the river simply vanished below the surface and were not seen again. Mexican horses without riders bolted through the Rangers and up the bank and away.

Grant saw Cavallin crash through a ring of Mexicans protecting the Pinto General. The Ranger fired his pistol and the general reeled under the impact of the bullet. Hard hit and sagging in the saddle the general reined his mount away from Cavallin and drove it into the river. His horse was large and swam strongly and made headway toward the opposite shore, being carried downstream all the while. The last thirty or so of the general's men still on horseback followed his lead, better to gamble with the river than certain death at the hands of the Americans with the guns that never went empty.

"Let them go," Grant shouted at a half dozen Rangers shooting at the men in the river. The chase had ended with slaughter, a simple task of shooting down men who had only empty guns.

Cavallin gave Grant a questioning look. "You getting kind hearted, Sam?"

"A few more dead Mexicans won't weaken the lesson we just gave them." Grant was staring at the bloody men and horses that littered the river bank so densely that he could've walked anyplace he wanted without having to step on the ground.

"I reckon not." Cavallin seemed disappointed the shooting had ended.

"Best we get back to the wagons," Grant said.

Cavallin shouted out to his sergeants. "Granger see to the wounded as best you can and get everybody moving back to the wagons. Pippin, round up all the sound horses and take every gun worth having."

* * *

"Listen to this," Chilton said and holding up a London newspaper in preparation to read and looking around at Grant, Hazlitt, and Cavallin seated at the table with him. "The paper quotes the Duke of Wellington, who as you know defeated Napoleon at Waterloo, is quoted as saying Scott has made the same mistake in Mexico that Napoleon did in invading Russia and trying to live off the land. And he further says, 'Scott is lost. He can't take Mexico City and he can't fall back upon his bases for he has none. He won't leave Mexico without getting the permission of the Mexicans.'"

The four men were in the Aztec Club in Puebla with more than half a hundred other officers. Some men were drinking or playing cards, most were reading newspapers, a large bundle of which had been recently brought up from Veracruz by General Pillow arriving with a division of volunteers. All around loud discussions were being held about the antiwar articles in the newspapers, articles calling the war "Polk's War" and demanding the troops be brought home.

"There is a similarity with Napoleon," Hazlitt said. "We're a damn small army in the heart of a country of seven million people who may at any time be goaded into rising up in all out guerrilla warfare against us."

"I'd say were in a better position than Napoleon," Grant said. "We can feed ourselves off the land."

"And don't forget, the winters are mild here," added Cavallin. He made a mock shiver. "I sure wouldn't want to fight in a Russian winter."

"What I like best about our situation is that we've got General Scott," Grant said. "He's done everything right so far, and if he keeps that up, we'll win this war. Once we get reinforcements we'll march and take Mexico City."

Because of his almost constant foraging, Grant was far behind in keeping up with the news. He sorted through the news papers until he found a copy of the American Star. His eye caught the heading of an article that read "Officers Promoted". Scanning the list for promotion to captain he saw the names of two of his classmates, Roswell Ripley and Frank Gardner, both had won a rank for their actions at Cerro Gordo. Grant had no chance to earn laurels at that battle. He must somehow twist old man fate, or luck, or whatever it was called into giving him the opportunity to perform some deed worthy of promotion. And importantly a high-ranking officer must see the deed or it meant nothing.

"Sam, what'd you read that you didn't like?" Hazlitt asked.

"Nothing," Grant said shortly.

"Fellows, I recommend that instead of sitting here and talking to each other that we go and see what Wade Ussing has in the way of entertainment at his gambling parlor?" Chilton said.

"It's not cards or the wheel that you want," Cavallin said. "You want to see Sophia, that pretty blond partner of Ussing."

"She's gorgeous and that's the truth of it," Chilton replied as a slight blush came over his face.

"I hope Ussing doesn't get mad at you for coming so often to see his girl," Hazlitt said in a serious voice. "I believe he's a mean one and would shoot you."

"I don't think Sophia is his girl," Chilton said. "And besides I'm not afraid of Ussing. A lot of men had tried to kill me in the last few weeks and I'm alive and they're dead."

"Even so, a little caution around Ussing might be smart for I don't think he's very particular how he'd kill a man," Cavallin said.

"I'd listen to Cavallin," Grant said. Chilton had become quite friendly with a woman, one of the camp followers who had part ownership of a gambling establishment brought from New Orleans.

"You going with us, Sam?" Cavallin asked.

"Just far enough to buy some tobacco. I've got some supply contracts to check." Grant had bargained with two large bakeries for fresh bread sufficient to feed his brigade and delivered daily to the brigade commissary. Also he had joined with the other army quartermasters as to how best to clothe their men, who had received no new uniforms since leaving the States. Puebla was known for its cotton mills so obtaining cloth wasn't a problem. Within three days the quartermasters had hired a thousand seamstresses and cobblers to make uniforms for the army.

"Let's go," Chilton said impatiently.

They filed out of the club, and moved off along the street crowded with townsfolk of the captured city.

Chapter Twenty-Nine

General Scott sat his horse on the green meadow outside the walls of Puebla and watched his army parade its skill at marching and maneuvering. He wore his full dress uniform with epaulets, gold braided cockade hat, and all his ribbons. His generals and senior staff officers, also in full dress uniform, sat their mounts on his right. On his left was Nicholas Trist, President Polk's special envoy.

The exhibition was ending with every company and regiment having strutted its stuff, drilling with practiced precision before their commanding general. Now they were marching in final review with their muskets at the correct slant over their shoulders and head snapping to the side to look at the general as they passed immediately in front of him.

Lee thought the soldiers had performed a commendable exercise. Even the recently arrived companies of volunteers had done acceptably well. From the expression on Scott's face he must be thinking the same thing. The last company passed by, the men were released from ranks, and Scott led his entourage of officers and Trist off the field and toward headquarters.

Trist was a man of average size with a thin face and curly brown hair. He had joined with one of the military detachments that Scott occasionally sent to Veracruz and returned with it to Puebla. For days neither would speak to the other. However kind-hearted Scott had taken pains to look after Trist's comfort by arranging for him to have mess with General Persifor Smith. Trist had become ill and Scott sent him a jar of guava marmalade. Trist sent a note of thanks and an invitation to come for a visit. Scott quickly accepted and Trist showed him the documents explaining his mission and the conditions for negotiating with the Mexican Government. Scott saw at once they contained nothing to usurp his authority as military commander. Trist's task was to lead peace negotiations and Scott to have authority over all military matters, strategy, safety of the army, and conditions of an armistice. That had ended all conflict between the two men and they had become warm friends.

Scott had now been with his army in Puebla six weeks. Immediately upon arriving he had ordered the troops be whipped into shape by drilling every day regardless of the weather. The officers practice with pistol and sword. Lee trained his engineers for the special work expected in the attack on Mexico City's defensive works. He prepared detailed maps from information gleaned from the maps and documents found at Santa-Anna's hacienda, El Encero, and from every available source in Puebla.

General Pillow had arrived ten days before with a long wagon train of supplies, 3,100 volunteers, and three hundred and fifty thousand dollars. President Polk had promoted Pillow to Major General and he now out ranked Worth, which further soured Worth's already foul mood. Lee felt regret that the army, even with Pillow's volunteers, was so small that Scott could do nothing but stand guard at Puebla and wait for President Polk and Secretary of War Marcy to carry out their promise to equip him for the battle to capture the capital of Mexico. Lee had come to believe that Scott would never have the 25,000 men promised him back months before in Washington. Further the morale of the army was low because of the lack of pay, and the depression caused by the almost daily drum taps of the death procession transporting one or more dead soldier to the cemetery outside the city walls.

Scott and his group arrived back at headquarters to find Edward Thornton, assistant to Charles Bankhead, British Minister and stationed in Mexico City, standing near his mount and talking with the lieutenant of the headquarters guard.

Thornton came to meet Scott. "Good evening, General Scott, and to you Mr. Trist."

"Evening to you, Mr. Thornton," Trist replied.

"You have a message for us?" Scott asked.

"Yes, sir."

"Regarding our Mexican general?"

"Yes, general."

"Let's not do business on the street," Scott said. "Come with Mr. Trist and me to headquarters. And you gentlemen come along too for this will effect you," Scott said to the assembled officers.

Lee believed he knew the reason for Thornton's appearance. Two weeks prior, British Minister Bankhead had sent his top aid Thornton to see Trist and Scott with the message that Santa-Anna, now in Mexico City and building a large army, had hinted that a cash bribe to him and certain legislatures might buy peace. Scott had invited his general officers and staff to consider Santa-Anna's proposal. Shrewdly knowing the scheme was dangerous, Scott had remained quietly in the background and let the generals and Trist carry the discussion. Pillow quickly came out in support for paying the bribe saying it was common practice in Mexico. Trist had recommended acceptance. So too did the other generals. Scott had released the ten thousand dollars advance payment Santa-Anna has requested into the care of Mr. Trist. Lee thought Scott had cleverly handled the hazardous situation. The down payment and a peace proposal had been given to Thornton to carry to the Mexican general's go-between. The British would certainly do all that they could to see that the scheme succeeded for they were being much harmed by the war.

Scott led the group directly to the war room in headquarters and closed the door behind them. He turned to Thornton. "Now, Mr. Thornton, your news."

"General Santa-Anna's go-between contacted us at our embassy and told us the general had been unable to convince any of the legislators to consider your peace proposal. That was three days ago and I've brought his answer as quickly as I could ride here. It seems the general and those he might have convinced to go along with the negotiations suddenly recalled the law recently passed by their legislature that to talk with an American about peace was a treasonous act and meant execution."

"What about the ten thousand dollars?"

"I'm afraid Santa-Anna has kept that."

"I've a suspicion that he never had any intention to carry through," Scott said. "This may be just another one of his tricks."

"I'm not sure that's it," Thornton replied with a thoughtful shake of his head. "The law had some bearing on his decision for he has enemies who would like nothing better than to see him stood up before a firing squad, but I believe he's convinced his new army can defeat you. I want to assure you that Minister Bankhead and I have done all we could behind the scenes to broker a meeting between you and the Mexicans officials."

"I'm certain that you did," said Scott. "What's the state of the city's defenses?"

"The general brags he has an army of thirty thousand men and many cannons in the city. And he may well have that number. As you will find out the city has many strong outer defensive works, and should those be breached, it is surrounded by marshes with access only by easily defended narrow, raised causeways."

Scott straightened to his full height and turned to his officers. "We have tried to end this without more fighting and bloodshed and failed. Now we have no option but to pursue the Mexican army to its capital and defeat it there."

Chapter Thirty

In the gray dawn of August 7 in the broad plaza of Puebla came the tramp, tramp of American infantrymen wearing boots made by Mexican cobblers of Mexican cowhide and uniforms of Mexican cotton, and the sharp clatter of iron-hoofed cavalry forming ranks.

The noise ceased as the men were called to attention and "Old Davey" Twiggs rode up on his big roan horse and stopped in front of his assembled division. He jerked off his hat and waved it above his head with its mass of white, brushpile hair.

"Give me a whoop like you did at Cerro Gordo," Twiggs bellowed out in his bullhorn voice.

His 2800 men let go with a shout that caused the windows of the surrounding buildings to rattle, made the hundreds of Mexicans flinch that stood watching, and sent hundreds of roosting pigeons into frightened flight.

Lee with his company of engineers, now reduced to forty-one due to illness, enthusiastically joined in with the shouting. Twiggs had a way with men and Lee was pleased to march with him.

Twiggs's division had been chosen to lead the advance upon Mexico City. He would take with him Colonel Harney and his three regiments of Dragoons to scout ahead and also guard the rear. Lee's engineers would build road and bridges and construct artillery sites and help place the cannons when the battle came.

General Franklin Pierce, former governor of New Hampshire and former U. S. Senator and another of Polk's civilian generals, had arrived at Puebla the day before with 2,500 volunteers, a long wagon train of badly needed ammunition, medicines, and other supplies. He had been struck six times by large forces of guerrillas but had fought through. Scott's army now consisted of 14,000 men, counting infantrymen, Dragoons, artillerymen, Marines, and Texas Rangers. However a large number of his men lay wounded or ill and unfit for duty, some 1,800 at Puebla and another 1,400 at Veracruz. By actual count the general had 10,738 men able to fight. Five hundred of them would stay behind at Puebla to guard the sick against 80,000 Pueblans and any force Santa-Anna might send to attack. The remaining men would march into the heart of Mexico to capture a city of a quarter million citizens and defended by a large Mexican army.

Scott had divided his force into four divisions, with Generals Twiggs, Quitman, Worth, and Pillow commanding them. Twiggs would march out first. Then on successive days, Quitman would leave accompanied by Scott and his entourage, followed by Worth, and lastly Pillow. Lee knew Quitman would have been a better choice for the lead division, but Twiggs outranked him. Worth being in third position to move forward was due to his lack of judgment and excitability. Pillow's bringing up the rear was right for he was a coward and lacked a grasp of military tactics. Also these last two men had no loyalty toward Scott, and he knew it.

"Forward march," Twiggs commanded.

The snare drums rolled and two of Harney's Dragoon regiments led off. The regimental bands struck up "The Girl I Left Behind Me". Lee and his engineers moved out. Then Twiggs and his staff, the heavy siege train, the two brigades of infantry, and in tail-end position the large supply train guarded by a regiment of Dragoons. The division, stretching for five miles along the National Road, began a hard, chilly, uphill march into the heart of the Sierra Madres. The waiting was over and the Halls of the Montezuma's lay but seventy miles ahead.

* * *

Lee was mounted upon his horse and close by General Scott when the division broke camp and rode into a clear, cold day in the high reaches of the Sierra Madres. They forded the snowmelt water of the Rio Frio, a powerful mountain river dashing foam flecked down its boulder-choked channel. After a stiff climb of four hours, the lead element came out on the rocky summit of the mountain range at 10,500 feet. There they halted to catch their wind in the thin, cold air.

Scott brought his horse to a stop beside Lee's mount. "Major, that's our objective, the reason for all out labor and fighting," Scott said.

"Yes, sir," Lee replied and raised his field glasses to look.

A feeling of awe and exhilaration came over Lee as below him 3,400 feet and twenty miles away the great city of Mexico came into focus. This must be how Cortez had felt when he reached this very point. The Americans had shown the same boldness as had the conquistador, cutting themselves off from their source of supplies and deciding to triumph over their foe or die in Mexico.

The remarkable clarity of the view made details visible. The city lay in the center of a green, bowl-like basin some forty miles across. He saw six broad sheets of water gleaming like pendants; the remnants of a great lake that was said to have once covered the whole valley. Though they could not be seen from his distance, Lee knew that within the city were many canals used as avenues of transportation, and the city was often called the Venice Of The Americas. There were large areas of marshes outside the city and randomly spaced about were ten small extinct volcanoes. A dozen or more white satellite villages showing like pieces of silver surrounded the main city. Sunlight glinted off the spires and domes of the churches and other large buildings, some peering out of the foliage of trees. Closer to him, individual fields of many crops, groves and orchards could be made out. At the foot of the mountain below the Americans were the miniature figures of horsemen. Lee thought they would be Lancers watching the Americans, but couldn't be sure due to the distance.

Lee swung his view back to the city bright with sunshine, and even with his field glasses, he could see no smoke, no tarnish, just its beauty. That magnificent place was to be the site of the final battle for the nation. Scott's advance had been one of conducting a moving siege against entrenched fortifications, and from all appearances would continue to be so to the very end. Sadness came over Lee for because of the Mexican's stubborn refusal to negotiate, he might have to direct cannon fire to destroy their grand capital.

"That splendid city shall soon be ours," Scott said, his eyes hard and determined.

"Either victory or a soldiers grave," said Twiggs who was riding up and heard Scott's words.

"Exactly so, General Twiggs," Scott said. He lowered his field glasses and stowed it away.

"General Twiggs, let us ride down and find a fitting place for our headquarters."

"Yes, sir. And see if they'll come out from their fortifications and fight."

"Not until the rest of our army arrives," Scott said.

Twiggs gave a signal to march and Harney moved out ahead and down the mountain road with his Dragoons. The two generals and their staff officers fell in with Lee riding at the head of his engineers. With the grade steep, the artillerymen and wagon drivers rode the breaks of their vehicles hard to prevent a runaway, creating a cacophony of screeches as break pads ground against iron rimmed wheels.

An hour later and rounding a turn of the road with the floor of the basin near at hand, Lee saw nearly a regiment of Lancers had gathered. Harney formed up his two regiments of Dragoons and rode steadily on. The Mexicans sat their horses and watched the Americans approach for a few minutes longer. Before the Americans were within carbine range, the Lancers reined their mounts about and faded away along the roads and through the orchards toward the city. Within the city a cannon boomed alerting the citizenry that the hated Yankees had arrived.

Twelve miles deep into the basin at the village of Ayotla, where every citizen had fled and the houses stood empty, Scott made his headquarters in a fine adobe hacienda with a large patio and a roof of cherry red tiles and all surrounded and shaded by huge olive trees. Lee and his company of engineers chose several houses close by headquarters for he knew Scott might call him at any time to go out to reconnoiter the enemy's fortifications.

Harney's cavalry advanced another one and a half mile closer to the enemy and took up a defensive position at the village of San Isidro. General Quitman had marched his division hard and in the late hours of the day, came down the mountain road and into the basin and began to make camp at the rear of Twiggs. Soon there was a huge wagon and ordnance park, and more than a thousand worn, dingy white tents erected in neat rows across a wide swath of the green land. Scott now stood guard and waited for his last two divisions to arrive.

* * *

Lee halted with his escort of Dragoons just beyond the range of any gun a sniper might be aiming at him from the hill named El Penon. Lee had expressed his opinion to Scott that the hill would be Santa-Anna's first line of defense and heavily fortified. Scott had directed him to reconnoiter it and report back. At the same time Beauregard had been dispatched to scout an alternate route to the capital, one that was much longer running west past Lake Chalco and through San Augustin before turning north to the city.

El Penon, located some seven miles from Mexico City, sat beside the National Highway that approached the city from the east and ran between lake Texcoco on the north and lakes Xochimico and Chalco on the south. The hill was more than four hundred feet tall, and made of layers of crimson volcanic rock and cinders. As Lee had thought would be the case, stockades, breastworks, parapets, and guns bristled on the summit and sides of El Penon. Additional defensive works at the broad base of the hill and in advance positions commanded all approaches. All the works had been skillfully designed and constructed. He counted thirty pieces of artillery, with each well placed for clear avenues of fire. To create more difficulty for an attacker, the Mexicans had flooded the meadows on one side of the hill. The waters of Lake Texcoco lapped upon and guarded the remainder of the hill's base. Lee estimated there were six to seven thousand men occupying the works.

He made sketches of the hill and its fortifications and then turned to a broad view of the land and routes to the city. He saw the maps he had prepared at Puebla were substantially accurate. The Spanish and the Mexicans after them had built a mighty defense for their capital city. Every approach was along a narrow raised causeway running through wide tracts of marshland that no artillery, cavalry, or wagons could cross. A series of strongholds and complex fortifications guarded each road. Whichever route Scott chose to launch his attack upon would funnel the Americans onto a ribbon of road that required running a gauntlet of forts from which cannon and musket fire could rake them.

Lee spotted a horseman coming along the road from the city and approaching El Penon. When parallel to the hill, the rider waved up at the men staring down at him from their elevated positions. He rode brazenly on and crossed beneath the frowning cannons and the thousands of muskets.

As the horseman drew closer, Lee saw it was Dominguez, leader of the Spy Company. He called out a greeting and Dominguez replied with a lift of his arm and a smile or recognition.

Lee turned to his escort of cavalry. "Any of you speak Spanish?"

"I do a little, major," one of the men said.

"Then come up here and help me."

The trooper brought his mount forward beside Lee.

"Ask Dominguez what he knows about El Penon." Lee chucked a thumb at the hill.

The trooper spoke and Dominguez responded.

"He says he's heard there are seven thousand men on it, and it's under the command of General Santa-Anna himself."

Lee nodded for he had heard the name Santa-Anna in Dominguez's answer. "Tell him to come with me to headquarters."

Again the trooper and Dominguez spoke together.

* * *

"General Scott, we could shell El Penon and then most likely take it by storm," Lee said. "But we'd suffer a fearful loss, one out of all proportion to what we'd gain."

Lee had described what he had seen, told that Santa-Anna personally commanded the fortifications, and showed his drawings of the hill and the other defensive works to Scott and the several other officers who had gathered at headquarters.

"That's regrettable for it would be to our advantage to fight and defeat Santa-Anna himself instead of having to fight several battles with his subordinates," Scott said. "However we can't sustain a large loss of men." He studied the map Lee had prepared of the area and that was spread on the table before him. "That leaves the southern route by way of San Augustin for our advance," Scott said and traced it with a finger. "I estimate the distance to be about twenty five miles."

"Yes, sir, and another ten or so to the capital," Lee added.

"We don't know if the road is passable for our wagons and heavy artillery," Scott said. "However Colonel Duncan and Lieutenant Beauregard should return from scouting it by tomorrow and then we will have that information."

183

Chapter Thirty-One

Grant, with Worth's division, looked down from the high mountain pass upon a vast valley brim-full of dense, gray mist, under which Mexico City lay hidden. He was disappointed in the view, not at the appearance of the valley for it looked intriguingly like an immense inland sea of unfathomable depth, but rather as a military officer, he would have preferred to see Mexico City from the vantage point of this elevated location.

Worth signaled the advance and led his men down into the mist, which at an elevation of two miles was damp and cold, and toward the hidden and unknown land beneath. Three thousand feet lower, the men broke through the bottom of the mist and spread in front of them lay a broad, flat valley that reminded Grant of a giant green garden. Surrounding the valley on all sides were brown, steep-sided mountains. Under the all-encompassing shadow caused by the thick layer of over-hanging mist, only the nearer objects were distinct, the more distant ones lost in the larger features of the landscape.

After another hour of marching and with the encampments of Twiggs and Quitman in sight, a patrol of cavalry galloped up and informed the general as to where he should camp. Worth marched another three miles to a little town on the shore of a shallow lake, both lake and town named Chalco, where he ordered his caravan to halt and the men to fall out of ranks.

Grant sensed rain threatening and hurried his quartermaster wagons to an open area where his men quickly began to set up tents for their tired and muddy comrades. The commissary officer hastened up with his wagons and soon had his field kitchen erected, cooking stoves unloaded and fires burning, pots and pans rattling, and cooks and their helpers sorting though Grant's wagons for food stuffs. After this warm meal, Grant's brigade had only four days of hard bread for rations. The entire army was in the same condition, and would continue so until the quartermasters could go foraging.

* * *

By first light, Grant had dressed, eaten his ration, and stood smoking a cigarette and watching his brigade come to life. This was the fifth morning since he had arrived in the valley. The discovery that Santa-Anna had built a formidable defense at El Penon had caused General Scott to move three of his divisions twenty seven miles to the west; Worth's, Pillow's, and Quitman's, in an attempt to find a route that would allow the Americans to flank the Mexican general. Twiggs had his division drawn up in a threatening manner before El Penon to hold Santa-Anna in place while Scott positioned the remainder of his army.

Grant saw Worth, and Major Seth Horton at the head of a platoon of his Dragoons riding toward Garland's headquarters. Knowing something was in the wind, he joined with the other junior officers and drifted toward Garland.

Worth finished his discussion with Garland and rode away, leaving behind the men that had come with him. Garland turned to his officers and spoke to one of them.

"Captain Branham, form up your company and go with Major Horton and the engineers to investigate the defenses of San Antonio."

"Yes, sir."

Grant started back to the camp area of his men. He stopped part way there and surveyed Branham's soldiers forming into ranks. Within three or four minutes the force of Americans was pushing north along the Acapulco Road toward San Antonio lying two miles distant.

Grant felt a powerful itch to go along. Without a conscious decision to act upon the urge, he reversed course and walked up to Garland still watching after the men marching off.

Grant saluted. "Colonel Garland, I request permission to go with Major Horton to San Antonio. I'm free for the next few hours from my duties."

"Lieutenant, there's enough of the men if there's no fighting, and too many if they should all be killed," Garland replied. He pivoted about and went off across the camp in the direction of the artillery company.

Grant stared after the colonel and thinking that hadn't been much of an answer to his request. Did the colonel say no? Not directly, merely saying that the number of men was large enough. Well, since he hadn't forbidden Grant going along, then he'd interpret the words as it suited him.

He saddled his horse and galloped up the Acapulco Road after the men now some half-mile away. The road ran on a raised causeway flanked by the waters of Lake Xochimilco on the right and on the left the Pedregal, an ancient lava field about five miles wide of volcanic rock and scoria broken into every possible form of jagged, sharp ridges and deep fissures. Both the lake and the Pedregal would be quite difficult for men to cross, and most certainly impassable for cavalry or artillery.

Grant overtook the Americans and worked his steed up through the marching infantry to ride beside Major Horton. Grant knew Horton from having fought beside him when both were with General Taylor on the Rio Grande, and liked the fellow.

Horton lifted his hand in greeting to Grant. "Maybe we'll get to see a little fighting after all these weeks of just drilling, or sitting on our butts," he said with a look of anticipation.

"Yes, sir. It's bound to happen soon now."

They marched along the causeway and a few minutes later San Antonio came into clear view ahead. From maps he had acquired in his foraging, Grant knew that the road continued straight ahead to Churubusco and onward to the capital.

Horton halted his Dragoons a few hundred yards from San Antonio, and Branham's infantry came to a stop behind them. Sitting side by side, Horton and Grant lifted their glasses. San Antonio was a great feudal hacienda lying astride the road and standing on flat land which was only a little above the water level of Lake Xochimilco. It consisted of several solidly built stone buildings on about three acres of ground with everything surrounded by a strong wall made of large pieces of lava rock. The two main buildings were two stories and the remainder single story. Tall pepper trees and silver leafed poplars shaded most every building.

The hacienda had been built as a major defense to block the Acapulco Road against invaders, and as Grant studied it though his glasses, judged it had been well constructed. A large Mexican flag floated from the top of the main building. He saw enemy riflemen lining the walls and the parapets on top of the two, long main buildings. The snouts of many cannon were visible pointing along the road toward the Americans.

Smoke jetted out from the top of the walls of the hacienda as heavy artillery began to fire. The first ball struck Horton full in the chest, crushing his ribs and breaking his spine. He was lifted from the saddle, carried backward off the horse, and dropped on the ground in two pieces, the body divided just below the rib cage. More solid shot came shrieking at the Americans and another seven men fell, and as many horses.

With Horton dead, the Dragoons were without an officer. Grant spun his horse to face them and shouted to reverse course. Captain Branham yelled at his foot soldiers. The full force of Americans, the Dragoons hard on the heels of the foot soldiers, beat a hasty retreat with cannon balls bouncing along the road after them and mangling the legs of men and horses and dropping them onto the roadway. Grant knew the Mexicans had pre-aimed their guns on the road and that was responsible for so much damage being done so quickly to the Americans. If the Mexican gunners had been wiser and used exploding canisters or grapeshot instead of solid shot, they could have decimated their enemy. As for poor Horton, he had wanted a fight and a little excitement. He had found a gruesome death instead. A man should be careful what he wished for.

Branham halted the Americans when out of cannon range and ordered men to bring back the wounded and dead. The chosen men stacked their arms. One of them tied a piece of white cloth to a limb he broke from a bush growing beside the road. Then holding the flag high and hoping the Mexicans didn't fire upon them, the men went warily along the causeway. The Mexicans held their fire.

Grant along with the three engineers and the line officers raised their glasses to complete their inspection of the heavily defended hacienda. He knew that with the lava field on one side and the lake waters on the opposite, San Antonio could not be flanked. If it were to be taken, it would have to be done by frontal assault. Worse yet, with no space for cavalry to maneuver, the attack would have to be made by infantry alone, and their movement must be along a narrow, level causeway with every inch covered by Mexican artillery and musket fire. He believed the hacienda should be by-passed and another route to the city found.

Chapter Thirty-Two

The Pedregal lay in front of Lee as a contorted black sea with its waves of frozen lava cracked and shattered into sword sharp rock slabs, and crevasses deep as the height of a tall man. The strong odor of volcanic ash riding on the west wind came to him. From his viewpoint the fearsome lava flow seemed impassable to man and weapons. But he must be certain of that.

Captain Branham and Lieutenant Grant had returned from probing the defenses of San Antonio and reported the strength of the fortress hacienda and the impossibility of turning it because of Lake Xochimilco and the Pedregal. Lee had requested Scott to allow him to search for a route across the southern end of the lava to the San Angel Road. If he could find a way, they could strike San Antonio by surprise from the rear.

He called out to the lieutenant commanding the escort of infantry and led slowly onto the lava. In the distance some two miles away, the volcanic hill Zacatepec rose about three hundred feet above the lava. The hill would be his first objective. From its top, he should be able to see to the far side of the lava field.

By avoiding the gaping fissures too wide to jump, and circling around the worst of the jagged mounds of rock, the men picked a way across the lava. Now and again a slab slid under a foot and threw a man, or a sharp edge tripped him and he fell. The men cursed the lava. Still Lee saw that infantrymen on foot and carrying hand weapons could navigate the Pedregal.

The lava field rose gradually to the base of Zacatepec and there Lee stopped with his escort. The hill was cone shaped, made of volcanic cinders and larger chunks of hardened lava, and quite steep. He directed the escort to wait for him, and set out to climb the hill.

The going was tortuous with the loose cinders sliding away from beneath his boots. At times he had to bend forward and make his way up by using both hands and feet. The exertion was worthwhile for as he rose higher, more and more of the lava flow came into view. He halted to catch his breath and look around.

A bullet came at Lee with a savage whine, landing with a splatter of lead against a rock by his feet. A second ball struck and glanced away with a whirring sound. Another sang by close to his ear. He ducked and scrambled to the side around the hill and out of the line of fire. Below him, his men leveled their muskets and returned the gunfire of the Mexicans who had seemed to appear magically out of the rocks a couple of hundred yards farther west.

Lee hurried to the top of the hill. He hadn't expected the presence of the Mexicans so far out on the lava. From the high point he saw them moving away west across the lava to escape the American musket fire. Some one and one-half miles farther away, the San Angel Road was in sight. To his dismay, infantry and artillery were visible moving south from the direction of the capital. Wily Santa-Anna had anticipated Scott's effort to turn San Antonio by shifting his army west and was staying one step ahead by marching part of his army to block the action.

Lee tracked the movement of men and weapons and determined the enemy was establishing a defensive position beyond the lava field on a hill between the villages of San Geronimo to the north and Contreras on the south. He checked his map and saw the name of the hill was Padierna. From what he could see, the hill stood alone and exposed and could possibly be taken. Scott must be quickly made aware of the situation and the enemy struck before they became strongly entrenched.

Lee swung his glass back to follow the Mexicans retreating before the fire of his escort, and to examine the lava they crossed. One thing was obvious, if Mexican soldiers could come so deeply into the lava and move so easily over it, then with work to fill in the crevices and flatten the lava piles, the Pedregal could be crossed not only with men but also artillery. He hurried down from the hill.

* * *

"Since the Mexican infantrymen can make their way over the lava from the San Angel Road to Zacatepec and we can cross from the Acapulco Road to the same hill, then we can cross the entire width of it," Lee said in winding up his report of exploring the Pedregal and observing the hill near Contreras being fortified by the Mexicans.

Upon Lee's return to headquarters, Scott had called a council of war with the generals of his four divisions and his staff officers. Twiggs was present due to Scott having called his division to San Augustin to consolidate the army.

"I'm certain that I can build a road suitable for moving both men and artillery," Lee added.

"Artillery?" Scott said, liking what he heard.

"Yes, sir," Lee replied. "With enough men, I can get it built before Santa-Anna can become too strongly entrenched in his new position near Contreras." Scott's keen military mind had immediately recognized the several possibilities that artillery meant as to how Santa-Anna could be assaulted. Lee knew Scott's tactics had been flawless so far, and on a personal basis, he liked the old general ever more as he had led the army into the mountains of the enemy.

"Then do it," Scott said with a warrior's gleam in his eyes. "How many men do you need?"

"Five hundred added to my engineers."

"You'll have them," Scott said. "Now some information that I've received from Dominguez of our Mexican Spy Company that agrees with the major's findings. He has reported that Santa-Anna is moving a major part of his army to the west. And further he has brought two hundred or so of our Irish deserters with him. Catch those bastard deserters if you can."

Scott focused on his generals. "As Major Lee said, the time to strike an enemy is before he erects his fortifications. Our objective is to drive up both the Acapulco Road and San Angel Road and occupy Tacubaya." He touched the location of the town on the map spread before them. "That will be out staging area for the final drive to crush the defenses of the Mexican Capital." He pressed the palm of his hand down on the map to cover the capital. "Unless you see a flaw in my reasoning, this is how we shall proceed."

Scott paused, and when no voice was raised, spoke with his voice quickening. "General Pillow, turn five hundred of your infantry into road builders for a time and place them at the disposal of Major Lee. Use the rest of your division to protect the workers."

"General Twiggs, follow General Pillow and his road builders and stand ready to assist them should they be attacked in strength. General Worth, place your division to threaten San Antonio and hold its defenders in place and prevent them from reinforcing the enemy near Contreras. When that fortification is taken, then move against San Antonio. General Quitman, you are to remain here at San Augustin and guard our rear. Now if there's discussion needed about these movements, let's hear it, and that includes anything the staff officers wish to say."

Silence held total sway in the war room and Lee knew why; the strategy seemed sound from the information available. And further, the officers saw the fire in Scott's flashing eyes and knew this wasn't a time to discuss minor tactics for they would depend upon what happened in the field once the action began.

"Excellent. You all are released to perform your duties."

* * *

Lee and his road builders hammered and hand-laid slabs of lava to build a narrow roadbed over the Pedregal. Two rifle companies were out in advance of the road builders, and the horse drawn artillery followed close behind them. The ambulance wagons that would haul wounded men to the hospital at San Augustin came last. By early afternoon, and driving a picket line of Mexican riflemen before them, the Americans reached the edge of the lava field. They halted on the border of a deep ravine full of swiftly running water lying a thousand yards from the enemy entrenchments on Padierna.

The batteries of artillery were brought up and Lee chose sites for them sheltered as much as possible from the cannons on the hill. The gunners began to pepper the Mexican position, throwing shells up at the entrenchments on the hillside, and receiving plunging fire from the big Mexican guns in return. The dueling was brisk, the Americans getting the worst of it with cannon balls pounding the lava rock and sending slivers of lead and rock fragments flying to cut and pierce the gunners.

Lee went to stand by the gun where Preston Johnston was one of the powder boys. Preston was the fourteen-year-old nephew of Lee's friend Joe Johnston, who had recovered from the wounds received at Cerro Gordo and now was an acting lieutenant colonel of a regiment. Preston, a brown-headed blue-eyed boy, had joined the army to come to Mexico with the uncle he idolized.

As Lee stood watching the bombardment, a Mexican solid ball struck Preston, knocking him down by his gun and ripping off his left leg just above the knee. Bright red blood spurted in great pulses from the torn, stub end of the leg.

Lee sprang to Preston and knelt by his side. Equally quick was the gunnery sergeant to come to help.

"Goddamn! Goddamn!" cursed the sergeant as he ripped off his neckerchief and speedily tied it around the stump of the severed leg.

Lee grabbed up a short piece of stick from a cannon ball shattered bush and twisted the cloth into a tight tourniquet to stop the spurting blood.

"Come here!" Lee shouted at two large infantrymen, part of the squad guarding the battery. "Carry him fast as you can to the ambulances," Lee ordered. The wagons were out of cannon range some quarter-mile back on the lava.

The men gathered up the limp and unconscious boy and hastened away. The last Lee saw of Preston was his pasty face, the tan from the sun gone with the draining away of his blood.

"Goddamn Mexicans," the sergeant yelled above the howling of the cannon to his men. "Give them hell, boys. I think they've killed poor Preston."

Lee thought the same thing for the wound was most grave. Joe would be heartbroken for Preston was his favorite nephew, and further Joe would feel responsible for having permitted the boy to join the army.

Lee went again to examine the ravine with its fast flowing water, and knew it would be slaughter to try to cross it in a frontal assault on the hill, also it was obvious they were out-gunned by the heavier Mexican artillery and couldn't remain here much longer under the deadly pounding. He looked at the San Angel Road and saw a flood of men and weapons coming from the direction of the capital. Santa-Anna was bringing in reinforcements. Some other way had to be found to get at the Mexicans before they became too strong to rout.

As Lee considered the situation growing ever more hazardous, an aid of General Pillow came up and called out above the boom of the cannons. "Major Lee, General Pillow wants to see you immediately at the rear."

Lee followed the lieutenant to General Pillow sitting on a mound of lava in front of his tent. He was studying one of the maps that Lee had prepared.

Pillow spoke, "Major, I'm considering sending two brigades under Riley and Cadwalder to turn the enemy's left flank by veering off to the right through the edge of the lava and westward across the San Angel Road. That would cut the men at Contreras off from retreat to Mexico City and give us a better place from which to launch an assault on his fortifications. What are your thoughts on this?"

"I like the plan, sir. Lieutenants McClellan and Tower can scout a route for them. The action should begin as soon as possible for our artillery and infantrymen up front are taking a heavy beating."

"Then we shall do it," Pillow said. "Report our plans to General Scott."

"Yes, sir."

Chapter Thirty-Three

Lee met Scott, with an escort of infantrymen and troopers, at the base of Zacatepec. The sound of the dueling artillery had brought the general from San Augustin and onto the lava. Lee gave his report of the situation and Pillow's plan for action. The general climbed a few yards up the side of the hill so as to be able to see over the ridges of lava and turned his field glasses onto the fortified hill near Contreras and the San Angel Road. After a few minutes he came down to Lee.

"I think it's the best we can do under the current circumstances. Return to General Pillow and inform him that I agree with his proposed action to take the Mexican fortification at Contreras. As always, watch what is happening, advise the general, and report developments to me so that I can give direction for co-operation of the other units.

* * *

Lee returned to Pillow's headquarters and informed the general of Scott's approval of their plans and to proceed with action against the Contreras fortification. In turn he was told that Persifor Smith's brigade of Twiggs division had been sent forward to join with Riley and Cadwalader.

Lee left Pillow, and climbing a high mound of lava, turned his field glasses to the northwest at the Americans, numbering some three thousand, west of San Angel Road. The brigades were in and around the small Indian village of San Geronimo one-half mile north of the fortified hill. The approach to the hill was across a ravine and up through orchards, standing corn and thick underbrush. Then as Lee rotated his glasses to look to the north toward Mexico City, his pulse rose to a rapid beat for the Americans were in growing danger from an army of Mexican infantry and cavalry mustering less than a mile distant on high ground. He estimated the enemy force at something near ten thousand men. The small force of Americans was caught between that strong enemy and the four thousand or more soldiers on Padierna.

Lee should be there with the men of the three brigades for that was where the fighting would be. He stowed his glasses and struck out along the edge of the lava. Half a mile later, he came down off the lava and crossed San Angel Road. A short distance later, he encountered the picket line Smith had set up outside the village.

"Where's General Smith's headquarters?" Lee asked the first picket he met.

"It's in the church, sir," replied the soldier.

Lee entered San Geronimo and proceeded to the church, the largest building in the village, and whitewashed as seemed to be the country's custom. The headquarters' guard saluted.

"Is the general here?"

"Yes, sir, in the big room on the right side. You can get there by going around to a door on the side of the church."

Lee circled the building and came to two soldiers standing guard. Through an open doorway, Lee saw Riley and Cadwalader were present and in conversation with Smith.

Smith's aid announced Lee presences and the three generals came outside. Smith, the senior general, looked up at the heavens where thick, dark clouds were gathering menacingly. "Going to be a wet night, major," he said.

"I believe so, sir," Lee said. He respected Smith's skill as a senior officer and his bravery and was pleased he was in command of the Americans caught in this perilous position between two powerful enemy forces.

"I'm glad that you've come," Smith said. "Have you talked with General Pillow?"

"Yes, sir."

"Any new orders from him?"

"No, sir."

"Good. Tell us what General Scott had to say about our plan?"

"He said to take Padierna."

"Then that's what we'll do, by God. And we've found a better way to get at the Mexicans there. McClellan and Tower explored the ground between us and Padierna and found a ravine that's unguarded and leads around to the rear of the hill."

"That makes it possible to come up behind them while they think we're going to strike from the front," Cadwalader added with a grim smile.

"What about the enemy force to the north of us?" Lee asked.

"Let's go inside and talk this through," Smith said.

The council of war went on with night falling and a heavy, cold rain driving in to drum on the roof of the church. Thunder crashed and jarred the earth and shook the church and rattled the window of the room. The four officers raised their voices and leaned closer over the table and maps so as to be heard by their fellow warriors. The discussion went on until at last a plan that all agreed to had been thrashed out.

Smith straightened and spoke to Lee. "It would increase our chances of taking the hill if General Scott would order a demonstration of infantry in front of it to draw the defenders attention from the true direction of our assault."

"I'll go and tell him the plan and request he order one," Lee said. They had reached a decision for Smith to attack Padierna with his nine hundred infantrymen from the rear and before daybreak. Smith requested Lieutenant Tower lead the way to the rear of the hill and Lee gave his concurrence. As for the larger Mexican force to the north, Riley and Cadwalader would stand with their brigades in its path should it move upon the Americans. They would have to hold off the much larger force until the capture of the hill was completed. Lee thought that it they could quickly rout the troops on Padierna, the larger force would not have time to attempt a counterstroke. This was a risky supposition, but taking Padierna was worth the gamble.

"I'd better get going," Lee said, and dreading the journey across the lava through the darkness. Just simply making the trip would be difficult and dangerous, and now he had the cold, driving rain to fight through.

"One last word, major. We can't delay this action because we're exposed here and the enemy out numbers us too greatly. It's either move on them or withdraw, and I'm not for withdrawing. I'll leave camp at 3 AM. And I AM going to attack even if you don't bring word from the general."

"I'll do my best to convince General Scott to accept our plan. And I believe he will." If any man could lead infantrymen to take Padierna, then that man was Persifor Smith.

Lee left the warmth and dryness of the church and went out into the thunder and lightening and the cold rain that swiftly soaked him to the skin. He crossed the San Angel Road, while behind him the heavy rain cut off the lights of San Geronimo. Now he had nothing to guide him except the wind he had marked coming from the northwest, and the view the light from an occasional jagged spear of lightening gave him. He groped his way forward and upon the lava and struck out on what he thought was to the east.

Lee went on step-by-step, and all the time holding the cold, wind driven rain to strike his face at a chosen angle. For a time much too long the lightening held back its light from him, then it flashed in multiple bolts, shooting down from the heavens to run like skeletons across the black lava. In the white glare, he caught a glimpse of the road his men had so laboriously built earlier in the day. He dashed forward onto it and was thankful for every pick and hammer blow that had taken some of the edges off the accursed lava. Yet even here he went slowly for he could so easily lose the road in the blackness.

He tripped and fell, and rose to hobble on through the pitch-dark night and gradually worked the pain out of his twisted ankle. He must reach Scott. The lightening was a savior, for without its now and again momentary flash of light he was certain he would drift left or right and lose the road. To wander off it was to court a broken leg, or worse. At times he knew he had lost the way by the feel of the lava beneath his feet, and he stopped and waited for the next flash of light, when he would veer back onto the road and hurry onward.

To his immense relief, in the ghostly glare of the light from a zigzag bolt of lightening, he caught a glimpse of Zacatepec ahead. Now he must find the American sentries and risk being shot before he could identify himself.

After three tortuous miles on the lava, drenched, and sore from falls, Lee passed through the sentries and into the American camp at Zacatepec. A sentry pointed out the headquarter tent.

"Come in out of the rain," General Pierce called to Lee upon his knock on the wooden tent pole. "You looked drowned."

Lee entered, shook some of the water off, and saluted. "Nearly am, general," Lee said. Pierce had been forced to his bed when injured by the fall of his horse upon the rough lava. Why did generals feel they had to be horseback when lesser men had to walk?

"What brings you out in the rain?"

"To inform General Scott that General Smith will attack Pedierna at first light tomorrow. He strongly requests a demonstration be made in front of the hill. Where is General Scott, sir?"

"General Scott and Twiggs both have returned to San Augustin."

"Then I must be on my way." He felt time running out for him to help Smith and his men.

Lee saluted quickly, pushed the flap of the tent open, and plunged back into the rain and wind. There was another three miles of lava to cover.

* * *

Close to exhaustion, Lee finally saw the dim lights of San Augustin. Dripping water from the rain and every muscle aching with weariness, he passed through the sentries and came to Scott's headquarters. He was surprised to find Scott up and writing at his desk for the time was near midnight.

"Come in, major!" Scott exclaimed upon seeing Lee at his door. He jumped up from his desk and came forward and clasped Lee by the hand. "My, God, man, you look beat. Take a seat." He motioned Lee to the nearest chair.

"You have news from the front?" Scott asked.

"Yes, sir."

"What's the situation?" Scott asked anxiously.

"General Smith will attack Padierna at daybreak, and he'll attack from the rear and has asked for a demonstration in front of the hill." Lee continued, "Santa-Anna has assembled some four or five divisions just to the north to threaten the operation. The brigades of Cadwalader and Riley will try to hold Santa-Anna off while Smith's assaults the hill."

Scott instantly grasped the situation and knew what was required. He turned to the door and shouted. "Sergeant, bring general Twiggs here on the double. On the double, I say."

"Now give me the details," Scott said to Lee.

They had talked but a moment when Old Davey entered. Scott faced about from talking with Lee.

"General Twiggs, a demonstration is needed before Padierna. And it's needed at first light." Scott turned back to Lee. "How many men would you recommend?"

"A full regiment to join up with the four companies and three batteries of artillery already there. We must convince the Mexicans that we're going to strike in strength."

"Make it a regiment," Scott said to Twiggs.

"I'll use one of Pierce's that's at Zacatepec for it's the nearest."

"Then be on your way," Scott said and prodding Twiggs to hurry.

"I'll need a guide," Twiggs said and looking at Lee with his meaning clear.

Lee heart sank at the general's words. He had been moving steadily without rest since daybreak, and had crossed the lava twice. He wanted to get dry and warm. Then something to eat, a long drink of water, and to sleep.

"Yes, sir, I'll go with you," Lee said.

"I'll have my horse saddled and be ready to go in ten minutes. Meet me at my quarters."

* * *

The rain dwindled down to a fine drizzle and ended shortly after Lee and Old Davey left headquarters. The clouds became broken and the moon found gaps in them and cast a pale silver glow down onto the lava road. The light allowed the men to hold their mounts to a fast walk with the iron sod hooves of the horses clanking dully on the black rock.

They reached Pierce's bivouac and the sergeant of the headquarters' guards let them approach. At the general's bid to enter, Twiggs pushed inside the tent and immediately plopped down on a chair. Lee wearily took a second one.

"General Pierce, form up a regiment, every man Jack of them, and get it to Pillow before daylight," Twiggs said without preamble and mopping his sweating, red face with a handkerchief. "Smith needs a demonstration in front of Padierna."

"I'm unable to walk," Pierce said from his bed. "I'll send Colonel Ransom and his 69th."

Pierce raised his voice and called, "Sergeant, do you hear me?"

"Yes, sir."

"Find Colonel Ransom and tell him to report here."

"Yes, sir."

Colonel Ransom, a large, strongly built man, came into the tent and saluted the generals. "Yes, sir," he said and looking at Pierce.

Pierce swiftly gave the colonel his orders to march his regiment. "And be certain that you have all your battle flags flying and bayonets fixed and that everything can be seen by the Mexicans on the hill," Pierce directed.

"General, none of my men nor have I been over the lava in the direction of Padierna. I don't believe it's possible to lead my regiment there until daylight."

Lee had been sitting with a stupor of weariness settling over him, but now it was washed away by the sudden flash of temper at Ransom's statement of inability to carry out a mission. He spoke quickly, harshly, and forever afterwards would blame his loss of control to his weariness "Colonel, General Smith is moving right now with nine hundred of our boys to attack more than five thousand Mexicans in strong entrenchments. By God, he needs your regiment in front of Padierna by dawn."

There was a silent gasp from the three senior officers, and their eyes whipped around to focus on Lee.

"So I'll guide you for I've been over the route four times," Lee hastily added to cover his lapse of protocol.

"I accept your help," Ransom said, his expression showing anger at Lee's rebuke, but also pleased that he had been gotten off the hook of his own blunder of complaining about the difficulty of carrying out an order.

* * *

Lee and Ransom with his regiment of infantrymen arrived at the western edge of the Pedregal in the first gray light of dawn. The three artillery batteries were directly ahead of Lee and he could see the infantry already present were spread equally left and right.

"I recommend your men would be most visible if they were to extend the line both directions," Lee said and pointing out through the murk lying thick on the lava.

Ransom hadn't said a word to Lee during the march from Zacatepec, and he didn't now. He looked at Pillow standing nearby for orders. Pillow was busy glassing the Mexican entrenchments on the hill rising steeply just beyond the swift creek at their feet. Ransom shrugged and turned to his company captains that had gathered behind him.

"By alternate companies file left and right to extend the line. Once in position, draw all charges and load fresh ones. Then fix bayonets and show your flags. Don't let your men hide in the rocks, but make them show themselves so they can be counted by the Mexicans. Stand ready to advance on the enemy at my command."

A murmur of "Yes, sirs" rose from the captains.

The dawn grew brighter and Lee could see the companies of American infantry in their blue uniforms standing on top of the lava and facing Padierna. Bayonets had been unsheathed and fixed to musket barrels, and the company flags were unfurled and the staffs held high. A strong sense of pride swept over Lee and he felt good despite his near exhaustion. He had done his part, but where was Smith and his nine hundred.

The Mexicans cannons began to roar. Iron balls fell upon the American position. Here and there a man fell. The American cannons answered the fire pouring down upon them.

Lee heard a slackening in the Mexican fire. Through his glasses he noted confusion of the men in the entrenchments, with men looking behind them and up the hill. Then came the roar of volleys of musket fire from the crest of the hill above the Mexican guns and men began to fall in the trenches.

Blue clad men came streaming down the hillside in a running charge at the Mexicans. Seeing Smith's infantry, Ransom shouted at his men and they dropped down the steep incline into the stream and up the far side through Mexican fire. Caught between the two American forces, scores of Mexicans leapt out of the trenches and fled. In other places Mexicans fought stoutly and fierce fighting with glint of bayonet and boil of gun smoke swirled across the hillside.

Lee saw Smith's men turning captured Mexican guns and hurling shot after shot into the fleeing enemy. They ceased firing only when Ransom's men got so close that they would be hit.

Lee saw the tide turn fully with enemy soldiers retreating in large numbers. Then the pockets of fighting ended. In but a quarter-hour after the first volley from American muskets, the firing was stilled, with the entire Mexican earthworks in the hands of the invader.

Those of the Mexican garrison who had abandoned the fighting early on were fleeing up the San Angel Road. Lee saw hundreds of the Mexican army on the plateau north of Riley and Cadwalader were also caught up in the panic and joining in the wholesale rout toward Mexico City. Riley's and Cadwalader's brigades were hustling to cut off the road and prevent more Mexicans from escaping. Already large numbers of prisoners were being rounded up.

Smith's brigade came down off the hill and onto the San Angel Road. Yelling shrill cries of victory, they ran full tilt to catch the fleeing Mexican soldiers. Mexican cavalry spurring their horses to outdistance the pursuing Americans, trampled many of their own infantrymen under the hooves of their mounts.

Now was the time to strike the remainder of Santa-Anna's army, Lee thought. He hurried to his horse and hastened back across the lava to tell General Scott of the grand victory at Contreras.

He met Scott and his escort hurrying west mid-way of the lava field. Hearing the news, Scott lead them on to the San Angel Road and then north on the seven mile ride to Coyocan.

Chapter Thirty-Four

For two days Grant with the Fourth Infantry of Garland's brigade lay threatening the fortified hacienda of San Antonio and listened to Pillows division trade artillery and musket fire with the Mexicans near Contreras. They waited for Worth to give orders to move his division forward along the Acapulco Road and upon San Antonio once the enemy positions at Contreras had been taken. Grant didn't want for this to be like Cerro Gordo where he was held back while other men did the fighting.

With the morning breaking, Grant and several other officers had gone into the Pedregal and climbed to a ridge of lava and were glassing to the west four miles to the enemy entrenched on the hill adjacent to the San Angel Road. Now the first sound of artillery of the morning reached them, and seconds later the roar of a huge volume of musket fire came rolling over the lava.

"The attack has begun," Hazlit said from beside Grant.

"Yes, the cat's in the cradle now," Grant replied and still looking westward. Through his field glasses he saw the defenders desert their positions and run down the hillside to the road. A much larger gathering of troops to the north of the hill was also breaking and flooding down to the San Angel Road and fleeing toward the capital.

The bugle call to assemble pealed out from where Worth had positioned himself in the forefront of his men and the officers hastened off the lava and to their assigned stations. Clarke's brigade moved out, veering left onto the lava to flank San Antonio and strike it from the north. Once Clarke was in place, Garland's brigade would drive straight ahead up the causeway in a frontal assault.

Grant felt ready for the battle, more than that, he was anticipating the exhilaration and danger of combat. The realization came that he was always ready for a fight. At that thought, a cold tingle ran up his spine. Was there something wrong with him? Or were there many men who felt as he did? One thing he knew, that a man who fought bravely could kill more enemies.

Grant kept a wary eye on San Antonio. Near noon Clarke's brigade drew opposite the hacienda, he spotted the defenders streaming out through the gates and hastening up the Acapulco Road toward the Churubusco River some two miles away. Clarke abruptly turned his men toward the causeway. They came again upon the raised roadway just ahead of Garland's brigade. Worth hastened his long, drawn out division of men after the retreating Mexicans.

The morning sun shone hot on the green maguey and cornfields lining the Acapulco Road, and on Grant and the Fourth Infantry as they led Garland's brigade chasing the retreating Mexican infantry, cavalry, artillery, wagons, mules, and carriages. After two miles, they approached the place where the causeway crossed the Churubusco River. On the left of the road and in front of the river stood the Franciscan convent of San Mateo. Grant was immediately apprehensive for he knew convents with their massive stone walls made stout forts.

As if his thoughts had caused it, cannons and muskets roared up ahead. Immediately there erupted a bedlam of shouts and cries from wounded and terrified men and horses. Grant raised his glasses to look. Worth had blundered upon heavily defended Mexican positions and the lead elements of Clarke's brigade were being shot all to pieces by cannon and musket fire from the convent and the earthworks that extended from it to the bridge, and from breastworks and entrenched rows of cannon and riflemen along the high bank on the far side of the river. The convent was the strongest position. It consisted of the convent building with its dormitories, a church with a parapet roof, a high stone enclosure, a broad water filled ditch, two outside bastions, and stout breastworks on the west and south.

Grant saw Worth and Clarke waving their swords and riding among the men and ordering them off the causeway and into the thick stands of corn in the fields. "Damn you, Worth!" Grant thought. You should've had scouts out front to spot the fortified positions. Worth with his usual impetuous manner had moved forward recklessly and now his men were paying the butchers bill.

Hazlitt ran up beside Grant. "That bastard Worth has done it again," Hazlitt shouted and almost crying.

"The Sixth is breaking," Grant said in a flat, unruffled voice and wanting to calm Hazlitt down. The Sixth was one of Clarke's infantry regiments. Grant saw men and horses falling under sheets of grape, round shot, and musket balls.

Grant and Hazlitt continued to move forward with the Fourth Infantry as the Sixth pulled back nearly in a rout for two hundred yards or so. They saw the officers moving among their men shouting at them and finally rallying them and sending them forward. Withering fire knocked scores of the men and several officers off their feet and the regiment broke and retreated. The remaining officers of the Sixth once more tried to rally their rattled men.

"We're next," Grant called to Hazlitt as he saw Lieutenant Buckner, one of Worth's aids, rush up to Garland and call out to him.

Garland shouted orders and the infantrymen of his brigade sprang off the causeway to the right and hurried forward through the corn standing six feet tall. A battery of American artillery, unable to leave the road, began to set up their guns to fire. The ground was muddy from the rain of the night just past and the men slipped and slid. They had gone but a short ways when crossfire from muskets and cannon firing canister and grapeshot struck them from the Mexican position around the convent and the entrenchments along the river. Cornstalks were mowed down. Men, riddled by lead, fell. It was the hottest fire Grant had ever seen. He hated grapeshot worst of all.

He glanced at Hazlitt, and found him looking in his direction. Grant motioned ahead for he knew there was no turning back; they had to take the Mexican positions. Hazlitt nodded and shouted at the men near him, and led forward blindly through the tall corn and across the muddy field into the withering fire. Within a few yards, they came to an irrigation canal too wide to jump and too deep to wade.

"Build a path," Grant shouted and holstered his pistols to grab up an armload of cornstalks cut by Mexican bullets and threw them into the canal. Others quickly joined him and a ford was built and the men ran across. They had advanced only a few more yards when they collided with the wounded and shattered companies of the Sixth Infantry hurrying to the rear.

Grant drew his sword and jumped in front of the leaders of the mass of frightened men, and shouted at the top of his lungs for them to halt. Every man was needed in the fighting and couldn't be allowed to abandon the battlefield. Coming straight at him was a soldier without his musket and his scared eyes seeing nothing but some place far away from the deadly bullets.

Grant had to stop the first men. He swung the flat of his sword and struck the man a powerful blow across the chest. The fellow stumbled and went down on his face. Grant hit the next one, knocking him to his knees.

Grant heard shouts beside him where Hazlitt and other officers of the Fourth, and a few from the Sixth were cursing and striking the men with the flat of their swords to stop the rout. The officers brought the stampeding soldiers to a standstill. The shamefaced men began to respond to orders to form ranks. Within a few minutes order was restored and the Fourth and the remnant of the Sixth were advancing across the field. Here and there cornstalks and men fell from their rows under the hail of bullets.

Hazlitt came up close beside Grant. "We almost didn't stop them," Hazlitt said above the sound of the cannons and muskets.

"Yes, but look at them move now. If the men had had time to prepare for the firing, they wouldn't have broke."

"It was all Worth's fault. We'd be better off if he let Garland or Clarke lead."

"Or even you," Grant said.

"Or even you," Hazlitt said. He tried to smile, but his taut face refused to obey and gave only a grim stretching of the lips.

They came to an area where more than a hundred of Clarke's men lay dead or wounded in less than an acre of corn. Agonized moans came from the wounded and suffering. A private struggled to his feet and gazed around with a dazed, befuddled stare. Another sat up and started to yell plaintively for help. There wasn't any help to be had.

The Fourth and Sixth kept on and reached an irrigation canal, and there the officers ordered the men to take shelter. Standing in water to their waists, the men fired over the lip of the canal and returned the sheets of musket fire from the breastworks and convent. Grant heard heavy firing, both cannon and musket, coming from what he judged were other American units. He listened closely and knew not one unit was making headway against the Mexicans. This couldn't go on, men exposed to the guns of entrenched positions must take them or retreat.

Chapter Thirty-Five

Lee was just behind the squad of Worth's men creeping through the cornfield when the cannonball struck. The solid ball hit a man, killing him instantly, and knocking his corpse more than fifty feet. The remaining soldiers threw themselves flat and hugged the muddy ground.

Lee glanced down at the men as he hurried on past. There was nothing he could do for the them. He must get to General Scott and report what he had seen of the position and condition of the regiments. He reached the causeway that carried the Acapulco Road, hoisted himself upon it, scuttled swiftly across, and dropped back down onto the ground. He was now in Pillow's portion of the American line. He hastened on toward Coyoacan.

Scott's army was stalemated. His eight thousand men couldn't break Santa-Anna's force, a number Lee estimated that more than doubled that of the Americans. The battle had gone on for three hours with the Americans constantly on the verge of defeat. A crisis lay upon the small American army and a way had to be found to breach the Mexican fortifications.

The army lay in an irregular arc around the south side of the Mexicans in the San Mateo Convent and the entrenchments near the bridge and north of the Churubusco River. Worth's men were on the east, Pillow's in the center and Twiggs's on the west. All three divisions had been stopped and lay exposed and taking heavy losses. Worth's division in the cornfield was in the worst condition for the general had botched his advance and sent his men into concentrated fire from the strong fortifications and they had suffered terribly.

Twigg's was next in the difficulty of his position. Twiggs exultant and over-confident after the victory at Contreras had attack the walled convent without reconnoitering. The rapid and accurate volleys of fire coming from the enemy in the convent were deadly. Lee had counted seven cannons and estimated a garrison of two thousand. The sound of firing had been one continuous roll throughout the fighting. He pitied the men standing under the deadly storm of metal.

Lee, weary to the bone for he had now been on his feet and moving for a day and a half, passed through Pillow's and Twiggs's positions and went swiftly the quarter mile to the village of Coyoacan. He climbed into the tower of the village church to where Scott and part of his staff officers stood out of musket range and glassing the battlefield.

Scott lowered his glasses. "Well major, what's the situation?" he asked.

"Bad, sir. I'd estimate that nearly fifteen percent of our men are down and out of action. General Worth is in the worst condition with half of Clarke's brigade gone. We must do something quickly."

"We dare not retreat!" Scott exclaimed. "To lose this battle means our total defeat and all the fighting our brave boys have done would have been for nothing."

"General Worth and I talked about flanking the Mexicans north of the river," Lee volunteered. "He said that if he had another regiment, he'd try to get round them on the east. I asked Clarke about the river in front of him and he told me it's shallow enough for a man to wade and but twenty feet wide."

"If the General Worth could do that then he could rollup the Mexican entrenchment. Anything else."

"Yes, sir. I believe there's another reason to give General Worth a regiment. We've got our men too much concentrated on the convent. It's too strong to take because it's too well supported by the crossfire coming from the entrenchments that are within musket range."

"We need to block the escape route toward the city," Scott said as he raised his glasses to look at the battlefield. "It appears Riley's brigade is nearest to Worth," Scott was reading the battle flags visible along the American line.

"Yes, sir," Lee said.

Scott lowered his glasses and turned to Beauregard standing nearby and listening. "Lieutenant, go with these orders. Riley is to send Worth one of his regiments. Worth is to move upon the entrenchments north of the river as soon as he gets the regiment into position. Further, inform Twiggs and Pillow they are ordered to assault the convent with every man when Worth reaches the entrenchments."

"Yes, sir." Beauregard left at a trot to the cornfield were the Mexican cannonballs and musket balls slashed and chopped the cornstalks as if an invisible reaper was moving through them.

"Major Lee, carry orders to General Shields to ford the river west of the convent and circle around to the Acapulco Road. Then he's to turn and come south blocking the road and striking the convent. He's to prevent the escape of the enemy. General Pierce is unable to ride, so have Shields take that brigade along with him."

Scott pointed down at a company of Mounted Rifles and a troop of Dragoons. These men were to protect Scott from capture by the enemy. "Take all of those men with you," he said.

"Yes, sir," Lee said. Scott had now committed every man of the small American army to the battle. With no reserves, it truly was win or die. He hurried down from the church tower and went to his horse tied to a tree in the yard.

* * *

"I'm going to go have a look around," Grant said out to Hazlitt standing in the water of the canal near him.

After more than an hour of intense firing from Americans and Mexicans alike, Grant could wait no longer to see what was happening. He pulled himself up over the top of the canal and crawled off with bullets whizzing close above his head and cleaving the cornstalks to fall upon him. He made it safely to where the corn ended and the land rose a few feet. Cautiously he raised his head and saw he was within easy musket range of the Churubusco River.

Through his glasses he surveyed the scene, focusing first on the convent some two hundred yards distant. The deadly musket and cannon fire from that place had struck many of his comrades of the Fourth. He saw white faces sighting over the guns at the walls and in the convent windows. It was the San Patricio Battalion made up of Irish deserters fighting for Santa-Anna. Looking to the west, he saw at least a regiment of Riley's division moving to reinforce Worth's penned down men.

Worth's order to prepare to advance came down the line. The bugle sounded and the Fourth with the remainders of Garland's and Clarke's division rose to its feet and with a whoop raced for the river. Grant sprang to his feet and joined in. The men plunged into the river to the right of the bridge, their front overlapping the Mexican entrenchments on the right. Holding their muskets and cartridge boxes above the water, the men waded the river and climbed up the far bank. They stormed over the parapets and pushed through the embrasures of the breastworks. Stabbing and slashing, they struck the Mexicans.

The fighting was fierce hand-to-hand, the Mexicans defending bravely, stoutly. Grant emptied his pistols one after another at point-blank range. Two men fell. He turned to his saber, cutting and stabbing with every ounce of his skill and strength. The screams, curses, and blows of the men in mortal combat around him were reduced to a muted, unimportant murmur for his mind was totally fixed upon but one thought, kill the armed Mexican in front of him, and then the next one. The passage of time was lost to him as he fought beside his comrades in the trenches.

Grant again sensed the flow of time when there were no more enemy soldiers coming at him with a bayonet or sword or swinging a musket. He stood gripping his sword and drew a long, deep shuddering breath. He was alive and uninjured. He glanced around at the dead, and wounded, and the living. The men still standing wore blue.

He looked about and saw that all along the river, the Mexicans were breaking and fleeing. He saw James Longstreet and George Pickett, off some hundred feet on his left, plant their regimental flag upon the Mexican breastworks. Some men hurried to the captured guns and turned them upon the fleeing Mexicans. Others began to round up prisoners.

Grant looked at the convent. Americans had captured a 4-pound cannon on the bridge and had turned it against the convent. American gunners at artillery pieces outside the convent, no longer pinned down by enemy fire from the bridge, had wheeled their batteries up close and were blowing gaping holes in the convent walls. Infantry were closing in on the east side of this last Mexican holdout. Grant saw defenders, some looked like the Irish deserters, fleeing over the walls on the opposite side of the convent.

Grant joined with Hazlitt and a few of his men and splashed back across the river to help take it. They merged with nearly a hundred of Twiggs's men and twenty of so of the Mexican Spy Company and struck the front door of the convent.

They were met inside the tall entryway by three score of the San Patricio Battalion wielding their empty muskets like clubs. The deserters fought madly for they knew a noose waited for them if captured. Grant, both pistols empty, swung his saber to parry a ferocious swing of a musket at his face, and speared the man in the stomach. Jerking the blade free, he brought it up and swung down and half severed the man's shoulder from the body. He jumped to the right and moved forward along the stone wall and on the right side of the melee. There he bore in swinging and cutting. The fighting was savage with men crying wild animal sounds. Men fell bleeding, wounded, dead.

The San Patricio men were forced back and back. At a stone archway leading into a large adjoining room, they made a stand and held their ground for a few minutes. Then they were caught from behind by a number of Americans that had entered through one of the cannon ball holes in a wall. The deserters, something over a dozen still on their feet, threw their muskets down on the floor and raised their hands above their heads.

"By, God, we got Riley himself," shouted a man of the Fourth. "You bastard, you'll surely get the hangman's rope."

Grant recognized Sergeant John Riley among the bloody San Patricios. He had known him in northern Mexico before he swam the Rio Grande at Matamoras and joined the Mexicans for the promise of three hundred and twenty acres of land. In total three hundred Americans had deserted at Matamoras for the same promise.

Grant walked toward the front door. He passed Dominguez who stood leaning against a wall and breathing hard. The spy had fought like a man gone mad. Dominguez, a man that had forsaken his country, had fought other men who had forsaken theirs. A strange battle indeed.

Grant left the convent and went into the front yard. There he saw more of the San Patricios, perhaps fifty or so who had tried to escape by a side door, under heavy guard.

Glad the fighting was over, at least for now, Grant shoved his bloody saber into its scabbard. He looked to the north where Americans were chasing the Mexicans in a full rout toward Mexico City. The enemy should not be allowed to regroup. He crossed the Churubusco River, using the bridge this time, and hastened after the retreating foe.

Chapter Thirty-Six

As Lee and General Shields approached the road between Portales and Churubusco, a large Mexican force of cavalry and infantry came into sight moving south from the capital to reinforce their men at Churubusco and San Mateo Convent. The enemy officers saw the Americans and shouted orders and their troops began to swiftly take up a defensive position along the road.

"Get the artillery firing on them," Shields called to Lee. He spun his mount and rode off calling orders to his regimental and company commanders to form ranks and prepare to fire.

Lee ran his horse to Lieutenant Reno commanding the Howitzer battery. "Reno, blast the head of the Mexican column with canister. Try to hit the officers."

"Yes, sir," Reno shouted back. He yelled at his gunners and they speedily spun their weapons. With practiced skill, the gunners loaded and fired. The exploding shells fell upon the lead element of the Mexicans and knocked several men and horses down and sending others fleeing.

Lee surveyed the land beyond the end of the Mexican line and then reined his horse back toward Shields sitting his mount and watching the battlefield. All along the American line, men were falling under heavy enemy fire.

"General, we can't outflank them because the ground's too boggy," Lee yelled out above the roar of guns. "And we can't just stand here for their fire is too severe."

"We dare not retreat," Shields replied, his face strained and his right hand gripping the hilt of his sword. "That leaves just one option."

Shields spurred his horse along the rear of the men and crying out to their commanders, "Forward! Forward! Every man forward! Give them the bayonet! The bayonet!"

The officers and the hundreds of infantrymen took up Shields's cry. "Bayonet! Bayonet!" The line advanced into the enemy musket and cannon fire. Lee felt a warm surge of pride at the courage of the men.

The Mexicans stood fast, and another volley blazed out at the Americans. Bullets flew true and more gaps appeared in the blue line. Still the men on their feet went forward into the face of the enemy guns.

"They're ready to break," Lee shouted as he saw a weakening in the firing from the Mexican ranks.

"I see it," Shields called back.

American officers with their men in the advancing ranks also saw the wavering of the Mexicans and they shouted out, "Now, boys! Now! Charge! Charge!"

A wild, shrill yell rose from the soldiers and they broke into a run at their foe. First to break was the Mexican cavalry and they spurred and lashed their horses back up the road toward Mexico City. The infantrymen were close behind running off in all directions, dropping their weapons so that they could flee faster.

Shields's men gained the road just as the defeated Mexicans from Churubusco came wildly up it closely pursued by Worth's regiments after capturing the convent and the bridge. The two forces joined together and chased after the Mexicans.

Worth halted the chase after two miles and ordered the officers to attend to their wounded, and to form up the remainder of their men for return to Churubusco.

Lee wasn't sure stopping the pursuit was the best thing for Mexico City might lay open to the Americans. Yet there was danger in rushing ahead, Santa-Anna still had thousands of men, and the strength of the fortifications defending the city was unknown. And the American army was scattered, and had many wounded to care for, and many soldiers had used up their ammunition.

The crisis that had face the American army had ended after nearly four hours of the most savage fighting. Churubusco with its convent and entrenchments was the last stronghold of Mexico City's outer defenses and had been taken. Its guns and powerful fortifications had offered Santa-Anna a chance to break the American Army before they reached the city. He had failed. The American victory could not be credited to the senior generals for through lack of reconnoitering and coordinated action they had lost control of the battlefield for more than an hour. The junior officers and the veterans and raw recruits alike, by simply refusing to believe they could be beaten, had saved the army from destruction.

Lee reined his horse and rode south before the infantrymen clogged the road. He was weary to the bone, his heady woozy and the world trying to spin. He had been on his feet for a day and a half without rest, had crossed the Pedregal three times, much of that in darkness and rain, had been in the fight at Contreras, Churubusco and now with Shields near Portales. It was time to report to Scott and then find his bed.

He passed Americans too exhausted to march sitting beside the road with their heads hanging down. Others more undone, lay prone on the ground. Wounded Americans by the score were limping and staggering south toward the hospital at San Augustin. Often an uninjured man was helping his wounded comrade to walk. And there were wounded Mexicans mad with pain and despair dragging themselves along with torn and mangled limbs toward Mexico City. The passing Americans gave them but a glance.

Lee in his deep weariness was little affected by the suffering of the wounded. A truth came to him, for a soldier to fully function, he must always be able to stand outside of himself and look dispassionately at the madness and carnage of battle.

Lee came up behind an American officer walking south in the direction of Churubusco. As Lee passed, the man looked up and Lee recognized the quartermaster Lieutenant Grant. The lieutenant was a nightmarish sight. His clothing was all wet and muddy, and his sword hand and lower arm were covered with blood and splotches of blood were scattered across his breast and some on his face, as if an artery had spewed out its red liquid onto him. Through this frightful mask, his blue eyes regarded Lee with a weary, but calm expression.

"Are your all right?" Lee asked, concerned that part of the blood was from a wound on Grant.

"Just dog tired," Grant replied.

"I know the feeling," Lee said. From the appearance of Grant, he was one of the young officers, one of the brave warriors that had driven the Mexicans in hand-to-hand fighting from their fortifications at Churubusco, and had the blood of his dead foes upon him to show what he had done. Lee had gathered information that resulted in the deaths of the enemy, carried orders for his comrades to fight, and had aimed cannon that killed men. However he had not yet stood eyeball-to-eyeball with an individual foe and fought him to the death with hand weapons. He thought that was when a man knew whether or not he had true courage.

Lee sent his horse ahead. At the crossroads near the convent, he turned right and rode to Coyoacan. There he made his report to Scott.

When Lee finished, Scott spoke, "You are released from duty, major, go and rest."

"Thank you, sir."

In a stupor of fatigue, Lee didn't feel up to riding to San Augustin. He slept like a dead man in all his clothes in a bed in a deserted house in Coyoacan. Around him many other weary officers and soldiers found shelter instead of traveling to their camps. He didn't hear the sentry's challenges during the night, or the snorts and tromps of his horse tied just outside his open window.

* * *

In the growing evening dusk, Grant passed through Churubusco and down the Acapulco Road. On the causeway opposite the cornfield, he encountered a long line of ambulance wagons drawn up. Medical orderlies were going empty handed into the field, with others returning carrying bodies. Pain filled moans and groans came from bullet torn bodies lying in the beds of the vehicles. Grant walked on.

Night caught him as he entered San Augustin. By candlelight in his tent, he soaked in a tub of water and washed the blood and grime from his tired body. He gave little thought to the men he had slain. He recognized that he had changed as the months of war passed, and was changing still, becoming a hardened warrior who was ever more unmoved by the deaths and destruction around him. What would all this mean for the future? He guided his mind away from those dark thoughts. He climbed from the tub, dried himself, and fell naked upon his bed and went to sleep.

* * *

Lee left his tent, saddled his horse and rode off to report to Scott. This was the second day after the battle of Churubusco. The 138 Americans slain at Contreras and Churubusco had been sewed into their blankets, placed in wooden coffins and, to the sound of drums and the chaplain saying prayers over the dead, buried in shallow graves in a meadow just outside San Augustin. The 865 wounded men were receiving treatment in commandeered houses in the town.

The American losses were staggering and Lee worried at what such a weakening of the army meant for there were more battles yet to be fought to capture the capital. Fortunately Santa-Anna's forces also had heavy losses. The estimate of killed and wounded were more than 4,000. The number of captured enemy was more precise, 2,645 with many officers, eight of them generals. Eighty-five of the San Patricio Battalion had been captured, along with their commander Colonel Francisco Moreno. Unfortunately about 200 of the deserters had escaped. Scott had directed court-martial boards be convened to hear the desertion charges against the captured San Patricios.

* * *

With a troop of Dragoons out front, General Scott and his staff officers, and accompanied by Trist, left San Augustin and struck out to the north along the Acapulco Road. A caravan of wagons loaded with headquarters paraphernalia and Scott's personal possessions followed.

A mile past Churubusco, a handsomely polished carriage drawn by a pair of fast stepping trotters came in sight on the road ahead of Scott and his entourage. The vehicle carried two military men, a general and a young lieutenant. The lieutenant drove. A large white flag on a tall staff was attached to the vehicle.

"Mexican officers," said Hitchcock.

"Yes indeed," Scott said. "I was expecting to see them after Mackintosh's visit." Edward Mackintosh of the British legation in Mexico City had come to San Augustin the preceding day to request safety for his consulate and the British citizens, and to intercede for Santa-Anna who wanted a meeting with Scott to discuss an armistice.

The captain of Dragoons, worried about Scott's safety, reined his mount up beside Scott. "General, should I halt them out aways until we know their intentions?"

"No, allow them to approach."

The driver pulled his team to a stop so that the seat of the carriage was opposite Scott's horse. The Mexican general was dressed in full dress uniform. He was thin of body and thin of face. He ran his sight over Scott's epaulets, and then stepped down to the ground.

"You must be General Scott. I am General Ignacio Mora y Villamil." He saluted smartly.

Scott returned the salute. He spoke to Trist. "Please interpret for us, if you would."

Trist faced the Mexican. "Yes, this is General Scott. And I am Nicholas Trist, special envoy of President Polk."

"I have heard of you, Mr. Trist."

"What can we do for you, general?"

"I have letters from Francisco Pacheco, Minister of Foreign Relations and Charles Bankhead, the British Minister." Villamil extracted two seal papers from a leather pouch on the seat beside him and handed them to Scott.

"Mr. Trist and I shall study them carefully," Scott said, and shoved the papers into the front of his tunic.

"Is there anything else?" Scott asked.

"Yes, I have a verbal message from General Santa-Anna." Villamil glanced at the other officers within hearing range, and evidenced obvious reluctance to speak in front of them.

"Yes," Scott said, and a slight smile played about his mouth at the Mexican's action.

Villamil gave the slightest of shrugs. "General Santa-Anna has directed me to inform you that he desires peace and hopes a treaty can be swiftly agreed upon."

"Tell the general that I have the same hopes," Scott said. "Should you have further need to find me, my headquarters will be at Tacubaya."

"I shall relay your words." Villamil stepped up into his carriage and spoke to the lieutenant. The man wheeled the carriage around in the road, tapped each of the horses once with his whip, and sent them trotting back toward Mexico City.

"Lead on, captain," Scott said to the captain of Dragoons.

Lee was worried. A liar and trickster such as Santa-Anna had proved himself to be, could so easily take advantage of an honest man like Scott.

Chapter Thirty-Seven

"Unacceptable! Totally unacceptable!" Scott's voice was harsh. He turned to Trist. "Nicholas, listen to this if you would. Pacheco proposes a year's truce to discuss 'the preliminaries of peace'. The PRELIMINARIES of peace, do you hear that, and not peace." Scott tossed the paper onto his desk.

"Perhaps so general, but consider what British Minister Bankhead has to say in his letter. I quote, 'I have been warned by intelligent neutrals and some of your American residents against a precipitous attack upon the city. And my humble opinion is the same. A treaty would be more likely to occur while the Mexican government officials were in possession of their capital, rather than have them scattered and the capital in the hands of an invader. Should the officials be driven to other towns, then it may not be possible to assemble a quorum to deliberate and reach a treaty'."

Lee sat with Hitchcock and listening to the two men discussing the letters delivered by General Villamil. Upon arriving at Tacubaya, Scott had established his headquarters in the sumptuous Bishop's Palace overlooking the town. From his window he had a fine view of Mexico City. The general's staff officers had taken quarters in commandeered homes close by. Tacubaya lay spread across a small, low range of hills south of Mexico City. The wealthy members of the British colony had summer homes there.

"There may be truth in what Bankhead writes," Scott said.

"Colonel Hitchcock, what's you thoughts on whether or not to grant a truce?" Scott asked his chief of staff.

"I strongly recommend against it," Hitchcock said with feeling. "Our experience with Santa-Anna tells me that it will serve no useful purpose."

Lee was surprised at the sharpness in Hitchcock's response. Usually the man couched his recommendations and suggestions in an unemotional manner.

"I see. How about you Major Lee, what do you think?"

"General, it isn't clear-cut whether or not to have a truce. Santa-Anna may be playing for time. Or he may be serious. I do have a recommendation, if the decision is to accept a truce, then Castle Chapultepec should be occupied before it begins. From its hilltop location and with its cannon, it dominates the main road into the city."

Scott frowned, and Lee wondered if it was because of his wishy-washy answer about the truce, or the recommendation of occupying Chapultepec Castle.

Scott spoke to Trist. "My goal is to gain the president's objectives and end hostilities. I'll do whatever is necessary to accomplish that. You need time to negotiate with the governmental officials. Should you succeed there would be no need for more fighting. A year is unthinkable, but a short truce that can be ended swiftly might be proper. However I shall continue to hold the army in a battering and assaulting position for I intend to immediately move upon the city if the talks fail."

* * *

On the eighth night after the beginning of the truce, Grant returned from Mexico City with five hundred pack mules with each loaded with about three hundred pounds of supplies. The trip had come-off without a hitch. Santa-Anna had made arrangements for the merchants of the city to open their doors in the night while the population slept, and the Americans using pack animals, that were less noisy than wagons, could come and buy provisions. Scott had cashed government drafts for $300,000 with the bankers in the city and Grant had money. The merchants smiled when Grant paid for his large purchases with silver and gold.

At army central stores, Grant set his quartermasters to work under O'Doyle to unloading the supplies from the backs of the mules. The time was near midnight, still he didn't feel like sleep and directed his steps toward the large cantina at the bottom of the hill upon which the Bishop's Palace rested. The cantina had become a favorite hangout for officers when off duty. He heard the rumble of men's voices while still half a block away from the cantina.

Grant estimated nearly a hundred officers in the spacious room, which was a surprise considering the late hour. Most of the tables were full. The ceiling was high, yet seemed low due to the dense layer of tobacco smoke hanging against it. He went straight to the bar on the far side of the room and ordered whiskey from the nearer of the two Mexican barkeeps. Holding his drink carefully, he wound a course among the tables and found a seat with Hazlitt, Cavallin, Chilton, and Lieutenant Steptoe of the artillery. He saw Lee, Beauregard, McClellan, Hitchcock, and Joe Johnston at a nearby table, and nodded at Beauregard who had caught his eye. Beauregard nodded back.

"Any trouble going into the city?" Hazlitt asked.

"Nope. Routine. Why such a big crowd tonight?"

"They're arguing about the truce and Santa-Anna strengthening the city's fortifications," Chilton said.

"A lot of it's whiskey talk," Cavallin said.

"We've won a wonderful victory and undoubtedly the greatest battle our country has ever fought, but instead of taking the Mexican capital we sit here and talk," Kirby Smith growled out his complaint. He was at a table nearby with Longstreet, Pickett and Hooker.

"The truce has merit from the point of giving Trist time to try and negotiate a treaty," Hooker said.

Grant agreed with the need for Trist to have time. Still he understood the men's frustration with the delay for he felt it too.

"From what I've seen in our dealings with the Mexs, I don't think any negotiation will lead to a treaty," Smith shot back. "In truth, I hope they don't agree to one. That'll give us a chance to thrash them proper. As scared and disorganized as they are, we could form up in the morning, march on them, and be sleeping in the city tomorrow night."

"Not from what I've heard," said Hooker. "Santa-Anna's pulled his army together and has strongly fortified the city."

Beauregard spoke to Grant. "Sam, you've been in the city several times. What have you seen in the way of Santa-Anna working on his defenses?"

"Not much. We go in at night and straight to the plaza and back out. The garitas and causeways are strongly fortified that's for certain. They'd be murder to take." Grant did not want to be drawn into the bickering and lamenting. Everything that would be said here tonight had already been said many times over during the days since the truce went into effect.

"General Scott should let us reconnoiter and know what the Mexicans have done to strengthen their defenses for I believe full well they are, day and night," Beauregard said.

Hitchcock gave Lee a knowing look. Both men had heard Dominguez report that Santa-Anna had reassembled his army and was working steadily to improve his defenses. Scott refused to do the same for he had given his word. No argument from Hitchcock or Lee could persuade him to do otherwise. Scott had told them that as long as Trist was negotiating, he would do nothing to break the conditions of the truce. Those negotiations might soon end for just this past morning, Trist had given the Mexicans a one day ultimatum to come to terms on a treaty of he would cease to meet with them.

Lee's main concern was that Scott hadn't required Santa-Anna to surrender Chapultepec Hill before the armistice went into effect. It possessed a strong defense and would be a difficult fortification to take. Still Scott was an honorable man and had done what he thought was best under the circumstances.

Hitchcock rose to his feet and his voice cut through the din of complaints. "Our commander has made a decision to allow time for Mr. Trist to try to negotiate a treaty that would stop further fighting. We must uphold him in this. Further, we as officers must be careful about what we say in front of our men." Every officer in the cantina listened to Hitchcock for he was a full colonel, the Army Inspector General, and Scott's chief of Staff.

Smith recognized he was being reprimanded. "I accept that colonel. If we can bring proof that Santa-Anna has broken the truce, can we present it to the general?"

"Certainly. In fact I will help you present it." Hitchcock reseated himself.

Grant knew Hitchcock had shut off the grumbling for now. He pointed at the American Star on the table in front of Hazlitt. "Okay if I have a look at that?"

"Sure. It's hot off the press."

Grant thought there was a sorrowful cast to Hazlitt's eyes. He was probably wrong. He began to scan the paper and came to promotions. The list was substantial for Scott rewarded those who served bravely and wisely. Among the names on the list were two of Grant's classmates at West Point, Buckner and Granger that had been promoted to captain. The twenty-year-old

McClellan had been promoted to full lieutenant. Lee had been made permanent major and recommended for lieutenant colonel. Garland had been recommended for brigadier general, and Hazlitt for captain. Hooker, Longstreet, and Pickett were recommended for promotion. Grant's name was missing.

Grant placed the paper back on the table. He picked up his whiskey and drank it down.

* * *

The third day of September was winding down to evening when Nicholas Trist returned from the city after a day of negotiations with the commissioners of the Mexican Government. Dispirited and fatigued he entered Scott's headquarters in Tacubaya where the general was discussing the army's supply of ammunition with Lee, Worth, Hitchcock, and Captain Huger, Chief of Ordnance. Trist had the privilege of coming directly to Scott's office without being announced by an orderly. Scott immediately bade him to have a seat.

"You have news," Scott said and looking into Trist's disturbed face.

"Yes, general."

Worth and the junior officers started to rise. Scott quickly motioned for them to remain seated. "Stay, gentlemen, for you should hear this first hand."

Scott spoke to Trist. "Your news of course has to do with the ultimatum you gave the Mexicans yesterday?"

Trsit nodded sorrowfully. "We can't agree on terms and so I've suspended the talks. They are willingly to give up Texas and upper California for they are distant from their capital and we've already taken them. They won't surrender New Mexico and President Polk has given me specific instruction that we must have it."

"What reaction do they have to the money that's being offered?"

"It doesn't seem to be of much interest to them. It's the loss of territory and its Mexican population that makes them unwilling to come to terms. There's another important reason the government officials won't agree to the terms we want. Some of the outlying provinces threaten to secede if peace overtures are accepted. The governor of Queretaro State has stated that any sale of territory would mean a general secession, and that he will certainly take his state out of the nation if a treaty is made with us. General, I fear further talks are useless."

"I had hoped to avoid assaulting their capital, but I have no alternative. I shall send a notice to Santa-Anna that the truce has ended due to his having violated the truce by strengthening his fortifications. General Worth, you shall have the lead in the coming action so prepare your men and weapons.

"Yes, sir," Worth said with a strictly military tone.

Lee had thought Worth might have shown some gratitude for Scott had just given him a prize by allowing his division to make the main assault. Yet there had been none. The hard feelings between Worth and Scott since Puebla, and even before that, hadn't eased one bit.

Scott turned to Lee. "Major, you and your engineers reconnoiter the roads leading into the city and their defenses and make reports on their use as avenues for the attack on the city."

Chapter Thirty-Eight

September 8, 1847. From Worth's command post on a rise of land behind the American lines, Lee watched the dawn unfurl its pale gray glow across the cloudless sky. The land took shape, the black night shadows in the valley bottom shrinking and dying. He lifted his field glasses to examine Molino del Rey, The King's Mill, which was becoming visible in the growing light some one thousand yards distant.

The Molino was a combination of a flourmill and a foundry for casting bronze cannon. He had examined its white walls many times during the past few days. It was a long stone building with a few smaller ones also made of stone, and all extending in a nearly straight line north to south. The narrow passageways between the buildings were strongly barricaded with sandbags. The heavy walls and the sandbag reinforced two feet high stone parapets on the flat roofs made the buildings fort-like. To the left of the Molino about three hundred yards and anchoring its right flank was Casa Mata, a squat stone citadel used by the Mexicans as a powder magazine. More than a score cannons had been placed in redoubts in the earthworks surrounding the structure. Lee had seen a regiment of soldiers guarding it. All in all the Mexicans were in a very strong positions. The cannon on Chapultepec Hill could cover the eastern segment of the battlefield, the guns of Casa Mata the western section. The Molino made a continuous breastwork covering the entire front. The line in total was nearly a mile long and he could see no weak point.

Behind the Molino was a large grove of cypress trees extending to the base of Chapultepec Hill, Grasshopper Hill, a two-hundred-foot high volcanic hill rising abruptly from the plain to loom over the main road leading into Mexico City. Chapultepec Castle, a massive masonry structure of two stories capped the hill. The Castle had been the resort of long dead Aztec princes and later used by the Viceroys of Spain.

Worth and Lee had drawn up an assault plan that Scott had approved. El Molino would be bombarded by cannon fire and then the infantry would rush in and mop up the defenders that hadn't been killed or fled. Though El Molino would be a tough fortification for infantrymen to take, its stone walls could be easily demolished by American siege cannon. Once El Molino had been taken, Worth would turn his men loose on Casa Mata.

Lee shifted his glasses to study the arrangement of the Americans assembled to assault the Molino. Lee didn't believe the assault was the correct thing to do. He and several other senior officers after intensive examination of the Molino had recommended to Scott that it be by-passed for it didn't threaten access to the city. It could prove to be a distraction and cost men's lives. Scott had rebutted them by saying he had information that he believed accurate that church bells were being brought from the city to the Molino where they were being melted down and made into cannon for the defense of the capital. Therefore the Molino had to be taken. Lee and the others had then argued that the news could be a rumor that Santa-Anna had spread, and further that any cannons made there after today would be too late to help the Mexicans since the Americans were ready to move upon the city. Scott could not be swayed to change his mind, saying that it would be but a minor effort to capture the Molino.

Lee focused his glasses on Garland's infantry waiting some three hundred yards directly south of the Molino, and just behind Captain Drum of the Fourth Artillery standing ready with four 6-pounders to fire upon the Molino and to ward off any flank attack from Chapultepec. On the ridge a little farther left was Major Huger with two 24-pound siege guns that would do the heavy work. Next on the left was Major Wright with five hundred volunteers drawn from Worth's six infantry regiments. Close on Wright's left was Kirby Smith's battalion waiting to support the five hundred. Farther left was Colonel Duncan with his wheeled artillery. Next left was Clarke's brigade of infantry facing the west end of the Molino and threatening the Casa Mata. Finally on the far left was Major Sumner with 270 Dragoons. His task was to hold off any Mexican cavalry that might try to enter the fray.

* * *

In the gray darkness, Grant sat on the hard surface of the road and marked time with the infantry of Garland's brigade. He had awaken at 3 o'clock, ate a little cold food Valere had prepared the evening before, and marched with the men from Tacubaya to participate in the battle to take the Molino. He waited silently with his thoughts turned inward to Julia and his family, mostly to Julia.

Yesterday as Garland's preparations for the assault on El Molino had been in progress, Grant had gone to him and made a strong plea to be formally assigned to join the men that would do the fighting. He had argued that the final battle to capture the Mexican capital was starting and that if they didn't win there would be no need for a quartermaster lieutenant. The battle was to be victory or death. If it was to be death, he wanted his to be fighting with his Fourth Infantry.

Without comment or expression, Garland listened to Grant's argument to the end. Then he gave Grant a bleak smile. "My orders are to help capture the Molino and to stop any reinforcements coming from Chapultepec. Your name will be on the roster of those men of the Fourth Infantry."

A noticeable lessening of the darkness came and with it there was a stirring of the men as a whispered order from Garland at the front passed down from officer to officer. The brigade crept another hundred yards nearer the Molino and just behind Drum's battery of 6-pounders and there halted on the road to again wait.

Grant saw the grim walls of the Molino form up ghost-like out of the morning dusk. He could make out the windows opening out to the front and the parapet extending above the flat roofline. Both were excellent locations from which enemy riflemen could shoot while still being protected from return fire. Had he been the commanding general he wouldn't be attacking the Molino and Chapultepec, but rather attacking the capital from the north. He had been in that direction on a foraging expedition and examined the gates through his field glasses and knew they were less well defended than the southern and western gates. Of course he must in honesty to General Scott, admit that getting the army there could be a problem.

He rose to his knees for a better view of the battlefield. The principal assault column, the five hundred "forlorn hopes", led by Major Wright was located in a low swale between the command post and the Molino. The name "forlorn hopes" came from the immense danger the men would face as they charged forward to capture the Mexican cannon entrenched in front of the wall of the Molino. Grant knew that many of the men of that initial charge would die. The cash bonuses and promotions promised to obtain the volunteers would mean nothing to dead men.

The WHUMP of one of the 24-pound, smoothbore cannon jarred the air. A gaping fissure appeared in the front wall near the center of the Molino as the solid ball struck. A section of the roof above collapsed, tumbling men and weapons into the void. Mexicans were dead. The battle had begun.

The two big siege guns continued to work, two shots per minute, shaking the ground. A cloud of hot gunpowder smoke formed in the quiet air and hung over the battery. Twelve rounds boomed out and then the guns fell silent. Much too soon, thought Grant. The defenses could not yet have been much weakened. He rose to his feet for an unobstructed view. The five hundred "forlorn hopes" were dashing toward the entrenched Mexican artillery. The presence of the men on the field had halted the firing of the big siege guns. Why hadn't Wright waited for the guns to knock the building into rubble with cannonballs and kill the Mexicans manning the artillery?

The Mexican cannon roared and flung a furious storm of grape and canister into the Americans. The charging blue line flinched. Men began to fall, a few, then by the tens as the cannon kept firing. The line of "forlorn hopes" was shredded and torn wholesale, the name proving too awfully true. Behind the line of soldiers still on their feet and moving forward, the ground was littered with blue-clad bodies.

Muskets crackled out from the windows and the roof parapets of the Molino, adding their blizzard of lead balls to do slaughter. Much reduced in number, Wright's men reached the cannons in front of the Molino, swarmed over them, and shooting and stabbing drove off the artillerists and the infantry stationed there to guard the guns.

The Mexican musket fire from the Molino proved to deadly and Wright's men faltered and broke. They whirled and ran toward the rear. Mexicans surged out of the Molino and onto the Americans left at the battery of cannon. Grant saw the Mexicans shooting the Americans left lying wounded on the ground. They began to search through the pockets to rob the dead.

Smith's battalion leapt forward down the slope of the hill from where they had waited and swept over the battery of cannon. Taking heavy losses, the battalion was brought to a halt. Smith stood among the hissing bullets and shouted at his men and they regrouped behind him. With Smith leading, the men again stormed toward the center of the Molino.

Grant felt a tightening of his chest for he feared for the safety of his good friend Fred Dent who was a commander of a company of Smith's battalion. Then his attention was yanked to the front by Garland's stentorian yell to charge. The brigade burst into a run at the Molino. They were met by withering canister and grape fire and Garland ordered a withdrawal to Drum's battery of guns.

Grant flung a look around to see from where the killing fire was coming. Sergeant Robertson, a man Grant knew was shouting and pointing. "There! There!" He was pointing at Mexican cannons on the thrashing floor of the Molino.

"Our boys are shooting at the wrong place," Grant yelled back to Robertson. "Help me."

Grant and Robertson ran to help the artillerymen place their pieces correctly and bring their fire against the Mexican guns on the thrashing floor. Taking advantage of the cover from the singing bullets provided by a stone wall, they shoved a pair of the guns to within less than two hundred yards of the Mexicans and opened fire with canister. The shells exploding among the Mexicans drove them from their guns to flee into the mill.

Grant and Robertson joined with Captain Thorn of the Fourth Infantry and his party of men and charged toward the mill. A short ways farther along, Grant halted abruptly; Fred Dent was slumped over unconscious and bleeding from a wound in his thigh. Grant swiftly examined the wound and found it wasn't too serious. He laid Dent upon the flat top of a nearby wall where the hospital orderlies could easily spot him when they came searching for the wounded.

Grant waited for a slackening in the enemy's fire, and then ran through the smoke to overtake Thorn and Robertson breaking down one of the barricaded doors leading into the Molino. As he drew near the two men he saw a Mexican running at Thorn and about to sink a bayonet into his back.

"Look out!" Grant yelled.

Thorn sprang out of the way. Robertson had heard the Grant's shout and whirled and seeing the danger, shot the Mexican through the head.

The interior of the cavernous Molino was full of the enemy and the fighting was ferocious, pistols popping and muskets banging. Grant quickly emptied his two pistols into brown-faced men. The firing stopped with all guns empty and the fighting became one of stabbing bayonets and swinging sabers.

The Americans took the big room and hurried to the door to the next one. There they halted, speedily reloaded, and shooting through the open door, emptied their weapons into the room. They charged in with bayonets and swords ready. Grant cutting ferociously with his steel blade and stepping over and trampling upon the fallen enemy, went forward with his comrades. The Mexicans gave ground slowly. He saw a young Mexican captain with a slender body and a aristocratic Spanish face swiftly dispatch two Americans with a narrow, two edged sword. After the second man fell, the Americans held back knowing their clumsy bayonets were no match for the agile man with the sword. With a taunting smile of belief in his skill, the Mexican motioned with his sword to come at him.

Robertson glanced at Grant as if to say, you have a sword so that man is yours to fight. Grant warily evaluated the captain. Mexico City was famous for its dueling schools where wealthy young men were taught the use of pistol and sword. This captain must be one of those pupils. Still there was nothing else to do but fight. Grant sprang forward and took on the Mexican. They parried, cut, thrust. Within half a minute, Grant wished he had practiced his swordsmanship more diligently. He was far out-classed.

With mastery and strength, the captain parried one of Grant's strikes. Instantly and with amazing speed he moved sideways to come in on the side while Grant's saber had been knocked out of position. Grant knew the Mexican had him. He was as good as dead.

The captain's foot came down upon a musket lying on the floor and he was thrown momentarily off balance. As he caught himself, the expression on his face of believing he had certain victory changed to one of sudden doubt.

Now! Strike! The warrior in Grant shouted. Grant lunged forward, and as he did so brought his saber in, aligned its point just so, and thrust it out fiercely at his foe. The honed steel point of the blade pierced the man's front just below his rib cage and exited out his back. With a great sense of his life given back, Grant wrenched his saber free.

The Mexican captain, his brown, pain-filled eyes locked on Grant, put out a hand to hold himself erect. His hand found only air and he fell to the floor of the mill.

Grant yelled out to the Americans around him. "Press them! Press them!"

The stalled Americans doggedly moved ahead stabbing and cutting. The Mexicans stubbornly gave ground toward the opposite side of the big room. Their backs came up against the far wall. One frightened foe spotted a door close by and broke and fled out through it. The remaining twenty or so Mexicans scrambled for the door, bunched up for a moment at the narrow opening, then broke out onto a paved courtyard. There they split up and ran swiftly into the cypress trees behind the Molino. Grant and the squad of men with him followed out onto the courtyard and watched the Mexicans fleeing in the direction of Chapultepec Hill.

He led his band of men into the next building, and there encountered a surviving squad of Kirby Smith's men. The squad corporal touched his ear and pointed upward. Grant listened and heard footsteps on the roof. He nodded and glanced around for a stairway up. He saw none, but there was a carriage with a long tongue. He motioned for the men to help him and they propped the tongue against a wall and chocked the wheels. Using the tongue as a sort of ladder that reached to within three feet of the top, he shinnied up it and came out onto the roof. Other men came close behind him.

A private was patrolling back and forth across the roof with his musket held ready to fire at nearly a dozen Mexican infantrymen, one a lieutenant. All alone he had corralled the soldiers and was holding them prisoner.

He saw Grant and smiled proudly. "Lieutenant, I always thought one of us was worth a dozen of them."

"Ppears you're right," Grant said.

The officer offered his sword and Grant accepted it. Then Grant spoke to his men. "Disable all their muskets."

With pleased smiles, the soldiers broke the muskets against the edge of the parapet and tossed them over the side to the ground.

"Take them to wherever prisoners are being held." Grant said and indicating the cowed Mexicans.

By way of a ladder at the wall of the building, Grant went down to the main floor. He joined with other Americans and they started a search through the buildings for the cannon foundry. They found a large forge for melting bronze, but there were no church bells. From the appearance of the forge, no bronze had been melted here for many months. Looking further, they discover a few old cannon molds. Santa-Anna had again made fools out of the Americans. And made them pay a terrible price in blood and death for their foolishness.

Chapter Thirty-Nine

Lee felt outraged as he looked down onto the battlefield in front of the Molino where hundreds of blue-clad soldiers littered the ground like broken dolls. He had witnessed the aborted cannonading by Huger's big siege guns because of Wright coming early onto the field, and Smith coming to help but not quite soon enough, and Garland fighting into the Molino. All the fighting had ended with the Molino in the hands of the Americans. But what a terrible waste of good men. Now Huger, Drum, and Duncan had turned their guns upon Casa Mata and Lee could see the damage being done to its walls as cannon balls hit.

Beside Lee, Worth spoke to one of his aids, "Tell Major McIntosh to take Casa Mata with the bayonet."

"General, shouldn't we wait for the cannons to do their work?" Lee asked quickly. Surely Worth had seen the horrible example of men dying because too few cannonballs had been thrown at the enemy's fortifications.

"That could take hours, and McIntosh and his boys can take it readily enough." Worth said impatiently and motioned at his aid to mount his horse.

The aid sprang astride and raced off to McIntosh waiting with his infantry. Lee felt like striking Worth for his lack of care for his men. Instead he put his glasses upon McIntosh and soon saw him leading his brigade upon Casa Mata. The Mexicans opened up on the Americans with a murderous fire from cannon and muskets. Major McIntosh fell on the slope of the ground in front of the powder magazine. Other soldiers toppled over by platoons. The remaining Americans threw themselves down behind the embankment and firing their muskets began to pick off the Mexicans at Casa Mata. After a quarter hour of so the Americans ran out of ammunition and pulled back out of range. This freed the guns of Duncan, Drum, and Huger and they resumed bombardment of Casa Mata with a vengeance. Within half an hour, the Mexicans raised a white flag.

* * *

Colonel Hitchcock had come up beside Lee and now spoke. "A few more such victories and our army will be destroyed." His voice crackled with anger.

"We must have lost 700 maybe 800 men in less than two hours," Lee replied. Worth and his aids had left the command post to return to headquarters. Lee had stayed behind and was watching the hospital orderlies load their ambulance wagons with the wounded and hasten away to the hospital in Tacubaya.

"Nothing could've been more badly bungled," Hitchcock agreed. "Wright and Worth acted like jackasses. If they had waited for the cannons to do their work, we need not have lost a dozen men."

Lee thought the same thing and promised himself that if he ever commanded an army that he wouldn't make the same mistake.

* * *

Grant arrived at Tacubaya sweating from a rapid pace under the hot September sun. He went directly to the town's church that had been appropriated along with several of the nearby buildings and converted to a hospital in anticipation of the coming battles. A number of ambulances were lined up along the street in front of the church and orderlies were carrying men on stretchers inside.

He saw Cavallin climbing the steps of the church and called out. "Tom, wait up and I'll go in with you."

"Who'd you going to see?"

"Fred Dent."

"Yeah, your future brother-in-law."

"How about you?"

"Mat Chilton got hit hard by an exploding shell."

Grant and Cavallin entered the hospital to the smell of medicine, disinfectant, and the cloying odor of blood. All the pews and seats had been removed from the high domed chapel and piled against the wall in the far end. On the left side of the chapel and across the back, more than a hundred wounded men lay on cots or blanket pallets on the floor. On the right near the front a score of surgeons were working over men strapped down on tables. At some operating tables, orderlies were adding their strength to hold the patients still while the surgeons operated. Some surgeons worked quietly with scalpels, probes, lancets, and needles and thread. Others plied saws that gave off an ugly rasping sound as they cut live bone. Surgeons were quick to amputate seriously damaged limbs of soldiers to lessen the chance of infection and gangrene and death. A skilled surgeon could remove an arm in five seconds, a leg in seven. Time was most important because the human body could stand just so much pain before it died.

A man lying on a pallet on the floor motioned Grant to come closer. He struggled to sit up, pushing with his arms for he had no legs below the mid-thigh to counterbalance the weight of his upper body. His eyes, hot and piercing, locked on Grant.

"Laudanum, damn you!" the man cried out in a tortured voice. "Surgeon, hear me. Give me laudanum. I'm not getting my fair share. Oh God! My legs hurt. You say they're gone, but you're wrong. They hurt to the very tips of my toes."

Grant turned away from the man, feeling repulsed by him and feeling shame that he was. He went on with Cavallin to Chilton lying pale and motionless on a table.

"How is he?" Cavallin said to the surgeon applying a bandage to Chilton.

"Gravely injured. I've just taken six pieces of shrapnel out of him with one being right against his heart."

"He looks dead," Cavallin said and staring intently at Chilton and looking for a sign of life.

"He's still alive. He looks that way for I've used some of the new medicine called ether that puts a man to sleep and prevents him from feeling the pain while he's operated upon. The lieutenant's life from here on is in the hands of God"

"Colonel, how about Dent there?" Grant asked and pointed at the cot where Dent lay with his eyes closed.

"He has a leg wound. He should recover unless infection sets in."

"Sam, our friends would heal best if they were moved someplace out of here." Cavallin pointed around at the men lying crowded together in the hot, crowded, and stinking chapel.

"Someplace on the hilltop where there's a breeze would be best," Grant said and pointed out a side window of the church at a line of twenty of so houses along the crest of the hill upon which the chapel rested. The houses were those of the rich people of the town and had been built on the hilltop to take advantage of the prevailing winds rising up over the hills and concentrating into cooling breezes.

Cavallin looked where Grant indicated, and then spoke to the surgeon. "I'd like for Chilton and Dent to be placed in that house with the biggest windows on the point of the hill. The one with the big tree in the yard. The breezes there would make them more comfortable and maybe help them to heal quicker. Would that be too far for you to look after him?"

"Certainly not. That's a place I've thought of as a hospital."

"Then Sam and I'll go and find beds in that house for our friends."

"You may have trouble doing that. The volunteer regiments have their billets in those houses. I've already asked them to vacate and give their rooms to the wounded. I'll need an order from General Scott to force the Missourians to move."

Cavallin glanced at Chilton lying so very still. "That could take a spell and we shouldn't wait."

"Colonel, you're the army's chief surgeon," Grant said. "If you write an order based on your rank, Cavallin and I'll deliver it. Right, Tom?"

"Damn right we'll deliver it" Cavallin said grimly.

"Such an order would most likely be beyond my normal authority. But this is war and our wounded need the space right now." He moved to a desk and quickly wrote a few lines and handed the paper to Grant. "The order is quite direct, stating that twenty houses along the hilltop road are needed for the occupancy by the wounded. That all officers of the regular army and those of the volunteers are directed to enforce the removal of any and all occupants of those structures at the earliest possible hour."

Grant folded the paper and shoved it into the front of his tunic.

"Try not to shoot anybody for the last thing I need is another patient," said the chief surgeon.

"We'll enforce your order as gentlemen should," Grant said.

"That's good. I'll have orderlies bring the wounded up when you report the houses are vacant."

* * *

"What in the hell are you doing in here?" growled a square built, muscular man coming into the room where Grant and Cavallin were rolling up the blankets from two beds of the Mexican owners that had fled the terrible Yankees. He ignored Cavallin and fastened his eyes on Grant. "You're not one of our officers."

Grant pulled out the chief surgeon's order. "I have an order here for this house and nineteen others on this street to be vacated so that our wounded can use them. Here read it."

The man merely glanced at the paper before looking back at Grant. "Who signed it?"

"The army's chief surgeon."

"Then it's not worth the paper it's written on. Only an order from one of our officers means a damn thing to me. We're not moving our stuff."

"Then we'll move them for you," Cavallin said and bent again to roll up the blanket on the bed near him.

The man shouted out the door. "Hey, Oscar, come in here. There's some fellows fooling with our stuff."

A large, bearded man stomped inside and looked at Grant and Cavallin. "What's going on?"

"The hospital needs more room for the wounded coming off the battlefield," Grant said. "These houses are the best places for them and I have an order to move the present occupants out."

"They don't have the right orders to make us move," said the first man. "And anyway none of our boys took part in the fight and got themselves hurt. So I reckon we don't have to give up our choice location."

Damn the callous men. Still Grant didn't want to fight with them. "These houses on the ridge of the hill are the best ones because of the breeze that blows here. Surely you'd help the fellows that's taken a ball or some shrapnel and needs a cool bed to lay in while he heals."

"We like the cool air too," Oscar said.

Both men stared truculently at Grant and didn't move.

"I'm a lieutenant of the regular army and I order you to remove your belongings from this house," Grant said. "Now get to it."

Neither man stirred. Oscar gave Grant a loose-lipped, lop-sided smile.

"You heard the lieutenant and that's all the Goddamn talking there's going to be," Cavallin said in a flat, deadly voice. He ripped the blanket off the bed near him and hurled it at the two men. "Get your gear out of here, and pronto."

"Damn you, that's my bed," snarled the first man and leapt at Cavallin.

Cavallin pivoted aside, then stepped strongly back at right angles to the charging man and stiff-arm him into the wall. The man was half dazed by the collision with the wall and remained leaning against it for support.

Oscar swiftly moved his hand to rest on the pistol in his belt.

"Don't do anything foolish with that," Cavallin warned. He had spun back to face the man. His hands gripped the butts of his revolvers.

Grant took hold of his cap and ball pistol. He would have to back Cavallin. But this was getting way out of hand. He glanced at the redheaded Texan. The rims of the man's nostrils were ice-white, and his eyes burned with a barely controlled fury. These men didn't know Cavallin like Grant did. Their lives hung by a tiny thread. One move by them, and they would be dead.

"He'll kill you," Grant said. The men deserved to be warned.

"Then after I do that, I'll ride back to Texas," Cavallin said. "Now, do I put my friend in a bed given gladly, or do I put him in a dead man's bed? Make up your mind and do it fast."

Oscar's hand fell from the pistol to hang by his side. His eyes held a glassy sheen of realization that he was close to death.

"Don't start a fight with them, Oscar," said the first man straightening up from the wall and edging toward his bed. "The lieutenant is carrying out the chief surgeon's order. I'm betting that our officers will honor it. And I've got a feeling that if we should try to kill this Texan, we'd have to kill this lieutenant too and he's regular army. We'd both hang for that. Best for us to get our bedrolls out of here."

Oscar glowered at Cavallin. "I won't forget you. We'll meet again."

"Maybe so. If we do, you'd better walk around me."

The men snatched their remaining blankets from the beds, grabbed up their other possessions and stomped out.

Cavallin looked into Grant's eyes. Then his gaze drop down and saw Grant's hand gripping the cap and ball pistol.

Cavallin laughed. "We bluffed them down," he said with a grin in his blue eyes.

"Yeah, it was all a bluff." Grant said with a smile that held no humor. Both Cavallin and he knew there had been no bluffing.

* * *

Lee climbed the steep stone steps and halted on the landing just under the bells of the church residing on the highest elevation in Tacubaya. He had been here at least half a dozen times before to study the magnificent capital city of Mexico lying some two miles distant. Still he wanted one last opportunity to see the city from this high perspective because the final battle of the war to conquer Mexico was close at hand. For the past day and a half, he and four of his engineers had been reconnoitering the defense of the roads leading into the city. They weren't by themselves in this effort. General Scott and the other generals were actively making their personal studies as to the best way to assault the city.

Lee lifted his field glasses and began to examine the capital from the vantage point of the church belfry. Today it was quite visible under the sun hanging in the top of a clear blue sky. Access was by eight roads coming in from the hinterlands like spokes of a wagon wheel, with the city being the hub. On their outer lengths, the roads cut through agricultural land growing fruits, vegetables, grain, cotton, and tobacco, and many other crops. Toward the center of the valley, the cultivated land gave way to marshes and then to canals and open bodies of water and here the roads were constructed upon causeways for the remaining distance to the city. Each causeway ended at the powerful stone buildings of a garita bristling with cannon laid to rake the road. Lee judged the best route for the Americans to take in their advance would be from the south along the San Antonio Road, or from the west over the causeways leading to the Belen Garita or the San Cosme Garita.

Both the Belen and San Cosme causeways had dual uses. Besides carrying roads, each causeway held a large aqueduct, resting on strong masonry arches about the height of a tall man, transporting water to the city. One of the aqueducts drew its water from a mountain stream and ran along the center of the wide causeway to Garita San Cosme. The second started at Chapultepec

Hill where it was fed by a spring and ran from there down the center of the road to Garita Belen. Sufficiently wide space existed along each side of the aqueducts for wagon and carriage roads. Lee noted that the thick arches supporting the aqueducts would afford protection for advancing American troops.

All three garitas, San Cosme, Belen, and San Antonio were strongly entrenched with cannon, and would be supported by riflemen on the nearby structures that were all protected by parapets of sandbags. At points on the San Cosme road breastworks were thrown across it with embrasures for a single piece of artillery. Deep, wide ditches filled with water lined the sides of all three roads for the last half-mile to the city.

Lee went down from the belfry of the church. To his surprise, he found General Scott just arriving.

Lee saluted. "Good day, general." The general's face held much gloom.

"Good day to you, Major Lee. I'm glad that I've run into you. Ride along with me for a look at Chapultepec Hill. I'd like to hear your observations about it."

"It'd be a pleasure, sir." Lee sensed there was more on the general's mind than Chapultepec and wondered what it could be.

Lee untied his horse from the hitching rail in front of the church and mounted, and he and Scott headed for Chapultepec a mile distant. Lee felt sadness at Scott's appearance. The general's shoulders sagged and his face was strained with anxiety. Lee believed it was from the coming battle for Mexico City, and from the past battle for Molino del Rey. When Scott had been told there had been no bells or cannon at the Molino, he had not been able to hide his misgivings about ordering the attack. Then adding to his woes had come the report of the heavy American casualties. One hundred and twenty-four had been killed and 582 wounded. Among them were 49 officers, with nine killed including Major Wright and Captain Kirby Smith.

Lee and Sciott halted a quarter mile back from Chapultepec to stay out of range of the Mexican snipers that would want nothing better than a shot at an American general. They lifted their glasses to view the fortified hill.

"The guns are well placed and could be a major danger to our troops unless we knocked them out of action first," Lee said.

"Exactly so," Scott replied, and without lowering his glasses continued to speak. "This time we shall insure no mistakes are made that cost men's lives."

Scott, in his way, was apologizing for what had occurred at Molino del Rey and Casa Mata. The general was saying it to Lee because he was more at ease with him than any of the other officers.

"Major, the issue of who wins a battle lies less in the officers than in the heart of the rank and file soldier. The lives of every one of them should be shown the most possible respect."

"Yes, sir, I fully agree." Lee understood Scott had added to his apology.

They fell quiet and concentrated on the rock strewn hill that sprang up two hundred feet from the flat plain. The distance across its base was about half a mile. On a broad level space on the top of the hill was the walled Chapultepec Castle, the home of Mexico's Military Academy. The Castle was of masonry construction, rectangular in shape, and two stories high. A tall flagpole carried the tricolor Mexican flag. Lee saw numerous cannons on the two sides of the Castle facing him. The park with the cypress trees at the base of the hill was surrounded by a thick stone wall six feet high and four feet thick. A roadway that wound up the steep flank of the hill was fortified with dirt trenches and cannon. There was a strong redoubt showing several cannons halfway up the slope of the hill. At the base of Castle's walls was a retaining wall at least twelve feet tall. Lee made a note that scaling ladders would be needed to mount the retaining wall. Many cannon were entrenched on the broad, flat top of the wall, and at several other places in recently prepared redoubts. Droves of men worked at building more fortifications. The cannons from their elevated position on the hill, could sweep the land all around.

"I've seen enough," Scott said to Lee. "I've called a council of war for six this evening at the church in La Piedad. Attend with your senior engineers."

"Yes, sir."

* * *

Lee and three of his engineers arrived on time and assembled with the army generals and Major Huger at the little church in La Piedad.

Scott entered the room last, his tread heavy on the wooden floor. His worried eyes, staring out from a drawn and creased face, swept the solemn gathering of officers. He began to speak in a somber voice. "Gentlemen, we now face the final and crucial battle of this long campaign. We are far from being

241

in a desirable situation. We're outnumbered, deep in hostile country, cut off from any thought of reinforcements, and caring for more than a thousand sick and wounded men. Our spies and other informants tell us that 15,000 men defend Mexico City, and that Generals Valencia and Alvarez with 8,000 men threaten our rear. To accomplish what must be done, we have 7,180 effectives."

Scott paused and looked around at his officers. "None of this is new to you. I mention it to impress upon you that there can be no mistakes, no failures in carrying out your duties and gaining victory in the coming battle.

"Now to the immediate question of what route to take in our advance on the city. I believe the options boil down to either the southern route by way of the San Antonio Road, or the western route by either San Cosme Road or the Belen Road. Now I don't want to influence your judgment, however I prefer the western route. First we take Chapultepec Hill and then follow the San Cosme causeway into the city. Now let's hear other recommendations."

Lee was surprised by Scott stating his preference for the assault route before first hearing the opinions of his subordinate officers. He should have waited so as not to stifle a free and candid discussion. Not only that, he disagreed with Scott's choice.

Huger spoke, "I agree with the western route. We can demolish Chapultepec with our cannon in one day."

"General, I recommend the southern route," Lee said. "The garita of San Antonio isn't nearly as strong as those of San Cosme and Belen. Further I don't believe we can take Chapultepec without a direct frontal attack by infantry. My opinion is that we should make the main thrust along the San Antonio Road and a feint along the Belen Road."

The generals and the other senior officers stated their preferences. Each was discussed in detail. For more than an hour, the argument went back and forth between the southern route and the western route.

Scott looked at Beauregard who had sat quietly throughout the meeting. "Lieutenant, you haven't voiced you opinion. What route do you recommend?"

"I have examined Chapultepec thoroughly and agree with Major Lee. An assault by infantry will be required to take it. And I agree with him that a feint should be made along the Belen Road. However the assault on Chapultepec should not be too costly if we use our artillery properly, thus the main attack should be made along the San Cosme Road. Once inside the gates the two columns will be close together and can swiftly merge to fight onward deeper into the city if that should be required."

Scott called for a show of hands as to which route, the southern or the western one, should be used to assault the city. Three generals and two engineers voted with Lee, and two generals and Beauregard sided with Scott.

"We've had enough discussion," Scott said and aggravated at the divided opinions. He rose to his feet and drew himself up straight. "We will attack the city by its western gates. A feint will be made along the Belen Road and the main assault along the San Cosme Road. The general officers, and Major Lee and Major Huger will remain for further orders. The meeting is dissolved."

When those men released had filed out of the room, Scott turned to Lee and Huger. "How long will it take you to position the cannon for bombardment of Chapultepec? A cannonade of the HEAVIEST sort?"

"A full day," Huger said.

"At least," Lee added.

"You have until daylight tomorrow," Scott said firmly. "We will begin bombardment at daylight, so that gives you not a day, but a night."

Chapter Forty

In the last hour of the night, Lee, Huger, Beauregard, and McClellan, directing gangs of artillerymen, finished positioning the howitzers, mortars, and the big siege cannons where they would do the most damage to the men and fortifications on Chapultepec Hill. Ammunition had been brought forward to each gun for twelve hours of continuous bombardment.

The four released their work crews and were congratulating themselves for having completed the task within Scott's allotted time limit when the first shift of the day gunners found them in the darkness. Lee and the other officers divided and led the crews to their assigned guns.

Lee was standing behind the battery of 24-pounders when the bombardment began at exactly 5 o'clock with the sun breaking above the eastern horizon and providing the gunners with light to aim their pieces. The din was horrific. The storm of projectiles filled the sky. He followed their flight toward the top of the hill and saw a hole knocked in the Castle and a section of the roof cave in. The final battle for Mexico City had begun.

The Mexican gunners on Chapultepec replied in kind, and as usual it was fine shooting that exploded sandbags from the parapets of the Americans batteries and made the gunners and powder boys dodge and duck. The American gunners quickly identified the most skilled Mexican pieces and concentrated their fire upon them. Lee saw two of the Mexican's most effective cannons disabled.

The American cannonading went on throughout the day and the Castle suffered much damaged and several of the enemy gun emplacements were knocked out. Still as the day waned and gave way to evening, Lee saw the enemy on Chapultepec standing firm and hurling their cannon balls down at the Americans. Huger's expectation that he could demolish the fortification in a day by cannon fire wasn't going to happen and an assault by infantrymen would be necessary. At dark the dueling cannons ceased to fire.

* * *

September 13, 1847. Shortly before daylight Lee made his way into the darkness of the Molino del Rey. All around him there was a rustling, a stirring, a murmur of low voice as the men of Pillow's division girded up for battle. The men had slept in the Molino so they could be quickly assembled for the attack on Chapultepec. Lee had spent the night directing the repositioning of the cannon for the morning bombardment and now had not slept for two days and was weary to the bone.

He made his way to Pillow's command post in the main building. Pillow and his officers were quietly talking among themselves. As Lee silently joined the group, Pillow gave him a nod of recognition. Lee was here on Scott's orders to, "Stay close to General Pillow. Advise him and encourage him to be aggressive. He must not fail to take the hill." Scott's countenance had showed his worry about Pillow's erratic behavior when under pressure. Scott's other words also resounded in Lee's mind, "I have my misgivings about today."

Scott had divided his army into four divisions for the final advance on Mexico City by adding loyal, trustworthy Quitman to his command generals. Pillow with his volunteers would take Chapultepec Castle. Worth would drive the main attack down the San Cosme Road. Quitman would make a strong feint along the Belen Road to the Belen Garita. Twiggs was held in reserve to protect the army's rear from attack and guard the sick and injured.

Pillow's division, spearheaded by a company of 250 "forlorn hopes" that had volunteered from Worth's division, would make the assault on Chapultepec Castle by crossing through the cypress grove lying south of the hill. Worth would support Pillow in the capture of the hill and then immediately advance on the city. Quitman's division with a detachment of fifty Marines would storm the hill just far enough to seize control of the steep, winding pathway that led up to the base of the Castle. He would halt there until the Castle was taken and then break away to make his feint at Mexico City along the Belen Road.

Lee peered out a rear door of the Molino and watched the day break clear, bright, and silent. The air, warm and growing warmer, lay dead on the land. A small flock of gray, dove-size birds sat in one of the big cypress trees beyond the thick stone wall and looked at Lee.

The signal gun broke the stillness and the American batteries opened fire. For two hours they shook the ground and rattled the walls of the Molino as the hurled solid shot and exploding shell up at the Castle and the fortifications on the hillsides. Then all guns ceased their growling. An eerie silence held for a minute. Then the guns began to roar again, hurling canister, shells, and grape into the park of cypress trees to try and clear it of the enemy for Pillow's advance.

Lee stood with Pillow just inside the Molino as the shells devastated the huge, ancient cypresses, blasting limbs free and sending them flying, bursting tree trunks, plowing the ground.

Pillow spoke in a low voice that Lee barely caught through the boom of cannon. "We shall be defeated."

Lee didn't like hearing such words from a general. Should a commanding officer think such thoughts, he most surely ought to keep them to himself.

"It's time," Lee said and looking at his watch. As he spoke, the American cannons fell quiet.

"I recommend we advance at the double," Lee said.

Giving no sign he heard Lee, Pillow shouted out to his bugler standing close by. The man raised his bright silver instrument and blew the call to advance.

The battalion of stormers with bayonets fixed burst from the center of the Molino. Yelling shrill cries the men ran toward the cypress trees in the park. The remainder of Pillow's division poured from other openings in the Molino and raced after their comrades. A ragged volley of musket fire met them from among the battered trees. Half a score men fell. The rest ran on, scrambled over the wall, and pushed in among the ancient trees. The Mexicans gave way grudgingly and shooting to the rear as they went.

Lee stayed by Pillow's side as they pushed though the wide cypress grove and struck the hill, where all the trees had been cut by the Mexicans, and started to climb. Above them the men of the division were swiftly mounting the slope, driving before them hundreds of Mexicans that had been chased from the cypress grove. Halfway up the hill was the redoubt to which the Mexicans were retreating. Above that another hundred yards was the great retaining wall of the Castle terrace. Lee cast a look to the right where some quarter mile away, Clarke's brigade of Worth's division was in sight advancing up the lower slope of the boulder strewn hill.

Shooting from the redoubt and the terrace and over the heads of their fellow soldiers, the Mexicans rained a murderous fire of canister and grapeshot down on the Americans. Men fell wounded and dead by the droves among the rocks and tree stumps. The men threw themselves down on the ground to get out of the hail of bullets, and returned the fire as best they could from a prone position. This went on for minute after minute, and then Lee saw Joe Johnston leap up into the face of the intense fire and gave a wild yell. His men surged to their feet behind him and he led them in a run up the hill. They struck the redoubt and after a minute of fierce fighting, swept over the defenders and chased the surviving enemy upward toward the tall retaining wall at the base of the Castle.

The Americans were now close and fully exposed to the enemy guns on top of the wall and the Mexicans let go with a furious hail of grapeshot and musket balls. Many Americans were knocked off their feet. The remaining Americans dropped to the ground and sought shelter behind rocks and tree stumps. From there they fired up at the foe on the high ground.

A packet of Mexican grapeshot struck the rocks close by Lee and Pillow. Pillow's feet were blown from under him and he cried out as he fell to the ground.

Lee felt a tug on his upper right arm, followed instantly by a sharp slash of pain. He looked at the torn tunic and the blood that showed. The wound would soon need a bandage. First the general had to be gotten to safety. He jumped to Pillow and scooped him up and slung him over a shoulder. Bent low, Lee hustled them both into shelter behind a boulder.

Pillow stifled his cries of pain and looked at his right foot where the boot had been torn away at the ankle and blood was flowing. Lee knelt beside him and taking his neckerchief, fastened a tourniquet above the wound.

Pillow motioned his orderly to him. "Go to General Worth and tell him we are in a bad way and need his men to press hard ahead. Make great haste or it'll be too late."

The Americans gunners that had been firing over the heads of their advancing comrades could no longer do so safely and ceased their cannonading. At that, a group of men leapt to their feet and ran forward and jammed up against the base of the retaining wall and under the parapet. Crouched low and pressed tightly to the stone wall, they were safe for the moment. A few feet above their heads the Mexican muskets and cannons cast a sheet of flame as they fired at the Americans farther down the hill.

Lee looked for the scaling ladders that should have been close behind the storming party. His heart began to thump angrily. Somebody had made a costly mistake. There were no ladders in sight.

Time passed, five minutes, ten minutes, fifteen minutes with the Mexicans pouring fire down upon the Americans and taking a heavy toll.

Clark's brigade was closer now and Lee saw Pickett and Longstreet out in front, with Longstreet carrying the regimental banner. He was hit by a bullet and fell. He handed the banner up to Pickett, who seized it and led on.

Lee looked again for the scaling ladders and saw they were being brought at a swift pace. Beauregard had seen the problem and was in among the company of ladder bearers shouting and cursing them and whipping the laggards with the flat of his sword.

The Mexicans on the retaining wall, realizing the significance of the ladders, turn their guns on the ladder bearers. Men fell and three ladders were lost. Beauregard drove the crew onward up the hill through the zipping bullets and in under the lip of the retaining wall.

Two ladders were quickly placed at a slant against the wall. The boldest Americans leapt upon them and climbed swiftly upward. Mexicans blew them off the ladder with muskets balls, and threw the ladders down.

Clarke's men came running in from the right and merged with Pillow's in a brilliant mix of regimental flags. Now with hundreds of willing hands more ladders were speedily set side by side upon the wall and men swarmed up them. The Mexicans increased their fire and mowed down the wave of Americans as they came over the top of the wall. Then there were enough ladders set that fifty Americans could climb abreast. Men were shot and bayoneted and fell, but men came over the wall faster than the Mexican could kill them.

The Mexicans fell back as the number of Americans inside the wall swelled. With a loud shout of triumph and shooting and yielding their bayonets with a savage fury upon the defenders, the Americans swept into the castle. To the right, other Americans broke through the main gate and into the castle.

Some Mexicans fought strongly, the cadets among the bravest. Hundreds of others began to flee the castle to the west. Some soldiers running in wild fright and cut off from escape leapt over the walls regardless of its height. The fighting died and the castle belonged to the Americans.

Pickett and two of Pillow's volunteers climbed to the top of the Castle, jerked down the tri-color Mexican flag, and hoisted Old Glory to the top of the flagpole. A mighty shout of victory rolled out from the hilltop. It was quickly picked up and added to by Worth's men and Quitman's men into a roaring ocean of American voices.

Pillow listened until the shouting ended and then spoke to Lee. "Major, it's time we reported to General Scott that Chapultepec Castle has been taken."

Lee looked to the east. The rising of the flag was the signal for the hanging of thirty of the San Patricio Battalion. The condemned men and their executioners were visible skylined on the crown of a hill near the Church of San Angel. Colonel Harney a strict disciplinarian was directing the hangings. Ten of the condemned men with their hands tied behind their backs and with nooses around their necks stood upon mule carts. The ends of the ten ropes were fastened in a row overhead to a gibbet made of a long pole supported at both ends by strong posts.

Lee heard a roll of drums, Harney's arm rose and fell, and the mules were whacked on the rump and lurched forward dragging the carts out from under the men's feet. The men hung dangling, choking, and kicking. Three long minutes passed, the limp bodies were taken down and another ten men were placed upon the carts. The mules went forward and left the men hanging. And yet another ten men were lifted upon the carts and hung. The executions ended. The lashing and branding began of those men spared being hung, each receiving fifty lashes and the letter D branded on their cheeks, and the grim job of digging the graves of those hanged. Lee was much saddened by such severe punishment. Still he couldn't find fault with Scott for discipline must be enforced or an army couldn't be held together and commanded.

Chapter Forty-One

Grant moved with a double-quick pace with Hazlitt and his Fourth Infantry of Garland's brigade that was in formation just behind the horse drawn artillery leading the way. From around Grant came the heavy, rasping breathing of men moving fast and the clatter of their boots on the pavement of the road. It felt good to be going into battle with these stalwart fighters that he knew from other battles.

As the brigade turned north onto the arrow straight San Cosme Road leading to Mexico City, Huger and his siege cannons came into view behind. The enlarged force of men and artillery divided into two columns and marched down both sides of the aqueduct toward the Garita San Cosme lying half a mile away.

Grant saw Worth looking to the east and measuring Quitman's progress driving down the Belen Road. Quitman was suppose to only make a feint, but in reality a race was being run and Worth wanted to be first into the city. Quitman had the shorter distance, however Grant heard heavy firing coming from the Belen Road and knew Quitman was having a tough time of it.

Grant's brigade pressed on and came within range of tremendous fire from the barricade at the garita. The only safety from the enemy's guns was the small areas behind the arches of the aqueduct. Houses clung to both sides of the roadway all the way to the garita with enemy soldiers occupying every one and shooting from windows and rooftops. The buildings penned the Americans into a narrow lane hot with exploding canister, grapeshot, and musket balls. Losses mounted swiftly.

Garland looked to the rear and motioned for Grant and Hazlitt to come to him. "Hazlitt, give Grant half your men," Garland ordered.

To Grant he said, "Bust through the houses like we did at Monterrey. Go as close as you can to the garita. Clear the houses and the rooftops of gunmen."

Grant speedily had his platoon of men equipped with pickaxes and sledgehammers borrowed from those carried by the artillery for entrenching their guns. With him leading, the men kicked in the door of the nearest house and vanished inside and began to break through the walls, tunneling from one house to the next. With hand-to-hand fighting they killed or drove the enemy soldiers out. In the taller houses they went to the windows or climbed to a roof and fired their muskets and pelted the enemy blocking the way ahead. Gradually they drew close to the barricade.

From the rooftop of a three-story house, Grant surveyed the buildings ahead for a way to flank the enemy and bring fire onto the enemy barricade and the redoubts of the garita. Looking forward past the garita, he saw a church with a high belfry that would command the ground behind the Mexican barricade. He thought there might be space in the church belfry for a gun. Leaving his men to continue to fire upon the enemy, he dropped down to the floor and ran back through the houses to the main American force.

Lieutenant Lendrum of the artillery saw Grant pop out of the house. "What in the hell have you been up to?"

"I believe I've found a place where we can put a gun and catch the Mexicans from the rear. I need a gun and help getting it there."

"I'll give you a gun and crew," Lendrum said without hesitation.

"I'll need some muscle power and guards," Grant said. He glanced around and saw a company of Marines. "I'll ask Captain Simmes if he's game to help."

Grant approached the captain standing with his Marines. "Captain Simmes, can I borrow a squad of your men to help me take a gun to that church you can see over the top of the garita?"

Simmes looked where Grant pointed. "That'd be a good place for one. Sure, take a squad."

"First let me see if there's room in the belfry," Grant said.

"Right." Simmes motioned at a dozen of his men and they gathered around him. "Go with the lieutenant," he ordered the Marines.

Using the cover of a low wall and ducking among the stone pillars of the arches, the men slipped forward a short distance. Then watching their chance, they darted across the road between grapeshot and stole forward on the right side of the causeway. Working past silent houses, stone walls and trees, and unseen by the Mexican riflemen and gunners, they came to the back side of the garita. To Grant's surprise the rear portion of the garita was unguarded.

He led his men to the church and banged on the heavy door. The door opened a crack and a priest, his eyes fearful, peered out at Grant. In Spanish, Grant asked to be let in. The priest shook his head and made to shut the door.

Grant blocked the door with a foot. "If you don't open the door, I'll have my men break it down and make you a prisoner."

The priest's expression changed at those words and he hastily opened the door wide.

"Watch the priest and keep him here," Grant ordered the Marines. "I'll take a look upstairs."

He ran up the stairs and found the belfry had a floor large enough for a gun. If he could get a howitzer up here, he could shoot the hell out of the enemy in the barricade and its redoubts not but a hundred yards away and below him.

Grant hurried down to the floor, and leaving the priest under guard by two Marines, stole back to his lines on the causeway. There he obtained a mountain howitzer from Lendrum, disassembled it, and distributed its parts and ammunition among the men.

Grant hoisted a wheel to hang on a shoulder and led the crew toward the church. Because of the bulky loads the men carried, the previous path wouldn't do and they drop off the causeway and slosh through the ditches filled with mud and water reaching to Grant's chest. Undiscovered by the enemy, they again reached the church and climbed to the belfry. There they swiftly reassembled the gun and loaded it with canister. With Grant calling directions, they hurled shot down upon the enemy below, wounding and killing men and throwing the rest into confusion.

As Grant worked with his crew, he felt a hand on his shoulder and turned to find Lieutenant Pemberton one of Worth's staff officers standing behind him.

"General Worth wants to see the officer manning the gun here," Pemberton said. "It seems that's you."

"Tell him that I'll report to him in a little while that I'm busy right now."

"I don't think that'll do," Pemberton said. "When a general says to report, it's best that a lieutenant does it promptly."

"That's probably good advice," Grant said. He called out to his gunners, "Keep firing."

The two officers went down to the ground and stole past the walls and houses to Worth.

Grant saluted. "Lieutenant Grant reporting, sir."

Worth returned the salute of the wet, muddy, young man stained with gunpowder smoke. "You must be the one with the gun in the church belfry?" he said.

"Yes, sir."

"That's mighty fine work getting the gun up there. Your shots are telling on the Mexicans. I'll send you another gun."

"Thank you, general," Grant replied. There wasn't enough room for another gun in the belfry, but it wasn't smart to contradict a general.

Grant returned to the church with a squad of men and the second howitzer. He let the gun set by the church door and took his men to the belfry to relieve the first gun crew. As he began to call out direction for sighting the gun, an American horse drawn gun came charging up the road toward the barricade.

One of Colonel Duncan's lieutenants rode horseback beside the cannon, nine gunners rode astride the teams, or clung to the caisson seats. For one hundred and fifty yards the men breasted the enemy fire. Then the horses and five of the men were hit by a pair of exploding shells and fell crashing to the pavement. The lieutenant and his remaining four men cut the writhing and screaming horses loose from the guns and swung them around and standing unprotected, naked to the shells whipping down the road, dueled with the guns behind the barricade.

As part of a coordinated assault, platoons of Americans had gone off both sides of the causeway and stolen along through the water as Grant had done. Now they pulled themselves upon the causeway and struck behind the garita. A company of men rushed forward along the road from the main body of Americans toward the garita. They made it half the distance before a devastating fire from the garita forced them to take cover behind the stone arches.

Grant and his men, and Clarke's men on the opposite side of the barricade, continued to fire down on the Mexicans. The volleys had now mangled or killed almost every Mexican gunner and artillery mule. The remaining enemy soldiers had deserted the garita and were dragging one of their guns with them toward a large building that appeared to be a barracks.

The American artillery lieutenant on the road fired a ball that splintered and weakened the garita gate. Seeing this fine shot, the Americans that had come in from the sides now quickly converged and sprang forward and crashed open the city's mighty defensive gate. The men were met by a barrage of canister fire from several cannons firing from the barracks. They pulled back and found shelter behind the garita walls. The two young lieutenants that had led the charge called out to their men and they sank down to sit on the pavement to rest.

Grant, in the belfry spoke to his squad of artillerymen and Marines. "You did good work. Now go and find your outfits."

The men filed away down the stairs from the belfry. Grant remained behind looking out across the land where a cloud of dense gray gun smoke had formed and stretched off over the valley. To the east at the Belen Garita, the thundering of the cannon and popping of musketry were ending in a ragged tailing off. To the west a blood-red sun was settling onto the horizon. The end of the day being so near surprised Grant for in the intensity of the fighting along the road and in the houses, he hadn't noticed the passing of time. The battle wouldn't be decided today.

He wiped at the sweat on his face and wearily went down the stairs and out of the church to sit on the pavement against the garita wall with the men of his Fourth Infantry. They had been marching and fighting all day, had had a terrible loss of comrades, and now it was time to rest and give thanks for still being alive.

A group of horsemen caught Grant's sight. On the road not a quarter mile away, Scott and nearly a dozen officers were making their way toward the garita. It's safe for you to come now thought Grant. Behind the horsemen came the ambulance wagons picking up the wounded. The dead must wait for tomorrow.

Chapter Forty-Two

Lee rode with Scott and half a dozen command officers on horseback through the litter of blue uniformed bodies lying dead or wounded on the San Cosme Road. The horses advanced by delicately placing their hooves so as not to trod upon the men. Both the San Cosme Garita and the Belen Garita had been taken. But God! Their capture had been a deadly affair for the soldiers. Worse yet, the enemy wasn't beaten. He must surely have thousands of fresh fighters to meet the invaders tomorrow as they continued their drive into the city.

Lee noticed movement from the wounded as Scott passed through them. Those that could stand did so; those too badly hurt to rise brought themselves to a sitting position. All of the men watched the general with their pain filled eyes. With their gray faces holding an expression of pride of what they had done, of the bravery they had shown, of the wounds they had taken on his orders, they saluted their general. Scott raised his hand in salute to the men, and rode on with his hand to his brow. 'Yes indeed, general', Lee thought, 'they deserve your full respect.'

Lee began to shake as the full weight of his exhaustion and the weakness caused by the wound swept over him. An infinitely dense blackness settled upon him. He reached out to catch hold of the pommel of his saddle. In the blackness he couldn't find it. He leaned to the side, then still further, and fell from the saddle and landed hard on the pavement.

* * *

As the thickening dusk became black night, Grant walked back along the road and entered one of the bigger houses he had fought his way through. He found a candle, lit it, and searched about and located a little food and a bottle of wine. He ate by himself in the abandoned house, and for some unexplainable reason was glad that he was alone.

Carrying the half empty wine bottle with him, he found a bed on the second floor. Ah, what a grand sight the clean, neatly made-up bed was. He drank again from the bottle, corked it, and sat it on a nearby table. He dropped down on the bed with his dirty clothes on, and placing his weapons within reach, closed his eyes.

From outside the house on the road came the rumble of the heavy wheels of Huger's big siege cannons. Tonight there would be little rest for the artillerymen because the guns must be positioned to support the final assault on the city. Grant heard the big 10-inch mortars fire five shots into the city as a good night message to Santa-Anna. That should make the Mexican general consider what was coming his way tomorrow.

Grant lay recalling the day's battle and what the morrow could bring. He knew first hand from the fighting for Monterey how dangerous combat was on the streets and among the houses of a city. Thoughts of Noah Grant came, what did that old man, no he would have been a man even younger than Grant was now, think as he lay resting after a hard fight during the battle for independence and faced another equally hard in the morning. He would like to have known that man, whose blood he carried in his own veins.

He reached for the wine bottle and took a long drink. He held it in his mouth for a moment, savoring the taste, and then let the fine liquid slowly slide down his throat. He was asleep by the time the last drop had left his mouth.

* * *

Lee awoke with someone gently shaking him by the shoulder. Beauregard sat beside his bed and watching him with a concerned expression.

"You all right, major?" Beauregard asked.

"Let me check," Lee said. He was still tired, his wound was painful, and he ached in other places when he moved. "I think I'll live," Lee said with a slight smile. "But I do ache here and there."

"I'm glad to hear that you'll live."

"What time is it?"

"About six thirty. I thought you might want to know what's happened since you fell off your horse."

"I guess that's why I hurt pretty much all over. What's the news?"

"The city might be ours without more fighting. Last night, or more accurately this morning about four o'clock city officials came to Scott and wanted to negotiate a surrender. They said Santa-Anna had left the city with his soldiers."

"And?"

Beauregard grinned. "Our old general has had enough negotiating and told them that he had fought his way into the city and now intended to have it without any further talking. The city must be surrendered or he would begin bombarding it at first daylight."

"So he's learned that it's not a good strategy to talk with the Mexicans."

"It seems to me that they're better at it than we are. Anyway, this morning at daylight, city officials brought a white flag to Quitman. Still Scott plans to enter the city in assault formation. Worth and Quitman are to advance at the same time, with Worth going to the Alameda, and Worth to the Grand Plaza and take possession of the National Palace. Scott will join Worth for the grand entry. The general sent me to find out if you're able to ride along with him."

"Most certainly I am."

"I thought you'd be unless you were completely dead. You'll need to be in full dress uniform for that's the way we're riding in."

Lee called out, "Connally, bring me my dress uniform."

"It's already laid out for you, major," Connally said and coming into the room, having obviously listened to the conversation. He chucked a thumb at the uniform draped over the back of a nearby chair. "And I've got a bath ready. Do you want me to shave you?" He nodded at Lee's wounded arm.

"I could use a little help in getting ready, that's for sure."

* * *

September 14, 1847. Under a yellow morning sun, Scott and Worth both on horseback took places side by side at the head of Worth's division. With Harney's Dragoons and Semmes Marines as escort, the division left the magnificent park Alameda amid the clatter of horses' hooves upon the cobblestone. Harney's regimental band struck up "Yankee Doodle" to lightened the steps of the men. General Worth wore his field uniform with its stains of the battle of yesterday. General Scott was resplendent in full dress uniform with saber and spurs, epaulets gleaming gold against his blue uniform and snowy plumes flowing from his cocked hat. He rode his superb bay charger, with all his staff officers following on horseback in prescribed uniforms and in prescribed order.

The two generals guided a course along the broad avenue toward a towering white building in the center of the city. Both sides of the street were lined with silent brown-skinned people watching the lean, sunbaked Americans parade past.

Grant marched with Hazlitt in front of his company of infantrymen. He had removed as much dirt from his uniform as possible and had scrubbed his face in a basin of water in the house where he had slept. Still he was dirty, but no more so than many of the soldiers and nobody seemed to mind. The rank and file and even the officers seemed to regard the dirt, gun smoke stains, and crude bandages as badges of their fighting.

Shortly the National Palace, a massive stone building with many balconies on the upper story, came into sight on the border of the Zocalo, the city's Grand Plaza. A scarred American flag whipped about from the staff on top of the palace. The sidewalks, and the windows, balconies, and tops of the houses surrounding the Grant Plaza were thronged with thousand of silent, watchful townsfolk.

In the center of the great square, General Quitman's soldiers were drawn up in orderly ranks facing the palace. The general paced back and forth in front of his ragged, bloodstained troops. At the foot of the broad stairs leading up to the palace, Quitman had assembled those city and national government officials that he could find. They fidgeted and glanced with worried eyes at the terrible, savage Americans.

Loud cheers sounded as Scott mounted on his charger came into sight of the soldiers in the plaza. He spurred his mount to a gallop and swept into the plaza with Harney's Dragoons, their swords drawn and leaning on their shoulders, galloping close behind him. Quitman's regimental bands struck up "Hail Columbia." Scott reined his big horse to a stop in front of the troops with their cheers drowning out the sound of the band.

The general, splendid in his dress uniform and so different from his battle stained army, listened another moment to the triumphant shouts. Then with a pleased expression upon his large face, he drew his saber and in a grand sweeping swing of the weapon saluted his men.

Scott spoke, lavishly praising his "Brave Rifles" for their grand victory. Then with his spurs jingling, he walked up the stone steps and entered the National Place of Mexico.

* * *

At the graveyard near Tacubaya, Grant stood in ranks with some two hundred officers and waited for the burial ceremony for those men killed during the fighting at Chapultepec Castle and the San Cosme and Belen Garitas. The wooden caskets were laid out beside the graves that were dug in perfectly straight rows across the meadow, and adjacent to the graves of the dead from the fighting at Molino del Rey. El Molino had cost the little American Army 789 wounded and killed; Chapultepec – 450; the garitas – 833; and in the three days and nights of rioting after the city fell -226. Grant didn't like funerals, and this one was especially bad because the corpses of his friends Calvin Benjamin and Sidney Smith lay in two of the coffins.

General Scott with a somber voice and his usual flowery words lauded the bravery of the men and the honor they had bestowed upon the army. The chaplain spoke and consigned the men into the care of the Lord. A bugle sounded a short lament, the honor guards fired their muskets in salute, and six field guns fired their tribute one after another.

Following the order to "fall out" Grant went to his wagon train of seventy vehicles drawn up for departure after the ceremony. Cavallin soon arrived with his company of Rangers, Hazlitt with his company of infantrymen, and Lieutenant Townsend with a company of Dragoons. In total Grant had some four hundred fighting men. The caravan moved off with Grant intending to go to the north side of the valley where there had been no fighting and the foraging for provision for his hungry men should be most productive.

Chapter Forty-Three

Lee reined in the black pacer and halted the buggy in front of the home of Edward Thornton, British Consul in Mexico. He climbed down from the buggy, that had been seized by one of the American patrols during the days of riots in the capital, and went up the long walk to the house.

Ten days had now passed since the surrender of Mexico City and the social life was in full swing. The opera was again holding plays, and the foreign nationals residing in the city were throwing festive parties in their lavish homes with wine, food, and dancing. The stated reason was to celebrate the end of the war without the destruction of the capital. Lee knew there was another reason for he sensed a pent up excitement among the young foreign women, the daughters, sisters, and other close relatives of the men. Those women now had more than two hundred and fifty American officers to choose among for escorts. Some two thirds of the officers were unmarried. Many romances and liaisons had already blossomed.

He rapped on the carved wooden door with the knocker that carried an English Coat of Arms that he couldn't interpret but must belong to the Thornton family. The Britisher had brought this piece of England with him to inform those people that came to his door that he was a citizen of the most powerful nation on the face of the earth. Lee smiled at that. After the conquering of Mexico by the Americans, the British standing in the world might be in doubt. The door opened to the hand of a ruddy-faced man in the uniform of a butler.

"Welcome, Mr. Lee," said the man.

"I wish to see Miss Thornton," Lee said.

"Yes, sir, Miss Thornton is expecting you. Please come in. She will be down shortly and asks you to please wait."

Lee doffed his hat and stepped through the doorway. He had advanced but a few steps when Elizabeth Thornton came hurrying into sight on the far side of the large room. She was tall, slender, quite fair skinned and with black hair in ringlets. Her sparkling blue eyes showed intelligence. She had a trilling laugh that delighted Lee. She was dressed in a summery blue dress that matched her eyes and wore a jeweled pendant around her neck, and for gaiety wore a pair of bracelets on one wrist where they tinkled pleasantly together as she moved.

"Robert, I'm so glad to see you," she called out gaily and hastened to take his hand.

"You look lovely," Lee said. He clasped Elizabeth's hand and tenderly squeezed it, feeling the slender bones inside their covering of soft skin and flesh. It gave him much pleasure just to touch the woman. She reminded him of a butterfly every time he saw her. Her movements were fluid and graceful and she always wore brightly colored dresses and a touch of rouge upon her cheeks and lips. He liked the fact that her face didn't have the sculpture of a perfect beauty. But pretty she was with a mouth that spoke gently and the lips that teased to be kissed. She was thirty and had been married to an army officer named Chadwick that had been killed in the fighting to subdue an uprising against the English in India. After that she had gone to live with her father and had traveled with him on his assignment to this foreign land.

"Give me three minutes and I shall be ready to go," Elizabeth said.

Lee bowed his acceptance of the waiting and watched the woman hurry away. He felt the urgent now of wanting a woman, wanting one to the center of his manhood. He thought married men used to having a woman when he desired her had a more difficult time doing without their presence than did a bachelor. But he didn't want a whore, which were readily available in any number of brothels. This was the woman he desired.

Lee had met Elizabeth at the first party he had attended and she had flirted and then danced with him. He had been a willing participant and they had found each other most agreeable companions. This was the fourth time they had spent the evening together. Lee justified his association with Elizabeth with the thought that a grain of lawlessness, of lust, especially in a soldier in a conquered land, was after all normal and a useful characteristic of a fighter.

Lee had much free time on his hands for his military duties were not difficult and were quite to his liking. He had been directed by Scott to prepare drawings of the fortifications at Churubusco, El Molino, Chapultepec Castle and the garitas San Cosme and Belen. Scott would include them in his report of the battles to President Polk and the Secretary of War Marcy.

The Americans now held total control of the capital. Following Scott's orders to proceed with vigor against those guilty of rioting and looting and attacking Americans, all criminal and guerilla bands had been subdued. Santa-Anna had surrendered his Presidency of Mexico and Luis de la Pena now held that office in a temporary manner until an election was held. On information provided by the spy Dominguez, Scott knew that Santa Anna was at Guadalupe reassembling his army.

Elizabeth returned hurrying and smiling. Lee drove them to a fine restaurant overlooking one of the many canals that served as roads for large sections of the city. Lee asked Elizabeth to make the selection of food, and she chose squab roasted in a delicious sauce, with a variety of side dishes, deserts, and wines. They ate leisurely and talked on unimportant topics, simply enjoying each other's company. Without a word having been said, both knew that tonight something special would occur.

* * *

Grant slept in the saddle as he rode through the darkness of the Mexican night lying thick on the National Highway. The long hours on horseback and the clop, clop of the mounts of the 380 Dragoons and Rangers riding four abreast behind him had put him to sleep. He awoke when his horse stopped. Around him riders were dismounting from their steeds. He also climbed down and stretched to get the kinks out of his weary body.

He could see mountains silhouetted against the sky off to the right. Closer to him on the left was a sleeping village with a few yellow lights burning in windows. He looked up at the half moon, high in the sky and surrounded by a hazy ring. There were two stars visible within the ring. If he had been back in Ohio, he would consider the ring with its stars as a sign that it would rain within two days. Perhaps that old farmer's tale wouldn't apply here in Mexico. He felt a deep longing to be back in the States.

The day just past, a messenger from Colonel Childs, who with a garrison of 400 men held Puebla and guarded the 1,800 men in the hospital there, had arrived at Scott's headquarters to report that he was under heavy attack by a large number of Mexican irregulars. Within an hour thereafter, the spy Dominguez had appeared and informed Scott that General Santa-Anna had marched south from Guadalupe toward Puebla two days earlier with an army of 6,000. Scott knew General Lane had arrived at Veracruz with a division of 2,500 volunteers and should now be approaching Puebla. Putting the information together, Scott reasoned that Santa-Anna planned to crush Lane's army of untested recruits with overwhelming numbers and then capture Puebla. A major defeat loomed, and the wounded Americans from Cerro Gordo now in a hospital in Puebla were in danger of being massacred. Scott had immediately ordered Colonel Sumner and Colonel Hays with all their available men to ride at once to warn Lane and help him to defeat Santa-Anna and hold Puebla. Grant and seven other officers that weren't part of the Dragoons or Rangers had requested permission to accompany Sumner. Knowing the importance of every man to the small force, Scott had given his approval. Dominguez rode with them as scout and interpreter.

Sumner had told the men that he meant to make a forced march all the way to Puebla within twenty-four hours, a distance of nearly seventy miles. Grant knew they would make it for the colonel had set a reasonable pace and was wisely halting at intervals to rest his men and horses.

"Mount up," Sumner called out and the word moved like a fading echo down the column.

Grant pulled himself upon his horse. He set his rump just so in the saddle, anchored his feet in the stirrups, lowered his head, and glad for the soft, rocking chair step of the horse, went back to sleep.

* * *

October 9 was born with a hot sun that grew into a sweltering fireball as the day wore on and baked the Americans riding on the National Highway hemmed in between steep, brush covered hills. Choking dust rose from under the iron hooves of the horses in a dense brown cloud. The men and horses, wavering and indistinct and wrapped in streamers of dust, moved like misshapen ghosts.

Cavallin and Dominguez, spurring their horses, broke into sight ahead. The two men had been sent out in advance by Sumner to find General Lane. They sped up to Sumner and pulled their mounts to a halt on their haunches.

"We found the general," Cavallin called. "He's got trouble. His mounted riflemen under Captain Walker are under siege at Humantla. Lane wants us to hurry forward and help Walker."

"What's the story?" Sumner said.

"Walker was scouting ahead when he found and attacked guerillas at Humantla. He whipped them but couldn't get out of the town before Santa-Anna with his army caught and penned him in. Now Walker's taking a beating. Lane's infantry is about three miles back and will take some time to come up."

"I know Walker," Hays said. "He's a hell of a fighter but too damn reckless."

"We'll go and help him," Sumner said. He signaled his men and kicked his horse into a run along the road.

Cavallin reined his horse in beside Grant. "Here we go again," he said and gave Grant his rakehell, battle smile.

Soon gunfire could be heard ahead of them. It grew loud as the column crested a rise and Humantla lay in front and below them. The town was long and narrow and strung out along the National Highway for half a mile. Four streets paralleled the highway, two on each side. Grant saw a brigade of Mexican cavalrymen in their red and blue uniforms, pennons flying, and a sea of lances was galloping along the streets and converging upon a giant building that appeared to be a warehouse on the southern end of the town. Companies of Mexican infantrymen were following behind.

"Walker must be near that big building for that's where those Mexicans are heading," Sumner said to Hays. "We'll fight our way there and try to hold out until Lane comes up." He twisted in the saddle and shouted out behind to the lieutenants. "We're outnumbered so stay together."

The Americans charged along the narrow street. Musket fire poured from the buildings lining the street. The Americans fired back at the men on the housetops and in the windows. Grant shot a sniper who was aiming a rifle from a rooftop. He saved his second pistol for a more desperate time.

Two Dragoons were hit and clutched their saddle horns to keep from falling. A horse went down throwing its rider. Both lay unmoving on the pavement. The Dragoons' weapons fell silent, empty and useless.

The revolvers of the Rangers kept on cracking, hurling lead balls at the Mexicans. The immense fire of the Mexicans emptied two Ranger saddles. Grant saw two other Rangers clinging to their mounts. He glanced at Cavallin and saw blood dripping from a wound on the side of the face. His crooked battle grin was twisted fiercely. Cavallin aimed his colt up and shot a Mexican from a rooftop.

A bullet exploded the right ear of Grant's horse. The poor beast screamed, shook its head and almost tripped itself. Grant fired his last shot up at the rifleman and saw him tumble backward and out of sight on the roof.

The charging Americans broke through the ring of Mexican cavalry, and sped on to halt by Walker's men. They leapt down from their mounts. Speedily they began to reload their carbines. Then using the horses as protection and shooting over their backs, they added their fire to that of Walker's men.

The Mexicans, taking heavy punishment from the concentrated balls, reeled back. They regrouped in the mouths of several streets, and continued the fight with long shots.

"Ration your shots. Make every one count." Sumner called out. "Where's Walker?" he said to a rifleman nearby.

"Captain Walker's dead." The man pointed at a body slumped on the ground at the edge of the group of Americans. "He was lanced in the side as we retreated here. He made it just this far."

A storm of rifle shots erupted on the south side of town. Grant recognized the crash of American muskets. Lane and his Yankee infantry had arrived and entered the fray. They were a quarter mile away and fighting their way through the town.

The shooting swelled for a few minutes and then gradually slackened. One of the companies of Lancers retreated. Others saw the first leave and they, too, rode away. The Mexican infantry melted away among the houses and off along the streets. The shots from the buildings stopped. In a moment the Americans stood alone with their dead and wounded.

Chapter Forty-Four

General Lane stomped up and down in front of the eight tents of the field hospital set up on the main street of Humantla. He was a big, burly man wearing an old blue coat and a black hat. A brace of pistols were buckled around his thick waist. He frequently cast a piercing look into the opening of the larger operating tent to gauge the progress of the surgeons with their instruments working swiftly on the wounded. Now and again he looked in the opposite direction at the blue clad body of Walker and others of his men that lay in a row on the pavement.

Except for the squads patrolling the borders of the town, the remaining men of his army was gathered in silent platoons and companies on the street close by. His staff officers stood nearby in a solemn rank as they watched the angry general. Not far off the wagon train was drawn up in the town square.

Two orderlies gently lifted the last wounded soldier, unconscious from the pain of the operation, and laid him on a stretcher. They carried him to one of he hospital tents. The chief surgeon came out of tent and onto the street.

"Is that the last one, colonel" Lane asked.

"Yes, sir," said the surgeon with a sad voice. "We've done as much as we can for them." He removed his bloody smock as he watched Lane for it was obvious he was going to speak.

Lane faced his officers. "Our wounded have been tended to. Our dead have all been found. This has been a costly battle. Captain Walker and many of his men have been killed. The Dragoons and Rangers have also suffered losses. Santa-Anna led the attack and has escaped again. But we'll catch him."

The general hesitated and his hard eyes swept over the gathering. He pointed at the men drawn up in long rows both ways along the street, and then at his officers. His voice crackled with hatred. "This town belongs to our men. They've paid for it with their blood and may take what ever they want from it. The women, the gold, the silver. Anything and everything. I want this place to remember the day they helped Santa-Anna. Go tell the men exactly what I said."

Lane called out in an even harsher voice. "This town is theirs and yours!"

* * *

Grant listened to the blood roar of the male hunting pack, deep and savage, coming from all parts of Humantla. It had gone on for better than an hour now as the Americans stormed through the town, yelling wildly as they destroyed and pillaged. He heard a woman scream now and again and his nerves crawled. Pistol shots rang out as soldiers fired their weapons in exuberance of their license to plunder and rape. Or they could be signaling a Mexican dying while defending his possessions and womenfolk.

The dusk of the day had fallen upon the town and Grant lay on a feather tick bed in the shadow filled room of some unknown family's home. Where had the people gone? Had they run from Santa-Anna, or later, during the attack of the Americans? It didn't really matter. Civilians were expendable during combat. But General Lane had been terribly wrong in his deliberate violence against the civilians after the battle had ended. Grant scowled at himself; that was a fine line to draw in war. However he wanted no part in further hurting the people of Humantla.

The door of the room opened and a young woman, more a girl stole into the room. Grant didn't stir, watching her closely and saw that she held no weapons. Watching the door, she sank down to huddled by the wall and cocked her head to listen. Her face was stark and she trembled with fright. The girl's fear saddened Grant.

A man shouted close by and a second answered. Grant heard running feet drawing nearer. The girl hunkered lower and seemed to shrink into herself.

The door was hit a powerful blow by a shoulder and slammed open half torn from its hinges. Two of Walker's mounted riflemen stormed inside.

Grant snatched up the two pistols lying on the bed by his side. He cocked them as he sprang to his feet.

The men slid to a halt in the center of the room. One of them was but a body length from Grant. His face blanched as he looked down the barrels of Grant's pistols.

"Hold it!" Grant commanded. He looked past the nearer man to make sure the second one wasn't drawing a weapon. Then swiftly back to the first man.

"Goddamn! I'm sorry lieutenant," said the man. "I didn't know you were here." He spun to the rear and shoved his cohort. "Let's get out of here."

The two men lunged out the door and were gone.

The girl stood rigid, surprised by Grant's presence in the room. She turned to the open door and edged toward it. She halted on the threshold and stared into the dusk, listening to the cries and noises outside and the danger that she knew existed there.

Grant spoke in Spanish to the girl. "You may stay here and be safe."

She gave no sign she heard his words. A pistol exploded close by and she began to shake.

"You will be safe here," Grant said again. "Please shut the door."

Watching Grant over her shoulder, the girl closed the door.

* * *

Lee hadn't seen Scott in such high spirits since the day he had marched into Mexico City as the commander of the conquering army. Scott with General Lane in tow was moving from one group of men and women to another and talking in a jovial manner with them. Some two hundred people; influential Mexicans, American officers, and foreign residents were gathered at the large, rambling hacienda of Alberto Salazar a wealthy business man of the capital who was throwing the party to celebrate the arrival of Percy W. Doyle the new British Minister replacing Bankhead who had left for England.

On a broad stone paved area adjacent to the hacienda, tables and chairs had been set up and an elaborate feast with food and wine of many kinds had been prepared. Servants stood ready to serve. Once the sun hid its warm face and the evening cooled, there would be dancing. Beyond the paved area were well-tended grounds with flowerbeds, trees, and a winding path leading down to the shore of Lake Texcoco two hundred yards distant.

Scott had reasons of his own for his festive manner. Four commissioners had been approved by the Mexican Congress to carry on negotiations for the treaty. General Lane had whipped Santa-Anna at Humantla, and then quickly lifted the siege of Puebla. Santa-Anna, following his defeat, had been removed as commanding general of the Mexican Army and told to make himself available to stand before a board of enquiry for his conduct of the war against the Americans.

Lee's companion at the celebration was Elizabeth Thornton. He spent much of his free time with the lovely woman and found her a very pleasant companion.

Lee had never seen so many beautiful women in one place at one time. Many of the officers had come with ladies on their arms. For men that had come alone, carriages were arriving one after another to stop in front and deliver another family with a marriageable age young woman. The moment the women placed their feet on the ground, their eyes darted about to examine the scores of American officers in dress uniforms. They smiled, obviously liking what they saw. The attraction between the officers and the women was a palpable force filling the space between them. Lee noticed more than one set of bright eyes showing interest in him. However he had a woman that satisfied him abundantly.

McClellan had arrived escorting Nachita Alaman, General Alaman's niece. She seemed but a schoolgirl, but then McClellan wasn't much older than the girl. Meade and Pickett, and Longstreet who limped slightly from his wound, showed up without lady friends. Beauregard came with Emerine Dupois, daughter of a member of the French Legation. Hooker appeared and catching Lee's eye as he went by, gave a knowing grin telling that he believed that this party should provide the opportunity for a conquest among the beauties.

"A glass of wine would be nice, Mr. Lee," Elizabeth said and took Lee by the arm. "And then let us go and talk with your General Scott."

"I'm sure he will find pleasure in talking with such a beautiful lady."

Elizabeth laughed lightly and squeezed his arm.

As he approached the wine, he saw Grant put down an empty glass and march off toward a group of young women that were talking among themselves.

* * *

Grant noticed upon arriving at Salazar's party that there were more women than men. That bode well for the evening. He approached the women who had no male escorts and had gathered together in groups of four or five and were talking. He would choose one from among them.

General Lane's division with the Dragoons and Rangers had reached Mexico City the day just past. After the defeat of Santa-Anna's army, Lane had remained in Puebla three days, and for all that time the Rangers and cavalry had been in the saddle from daylight to dark and scouting the surrounding countryside. Three times they had encountered companies of Mexican soldiers that had stood and fought. The Americans had sent them running. Guerillas were treated differently from soldiers. In a town where the Americans fought and defeated guerillas, the town was burned for harboring the guerillas.

Grant missed a step as he observed one of the girls scrutinizing him with a keen interest. To his amazement she came toward him a short distance before abruptly stopping. She glanced quickly at the other girls, then back to Grant. He recognized the girl as the one that had endured his poor dancing at Toluca. His heart did tattoo against his ribs. He lifted his hand to her and hastened forward.

"I'm surprised to see you here," Grant said in Spanish as he clasped her offered hand. "But I'm glad that you are."

"So am I. My uncle lives in the city and I'm staying with him now."

She was telling Grant that she would be here for a time. "My name is Ulysses Grant." He should have told her his name at Toluca.

"Mine is Charlolita Paz."

"Charlolita Paz," Grant said. "That has a nice sound to it. Would you walk with me?"

"Certainly. Where should we go?"

Grant pointed at the grounds with the flowers and the path leading down to Lake Texcoco. "To the lake, if that would be all right."

"That should be an enjoyable walk."

Grant held out his arm for her to take. Keep it formal until later.

As Grant and the girl strolled down the slope, the sun rolled down the last length of its ancient sky path and disappeared behind the lava mountains surrounding the valley. The big stars came out in the evening dusk. An orange glow formed on the eastern horizon, heralding the rise of the full moon. The evening was turning out to be a beautiful one.

Grant took hold of the girl's hand and she didn't pull away. A good first step toward friendship.

Chapter Forty-Five

Grant sat on the rocking chair with his feet braced on the sill of the open window in Chilton's quarters and rocked back and forth and gazed out at the valley of the Aztec's. He was impressed by the striking beauty of the land lying within its sheltering circle of mountains; the three lakes, the city with its canal streets, large buildings painted with bright colors, and the hundreds of farms with their fields and orchards. What it needed was a government that worked for the people instead of for the self-interests of the politicians, the army generals, and the church officials.

He waited for Mathew Chilton who slept on the bed behind him to awaken. Chilton had been seriously wounded by a lance thrust through his chest during the Dragoons' battle with the Mexican Lancers at the battle for the Molino. He had healed slowly but had now left the hospital and taken quarters with other wounded officers in a commandeered home. Grant worried about his friend's health and the fact he brooded too much about the deaths of the men he had led in the battle. Death was to be expected in war. An officer must guard the lives of his men and that was true enough, but once they were dead, he must keep his mind off them. Grant heard a stir behind him.

"Sam, what do you see out there?" Chilton said and rose to sit on the edge of his bed.

"A beautiful land, perhaps one of the most beautiful in the world," Grant said and twisting the chair around to face Chilton. "How do you feel?" Chilton's face was haggard and his eyes held a tormented look.

"Getting better. I can ride some now."

"You had a bad wound."

"It came close to doing me in." Chilton rose from the bed and came to sit in the second chair in the room. He too stared out the window.

"How are you doing?" Chilton said.

"Just soldiering along."

"I heard you're giving the profit from your bakery to the Soldiers Fund."

"Yes, that's so." Grant had rented an abandoned store and hired six Mexican bakers. His bakery was in constant operation with the fires of the ovens never out. He was supplying bread for his men, and selling bread to the other brigades. His profit was forty percent and he gave it to the Soldier's Fund that provided financial help to the wives and children of crippled and dead soldiers.

"I think that's a fine thing to do. I'd like to do something for my dead and those that'll be crippled for the rest of their lives. In the fight for El Molino, I lost a third of my men in less than a minute of fighting. That counts to more than a 1,000 years of my men's future that won't be lived, that's destroyed and lost forever. And we have some men so badly wounded that they'll also die."

"Mat, I think you fret too much about your men for it can get you down. In battle there's death, and those still living must not anguish too much over it."

"Sam, how do you discharge a debt to dead men?"

"The only way I can think of is to help their families with money to live on."

"Like you're doing by giving money to the Soldier's Fund. Yes, I can see that's a way. I'll give the idea some serious thought."

"The army should pay pensions to the wives and children of men killed in combat. Maybe one day it will. For now think of something else. Spend your time with a pretty woman and that'll keep your mind off your men."

* * *

Grant lengthened his stride along The Street Of The Silversmiths toward the Aztec Club. The club was the commandeered splendid mansion of Senor Bocanigra, former Mexican minister to the United States. The mansion contained all it furnishings, china plates, cups and saucers, with gold and silver table utensils, and fine tablecloths. The officers had added eight round tables to the bottom floor for gambling. The top floor had billiard tables, a dance floor, and a well stocked bar. Grant was anticipating an evening of cards and some drinks.

As Grant drew close to the entrance of the club, Dent and Hazlitt, and several other officers came hurrying out. "Where's everybody going in such a hurry?" Grant called out.

"Someone said the new promotion roster has been posted," Dent replied as he and Hazlitt stopped by Grant. "Those fellows who think they've earned another bar are going to check it out."

"Come along with us," Hazlitt said. "Maybe you've gotten lucky."

"Bob, you already got your captain's bar," Grant said.

"Well I'd accept another one to major."

"Sure you would. Let's go."

They arrived at the National Palace and went inside to the bulletin board where copies of all official announcements were posted. The men that had arrived ahead of them blocked the way for a couple of minutes. Words of approval and gladness rang out, and some mutters of disappointment sounded as men turned away from the board. Then Grant and the men with him moved close enough to read the list.

"Mat, you made captain," Dent exclaimed. "Congratulations."

"So did you, Fred," Grant said reading down the alphabetical listening.

"Sam, you lucky dog," Dent said his voice rising. "You got two promotions from second lieutenant to first and then to captain."

Grant felt his heart suddenly pounding. He had known the battle for Mexico City was his last chance to earn a promotion. But two of them! He had been correct in convincing Garland to formally assign him to a fighting unit.

"I didn't make major," Hazlitt said. "But I can live as a captain. So let's four captains go and celebrate with a drink."

"I'm buying," Grant said.

"Any man who gets two promotions at one time sure as hell should."

* * *

"Big lies, that what it is," Beauregard exclaimed.

Beauregard was with Lee and Hitchcock at a table in the Aztec Club and reading the American Star. The paperboy had just passed through selling the latest issue. Twenty or so other officers were present and bent over their copies.

Lee's attention was riveted on two articles on the front page, a reprint from the Pittsburg "Post", and another from the New Orleans "Delta". The article from the Post was a letter that claimed General Worth and Colonel Duncan had rescued General Scott from his own bad judgment by persuading him to adopt the Chalco Road for the assault of Mexico City rather than the National Highway running past El Penon. Lee had been present when that decision had been made and knew first hand that Scott had personally chosen to march west to Chalco and assault the capital from the south.

The Delta article was a letter extolling Pillows military genius and signed by Leonidas. The letter took up half a newspaper column. Lee read it through and then went back and reread the highlights of the article. "General Pillow's plan for the battle of Contreras and the disposition of his forces, were most judicious and successful. He evidenced in this, as he has done on other occasions, that masterly genius and profound knowledge of the science of war, which has astonished so much the mere martinets of the profession . . . During the great battle, which lasted two days, General Pillow was in command of all the forces engaged, except General Worth's division, and this was not engaged . . . (General Scott gave but one order and that was to reinforce General Cadwalader's brigade.)"

Beauregard finished reading and spoke to Lee. "Colonel, what do you think of this letter about General Worth and the Chalco route?"

Lee shook his head. "You know it's not accurate. You were there at the meeting same as I was when the decision was made and you know Scott chose the Chalco route."

"I remember well enough for it's the one I recommended. And this piece about Pillow is all lies. He's the worst general we have."

"Robert, who wrote the Leonidas letter?" Hitchcock asked.

Lee almost said Pillow, but caught himself. He didn't know that for certain, however if he were to bet, that's the man he would choose. "I don't know. But what could he have been thinking to brag so shamelessly when other people would know the truth?"

"We both know who," Hitchcock said sternly. "Only Pillow could brag himself up and belittle Scott at the same time. General Scott will know it too."

All around Lee, other officers were discussing the news items in loud voices. Laughter broke out and quickly spread throughout the room. Lee knew the cause of the laughter for there had been a previous letter written by someone calling themselves Veritas that had puffed Pillow's actions on the battlefield. The general was making a fool of himself. However back in the States, many people might believe it.

Beauregard joined the laughter. Lee couldn't even manage a smile because he saw much trouble ahead. He noticed Hitchcock's face was glum. Pillow and the person who had written the Worth and Duncan letter had gone much too far this time and Scott would have to take action.

"Scott will find out who wrote it," Hitchcock said. "Then somebody's ass will hang."

Lee agreed with Hitchcock, for the letters hit Scott in his most vulnerable spot, his vanity.

* * *

Trist and Lee rode into the Grand Plaza and to the National Palace. They dismounted and the sergeant of the headquarters' guard saluted them past and onward down the wide hallway to Scott's office. The office door was open and Scott was visible pacing about the room with his ponderous strides, and Hitchcock, and Colonel Tipton the Chief Provost Martial sitting at the table with newspapers spread in front of them.

Scott stopped and looked down at the seated men. "I have given this matter much thought as to what action to take against the three officers. I have decided there can be but one response. Any general-in-chief who once submits to an outrage from a junior officer such as these, must lay himself open to suffer the same from all the vicious men under him, and even the great mass of spirited and intelligent among his brothers in arms would soon reduce such a commander to scorn and contempt."

Lee knew Scott was talking about Pillow, Worth, and Duncan. Scott had reissued an old army regulation that forbade the publication of any private letters, or reports describing military operations before the end of the campaign, and further any officers found guilty of making such report for publication would be dismissed from the service. Scott had used the regulation to strongly castigate the writers of the Leonidas and Veritas letters by adding words not in the original order such as, taking false credit, self-aggrandizement, self-puffery, and malignant exclusion of other honorable officers who love their country, their profession, and the truth of history.

Following the issuance of the order, he had questioned Pillow about the authorship of the Leonidas and Veritas letters and Pillow had denied writing them. Duncan had admitted writing the Chalco Route letter but said it had been to his brother and not for publication.

Worth had taken affront at Scott's wording of the order, and in the discussion with the general about it had become abusive in his language. Following that episode, he had written Secretary of War Marcy and President Polk a derogatory letter about Scott.

Scott spoke to Tipton. "Place General's Pillow and Worth, and Colonel Duncan under arrest. We'll allow a board-of-enquiry to sort out the truth of the matter regarding each of them. The three shall be restricted to the city limits until the board meets."

"Yes, sir," said Tipton and left the office.

Lee believed Scott had just condemned himself to much trouble in the future. Pillow was a favorite of President Polk and it was doubtful if he would allow harm to come to the general. Lee felt saddened that Duncan, a skilled and brave officer and a good friend, was caught up in this with Pillow. Still Scott was correct in his action against the officers. The duties of a commanding general in the heart of an enemy country, the army flush with victory, and with little to keep the men busy, must maintain control of his troops with firmness and discipline.

Scott saw Trist and Lee in the hallway. "Come in gentlemen and give me some good news."

"I wish to God that I could," Trist said. "The commissioners are most inflexible and won't negotiate to resolve anything. They become angry when I point out to them that they are totally defeated with General Kearney controlling New Mexico and California, General Taylor occupying Monterrey, Saltillo, and Matamoros, and you, general, the center of the nation including their capital city. The commissioners won't even agree to a boundary for Texas that has been independent of them since 1836. At the end of each meeting, they promise to discuss our proposal with the president, but nothing ever comes of it."

"We must take an action that will force them to come to terms," Lee said.

"You're correct, colonel. We've learned by now that talking does no good."

"We can't occupy more of Mexico just now for we barely have enough troops to hold the capital and Puebla and Veracruz," Hitchcock said.

"But we can levy taxes, huge taxes," Scott said, his harsh words showing his exasperation. "This war is costing our government millions of dollars. We'll make Mexico pay part of it."

"President Polk will think that an excellent plan," Trist said. "That'll help him defend the war against those who condemn it for its high cost."

Scott spoke to Hitchcock. "I think a tax levy of $3,000,000 should get their attention. Divide the levy according to the best estimate of the populations of the nineteen states and the Federal District holding Mexico City. Then prepare an order levying the tax for my signature."

"With pleasure, general," Hitchcock said.

"General Scott," the sergeant of the guard spoke at the doorway, "mail riders have just arrived from the coast and there's an official mail packet for you. Do you want it now?"

"Yes, sergeant, bring it in."

The sergeant came into the room carrying a leather mail pouch and placed it on the desk and retreated.

"Should Lee and I leave, general?" Hitchcock asked.

"No remain for there are other things to discuss."

Scott focused on the mail. "Let's see what Washington has to say to us." He unbuckled the strap that held the pouch closed and removed a sealed packet. He broke the seal and removed several letters.

"There's a letter from the president for you, Nicholas." Scott handed him the envelope with its maroon colored wax seal.

"And several for me, one from the president himself."

Lee sensed the general's reluctance to open the letter. It was well known that there had been friction between Polk and Scott almost from the day Polk had become president. The ill feeling had grown steadily worse since Scott had led the army to Mexico. This past May, Scott had offered to resign as commander in the field. Polk had declined the proposal and Lee was glad for it.

The two men broke the final seals and began to read.

"My, God, this can't be true!" Trist exclaimed. "I've been ordered to cease negotiations with the Mexicans and return to Washington. The president says he's much disturbed by our lack of progress in obtaining a treaty."

"My orders are equally astounding," Scott said. "I'm to prosecute the war with increased energy. Now who would I battle for we have totally beaten the Mexican Army?"

Scott and Trist looked at each other, both stunned at the sudden turn of events. Then Scott spoke. "Nicholas, all our plans are for nothing."

Trist, his face showing disbelief, reread his letter. He looked at Scott. "Perhaps it is best that I go to Washington and discuss the situation directly with the president. The mail requires four weeks or so to make the round trip, and I think President Polk is getting too much slanted information from the newspapers and private reports from some of our officers."

"The British have been working behind the scene to help us in our negotiations with the Mexicans and should be made aware of these developments. Colonel Lee, ride and bring the Britisher Thornton here. Ask him to come at once if it's possible for him to do so. Say nothing to him as to why I ask for his presence."

"Yes, sir."

Chapter Forty-Six

Thornton came into the room flashing his usual broad smile. The smile faded swiftly as he saw the gloomy faces in the room. "What has happened?" he asked.

"Bad news, I'm afraid," Scott replied. "Nicholas has been ordered back to Washington. And I've been ordered to restart the war."

"But, general, the war is won. And you, Mr. Trist, must not leave. The negotiations have to be brought to a conclusion. To fail to seize this opportunity could indefinable postpone the settlement."

"I'm a discharged official and have no authority to do that, and should I, I could be arrested for treason."

Lee saw Thornton was shaken. The financial interest of the British had been hurt by the war and the occupation. They were actively trying to bring about a treaty and a speedy return to business as usual.

"It's just as well that I go to Washington for the Mexicans officials don't seem truly interested in making a treaty with us," Trist said.

"There are several reasons for their slowness in coming to terms," Thornton said. "A large group of Mexicans want the Mexican Army substantially weakened and since you Americans have taken control of much of the country, it no longer plunders the people as it used to. And the church isn't so demanding in its request for tithes. The businessmen like the fact that you pay a fair price for the supplies you take for your army. You may not know it, but the city with General Scott as the ruler has never been run more fairly for the people. Most importantly, Mr. Trist, the commissioners and the president consider you an honest broker of peace and will eventually come to an agreement on the terms for a treaty. I assure you that we of the British legation will do all in our power to assist you."

"Eventually won't do," Trist said. "It's too late now. And they should know that there is much talk, and many editorials are appearing in our newspapers that we should annex all of Mexico as the right of our conquest. President Polk may soon come to the same conclusion for he isn't a patient man.

In fact his order to General Scott to start the war again may be leading to that very end."

"I've been hearing the same thing and that worries me," Thornton said. "How will the negotiations proceed with you gone?"

"Pena will have to send the commissioners to Washington and deal with my government there."

"They'll never do that."

"Then I'll be forced to occupy the entire country," Scott said. "And soon I will have the troops to do that. Then the Mexicans will lose everything."

"I must go immediately and see President Pena," Thornton said and deeply concerned. "General, would you provide me an escort to Queretaro?"

"Certainly. Colonel Lee, go with Mister Thornton to Colonel Sumner's camp and see that an escort of twenty troopers accompany him."

"Yes, sir."

"Mr. Trist, I urge you most strongly, please remain here and carry on with the negotiations."

"That would be a treasonable act now that President Polk has taken away my authority to do so."

* * *

"Eighty men were killed in the brothel district last evening." General Scott's voice was a growl and his face was flushed with anger. He leaned forward over his desk and aimed his scalding glared at Colonel Hays. "Our investigation has shown to my complete satisfaction that your Rangers did the killing. They were seen entering the street where it occurred, and that was just minutes before the shooting began. It was a slaughter and there's no other way to describe what happened."

The general slammed his hand down on the desktop. A pile of written reports bounced into the air and fluttered like crippled birds to the floor. He looked down at the scattered papers and scowled.

"One of my men named Adam Allsens was cut to pieces there," Hays said. "Those Rangers that I questioned swear that they were fired upon when they went to find out who did the cutting. That they merely defended themselves against the thugs and pimps who run that district. That's permitted by your orders. And there's something I'd like to bring to your attention. The men call that place Cutthroat Alley for the reason dozens of Americans have been killed there. I'd say it was time those criminals were taught a lesson."

Lee, watching the exchange between the two men, was impressed with the Ranger colonel's relaxed composure. He acted as if he was merely discussing the weather with the angry Scott.

"It's not up to your Rangers to teach them a lesson. That duty belongs to our patrols and the Mexican police."

"Yes sir, that's who should do it," Hays said. His tone stated clearly that the patrols and police weren't doing their job.

Scott rubbed his jaw and a flinty look came into his eyes. Then that faded and his usual gentlemanly expression came over him. "You may have a point there, colonel. Here's how we'll handle this. You'll put yourself and your regiment of men under the command of General Lane."

Scott picked up a piece of paper. "I've prepared an order directing the general to be even more aggressive in his efforts to capture the leaders of the guerillas forces, Generals Rea, Paredes, Alvarez, and the renegade priest Caledonia Jarauta. He can use your men to help him do that for now with the Mexican army mostly disbanded and many of the soldiers having joined the guerillas, they're larger in number then in the past."

"What about Santa-Anna, general," Hays asked.

"He's on the top of the list. Find him and bring him before me. Look at Tehuacan first for I've had reports he's there. As for the guerillas, give them no quarter. I want them destroyed. Any man caught should be immediately tried by three officers and if there's no doubt as to his guilt of being a guerilla, execute him. Take what you need in the way of provisions and horses from the alcalde of the town nearest the place where you find the guerillas. Charge him three hundred dollars for each one of your men that's killed."

Lee knew Scott had put together a tough, merciless group of men, and many guerillas would die over the next several weeks. Lane's mounted riflemen and the Rangers together would number about 350 men. Lane was the best of the regular army guerilla fighters. During the past weeks patrolling the National Highway, he had attacked General Rea at Atlisco thirty miles from Puebla and killed some 500 guerillas. A week later he had again caught up with Rea and killed thirty more. Then in a joint operation with the Rangers, they had attacked Izucar de Matamoros and killed eighty of General Alvarez men and freed twenty-three Americans. There had been many attacks on smaller guerilla bands. Though deadly in dealing with guerillas, Lane had changed from what he had allowed at Humantla. He had hung two of his teamsters for killing a Mexican boy, and hung one of his soldiers for murdering a woman.

"Do you have any questions?" Scott said.

"No, sir," Hays said.

"Then carry out my orders."

Hays saluted and left.

"The Rangers are as fine a company of fighting men as we have," Scott said as he watched Hays disappear down the hallway. "But they can't be controlled," he added with regret.

That unruly, vengeful attitude makes them what they are, thought Lee.

Chapter Forty-Seven

Grant and Charlolita rode horseback across the Mexican valley on a mild December day. The sun was a golden globe floating high in a clear sky. A gentle breeze barely moved the knee-high grass that surrounded them. Beyond Mexico City and over the faraway south rim of the valley, a thick blanket of dark gray clouds poured rain down upon the mountains.

The well-used road had carried them beyond the cultivated land of the valley center and now crossed over grazing land at the base of the northern mountains. Grant knew it led up through a pass and onward to Pachuca, a town some forty miles distant and known for its rich gold and silver mines. The man and woman rode at a gallop, Grant's favorite gait for a horse. With each bound of the horse, he felt its muscles coil and bunched between his legs and then release as mighty springs to launched the steed forward in long, graceful leaps. Grant much enjoyed the rocking motion of the horse's gallop.

He glanced at Char on his left. She rode effortlessly, head held regally erect and her supple body swaying easily to the stride of her steed. He had enjoyed her pleasant company several times since they had met at the celebration of the arrival of British Minister Percy Doyle.

Char looked, and catching Grant's eyes upon her, gave him a gorgeous smile and a wink. Then to Grant's surprise, she raised her face to the heavens and gave it a strong, lilting shout full of pure animal joy at being alive. Grant couldn't resist joining her, and turning his face up as she had done, gave the heavens a second joyous cry. He was pleased that he was alive with this woman at this moment in time.

They looked into each other's eyes without the slightest embarrassment for yelling at the sky. With the knowledge they were amazingly alike, they broke into laughter. Grant had found a companion with the same passion for life as he possessed, and that person was a lovely woman.

Char gave every sign of enjoying herself when with Grant, always quickly accepting his invitations to parties, dinners, and especially horseback riding as today. She had asked him to call her Char, explaining everybody else did for Charlolitta was much too long of a name. He was surprised at the intensity with which she embraced life, as if she were having a last fling before some type of confinement. He was amazed at the degree of freedom she possessed to accompany him without a chaperon, though he had noted that this occurred only when they rode horseback away from the city, or went on one of the brightly painted canal boats to explore the city, or when she guided him to some small out of the way restaurants to dine. An older woman was always present in the background when they attended parties or gatherings of people.

The thought came unbidden that it could be an enjoyable life to remain in Mexico. Many other men had come to the same conclusion for there had been more than three thousand desertions since the army left Veracruz. As the weeks passed and the monotony of occupying a conquered city wore on them, some of Grant's officer friends had taken apartments in the city and found local girls to live with them full time.

Grant sensed Mexico wasn't to be his future, not even by being slain and buried here. Every enemy bullet had missed, whipping past with an angry hiss of disappointment at not being allowed to strike him. Not understanding how it was possible, he had believed fate, that unknowable yet controlling element of every man's life, had something large in scope for him to do in the future. For now though, he was a soldier in a land conquered by his army and would make the most of it.

Char reined her mount off the road. A short distance later she halted by a spring in the shade of a grove of trees on the mountainside.

"Will this do?" she asked.

"For what?"

"For our picnic."

Grant checked the height of the sun as if determining the time of day.

"Stop that, you know you're hungry," Char said.

"Actually I'm starved. I thought you would never feed me." Grant said with a laugh.

Grant stepped down from his horse. Before he could get to Char to help her dismount, she jumped down to the ground.

"You just take care of yourself," she said with a mischievous light in her eyes. "I'm quite capable of getting off a horse."

"I think you could do whatever you set your mind to."

Char gave him a smile with her perfect lips, and turned to removing packets of food and a white cotton tablecloth from her saddlebags. In half a minute she had the picnic spread, sliced braised lamb, fresh bread, a dark wine, and peach pie. They ate leisurely talking and laughing.

From their position on the mountain, they could look down on the wide, nearly circular valley and Grant took out his field glasses to survey the wide sweep of land. The capital city was plainly visible. Lake Texcoco to the left of the splendid city caught the sunlight just right and sparkled like a great silver coin. Char pointed out the ranchos of relatives and friends. Her father owned one near Toluca. He had a stable of excellent horses and everybody rode, including Char's mother. Her uncle owned a sizeable wholesale business in Mexico City. Grant had discovered that he had purchased supplies for his brigade from the man, and once knowing who the man was, made more frequent purchases from him. Altogether her family was one of importance in Mexican society.

"I've never looked through that," Char said and indicating the field glasses. "May I use them?"

Grant handed the glasses to Char. For a long time she viewed the scene, and uttering little cries of pleasure and surprise as she saw something she recognized.

"It's amazing how well you can see with them. I must buy a pair."

"I'll have a pair for you the next time we meet."

"That would be a nice present. But the very best present you could ever give me you already have."

"What was that?" Grant asked surprised.

"It happened that day you came to Toluca and asked me to dance."

"That was sure my lucky day," Grant said, and meant it. They never mentioned the war between their two peoples. Grant believed women were more practical and forgiving in that regard than were men.

Char turned back to the field glasses. After a couple of minutes, she lowered them and pointed at the storm that had come down into the south end of the valley and was almost to the city. "Maybe we should find shelter before the rain catches us."

They gathered up the remnants of the picnic, stowed all away in the saddlebags, mounted, and rode down into the valley. With the imminent arrival of the rain, they passed other travelers on foot, horseback, or some type of vehicle hurrying along the road to find a roof to protect them from the rain.

* * *

"Best we find a dry place quick," Grant said and feeling the cool dampness of the winds sweeping out ahead of the storm that blanked out half the sky.

"Let's take a look in that old hacienda," Char said and pointing ahead at a long, low adobe structure sitting close beside the road but a couple of minutes ride away.

"Right."

They lifted their horses to a fast gait for the short distance, and then drew rein in the yard full of tall grass and flowers gone wild.

"It's deserted and part of the roof's caved in, still it'll keep us dry," Grant said.

"We'll take the horses inside with us," Char said and glancing at the rapidly approaching storm as she dismounted.

Leading their mounts they entered the open main door of the abandoned building. The old adobe house was cool and musty smelling and with dark shadows in the corners. Dust lay thick on everything. All the windows were open to the outside for the valuable glass panes had been removed. Grant unsaddled the horses and spread the saddle blankets on the earthen floor under a section of intact roof near an inside wall.

"We should be dry here," he said.

He dropped down on the blankets to lie on his back and look up at Char. She gazed at him, however with her face hidden in shadows of the room, he couldn't read her expression. Then she lay down beside him and pressed close and her touch held promises of things to come.

"This isn't too bad," she said, with a smile in her voice.

"I totally agree," Grant said and put his arms around Char's warm body. He hugged her close and kissed her lips, and felt them kissing him back.

He felt a twinge of guilt, of betrayal of Julia, for the comparison that came unbidden that Char was more beautiful than Julia, and certainly more affectionate. He shoved the feeling away. He was a young man with a girl in his arms while Julia was three years in the past and most likely months in the future. And maybe never, for life held huge uncertainties. Concentrate on what's in your arms. His kisses became more passionate, and to his joy, Char responded with sweet ardor.

The shadows grew darker and a mist like rain came to run softly as the feet of spiders across the housetop. The rain gradually thickened to a muted drum on the rooftop. Water leaked through the aged roof in a score of places and fell to puddle on the earthen floor with wet plopping sounds. Still the storm built in intensity. Lightening flashed and thunder rumbled. One of the horses snorted in fright. The clouds opened to dump a torrent upon the old hacienda. Grant and Char lay wrapped in their own world of each other's arms.

Grant woke from a short sleep to the rain slackened to a steady drizzle on the rooftop. Char lay beside him. Her finely chiseled face in relaxed sleep was a wonderful sight. He rose quietly and went to stand to look out one of the open windows. The wind blew mist in to strike his face. Water ran in the grooves cut in the road by the wheels of wagons and carts. Even when the rain ended, the ride to the city would be sloppy, muddy.

He caught movement and looked to the left. A band of riders, he guessed nearly twenty, was coming along the road from the direction of Pachuca. He hastily stepped to the side and peered around the edge of the window frame. Any riders out in this kind of weather could be guerillas and they would be horrible to Char should she be caught with one of the hated Yankees.

The horsemen came into better view on the road in front of the house. They rode slouched forward with shoulders humped against the soaking rain, and faces turned down to escape the strike of the plummeting raindrops. Their wet clothing was plastered to their bodies. To Grant's surprise, the men's clothing was a mixture of boots, pants, shirts, and hats of American Army uniforms. The pants and boots were those of the Dragoons, the shirts and shoulder insignia those of the Missouri Mounted Riflemen, and Pennsylvania Infantry black shako caps with short-billed visors crowned their heads. A tall, thin man in front, Grant thought he would be the leader, had captain's shoulder straps. The man seemed somehow familiar and Grant tried to make out his face through the rain but couldn't because it was angled too steeply down and into his collar. The riders passed on vanishing into the rain in the direction

of Mexico City. Grant knew they were Americans and in disguise and believed they were one of the bands pillaging the outlying towns, and had been
to Pachuca for its gold. He would make a report of what he had seen to the
colonel of the provost marshals.

Chapter Forty-Eight

Lee played poker with Longstreet, Johnston, and Pickett on the second floor of the Bella Union. He enjoyed the Union with its boisterous talk, laughter, spirited music, and the stomp of dancing feet resounding throughout. This was the place of choice of enlisted men and officers that wanted a rousing good evening with a woman, or gambling, or lively discussions on army politics, or the politics of the president and others back in the States. Arguments about the purpose of the war and whether or not the land that would be taken from the Mexicans was meant for slavery sometimes ended in fistfights. Lee thought the reason for the war was simple, President Polk meant for the United States to expand to the Pacific Ocean.

The Bella Union had been acquired on that first day of occupation when shots had been fired from it and a squad of Americans had charged in and killed some of the snipers and routed the remainder. The Americans quickly recognized the possibilities of the Bella Union, a wide, three-story building with the first floor a restaurant and dance floor, the second a card parlor with more than two dozen tables, and the third the realm of a bevy of pretty whores. The Americans took possession of the building instead of destroying it as was their right because of shots having been fired from it.

The rollicking, rowdy nature of the Bella Union came from the fact that an army of occupation was an entirely different animal from a fighting one. Much of the energy and daring that had won battles was now turned to gambling of various kinds; horseracing, cards, spinning wheels of chance, and whoring. Gambling was an epidemic and running rampant in the army from the generals down to the lowest private. Drink, women, and cards made a volatile mix. Men fought over cheating at cards, over a woman, or from simply being mean drunk. The fighting was always by fists for General Scott didn't allow dueling with weapons.

Some Americans had turned to robbery and murder of the native people; the town banks were frequent targets. Some thirty Americans caught committing crimes, had been lashed in the public plaza, five had been hung on the

gibbet that Scott had had built there. Nearly four hundred Mexicans had received punishment in the same place and manner and before a large throng.
Any Mexican caught carrying a weapon was given twenty lashes on the bare
back. When an American was punished, Scott often ordered the one-third of
soldiers on standby duty to witness it. He wanted a peaceful city and meant
to have it.

For officers who didn't like Bella Union because of the gambling and the
presence of whores, a higher class of women could be found at the dances in
the gentlemanly Aztec Club. For enlisted men of the same bent, a dance partner was available at the dances held every Sunday at the former convent on
Bellemintas Street.

Lee's luck at cards was running the wrong direction and he had lost several dollars. Longstreet was the big winner.

"We need to break Longstreet's winning streak," Sumner said.

"Another player or two just might do that," Lee said.

"One of our new captains just came in," Picket said and nodding toward
the entryway to the second floor. "I've seen him playing cards."

The other three men looked in the direction of the entryway where Grant
stood checking the room.

"It's about time Garland and Worth promoted him," said Longstreet as he
observed the smallish, slouched shouldered man. "I saw him at Churubusco.
He was the fastest of any man there to get to where the fighting was the hottest."

"He doesn't look much like a fighter, but he was in the thick of it at Humantla," Sumner said.

"He can join my brigade any time he wants to," Longstreet said.

Lee climbed to his feet and called out. "Grant, we need another player
over here. Are you game?"

Grant knew he had come to the right place when he stepped thought the
door of the Bella Union and the music and the noisy camaraderie of the soldiers struck him with a pleasant physical force. He bought a drink at the bar,
took a sip, and watched the whirling dancers for a minute before climbing to
the second floor and the card games.

He was surprised when Lee called out to him. He raised his drink in
acknowledgement of the invitation, and wound a way through the tables with

the sound of the clink of coins, the call of bets, and the shuffle of cards all around him. He felt self-conscious with the new captain's straps on his shoulders as he came toward the table of the four older men, all colonels. Looking at the situation another way, he had fought in as many battles as any of them, and twice as many as Scott's favorite officer, Lee. He felt better after that comparison.

Grant stopped at the table. "What's the game?" he asked as he took a seat.

"A friendly game of five card draw," Longstreet said.

"I hope you brought plenty of money for Longstreet's on a roll." Lee said.

"Let's play," Longstreet said and began to shuffle the cards.

The cards were dealt and the playing began with each man measuring and challenging his fellow officers' luck and skill.

"How're the negotiations for the treaty going?" Sumner asked Lee.

"Nowhere as far as I know," Lee replied. "At the rate we're moving, I don't know when we'll have a treaty." He could say nothing more for he had been ordered not to discuss Nicholas Trist's decision. Scott, Thornton, and President Pena had for the past several days been urging Trist to remain in Mexico and continue the negotiations on a treaty even though he had no authority to do so. Scott had made the argument that if a treaty was agreed upon and it conformed to Trist's original instructions, that Polk and the congress would accept it. Lee thought the same. Trist had finally made his decision, and that was to stay in the Mexican capital and meet with the commissioners and try to reach an agreement until the president had responded to his letter requesting a delay in leaving for Washington. He had insisted the meetings would be unofficial and must be held in secrecy. Scott had promised Trist his full support in the event Polk or anybody else should accuse him of a traitorous act.

"I believe by the laws of conquest that we have the right to dictate the terms of the peace," Longstreet said.

"And take as much of their land and wealth as we want," Pickett said.

"I agree, though we did bully Mexico into war and she was the weaker nation," Grant said. "However now that we're here I'd set a time limit and if the Mexican government didn't come to terms on a treaty, then we should march across the country up to the boundary of Texuantepec or Osaqualco or whatever southern line Polk or the congress should think proper for the U. S.

I'd think the Mexicans would then waste no time in making a treaty. I might make a rough diplomat, but a tolerably quick one."

"General Scott feels the same way," Lee said. "And to force the Mexican hand, I'm to start tomorrow to guide army detachments to occupy Cuernavaca, Toluca, Pachuca, and Orizaba where they'll collect taxes. And other towns later if the first four don't bring the negotiations to an end." Scott's army had grown to 15,000 strong and large enough to occupy outlying towns. This increase in size had occurred within the past three weeks when General Patterson, one of Lee's favorite officers, had returned to Mexico with a division of 3,000 men. Then General William Butler had arrived with 4,000, and Colonel Joseph Johnson with 1,500.

"I've been to Toluca and nearly to Cuernavaca on foraging trips and have maps of the roads in those directions that you're welcome to use," Grant said.

"I know the road to Toluca for I've been there," Lee said. "I'll be going to Cuernavaca first and would like to see your map."

"I'll bring it by your quarters after we're finished playing cards."

"I've a better idea. Why not come with me and be the guide?

"My duties are caught up and I'm sure I can get permission to do that."

"Then I'll plan on it," Lee said.

"Back to the game, fellows, for I want to at least break even before we stop," Sumner said.

* * *

Grant and Lee halted their horses on the summit of the mountains rimming the southern boundary of the valley that held the Mexican capital. As the mounts caught their wind after the steep climb, the men rolled and lit cigarettes and surveyed the land about them. In the bright mid-day sun the valleys and the forested mountains stood out in sharp relief. On the winding road behind and before them, people on foot, donkeys pulling carts, horses and oxen drawing wagons, and men on horseback were seen coming and going.

"No country was ever more blessed by nature than Mexico," Lee said and indicating the land with a broad sweep of his hand. "Every fruit and grain and vegetable grows on the rich volcanic soil. And there's grazing land for hundreds of thousands of cattle, sheep, and goats. Yet most of the people are poor with the wealth concentrated in the hands of the Creoles, the Catholic Church, and the army generals. What's needed is a stable and fair government so that the ordinary people can get what's due them."

"I agree," Grant said. "I've heard that many influential people in the States are pushing a plan for us to take all of Mexico and annex it, and then give the 300,000 immigrants pouring into our country from Europe each year land here in Mexico. They say that Mexico with democracy and Europeans would bloom."

"I don't agree with taking all of Mexico."

"I don't think we should either, but we are an army of conquest," Grant said. "I see one benefit from us being here. We may have headed off some other strong nation, most likely France or England from eventually taking Mexico over entirely. The question is, how much of Mexico will President Polk settle for, and how much will he pay for what he takes."

"Best we be on our way," Lee said. He knew the terms of Polk's proposal but it wasn't his place to disclose them.

Lee sent his horse off along the road. Grant reined his horse in beside the colonel. They rode at a trot down the road that would lead them past Popocatepetl with its snow capped peak and onward to Cuernavaca.

Both men were armed with a pair of pistols, a carbine, and their sabers, still Grant would have preferred a few Dragoons to be with them. Guerillas were frequently striking groups of Americans caught on the highways. The colonel hadn't mentioned taking along an escort, and for a mere captain to suggest it would seem to say the colonel didn't know what he was doing.

* * *

When Cuernavaca came into view two miles ahead, Lee and Grant examined it for a few minutes and then turned back along the road on their return journey to Mexico City. They had added features to Grant's map, plotting the cross roads, the streams, and campgrounds suitable for the detachment of American soldiers that would soon come marching this way. A copy of the completed map was made for Lee.

They had gone a short ways and were drawing near dense woods that the road cut through, when six riders came out from hiding among the trees. At a word from the leader, a spindly man with a hatchet sharp face and bulging black eyes, and mounted on a cream colored horse, the riders divided with three on each side of the road. Holding their lariats coiled with the nooses open and positioned for quick throwing, they sat their horses and waited as the Americans came closer. Long endured hate showed in the leader's black eyes. Now too there was a look of anticipation of inflicting punishment upon the Yankees.

"They want us to run and then they'll lasso and drag us," Grant said as he and Lee stopped their mounts back some fifty feet from the Mexicans. He had seen the battered corpses of Americans that had been roped around the neck and dragged behind a running horse until dead.

"Well I don't feel like playing the hound and hare game with them. Or riding around them either." Lee's voice betrayed no emotion.

"Neither do I," Grant said and felt his urge to fight come afire.

"Captain Grant," Lee said being very formal, "I've heard that you're an excellent pistol shot, is that so?"

"Colonel Lee, I usually hit what I aim at." Grant wasn't going to be out done in formality.

With a deliberate motion, Lee pointed a finger at the horseman who had given the order to the others, and was on Grant's side of the road. With a sharp, commanding voice, he said, "Captain, kill that man if one of them moves to throw his lariat, or to pull a gun."

"Yes, sir." Grant had drawn both of his pistols and eared back the hammers. Now he raised the guns above his horse's head where the Mexicans could plainly see them. He wished he had a couple of the five-shooters of the Rangers for then he could have killed all six of the Mexicans. He focused on the man at whom Lee had pointed, and the two nearest him. He saw the leader's face lose the look of anticipation and take on one of much uncertainty.

Lee drew his pair of pistols and cocked them. "Forward, captain, and we'll see if they really want to use their ropes, or go for their pistols."

They touched their mounts with spurs and walked them down the road. They came within forty feet of the waiting Mexicans, thirty, then less and were within reaching distance of the lariats.

Grant pointed his right hand pistol at the center of the leader's face, giving him a good look down the open bore of the gun. He saw the man's eyes waver as his will to fight crumpled. The man called out and Grant understood the words, "Do nothing. Let them pass."

The Mexicans parted, backing their horses off the road.

Lee and Grant rode on, and turning in the saddle so as to always have the Mexicans in view and under their guns. They moved on until past their foes.

"At a trot, captain," Lee said.

Still looking to the rear, the officers rolled spurs gently across the flanks of their steeds and raised them to a slow trot. The Mexicans remained motionless and staring after them. They fell from sight as the road curved away through the woods.

"They didn't want to fight with guns, captain," Lee said.

"No, sir, just throw their lariats that's all," Grant said. The colonel was all right.

* * *

"Captain, I'll part company with you here," Lee said. He and Grant had arrived on the outskirts of Mexico City after three days of hard riding and now he wanted food, a warm bath, and a night's sleep on a soft bed.

"Yes, sir," Grant said.

Lee rode on along the Belen Road toward the capital. In the morning he would leave to scout the road to Orizaba, and then when that was completed the road to Pachuca. The days ahead would be busy ones.

Grant turned left on the road to Tacubaya and his brigade headquarters to announce his return to Garland, who had been promoted to brigadier general for his stalwart action at Churubusco.

Chapter Forty-Nine

The four men dipped their pens in the inkwells and signed the duplicate copies of the three-page peace treaty as they were passed to them. Nicholas Trist and the Mexicans were meeting in secrecy as they had since President Polk had stripped Trist of his authority to negotiate. They had chosen Guadalupe Hidalgo the location of Mexico's most venerated shrine for today's meeting because what they were doing was an event of memorable importance to both nations.

Lee was once again accompanying Trist during his discussions and acting as guard and General Scott's military representative. The Mexicans had been tenacious and difficult bargainers and found fault with every one of Trist's offer of terms for a treaty. Still Trist had finally brought the commissioners, with President Pena approval, to the signing of the treaty.

Reaching this point had been very difficult. The date was February 2, 1848 and four months had passed since Trist had placed himself in jeopardy of Polk's anger by continuing with the negotiations. Just three days past, Trist had made his final offer of $15,000,000 for the land Polk had instructed him to acquire. The Mexicans had immediately demanded $30,000,000. At that Trist lost his patience with the intransigent commissioners and declared the negotiations at an end and he was returning to Washington. In the strongest language he told then that by their refusal to accept the reality that the Americans controlled their country that they were in the greatest danger of losing all of it to the Yankee President. With that said, he and Lee had left to report to Scott.

British Minister Doyle upon hearing of Trist breaking off negotiations came with Thornton to Scott's headquarters. He explained to Trist and Scott that President Pena feared a revolution against him and that was the reason he and the commissioners wouldn't come to an agreement. To that Scott had spoken with much heat. "Then tell Pena that I will protect him against any revolution should a treaty be signed. But if not signed promptly, then I will dislodge his government myself and hunt him like a deer through the mountains." Upon being told this by the Britishers, Pena quickly responded by asking Trist to meet with the commissioners.

The last signature, Trist's, was attached to the treaty and the scratching pen laid down. Trist picked up one copy and gently folded it.

"We have what President Polk wanted," he said in English to Lee and radiating relief and satisfaction.

"You did it, Nicholas," Lee said. Trist was a brave man and Lee was glad his huge gamble paid off. However there were yet obstacles to overcome; Polk had to give his blessing to the treaty and then the American Congress must ratify it. Following that, the Mexican Congress had to be persuaded to approve it.

Trist and Lee solemnly shook hands with the Mexicans and left by the rear door of the private residence loaned to them for the meeting. Waiting for them in the rear yard were Dominguez and three other men of the Mexican Spy Company. All were well armed. They were here to protect Trist and the Mexican negotiators from being assassinated for there were powerful men who did not want a treaty that gave land to the Americans.

Lee and Trist mounted and followed the Mexican riders through the gate in the wall and into an alley. As they came out onto the main street, three more of Dominguez's men fell in behind them. Lee felt safe with the men of the Spy Company for they had proved their dependability time and again.

* * *

"Let me see the document," General Scott said, his broad face wreathed in a smile of anticipation.

Trist unfolded the pages of the treaty and in a slow, almost teasing way, and handed them to Scott. Present also in the general's office were Lee and Captain Scott.

General Scott read to the end and nodding from time to time. He looked at Trist and his eyes were misty, the most intense emotion Lee had ever seen from the general. "Nicholas, my friend, you've done it in a grand fashion. Everything the president desired from the Mexicans you've gotten for him. I hope he and the country appreciates your unselfish action."

"It was possible only because of your victorious march to take the Mexican capital."

"We make a fine team," Scott said in a hearty voice and clapped the smaller man soundly on the shoulder.

Scott handed the document to Lee. "Read, colonel, and see how your country had been increased in size by a third in one fell swoop and reaches to the Pacific Ocean."

Lee read the twenty-three terms of the treaty. The boundary between the two countries would run along the Rio Grande to the southern boundary of New Mexico, then west along the Gila River to the Gulf of California. From there it would run westward along a line just south of San Diego to the Pacific Ocean. The United States would pay $15,000,000 for the territory. Lee thought it fair when looked at from the point of view that the Americans were giving up a large area of conquered land. One of the terms spoke to the Mexican people in the transferred territory. They could go or stay and would retain ownership of their property. Should they remain, they would become American citizens.

"Captain, make a copy for us to keep here at headquarters." Scott said to Captain Scott. "The original must be sent at once to the coast and put aboard a mail packet to Washington."

"Nicholas, you should have the honor of transmitting the treaty to Washington?"

"I'll prepare a letter to President Polk at once. I hope he'll accept it since I had no authority to negotiate with the Mexicans."

* * *

"Pillow should be taken out and shot like the cowardly, treacherous dog he is," Hitchcock said in a malevolent voice to Lee. "This is his doing by writing President Polk lies about the general."

Lee said nothing. Exactly one week after the signing of the peace treaty, a messenger had arrived directly from Polk with a dispatch containing an order directing Scott to turn over the command of the army to General Butler. A second order had directed him to convene a court of enquiry to hear his charges against Pillow, Worth, and Duncan. The same court would also hear

298

Worth's charges against Scott. Hitchcock and Lee had left headquarters with Scott somber and thoughtful writing out his final order for the army he had led in victorious battles, an order relinquishing his command in ten days and placing General Butler as commander of the army in central Mexico.

"Well, what do you say?" Hitchcock asked, and aimed a questioning eye at Lee.

"The general could've handled Pillow and Worth in a more subtle way. His vanity led him to speak too bluntly and do things that played into the hands of Pillow and Polk."

"Maybe he could've. But it's hard for an honest man to deal with a liar and braggart like Pillow. The general will have his chance to prove what kind of an officer Pillow is when he has him before the court of enquiry."

"Scott must also stand before the court and face questioning about Worth's charges against him."

"I'll demand to testify at the hearing. I want to have my say about Pillow."

"We'll both have our chance to testify, I'm sure of that," Lee said.

He glanced around the large reading room of the Aztec Club that was jam-packed with more than a hundred officers engaged in intense conversations. Men gestured and talked with high emotion as they made their point. The news that the general was being replaced had struck the army like a bomb-shell. Officers had flocked to the club knowing that here they would find others to discuss and argue such a startling event. Pillow, Worth, and Duncan were absent and for good reason, by forming a cabal against the popular Scott, they had alienated most of the other officers of the army that had marched inland with the general and held him in high regard. Several officers of Butler's staff were present and in a good mood for with him soon to be the commanding general of the army their own status would be substantially increased.

Lee saw Captain Grant sitting off by himself with a newspaper. He was the only officer in the reading room who was actually reading. Lee had never seen the captain show his inner thoughts or feelings, always unruffled and with a calm voice.

Grant sensing eyes upon him looked up from the newspaper. Seeing Colonel Lee watching him, he nodded, got a return nod, and went back to his reading. Grant couldn't but help hearing the loud talk among the officers surrounding him. Scott's staff officers, especially Hitchcock, Beauregard and McClellan were condemning Pillow in the roughest of language, cursing and denouncing him for lying and betraying their general. Worth's and Duncan's name came up now and again in a derogatory way. Scott's staff men had glum expressions, which were rightfully possessed since they had much to lose by the change in army commanders. Lee especially must dislike it since he was Scott's favored staff officer. Or at least that was the word in the army.

Grant thought Polk's treatment of Scott to be harsh and unjust, and further that it was poor strategy to take a victorious general's army away from him in a foreign land before the war was officially ended and a treaty signed, sealed, and delivered. He was confident that Polk's action was caused by politics with him wanting to lessen Scott's chance of winning the nomination for president on the Whig ticket.

* * *

General Scott met with Lee and Hitchcock in his plush quarters in the National Palace. He had surrendered his office at headquarters when General Butler assumed command of the army two weeks past. The two colonels had come at Scott's request and were seated and facing him.

The general was in a thoughtful mood, yet that did not distract him from his usual courteous manner and he was pouring wine into tall glasses for the two men and himself. The wine merchants of the capital kept the general well stocked with the finest of the country. Scott took up his drink and seated himself across from the two colonels. Holding the wine glass delicately in his large hand, he took a drink and focused on the junior officers.

"We three have soldiered together for a year, almost to the day. During that time we have had time to take each other's measure. I judge both of you fine soldiers and honest and fair men and for that reason I want you to consider the following proposition that has been brought to me." A trace of a smile came and went on his face.

"Several prominent Mexicans, businessmen, government officials, and military have come to me and propose that I resign from the American army and issue a proclamation declaring myself dictator of Mexico for the next six years."

The statement amazed Lee, believable only because Scott never joked, and certainly never lied.

Hitchcock cackled and slapped his leg. "By, God!" he chortled.

Scott smiled at their reaction. "Ah, I see that has your attention. And you're wondering why the Mexicans would do such a thing. I have the answer for they told me. They want me to make Mexico a country where the law applies to all citizens equally, to make it a true democracy, to stop insurrection and the extortion and tyranny practiced by the military and the church. A period of dictatorship would give time for them and me to organize a government that would give the people what they rightfully deserve. They also fear invasion from another foreign power once we leave, and this would quiet likely happen for they have no army and a very weak and fractured government. They even mentioned that they would seriously consider annexing Mexico to the Untied States as Texas did."

"How sincere do you think they were?" Lee asked.

"Quite sincere. To seal the deal, five of the richest men in the capital have guaranteed me $250,000 each for a total of $1,250,000 and the salary of the president for the six years. That's quite a fortune."

"Even for a dictator," Hitchcock said. He gave a chuckling laugh enjoying the news immensely.

"Yes, even for a dictator. Should I accept the offer, I'd want you two to join me as my principal staff officers, and of course with the proper promotions and increase of pay. As you know, we can all resign our commission so that there would be no reason why we can't legally do as we wish."

"When would this take place, if it did?" Lee asked.

"When the treaty is finally approved by the American and Mexican congresses. At that time, about seventy percent of our men will be discharged in place. That would be some 10,000 soldiers. With a handsome pay raise most of them would sign on with us. In addition, the Mexicans say that I could choose another 10,000 Mexican troops from their army. With that size of an army we could defeat any nation that might try to invade Mexico."

Scott sat back in his chair and observed the men. "It's tempting, isn't it?" he said with a chuckle.

Lee was flabbergasted with the proposal. Scott with his intelligence and honesty and immense prestige could in truth make it work.

"I agree with you about the number of men that would sign on," Hitch-cock said. "And we already control the arsenals and occupy all the major cities and seaports, and have a tax on the output of the gold and silver mines."

"I don't expect your answers now for even I haven't made up my mind. Before I could, I would need to know approximately how many officers and men would be with me. Talk quietly with those officers that you think would be the right ones for such a venture and see how many of them would come along. The Mexicans expect an answer and we will give them one."

A series of faces and names came to Lee of the colonels, majors, and captains that he would choose to serve with him. They could all become wealthy, and life here would be enjoyable.

"This is a strange situation to be in," Hitchcock said.

"How do you feel about this offer?" Scott asked Lee.

"I like serving with you and will give this serious thought. One thing for certain, Mexico needs something like this to have time to get its house in order."

Chapter Fifty

Grant left the conclave of army captains with a feeling of uneasiness about what was being proposed. Captain Porter of Quitman's division had sought Grant out and persuaded him to attend a secret meeting of other captains in his quarters to discuss the Mexican proposal to Scott. The news that Scott might declare himself dictator of the country and would need officers to command an army had spread like wildfire. The men discussed the possibilities for acquiring wealth should he become part of an army of Americans controlled by an American general. Some men thumped the table and boasted about what they could achieve in the way of promotion, or starting a private businesses. In Grant's case, he already had a bakery business in operation and could keep all the profit instead of contributing it to the Soldiers' Fund. Further he might get promoted to the rank of major, which wouldn't be all that bad.

Grant's apprehension grew as he considered what signing on with an American dictator ruling Mexico might mean. As an American soldier, the scheme to overthrow the Mexican government seemed wrong. This was so even given how poorly the government functioned. In addition, he was opposed to the annexation of Mexico. No, Grant wouldn't sign on to a dictator's army in Mexico. With that decision resting easy on his mind, he struck off to the army hospital where he had been headed when sidetracked by Porter.

* * *

Grant came to the hospital consisting of scores of tents and an even greater number of houses that had been taken over by the army on the border of Tacubaya. Thirty-six hundred soldiers, one out of every six men of the army, lay wounded or ill with disease. Most of them were here in Mexico City, with a lesser number at Puebla and Veracruz. Men had been wounded in battles and in fights in the grog shops and low dives of the city. However it was disease, mainly typhus and dysentery that was the biggest killer of the soldiers.

General Butler had ordered all the injured and sick men that were able to travel to be taken to Veracruz for transport to the army hospital in New Orleans. When well enough, the men would to be released from the army and sent on to their homes. Grant was to get the expedition started just as soon as he could put together the necessary wagons and teams. He entered the office of Colonel Samson, Chief Surgeon.

"Colonel, I'm Captain Grant. I've been ordered to take your sick and wounded to Veracruz. How many will I need wagons for?"

"Eleven hundred and ninety are well enough to travel," Samson said. "When can you leave with them?"

"Mid-morning tomorrow, sir. Say nine o'clock."

"I'll have them ready. I'll send along two surgeons and their medical assistants to look after the men. All you have to do is get them safely to the coast."

"I'll do my best, sir."

* * *

Grant found O'Doyle and directed him to gather the men and start assembling three hundred wagons and rounding up the needed teams of horses and mules and prepare everything for the journey to Veracruz. The army had nearly three thousand wagons in a yard occupying a large area west of Tacubaya, and more than eight thousand horses and mules grazing in rented pasturage round about the south end of the valley. He ordered the men to start their work at once and continue until dark. They had been loafing for days and that wasn't good for soldiers.

He thought of Char. He would like to spend the evening with her but preparation for the journey must come first. As he passed the army cemetery heading to his quarters to grab a bite of food, he saw Chilton standing among the graves. The cemetery was rapidly adding new graves for the drum taps of the dead march sounded almost every day as two, three, and sometimes four corpses of soldiers were brought for burial.

Chilton appeared very lonely there in the cemetery with his shoulders slumped and his head turned down to a grave. That posture of Chilton's brought to Grant's mind the band of horsemen he had seen that day when Char and he were in the abandoned house and men had passed in the rain. Chilton closely resembled the leader of those riders. Grant caught himself up short for he was confident those men were some of the Americans that had been robbing the outlying towns and thus it was best not to think of Chilton being one of them. He went to talk with his friend who worried too much about the dead.

As he walked across the cemetery, he read names carved into wooden markers driven into the ground at the head of each grave. The old sorrow for his friends moldering in their graves came over him. He shoved the thoughts out of his mind.

"Hello, Mat," he called.

Chilton lifted his arm. "Hi, Sam."

"How you doing?" Grant replied. Chilton had been a slender man at the beginning of the march from the sea. Now he was gaunt, unhealthily so with hollow cheeks and blue eyes unnaturally large in his bony face. At the moment they held tears. Some men weren't meant to be soldiers because the death of comrades was too much for them to bear.

"Surviving, Sam, surviving."

"What're you doing out here?"

"Another one of my fellows died." Chilton pointed at the fresh dirt of the grave near his feet. "Once I thought a man who had no fear could do anything he wanted. How bitter that thought is today with so many of my men lying buried here."

"Mat, the army is no place for you, so why not go home. I believe the chief surgeon would approve a discharge for you, or at least a release to inactive duty."

"I've already got permission to leave. A wagon train will soon be going to Veracruz and I plan to be with it."

"I'll be leading it."

"That's good. We'll have time to talk. When will you be leaving?"

"Tomorrow mid morning."

"I'll see you then." Chilton turned back to stare at the graves.

Grant watched Chilton for a moment, and then walked away.

* * *

Grant bathed, donned a fresh uniform, and ate a meal prepared by Valere. He complimented Valere for the fine food and left his quarters and walked to the center of Tacubaya where he stopped at a tobacconist shop and ordered six cigars be freshly rolled. While he waited, he went next door to a barbershop and bought a shave and had his raggedy hair shortened. Since arriving in the capital he'd gone clean-shaven. Spruced up, he struck out for the capital to see Char.

Grant knocked on the door of the Paz home with a pleasant feeling of anticipation at seeing Char. The young woman had built a warm place in his heart.

The older woman that chaperoned Char opened the door. Her face tightened with displeasure at sight of Grant. Why was that? "I wish to see Senorita Paz," Grant said.

"The Senorita isn't at home," said the woman and started to shut the door.

"Wait. Please tell her that Senor Grant came to see her?"

"She will be told," the woman's voice had finality in it. She shut the door in Grant's face.

He walked across the yard to the street. There he turned to look at the house. For the briefest of moments, he saw someone peeking from an upstairs window before they drew back hastily out of sight. The person could have been Char. Grant's relationship with the people of the house had drastically changed.

* * *

Approaching Jalapa with his wagon train, Grant came upon the bivouac of the Rangers in a grove of trees beside a small stream just off the National Highway. The men lounged about on their blankets on the ground smoking and talking. The camp of Lane's Mounted Riflemen was just downstream from the Rangers, and they too were lazing about.

Grant brought his caravan of wagons into the upper end of the meadow and halted to rest men and animals until the coming morning. The sick and wounded men, those that were capable, climbed down from the vehicles to walk about. The surgeons and their assistants hurried to help the men who had lost a leg or were for some reason unable to dismount from the vehicles. The teamsters began to unhook their animals and take them out to graze, and the cooks hastened to gather wood for their evening cooking fires.

Cavallin came up from the camp of the Rangers. He called out ahead. "Sam, I didn't expect to see you coming with a wagon train."

"The general wanted a load of sick and wounded taken to ships waiting at Veracruz. Then it's on to New Orleans for them."

"They'll be glad to get home."

"Where are Hays and Lane. Since I'm going to Veracruz, I thought that I could take any of their men that are wounded with me to the hospital there."

"Both rode into Jalapa to buy provisions. We've been chasing guerillas long and hard and are short of everything."

"I'll talk with them later on this evening."

Cavallin was looking past Grant. "Here come one of my boys and he's in a hurry."

The Ranger stopped by Cavallin. "Lieutenant, I heard something in town that you'll be glad to know. Santa-Anna's coming, and he's just a few miles up the road. People are saying that he's leaving the country."

"That sonofabitch has his nerve coming past us," Cavallin said.

"Tom, he probably doesn't know you're here," Grant said. "He's got a safe conduct pass from General Butler so you can't bother him."

"I know about the pass for we've been told to stop hunting him."

"I'll tell the other men," said the Ranger and hurried off through the camp and calling out, "Santa-Anna's coming and will be here soon."

"We almost caught him once," Cavallin said. "I wish to God that we had. We were so close on his trail that he ran leaving seventeen trunks piled on the patio of the house, and candles burning on the table, and food ready to eat. We opened the trunks and found his wife's clothing, dresses by the hundreds, shoes, all kinds of woman things. One of the dresses must have weighed fifteen pound from all the gold decoration on it. And we found a cane of the one-legged bastard. It was studded with all kinds of jewels. We gave it to the colonel."

"Tom, you can't let the men kill Santa-Anna, not with the pass he's carrying. Butler will hang any man that takes part in it."

"Maybe he would, and then again maybe we wouldn't stand for him to do that. And anyway I couldn't stop them from going after that butcher even if I wanted to. Best you get out of here for you don't want to be part of what's going to happen."

Grant went to his horse and rode in the direction of his wagons. Once out of sight of the Rangers, he put spurs to his horse and hurried into Jalapa. He had to try to save the Rangers from themselves. Only Hays would have any chance at all to prevent Santa-Anna's murder.

Chapter Fifty-One

Hays and Grant brought their running horses to a prancing stop in front of the Rangers gathered silently along the side of the road that Santa-Anna would be traveling. With hooded eyes, the men stared at their colonel. They weren't in any mood to listen to what he might say. Cavallin gave Grant an angry stare.

Hays sat his saddle for a moment and looking at the bleak faces of the men. Then he dismounted and began to pace up and down in front of them. His voice rang out. "The bastard Santa-Anna massacred our people at Alamo and Goliad, and don't forget the drawing of the black beans at Perote where one man out of each ten was shot, and all the killings at other places. He deserves to be killed like the dog he is. Now isn't that right?"

A mighty roar of voices rolled out across the land. "Goddamn right." "Kill the greaser." "Skin him alive and even that'd be too good for him." "We're with you colonel."

Grant was flabbergasted by Hays speech. The colonel was goading the men to kill Santa-Anna and this wasn't why Grant had brought him.

"Some of you men had relatives killed, isn't that right?" Hays voice was grim.

Another cry of angry curses and threats rang out.

"Yes indeed, he deserves killing." Hays ceased pacing and ran his eyes down the line of men, every one of them a larger man than he was, and not missing one eye that was watching him back so intently. "But if we do, then we're no better than he is. Hell, I'm not going to stand here and tell you not do it for that's your call. Still I'll say this, Santa-Anna has been condemned for killing prisoners. The world knows it and detests him for it."

"But Colonel Hays," a tall, gangly Rangers spoke up, "he's a free man and I'm damn sure he's got money stashed away, and a hell of a lot of it too."

"He's as good as being a prisoner for he's forced to flee his own country. If you kill him you'll dishonor Texas. You sure don't want that."

A man looked up the road, and then another, and another as the rumble of wheels, the jangle of trace chains, and the clop of horses' hooves came to the group. A string of vehicles came around a bend in the road and into sight. The caravan was made up of four coaches and eleven wagons and thirty of so mounted and armed riders as escort.

"You're right, colonel," Cavallin said. "It would dishonor Texas. We can't shoot the sonofabitch no matter how bad we want to."

There was a general nodding of heads among the Rangers.

"Then let him pass without a word. No cat calls. Nothing." Hays said.

Grant dismounted and stood with the motionless, silent Rangers as the approaching vehicles and riders came abreast. Just behind the four lead horsemen was Santa-Anna's big, fancy coach painted red and gold and drawn by four matched gray horses. Santa-Anna in resplendent civilian clothing, his army rank had been stripped from him, sat with an arm resting on the top of the half door of the coach. His pretty young wife sat beside him.

Grant was surprised when the woman waved at the Rangers, she must not know the deadly enmity the men held for her husband. Santa-Anna looked out the window and alarm flashed across his face at seeing the shaggy haired Texans with their hate-filled eyes and pistols. He hastily caught his wife's hand and stopped her waving. He looked stonily back to the front. The eyes of every Ranger followed the coach.

The last coach came in front of Grant and to his astonishment he saw Charlolita Paz looking out at the men near the road. Grant's eyes found hers, and he felt an instant surge of pleasure. He stepped close to the side of the coach, caught hold of the half door, and paced along beside it.

"Char! What are you doing here?"

She gave him a radiant smile and laid her hand on top of his. "I'm being sent to Spain. This is my brother Raoul who is going with me." With a motion of her free hand, she indicated the second occupant in the coach.

Grant could see the resemblance between Char and the man, who was about his age. The fellow was scowling, which didn't bother Grant at all.

"Why to Spain?" he asked and hating her leaving.

"To be married. My parents arranged it."

"You don't know the man?" Char's coming marriage with a man chosen for her in a distant land explained her actions of taking every opportunity to be free of her chaperon and out with Grant. All their pleasant days and evenings together, all her many carefree, happy smiles meant she had been cramming into the limited time still remaining to her as much pleasure as possible before the constraints of a married woman confined her.

"No I don't. But I have several months to get to know him for the marriage isn't until June. They ordered me to leave now for they were afraid I was becoming too fond of a Yankee and would do something to disgrace myself. Of course I would never even think of doing something unladylike." She winked impishly at Grant, and with her face turned away from her brother, the wink was hidden from him.

"Certainly not," Grant agreed. The lie felt good on his tongue.

"Any man who gets you for a wife will be very lucky." Grant knew events had been set in motion and he could do nothing to alter their course. Best to talk of something else. "How did you become part of Santa-Anna's party?"

"My father knows him and asked permission for Raoul and me to travel with his group to the coast. With the general we are safe from guerillas and bandits, and with his safe conduct pass we are safe from you Yankees."

"I will miss you very much," Grant said.

"And I will miss you, my Yankee friend." Char removed her hand from Grant's. "Now I must say goodbye."

Grant felt much saddened. She was the type of free spirited and giving young women that a man should meet at least once in his life. "Goodbye, Char," he said.

He halted, and as the coach carried Char on, she leaned to look out the window and their eyes held. The coach moved on a few yards more and she lifted a hand and gave him a wave and withdrew into the coach. She was gone from his life. Mexico suddenly lost its luster and charm because of her going.

Grant watched after the coach carrying Char and the long line of wagons heavily laden with Santa-Anna's rich possessions until they vanish from sight.

Cavallin came up. "A very pretty girl there," he said.

"Yes she is."

"Sam, you did right in getting the colonel, so there's no hard feelings."

"Thanks, Tom."

"I'll even buy you a drink in Jalapa."

"I accept for I need one. Let's get Mat for he has some heavy thoughts on his mind."

Chapter Fifty-Two

General Scott came out of his quarters in the National Palace and onto the Grand Plaza. He was dressed in a blue field uniform and wearing his usual weapon of a cap and ball pistol in a holster on his belt. His face lit up at sight of the huge gathering of officers waiting to greet him before he departed Mexico City for the coast. He lifted his arm to them and climbed up into the wagon outfitted for his travel.

He straightened to his full height. "Farewell, brave and loyal officers I must leave you now," he said and trembling with emotion and his voice breaking. "You are warriors of the highest order. To you and all your men go the credit for battles fought and victories won. I merely gave you the direction to march."

Scott controlled his feelings with a will and his voice took on a somber tone. "As you go forth in your future duties as soldiers, I give you this to ponder.

That crown with peerless glories bright,

Which shall new luster boast,

When victor's wreaths and monarch's gems,

Shall blend in common dust."

He saluted the men smartly and took a seat.

Hitchcock, standing with Lee in the front of the crowd, shouted out, "Three cheers for our general. Hip! Hip! Hooray!"

The other officers caught up with Hitchcock on the second cry and the Grand Plaza resounded to. "Hip! Hip! Hooray! Hip! Hip! Hooray!"

A young lieutenant called out, "God bless you, general!" This was picked up by other men and repeated over and over.

Scott lifted his hand again in salute of the honor the men had shown him. He spoke to the wagon driver. The man popped his whip over the heads of the team of horses. The officers gave way to provide an avenue for the vehicle to move.

Scott's staff and several other officers had brought their horses to the plaza and they now mounted and rode along with the wagon. A company of Dragoons assigned to escort the general, formed up ahead and riding four abreast led from the plaza and off along the street leading to the National Highway. A train of wagons carrying Scott's servant, his aide a crippled soldier, and provisions for the journey fell in at the tail of the cavalcade.

The procession proceeded with the sounds of the hoof falls of the horses, the rattle of the iron-rimmed wheels on the stone pavement, and the creak of saddle leather echoing back from the walls of the buildings lining the street. There was no conversation and Lee believed all of the men were like him reflecting with a feeling of heavyheartedness upon the events surrounding the general.

Scott had rejected, after four days and with the most polite language, the Mexican offer to become dictator of Mexico. He had explained his decision to his staff, that he was too old and dedicated a soldier to enter into an arrangement so questionable in terms of his country's interests. "I want to return to Washington and face my enemies", he had said. Lee believed the general never at any time had any intention to accept the proposal, but rather he had told about the offer so that word of it would get back to Polk, Marcy, and Congress, and other influential men in Washington.

The court of enquiry had taken testimony on Scott's charges against Pillow, Worth, and Duncan during six days in late March and early April. Two generals and a colonel from Butler's division had been directed by President Polk to make up the court. Scott's case against Pillow was practically destroyed when the wily Pillow persuaded his paymaster, Major Archibald Burns to come forward and swear he had been the author of the Leonidas letter. Duncan took responsibility for the Veritas letter. Lee couldn't imagine what Pillow could have promised Duncan to make him lie under oath. He was confident that Pillow, Duncan and Worth had conspired against Scott for he had seen them talking quietly with their heads together at the Aztec Club.

As the enquiry went along, Polk learned of the July attempt to bribe Santa-Anna and ordered the court to look into the matter as to whether it had occurred and if so had it influenced Scott's military actions. At this point the hearing became more an inquisition of Scott. Pillow lied under oath, swearing that he had opposed offering the bribe. Trist refused to testify on the subject.

So too did Scott, stating that he would discuss the matter only with the president.

Lee thought Scott had handled himself well despite the practiced courtroom tactics of Pillow the consummate lawyer. Trist and Hitchcock had been very compelling witnesses for the general. Trist lauded the general's honesty and loyalty to the United States. Hitchcock went even further, once stating that there were liars, braggarts, and insubordinate officers trying to pull down a great general. At this Worth who was present in the courtroom, sprang to his feet in anger and asked General Butler, also in attendance, to put Hitchcock under arrest. Butler calmly refused and told the court to continue. Lee had been asked but a few questions during his appearance before the court of enquiry, and those had been limited to the orders that he had carried from Scott to the commanding officers of the forces fighting at Contreras and Chapultepec, and the troop movements at those battles. Other witness testified and several officers were directed to submit written responses to questions. The hearings had concluded and the findings and recommendations of the court members had gone to Washington for Polk's review. The official response had been that no payment of money as a bribe to Santa-Anna could be proved, and that military operation had not been influenced. All charges were dropped and President Polk ordered the court to disband. Lee knew that a brilliant campaign had been tarnished by the actions of a few unscrupulous officers.

Grant rode along with the other officers accompanying Scott. After an hour they arrived at El Pinon and Scott called out to his escort of Dragoons and halted them. He climbed down from the wagon and moved among the officers, all of whom had dismounted and removed their hats to show affection. He called the men by name, said a few words to each one, and shook his hand. Grant found himself standing near Lee as Scott came up and caught the man by the hand.

"Colonel Lee, when you return to Washington be sure to come and visit me." Scott clasped him by the shoulder with a friendly grip.

"It has been an honor to serve under you, general," Lee said in a tone that told much about the depth of their friendship

"Good man," Scott said.

Scott turned to Grant and pumped his hand. "You are Captain Grant. The colonel has spoken of you."

"Yes, sir." Grant was pleased Lee had mentioned his name to the general.

Scott completed his circle through the men and again mounted his wagon. He gave a smart salute to the bareheaded group and seated himself. The caravan began its days long journey up into the high Sierra Madre and then down the far eastern slope of the mountains to the seacoast.

* * *

May 30, 1848. The great central chamber of the National Palace was packed with Mexican governmental and church officials, officers of the foreign legations, and high ranking American and Mexican army officers. Sunlight streamed in through the windows surrounding the high dome of the room and lighted the interior with a fine golden light. All eyes were on President Luis de la Pena and General Butler standing together in the center of the room. Each man held a leather bound document containing the terms of the peace treaty agreed to by the two nations.

Butler, standing erect and very military, offered his copy of the treaty to Pena. The Mexican President accepted the document with a slight nod of his gray streaked head, extended his copy to the American and the exchange was made. General Butler turned to the gathering of dignitaries; he spoke for exactly three minutes wishing peace between the two nations and prosperity for Mexico. Pena spoke for only one minute. He turned to Butler and put his hand. The two men shook hands and the ceremony ended.

The people moved in mass toward the wide doors standing open. Lee went with the flow and looking about over the heads of most everybody around him. He saw Elizabeth off on his right a short ways and his heart sped its beat. Days earlier she had sent him a short letter stating she had found pleasure in his friendship, but knew that nothing could come of it. That she had accepted a proposal of marriage from Minister Doyle's chief assistant. Even so, Lee wanted to speak to her one last time and waded across the current of people to her.

"Hello, Elizabeth," he said and catching her by the arm.

She turned, and seeing who had hold of her, gave him a pleased smile and took his hand in both of hers. "I had hoped we would see each other before you left the city."

"So had I." Her warm, smooth hand brought back memories of the other times he had touched her. Everyone of them was a time to remember for she was a most appealing woman. His hand tightened on hers.

"When do you leave?"

"In an hour or so. My engineers and I are the very first to go."

"You must be happy to go home after so many months away."

"A lovely woman made my time here very pleasant. I wish to thank her now."

"And I too enjoyed our friendship. I shall miss you, Robert."

"And I you."

"Perhaps if we had met at some other time this all might have turned out differently," Elizabeth said in a low voice.

Then she smiled brightly. "Goodbye, Robert. Have a safe journey." She spun quickly away and merged into the moving crowd, some of which had turned to glance at the two making an island in the current of people.

Lee went at a slower pace and watched Elizabeth draw away. She never looked back. This chapter of life was closed for both of them.

* * *

The long caravan of cannons and wagons rumbled and rattled on the National Highway toward the seacoast and the docks at Veracruz. Every heavy siege cannon was tripled-teamed and every loaded wagon double-teamed by either mules or horses. The teamsters cursed their animals and laid the whips on their backs to drive them up the steep mountain grades. The thousands of marching infantrymen grumbled and sweated.

General Butler and General Patterson and Lee led the caravan. Butler and his staff had joined with Patterson's division for the journey to the coast. Lee liked the two men and was pleased the three of them were traveling together. Lee's company of engineers came next for their duty was to repair any bridge or section of road that had been washed out by the spring rains. Next came the heavy siege cannons and field artillery, then the infantry, the wagons carrying the sick and wounded from the hospital in Mexico City, the wagons of the quartermaster and commissary officers, and the extra horses and mules. Lastly came the camp followers with their wagons and saddle horses. Those men and women seemed as anxious as the soldiers to return to the States.

The caravan was approaching the last mountain pass and beyond that the going would be easier. So far Lee and his men had had only one landslide to clear off the road and one bridge to strengthen. He praised the skill of the Spanish engineers that had done the original construction.

From the first day after leaving Mexico City, Lee had observed soldiers dropping out of ranks and disappearing into the forest. The rate of desertion was increasing as the distance from Mexico City grew. Butler and Patterson were informed, however they forbade the provost marshals pursuing and attempting to arrest the runaways. Lee believed the deserters would return to Mexico City, where many had girlfriends, and join the well-paid Legion of Foreigners that President Pena was hiring to guard the National Palace as soon as the Yankees had gone, a sort of Swiss Guard like that which protected the French Bourbon kings, and the Catholic pope.

Chapter Fifty-Three

In the early afternoon on May 9, 1848, Patterson's army reached Veracruz. On the outskirts of the town, Lee spotted a white pony in a pasture beside the road, and thinking it would make a nice homecoming present for his children, turned aside to see if he could buy it. The grizzled old Mexican agreed to sell when Lee flashed six silver dollars before his eyes. Lee directed Connally to take the pony in tow and see that it was put aboard the transport ship with Lee's horse.

El vomito had arrived and lay with its deadly hand upon the town and Patterson hurried his troops along the main street past the whitewashed houses, the central plaza, the town's largest church, and onward to the docks. The harbor was crowded with every pier lined with ships, every anchorage in use, and ships occupying all the open water from Veracruz to Isle de Sacrificios.

Most of the vessels were American with a wide variety of sizes, hull shapes, and rigging. Some score of them were steamships, the preponderance were sailing ships. Lee thought the army purchasing agents must have contracted all the ships on the southern coast of the States to transport the soldiers and their weapons home. Still he knew there weren't enough vessels to do the job. The division coming last down from the mountains would have a long wait.

Lee, with Beauregard, McClellan, and Tower and the others of the engineering company went aboard the Steamship Portland that would carry them to New Orleans. Beauregard came to stand beside Lee as the stevedores and seamen loaded the horses and other personal possessions of the engineers and the other officers assigned to the Portland. On the wharf the quartermasters and their men were busy inventorying the thousands of governmental items in their charge and dismantling the wagons and weapons for compact stowing aboard the ships. Their tasks would keep them here for days.

"We fought a war and are going home all in one piece," Beauregard said.

"I think my wife and kids may approve of that." Lee had been away from the States twenty-one months during which he had journeyed long distances upon the sea and across a foreign land. The time had contained periods of calm, of storm, of bivouac, of battle and death. And as for death, he had come close to it many times, yet had escaped while men nearby had died. He had been wounded, but only slightly, had caught no diseases and was in excellent health.

He had learned much in the war; that reconnaissance and planning and audacious officers leading well-trained men won battles. That to engage in war was to attack for no victories could be won holed up in a fort or city. A defensive position was only to gain time and opportunity to resume the offensive. He had seen bravery in men that he would never forget. Regardless of all the wrongs of the war, it had solidified his role as an army man.

Now it was time to turn away from a warrior's life in a foreign land where he had felt free and life enjoyable to the highest order even in the times of battle. Now he must return and accept the tasks of father and husband, at least be as much of a father and husband as his military duties and his nature would allow. A pleasant feeling of anticipation at seeing his wife and children came over him.

The captain shouted from the bridge and the lines holding the ship to the dock were cast off. The throb of the steam engine pistons grew louder, water swirled along the ship's side as it pulled away from the dock.

* * *

In the darkness of the late Mexican night of June 12, Grant sat slouched in the old wicker chair in the quiet garden at the rear of the monastery. This was a place he often came to loaf and enjoy the quiet hours. Also it was where he had spent so many pleasant hours studying Spanish with the gentle monk Sebastian. He breathed the fragrance of the flowers that were in full bloom and watched the diamond stars drift across the ebony sky. Close above him a lone bat wheeled and dove and chased the nighttime insects through the black air.

All was as it should be. Yet Grant felt unsettled because a great adventure was coming to an end. His brigade would be leaving Mexico City in a few hours. He would be glad to see Julia, yes indeed, but knowing that he would never journey this way again left a strange emptiness in his heart. He hadn't expected that.

He remembered Char and her gay laughter, and her lovely body that she so willingly gave him. Julia would never know about her for there were some things a man should not tell a betrothed, or a wife. As the years passed he would recall those days from that special place in his memory where he kept his secrets and relive them through his inner eye. Nothing was ever totally lost until all memory of it had been erased by death.

One truth came very clear to Grant, a man must participate in important events, to engage in outrageous adventures so that he would have them to marvel at when he was old and to frail to ever do them again. And he would smile in wonderment and think, had he really done such foolish things, or maybe if he had been lucky, had he truly performed such brave deeds. He was only twenty-six years old. Should the opportunity present itself to join in a future campaign of importance, he would seize it with the utmost gusto.

He saw a pale yellow light from Valere's lamp brighten the window in the man's quarters just a stone's throw away. Morning was near and Valere would shortly have food ready for the day's march. Grant rose from the wicker chair for the last time and went into his quarters to prepare for the long journey to the sea.

* * *

By noon of the day of July 21, every cannon, horse, musket, pound of gunpowder powder, saber, medical supplies and instruments, and even the horseshoes and army eating utensils had been counted and recorded in the proper category, carried aboard the transport ships, and stowed away in the holds or lashed down on the decks. The ships began to pull away from the docks.

On the deck of the last ship to depart, Grant rested, smelling the hot tainted air of the waterfront. On the docks, the brown skinned stevedores that he had hired to help load the ships stared after them. Overhead the buzzards sailed in their eternal circling and looking down for death below. The Americans had given them plenty of death.

The steamer came alive with a rumble of the steam engines and a quiver of her decks. The big side-paddlewheels began to spin and the vessel pulled away from the dock.

The strip of blue Gulf between the ship and shore widened and the smell of the waterfront vanished. The western wind that overflowed the city brought the true scent of the land down to Grant; the heavy vanilla perfume of acacia, the spicy fragrance of uncountable flower blossoms, the odor of hundreds of species of tropical plants decomposing, and all blending together into a smell he would never forget. Then a few hundred turns of the paddlewheels and there was only the moist, briny air of the sea in his lungs. All that remained of Mexico was the Starry Mountain, Orizaba, its snowy cap suspended there between the earth and sky.

Epilogue

The Treaty at Guadalupe Hidalgo gave the United States the land that now encompasses all of Texas, California, Nevada, Utah, Arizona, New Mexico and parts of Wyoming, Colorado, and Kansas.

One year after the treaty was signed, gold was discovered in California and then began the greatest gold rush the world has ever seen.

Lee remained in the military. At the beginning of the Civil War in 1861, General Scott, still Commander and Chief of the army, recommended to Lincoln that he appoint Lee as the commanding general of the Union Army. Lincoln made the offer, but Lee declined it and went south to fight with the Confederate Army.

Grant went into private business after his required term with the military ended. President Lincoln recalled him to active duty in 1861 at the beginning of the Civil War. Following their service together in the Mexican War, Lee and Grant never saw each other until April 9, 1865 at Appomattox Court House.

General Zachary Taylor bested General Scott for the candidacy of the Whig Party and went on to be elected president after Polk's term ended in 1848.

President Polk died in Nashville three months after leaving office, at the age of fifty-four.

General Scott retained his position as U. S. Army General and Chief. Once Scott reached Washington his friends rallied around and feted him as a hero. Congress presented him with a medal for his services, and New York held a grand celebration for him. In the second year of the Civil War, McClellan maneuvered Scott, then seventy-six, aside and became the General and Chief of the Union Army.

General Pillow went back to civilian life after the end of the Mexican War. At the beginning of the Civil War he returned to uniform, the uniform of gray of the Confederates. A young general named Ulysses S. Grant defeated him at Fort Donelson on the Cumberland River in 1862 and sent him into obscurity.

General Worth remained in uniform and died in 1852. A fort he established on what was then the Texas frontier, Fort Worth, immortalized his name.

Santa-Anna returned from exile to Mexico in 1853 and again became president. In 1855 he was exiled again. In 1874 he was permitted to return to Mexico. He died in Mexico City in 1876 at the age of ninety-two.

The Mexican War was the training ground for many Union and Confederate officers. More than 200 of the officers that fought in that war became Union or Confederate generals in the Civil War. A person could easily believe that this training in warfare led to the length and deadliness of the Civil War. Some of the most notable of the generals were:

Ulysses S. Grant
Robert E. Lee
Jefferson Davis
George McCllelan
P. G. T. Beauregard
Thomas Jackson
Joseph Hooker
D. H. Hill
George Meade
Joseph Johnston
Fitz-John Porter
Roswell Ripley
William Sherman
Zealous Tower
Don Buel
Ambrose Burnside
John Magruder

In May 1846 at the beginning of the Mexican War there were 637 officers and 5,925 enlisted men in the army. During the war 1,016 officers and 35,009 enlisted men joined the regular army, swelling its ranks to 42,587 men, while an additional 73,532 men appeared on the rolls of the various volunteer units. The table below lists the losses suffered.

Killed in action	1,192
Died of wounds	529
Disease, etc.*	11,155
Wounded in action	4,102
Discharged for disability	9,754
Deserters	9,207

*Includes deaths from disease, accidents, executions, and miscellaneous causes.

The 12,876 deaths make this war for its size the deadliest in American history.

The war cost the United States about $58,000,000 in direct costs for military operations. Another $15,000,000 was paid to Mexico under the treaty. Miscellaneous other costs ran the total cost to about $100,000,000.

The U. S. annexation of Texas in 1845 set the stage for the war. Mexico in early 1830 had granted permission for people from the U. S. to come into Texas and take up land and make a home among the few Mexican citizens living there. By 1836 the number of Americans living in Texas had grown to several thousands and they felt the need to be independent of Mexico. The revolting Texans were beaten and massacred at the Alamo and Goliad. A few weeks later Sam Houston with an army of 783 men defeated the Mexican Army of two thousand at San Jacinto and declared Texas an independent and sovereign nation. Mexico did not accept this, but considered Texas still part of that nation and a wayward province in revolt. When the United States annexed Texas as a state, the Mexican government declared the annexation an act of war. Further complicating the situation, Mexico claimed the Nueces River was the western boundary of Texas while the Texans claimed the boundary was the Rio Grande some one hundred miles farther west and south.

President Polk, and indeed most of the people of the U. S. believed in Manifest Destiny, the American people's right to control all the land between the Atlantic and Pacific oceans. To reach this end, Polk sent a representative to Mexico City with an offer to pay Mexico thirty-five million dollars for California, and New Mexico and to give up its claims on Texas. Mexican officials refused to listen to the offer, and their congress quickly passed a resolution that even to speak with an American official about the subject was treasonous and punishable by death.

To defend the Texan claim of the Rio Grande as the western boundary of Texas, President Polk ordered General Zachary Taylor with three thousand men to the disputed Rio Grande. Instructed not to start hostilities, Taylor built a fort above the river and settled down to wait for the Mexicans to begin the fighting.

At this same time, the British and the Americans seemed to be girding for a war over the boundary of the Oregon Territory. The American's slogan was "54-40 or fight", meaning the border would be 54 degrees and 40 minutes north latitude, which would put it at the southern border of Russian Alaska, while the British wanted it much farther south. The British would not allow a large slice of Canada to be taken. A war seemed imminent.

The British were also vehemently against the Americans move against Mexico for they had many valuable investments there. After the Mexicans drove out the Spanish, British businessmen had poured into the country to develop gold and silver mines and establish trading companies and mercantile businesses.

Britain was not alone in considering the United States an upstart nation driven to expand its borders, so too did France and Spain. Polk was aware of a meeting held by the three countries in early 1846 wherein they had discussed a scheme to install a monarchy in Mexico, one ruled by a Spanish Prince with his reign enforced by the armies of the three European nations. Polk, to forestall the plan and also to prevent any military assistance from foreign powers reaching Mexico, ordered Admiral David Conner, Commodore of the American Home Fleet to take his warships and blockade the eastern coast of Mexico. With a foreign army on its territory and a navy blockading its seaports, Mexico was now in a position to either sell a large piece of their country to Polk, or go to war with the U. S.

A large minority of people in the U. S. felt the war was little more than a land grab by politicians who were determined to expand the nation regardless of cost in American blood and treasure. The editorials of many U. S.

newspapers wrote strongly against the war. Dissension became fierce between the states, with the northern congressmen and senators fearing any land taken from Mexico would become slave, and the southern congressmen and senators wanting more land for the spread of slavery and thus keep equilibrium between free and slave states. Anti-war riots broke out in a number of cities.

The Mexicans believed they would have a strong ally in the British, and were encouraged in this belief by editorials in British newspapers. With this in their thoughts, and seeing the controversy in the U. S. about the war, the Mexicans declared war on the U. S. The Mexican Army crossed the Rio Grande and attacked a company of Americans, killing several men. In retaliation, General Taylor crossed to the south bank of the river, and on May 8, 1846 defeated the Mexican Army at Palo Alto. A second battle at Resaca de la Palma was fought on May 9 and again the Americans were victorious. Taylor kept marching deeper into Mexico and in four days of savage fighting, September 20-24, captured Monterrey. Here he settled down to wait for the Mexicans to call for negotiations to resolve the disputes.

And wait he did, as did President Polk in Washington. However, regardless of the defeat of its northern army, the Mexicans refused to negotiate with the Americans. Worried about the anti-war uproar increasing across the United States, Polk ordered Winfield Scott, General and Chief of the American Army, to assemble an army and invade Mexico at Veracruz and march inland and capture Mexico City, Mexico's capital and seat of government. He thought that must surely force the stubborn Mexicans to come to the negotiation table. With Polk's promise of a 25,000 man army, Scott assembled his first contingent, two divisions of battle hardened regulars from Taylor's army in the north and a new division of volunteers. On March 2, 1847, Scott set sail for Veracruz with 9,000 men on 100 ships.

Among the soldiers journeying south with Scott were the battle toughened Lieutenant Ulysses S. Grant, who had fought with General Taylor in all of the battles in the north, and the untested Captain Robert E. Lee.

* * *

Robert Edward Lee was born on January 19, 1807 in the grand manor house Stratford Hall in Westmorland County, Virginia, the birthplace of many famous members of the illustrious Lee family. The East India Company, aided by an ample donation from Queen Caroline of England, had built the seventeen room Stratford Hall for Thomas Lee in 1730. Its paneled walls were hung with portraits of many earlier Lees. The oldest portrait was of Lancelot Lee who entered England with William the Conqueror in 1066. Lancelot distinguished himself at the battle of Hastings and acquired a large estate in Essex County.

A later member of the family, Lionel Lee at the head of a company of cavaliers, took part in the Third Crusade, following Richard Coeur de Lion in 1192 to Palestine. He displayed great gallantry at the siege of Acre and in return for his services was made Earl of Litchfield. Robert could trace his line of descent from Richard Lee, a younger son of the Earl of Litchfield and Knight of the Garter in the reign of Queen Elizabeth. Richard Lee, in 1641, came to American as colonial secretary for Governor Sir William Berkeley, and this began the American line of Lees.

Three generations later, Robert's father Henry Lee was born in Stratford Hall. He was nineteen when the colonies revolted against England. He fought with General Washington and rose rapidly up through the officer ranks. Due to his daring actions, he became known as "Light-horse Harry". After the war he served in the Continental Congress and three times as governor of Virginia.

The sort of recklessness that had brought Henry Lee success on the battlefield ruined him in his personal life. He squandered most of his first wife's tobacco fortune in wild schemes. He began land speculating with the money of his second wife, the mother of Robert E, and when unable to pay a $40,000 debt was thrown into debtor's prison. President Monroe "arranged" for "Light-horse" to escape his debts in the States by fleeing to the West Indies. This was the last time six-year-old Robert ever saw his father, who died five years later in exile. Because of the absence of his father, black haired and brown eyed Robert grew up with much responsibility while but a boy.

With a long list of illustrious ancestors, English earls, American governors, Speaker of the House, generals, signers of the Declaration of Independence, diplomats, and judges, Robert had much to live up to, and a father's black actions to live down.

Believing the military was the best way to accomplish his goals, he decided upon West Point as a starting point. He had been the most sponsored cadet to have ever entered the Point, with five U.S. Senators, three Representatives, and the Secretary Of War endorsing him.

A full grown man standing six feet tall, Lee was accepted at the Point in 1825 and graduated in 1828 as Adjutant of Cadets, the highest rank possible. When the Mexican War began he urgently requested transfer to the front to take part in the fighting. He was ordered to join General Wool's army in northern Mexico. After marching for six weeks looking for a Mexican army to fight and finding none, he was ordered to join General Scott in the invasion of central Mexico.

* * *

Ulysses Hiram Grant was born April 27, 1822 at Point Pleasant, Ohio in a two room, clapboard house 18 feet by 19 feet. His father, Jesse Root Grant, named him Ulysses after the Grecian warrior Ulysses in Fenelon's epic tale Telemachus. Ulysses was of the eighth generation in the United States. His ancestors, Mathew and Priscilla Grant were of Scottish descent and came from Dorset England and landed at Plymouth Massachusetts in the summer of 1630 on the sailing ship John & Mary. By the time of the revolution, their descendants had formed a core of a moderately prominent family in Connecticut.

Ulysses's grandfather Noah Grant fought in the Continental Army throughout the Revolutionary War, starting as a Minute Man on Lexington Green and rising to captain by the time the British were defeated. After being discharged, he turned to drunkenness and wasted a substantial inheritance on whiskey, and abandoned his wife and children.

Grant's father, Jesse, was eleven years old at the time of his father's abandonment. He made his own way as a farm hand, and then for several years as a tannery worked soaking hides in lime and oak bark sludge and scraping off the loosened flesh and hair. When Ulysses was two, Jesse quit work in the tannery and moved the family to Georgetown, Ohio, on the banks of the Ohio River. There he started his own tanning business.

Brown haired and blue-eyed Ulysses could read well at six. His true love was horses, and he had a way with them. He had a remarkable visual memory of landscape and terrain and at the age of eight was driving horse and wagon by himself all over the backwoods of the county hauling oak bark for his father's tannery. Neighbors brought colts for Ulysses to break to ride. To show his horsemanship, he would sometimes gallop his steed down the main street standing on one foot on his horse's back. At fourteen Ulysses provided limousine service with a two horse carriage taking people from Georgetown to Chillicothe sixty miles away and return, and to Cincinnati forty miles distant, and delivering mail about the county.

Ulysses had but a few years of formal schooling, however Jesse had a thirty-five book library and required the boy to study. Jesse decided Ulysses should go to West Point, and persuaded his representative, Congressman Hammer, to sponsor Ulysses. Ulysses didn't want to go, but Jesse insisted, and when Jesse insisted that was the way it went.

So at seventeen, standing five foot one inch and weighing one hundred and seventeen pounds, Ulysses set off for West Point on the Hudson River in New York. Worried about passing the entrance examination at the Point, Ulysses took a book from Jesse's library and taught himself algebra during the ten-day journey. He passed the exam and signed the enlistment papers on September 14, 1839. Ulysses graduated in 1843, and being unwilling to apply himself diligently to his studies, ranked twenty-one out of a class of thirty-nine. He was assigned to the elite Fourth Infantry under the command of General Worth.

About the Author

F.M. Parker has worked as a sheepherder, lumberman, sailor, geologist, and as a manager of wild horses, wild, free roaming buffalo and livestock grazing. For several years he was the manager of five million acres of Public Domain Land in eastern Oregon. His highly acclaimed novels include the *Coldiron* Series, *The Searcher*, *The Assassins*, *Predators and Prey*, and *The Shadow Man*.

Coming Soon!

F.M. PARKER'S

DREAM HITCHER
(a.k.a. The Hitcher)

Dan Gallatin, ex-Marine with multiple battles, is a violent man. He makes his living bare knuckle fighting on the Chicago waterfront and as a bouncer at the tough, rowdy country western Bank Vault Club.

A man, calling himself Anubis' can't dream. He slays veterans and men who have adventurous lives and hitches onto their dreams and their final journeys into the afterlife.

Colonel Granville, wounded and blinded in combat, has the ability to see human auras. He guides groups of injured veterans into dream sessions, in which the blind vet can see…

Colonel Granville is being stalked by the dream hitcher, to journey with him in his death dream. The colonel reads Dan's aura and sees his violent nature…

For more information
visit: www.SpeakingVolumes.us

Now Available!

SPUR AWARD-WINNING AUTHOR
ROD MILLER

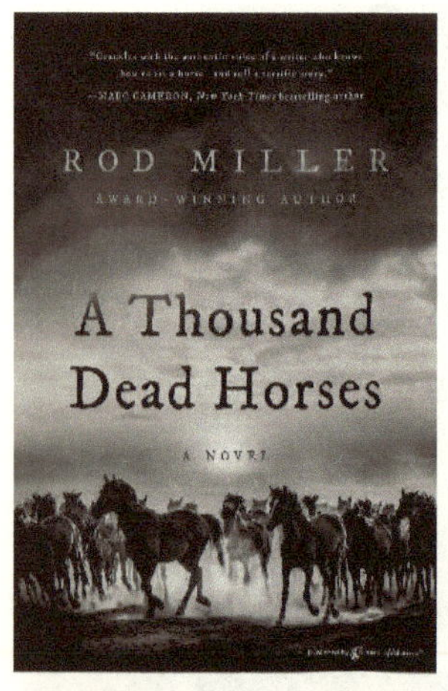

**For more information
visit: www.SpeakingVolumes.us**